Imagine a family tree that includes Texas cowboys, Choctaw and Cherokee Indians, a Louisiana pirate and a Scottish rebel who battled side by side with William Wallace. With ancestors like that, it's easy to understand why *USA TODAY* bestselling author and former air force captain **Delores Fossen** feels as if she were genetically predisposed to writing romances. Along the way to fulfilling her DNA destiny, Delores married an air force top gun who just happens to be of Viking descent. With all those romantic bases covered, she doesn't have to look too far for inspiration.

# *Chapter One*

Marshal Harlan McKinney heard a soft clicking sound.

He waited, heard a second one and eased back the covers on his bed. In one smooth motion he snatched up his Glock from the nightstand and got to his feet.

Just as someone opened the back door of his house.

Harlan listened, hoping it was one of his foster brothers who sometimes crashed at his place. But no such luck. Since all of his brothers were federal marshals, they wouldn't have risked sneaking in at 2:00 a.m., knowing that he was armed and a light sleeper.

He heard the door being closed. Then footsteps. They were barely audible on the tiled floor of the kitchen, but the person seemed to be making a beeline for the hall that led to his bedroom and home office.

There was no time for him to pull on his jeans or boots. It was bad enough that he had an intruder, but now he'd have to bring down this person while he was wearing only boxers.

Harlan ducked behind his bedroom doorjamb and kept watch. There were no lights on in the house, but there was enough moonlight seeping through the windows that he could see the shadow that appeared on the wall.

Just a few feet away.

He didn't move. Didn't make a sound. He wanted to see if the person was armed, but he couldn't tell.

"Put your hands in the air," Harlan growled, his voice shooting through the silence.

The intruder gasped and turned as if to bolt. Harlan wasn't going to let that happen. He darn well intended to find out who was brassy or stupid enough to break into a lawman's house in the dead of night. He lunged toward the person, slamming him back against the wall.

Except it wasn't a *him*.

It didn't take long for Harlan to figure that out, because his chest landed against her breasts.

"It's me," the woman said, her breathing heavy.

Harlan instantly recognized that voice, and he reached behind him and slapped on the hall light.

Caitlyn Barnes.

It had been a few years since he'd seen her, but there was no mistaking that face.

Or that body.

Harlan had firsthand knowledge of her breasts—bare, at that—pressing against him. And while that was a pretty good memory made years ago, there weren't too many recent good memories when it came to the woman herself.

He stepped back, met her wide blue eyes. He caught just a glimpse of panic in them before she lifted her chin defiantly. He knew she was trying to look a whole lot more confident than she was. That's because he was six-three, a good eight inches taller than she was, and he outsized her by at least eighty pounds. He was a big guy, and no one had ever accused him of looking too friendly.

Plus, there was the part about him having a Glock aimed at her pretty little head.

"Most visitors just knock, even the uninvited ones,"

he snarled, easing the Glock back to his side. However, Harlan didn't ease up on the glare.

She made a sarcastic sound of agreement, huffed and put her left palm on his chest to push him back. "I didn't think you'd be here."

Well, that wasn't much of an explanation for breaking and entering or for driving all the way out to his family's ranch. The place wasn't exactly on the beaten path and was a good fifteen miles from the town of Maverick Springs, where he worked. Much too far out of the way for a friendly spur-of-the-moment visit, and Harlan let her know that with the hard look he gave her.

Caitlyn stared back, and then her gaze drifted lower. To his chest. Then lower. To his boxers. Since it wasn't anything she hadn't seen before, and because he was still waiting on that explanation, Harlan didn't budge.

But he felt that old kick of desire.

Hard not to feel it, since they'd been lovers. Well, one-time lovers anyway when they were teenagers. But once was enough. Stuff like that created bonds that weren't worth a thimbleful of spit.

Unless…

The heat was still there. Much to Harlan's disgust, it was. Probably because Caitlyn and he had spent way too much of their teens driving each other hot and crazy. He didn't intend to let it cloud his head.

For Pete's sake, the woman had broken into his home.

Just as he would have done to any other criminal caught in the act, he took her by the arm, turned her and put her face-first against the wall. Another gasp, and she tried to fight him off, but he grabbed the Colt she had tucked in the back waist of her jeans.

So not only had this blast from his past broken into his house, she'd come armed.

Harlan turned her back around and dangled her gun in front of her. "Last I heard you were a reporter," he said.

"Still am." She managed to hold her glare a moment longer before she lost the staring match and glanced away. "I came because I needed answers."

Again, no explanation for the gun or her presence, but Harlan made a circling motion with the Colt so she'd continue.

Her blue eyes snapped back to his. "Do you want me dead?"

Now, that wasn't a question he'd expected. "No," Harlan answered, and he stretched out the word a bit. "Is there a reason I'd want you dead?"

"You might think there is."

Another puzzling answer, and Harlan was getting tired of them. He wasn't a patient man, even on good days, and this didn't qualify as good in any way, fashion or form.

"A Texas Ranger came to visit me," Caitlyn said.

His heart slammed against his chest, and things became a lot clearer. "About Kirby?"

But it wasn't really a question. The Rangers were indeed investigating the sixteen-year-old murder of Jonah Webb, the SOB headmaster of the pigsty of an orphanage where Harlan and his five foster brothers had been raised.

Caitlyn, too.

Several months ago the Rangers had identified the headmaster's killer, Webb's own wife. Webb had been physically abusive, and she'd killed him during one of his beatings. But there'd been an accomplice. Neither Harlan nor any of his foster brothers had been ruled out as suspects, but the Rangers no doubt had their foster father, Kirby Granger, at the top of their list. Kirby had motive, too.

Six of them.

Because that was how many kids he'd saved from the orphanage—Harlan and the five other boys who'd become his brothers. But Kirby hadn't saved them until after Webb had been murdered.

"What'd you say to this Ranger?" Harlan asked. And it better not have been anything incriminating.

"I told him there was nothing to tell." Caitlyn paused, pushed her choppy blond hair from her face. "But he didn't believe me. He thought I was covering for one of you—even though I told him I haven't seen you or any of your foster family since we left the Rocky Creek facility after it was shut down."

That part was true. Caitlyn had been sent to another children's home, and Harlan and his foster brothers had left with Kirby. Harlan had written her, for a while anyway, and then they'd lost touch.

Until now.

Of course, he wasn't ignorant of what had happened to her. Nope. Caitlyn had become a high-profile investigative journalist. Heck, he'd even seen her on TV a couple of times while reporting stories. But then she'd practically disappeared. Why, he didn't know, and he hadn't given it much thought. Until now.

"I don't want you dead," Harlan clarified. "But I also don't want you saying anything that might get Kirby arrested. He's sick. Going through cancer treatments. And I won't have you or anyone else making his life harder than it already is. Got that?"

She nodded. "And that's why I thought you might want me out of the picture, to make sure I wouldn't implicate Kirby in Webb's murder."

Harlan didn't roll his eyes, but it was close. He tapped the top of his boxers. "Normally I wear a badge there, and I took an oath to uphold the law—"

"An oath you'd break in a heartbeat to protect Kirby," Caitlyn interrupted.

Harlan shook his head. "I can't argue with that. But murder? Really?"

"There's no love lost between us," she reminded him.

Yeah, thanks to her renegade brand of journalism that had trashed the marshals and others in law enforcement. Heck, a couple of times she'd revealed names on investigations that had come under fire, including Harlan himself. So she was right—no love lost. Still, something about this didn't make sense.

"If you thought I was out to kill you, then why come to my house?" he demanded.

"As I said, because I didn't think you'd be here." She cursed under her breath. "I wanted to search the place, to see if there was any evidence."

"Sheez. Evidence of what?"

"That you hired someone to come after me."

Harlan tried to hold on to his temper, but this was a very frustrating and confusing conversation. "Start from the beginning," he insisted.

Her gaze dropped to his boxers again. "Get dressed. Your file is in my car."

He didn't budge. "My *file?*"

"Yes, with a sworn statement from a criminal informant that you paid him to scare me, 'or worse.'"

Now it was Harlan's turn to curse, and he didn't keep it under his breath. "I've hired no one. And I want to see this file."

Another glance at his boxers. "Then I suggest you put on your jeans, because I'm parked at the end of the road."

Of course. A good quarter of a mile away. Harlan didn't mind the walk, but his mood was getting more ornery with each passing second.

Why the heck would Caitlyn think of him as a killer?

Harlan turned to go into his bedroom but decided he wasn't going to take any chances where she was concerned. He latched on to her wrist, pulled her into the bedroom with him and shut the door.

"How'd you know I lived here?" He put both her gun and his on the dresser while he pulled on his jeans.

"Research." She glanced around. Not much to see, though. A bed, dresser and nightstand. The entire house was the same—a no-frills man cave, exactly the way Harlan liked it.

"The place used to belong to Kirby's father," she remarked, probably to let him know that she had indeed done her research. "And the main ranch house where Kirby and the others live is about a mile that way." Caitlyn tipped her head in the opposite direction from where she'd said her car was parked.

"My brother Dallas doesn't live there," he disagreed, just to show her that her research sucked. And it did. Because there was no way she had any real proof that he'd hired someone to kill her.

She nodded and didn't look away when he zipped his jeans. "Because Dallas married Joelle, and they built a house on the property."

Joelle, a woman who'd once been Caitlyn's friend at Rocky Creek Children's Facility. He doubted his sister-in-law knew anything about this little visit, but he would ask her first chance he got.

Harlan put on his boots and a shirt and stuffed her Colt into the back waist of his jeans. "Why'd you think I wouldn't be here?" he asked, heading for the door.

"The P.I. that I hired said you were transporting a prisoner to Dallas."

He had been, but had finished early. The transport of a prisoner wasn't usually classified info, unless it was a high-risk, high-profile case. In this case, it wasn't. Still, it wouldn't have been common knowledge, and along with all the other things he wanted to know, Harlan would need to address that.

"What's the name of this P.I.?" He opened the front door and held it for her so that she'd be in front of him.

"I'd rather not say."

"I'd rather you did say," Harlan insisted. "In fact, I've got grounds to arrest you for breaking and entering. Don't add failure to cooperate to those charges."

Caitlyn whirled around and would have tumbled down the flagstone steps if Harlan hadn't caught her. "You're not going to arrest me."

"Who says? Give me the name of that P.I."

"Mazy Hinton." Her teeth were clenched so tightly that he was surprised she was able to speak. She tore herself from his grip and stomped through the yard toward the road.

Harlan didn't recognize the name, but within an hour or two, he'd know everything there was to know about this P.I., who was either incompetent, stupid or an out-and-out liar. None of those possibilities sat well with him.

He glanced up the road, spotted her car right where she said it would be, and he cursed both it and the August heat. There was a breeze, but it was muggy and still hot despite the late hour.

"What exactly did you think you'd find in my house?" he pressed.

She shook her head. "I wasn't sure. An email, maybe.

Or a paper trail to prove you hired someone. I wanted something in your own handwriting or from your personal computer."

Something she wouldn't find, because he hadn't done anything to set this crazy visit into motion. "I guess it didn't occur to you that if I was really a rogue marshal you should go to the cops?"

"Wasn't sure I could trust them." Ahead of him her steps slowed, and she wiped her forehead with the back of her hand. "I wasn't sure I could trust anyone. Like I said, someone's trying to scare me...or something."

"Considering your job, is that much of a surprise? You've riled a boatload of people, including me."

She turned, and in the moonlight he got a glimpse of her expression. Not the fake bravery she'd tried to sport in the hall. Not the emotions from their past. But something else. Something Harlan couldn't quite put his finger on.

"Some people do hate me," she said, as if choosing her words carefully. "But this isn't about that. The threatening notes had, well, personal details in them."

"Personal?" Harlan caught up with her, and even though they were still yards from her car, he stopped her. He whirled her back around to face him.

Not the brightest idea he'd ever had.

That whirl put them too darn close, and the breeze hit just right so that her scent washed over him. Through him, actually. Yeah, not a bright idea.

*"Personal,"* Caitlyn verified. She took a deep breath. "The notes were typed, and they warned if I said anything about the investigation into Jonah Webb's murder, I'd be sorry. Your name was on them."

It didn't take Harlan long to figure out what this might be. "So? Anyone could have typed them."

"No. Not anyone." She didn't say anything for several moments. "Remember when we were together that night at Rocky Creek?"

Even though they'd had a lot of nights at that hellhole, Harlan figured he knew which one she meant.

"Jonah Webb went missing that night," she continued. "And we heard they were closing the place, that we'd all be split up and sent to other facilities. Well, except for Kirby Granger's *boys*. Kirby was getting all of you and some of the others out of there."

"He couldn't get you out," Harlan reminded her. "He couldn't locate your next of kin to get permission to request guardianship of you."

She gave that a dismissive nod and started walking again. "And that night we met down in the laundry room."

Their usual meeting place, where they'd talked, and kissed, for hours. They'd been barely sixteen then, but the making out had started a month earlier. It had escalated that night, and they'd had sex.

With a surprise ending.

Caitlyn had had one of the worst reputations at Rocky Creek, but Harlan had found out unexpectedly that she'd been a virgin.

"Remember what you said to me?" Caitlyn asked. *"Afterward,"* she clarified.

Yeah, he did. After sixteen years, he still did.

It had been Caitlyn's first time. Not his, though. He'd gotten lucky a few other times with girls who'd found him attractive. Sometimes he regretted that and had regretted even more that Caitlyn had given him something special—her virginity.

*You'll always be my first, Caitlyn,* he'd said to her. And in his crazy sixteen-year-old mind, that meant something, even though he'd omitted the critical word—*love*.

That was probably for the best, considering how things had turned out between them.

Caitlyn got to the car and threw open the passenger door. "Did you ever tell anyone else what you said to me that night?"

Harlan didn't have to think about that answer. "No. It's not the sort of thing a teenage boy chats about with his friends."

Caitlyn made a sound of agreement, fished her keys from the front pocket of her jeans and unlocked the glove compartment. She pulled out a manila folder and used her phone as a flashlight on the pages.

Harlan thumbed through the pages and saw that the first three were all typewritten and were just a few lines long.

Each had his name typed at the bottom.

But it was the threats that caught his attention.

*Talk to the Rangers about Kirby and you'll be sorry,* the first one read.

The second escalated. *Talk to the Rangers, and you'll die.*

He flipped the page, and he felt the knot tighten in his stomach.

*Don't make me kill you* had been typed in bold letters. And beneath it, *You'll always be my first, Caitlyn.*

"Hell." And that was all Harlan could manage to say for several seconds. "Believe me, I didn't send you these. If I'd wanted to warn you to keep quiet, I would have said it to your face."

She studied him, as if trying to decide if he was telling the truth, and then huffed. "There's more. Look at the next page."

He looked at the next page, but saw only a list of names and contact information.

"I'm sure you recognize them," Caitlyn said.

Harlan did. There were three names, including Caitlyn's. The two others were girls who'd lived in her dorm at the Rocky Creek Children's Facility.

Sherry Summers and Tiffany Brock.

"The three of us lived in the room nearest Jonah Webb's family quarters," Caitlyn supplied. "We were all questioned at length when Webb disappeared."

Harlan shook his head. "You think one of them sent you the threatening notes?"

"No. Tiffany's dead, killed in a car accident about two weeks ago near San Antonio." Caitlyn drew in a breath, blew it out slowly. "Her fiancé said before she died, she was getting threatening letters, warning her to stay quiet about the Webb investigation. Maybe the threats came from you. Maybe from one of your foster brothers or Kirby."

"Not a chance," Harlan jumped to answer. "Did those have my typed name on them, too?"

"No," she repeated. "And until I talked to her fiancé, he had no idea who might have sent them."

"How kind of you to fill in the blanks for him. I just wish you'd filled them in with a little truth and not some stupid speculation." He glanced at the other names. "What about Sherry?"

Another deep breath. "She's missing—for nearly three weeks now. I'm the only one left on the list, and earlier tonight I found this on my car windshield." Caitlyn turned to the next page.

It was two typewritten lines. Just a handful of words, but they caused Harlan's heart to slam against his chest.

Hell, what was going on?

*Time's up, Caitlyn. Tomorrow you die.*

# Chapter Two

*Time's up, Caitlyn. Tomorrow you die.*

Caitlyn had read the latest threat so many times that she didn't need to look at it again. It was branded into her memory now, but Harlan kept his attention fixed on it for several long moments.

"I got that before midnight, which means tomorrow is already here," she added, though he no doubt had figured that out. Now what Caitlyn had to figure out was if Harlan had anything to do with it.

Judging from his reaction, the answer was no. But there was still the likelihood that someone very close to him was responsible.

He cursed and scanned the area as an experienced marshal would do to make sure they were safe. A moment later Harlan held up the note for her.

"You didn't report this to the local cops?" he demanded.

Caitlyn huffed. "If I couldn't trust you, how could I trust them?"

He cursed again. "Hell's bells, Caitlyn. According to you, a woman's dead. Another's missing, and the whack job behind all of this has clearly got you in his crosshairs." Harlan added a few more words of profanity. "How the devil could you think I'd do this to you?"

"Partly because of our last phone conversation." She gave him a moment to recall the call in question, but judging from his instant smirk he remembered it readily.

"You'd trashed the Marshals Service and me in one of your so-called pieces of journalism," he said. "And I told you what you could do with your *story.*"

Exactly.

Caitlyn had only reported the facts of the case in question, but they had clashed with Harlan's version of events. Yet a dangerous criminal managed to escape while in custody of federal marshals, and that was what had happened.

Too bad it'd been on Harlan's watch.

She'd felt duty bound to report it and equally duty bound to do a follow-up piece when Harlan had been cleared of any wrongdoing. However, the follow-up hadn't soothed Harlan much.

"That phone conversation wasn't a threat," he insisted. "I was riled because you didn't wait for the whole truth before you got on TV and blabbed about it."

"It wasn't just that conversation." Caitlyn tapped the pages to remind him of something else, and in doing so her hand brushed against his. The jolt was instant.

She silently cursed it.

How could she possibly still be attracted to Harlan?

She wasn't a starry-eyed teenager anymore. She was thirty-two. Yet her hormones were zinging with just a simple touch. She blamed that on his hot cowboy looks. That black hair. Those gray eyes. Oh, and those jeans. No one should look that good in such basic clothing.

Well, it ended now. She couldn't be one of those women attracted to dangerous men.

Or potentially dangerous anyway.

Her obsession with bad boys was over, even if once she'd been proud of her own bad-girl reputation.

"It wasn't just that conversation," Caitlyn repeated after she cleared her throat. "There's the part about what you said to me that night in the laundry room at Rocky Creek. We're the only two people who knew about that." She paused. "Weren't we?"

"I thought we were." He groaned. "But obviously not. Unless you told someone."

"No." And she couldn't answer it quickly enough. "Before you ask, I didn't keep a diary. I said nothing about it in a down-memory-lane blog post. Didn't mention it in a drunken stupor either."

But yes, Caitlyn had gone through all those possibilities before she'd decided it was Harlan.

Or someone Harlan knew well.

"Maybe one of your foster brothers overheard us?" she suggested.

"And wrote the threats sixteen years later?" he finished for her, after he glared at her. "Not a chance."

"Harlan, none of you is a bloomin' Boy Scout. Kirby and all of you have reputations for bending justice now and then."

"Never justice, just the law. Something you know all about." He stared at her, practically daring her to disagree. She couldn't, especially since she'd just broken into his house.

Caitlyn did know the difference between the law and justice, but at the moment she would settle for just knowing the truth.

"How about Kirby, then?" Caitlyn tried for a slightly different angle. "Maybe he wrote the threats to keep me from talking to the Rangers?"

"No way. He's too sick. And besides, he'd rather implicate himself than me or the others."

Yes, that was exactly what she'd thought. Kirby wouldn't sell out any of them. And if Harlan had wanted to threaten her, he wouldn't have used typed notes with his name at the bottom. Still, she'd had to rule him out because of that one intimate line added to the threat.

Harlan looked at the third threat again. "The wording is exact, so it means someone overheard us. And watched us."

Caitlyn had already considered that possibility, but hearing it confirmed made her a little queasy.

*Mercy.*

She'd been butt naked. Harlan, too. And someone had perhaps not only watched them have sex, they'd also remembered verbatim what Harlan had said to her.

Now it was her turn to curse. "This would have been a lot easier if you'd written the notes."

He gave her a look, as if she'd sprouted a third eyeball or something.

"Easier because I'd know who was behind this," she clarified.

"Maybe, but it's obvious that someone's trying to set me up. Someone who would have been at Rocky Creek that night." Harlan looked around again. That quick, edgy sweep of the road and the pasture on both sides. "Come on. If this nut job is planning to try to kill you today, you shouldn't be out in the open like this."

That reminder unnerved her even further. She felt as if she was walking barefoot on razor blades. But she wasn't stupid, and she had taken precautions.

"That's why I brought the gun. And besides, no one followed me," she insisted.

"No one that you saw," Harlan growled. He tucked

the folder under his arm, shut her car door and took her
by the shoulder again.

Caitlyn wanted to argue with that. Heck, at this point
she wanted to argue with anything and anybody. She was
exhausted, scared, and she'd been forced to come to the
last man on earth who wanted to see her.

"Let's go back to my house so I can check some things
on the computer," he added, and he got her moving in
that direction. "Other than the threatening notes, has
anything else happened?"

"A while back. But that had nothing to do with this."

He smirked at her again. "You got more than one person threatening you?"

"Lots of people threaten me." Caitlyn returned the
smirk. "I don't exactly make a lot of friends in my job."

"That's not hard to believe," Harlan mumbled. "Anyone specific?"

She lifted her shoulder. "I had a stalker named Jay
Farris. He'd leave me marriage proposals stuffed into
bouquets of roses. When I turned him down, the roses
became bunches of dead rats and death threats."

That required a deep breath. Caitlyn still had nightmares about him. Always would.

"The rats escalated to an attempt to strangle me one
night after he'd seen me on a date with another man,"
she explained, not easily. Nothing was easy when it came
to talking about Farris. "He wanted to kill me to prove
how much he loved me."

"A real charmer, huh?" But there seemed to be more
anger than sarcasm in his voice. "What happened to
him?"

"He was diagnosed as a paranoid schizophrenic and
placed in a mental institution. Haven't heard from him
in nearly a year."

But what she left out was that Farris still had mentally haunted her all these months later. Haunted her to the point that she'd moved five times and had rarely gone into the office. She'd done most of her work from home.

"You're sure you haven't heard from Farris?" Harlan asked. "He could have sent you those notes."

Caitlyn shook her head. "No way would he have known what you said to me that night. He's seven years younger than we are, and that would have made him only nine when we were together. There weren't any kids that young in Rocky Creek."

Besides, she would have recognized an all-grown-up Farris if he'd been a fellow Rocky Creek resident. Those hard times had created bonds. Not necessarily good ones. But Caitlyn had no trouble remembering each face.

Including those of the dead and missing women.

They'd been her friends. One, Tiffany, had been her bunk mate. They'd shared every secret but one—Caitlyn hadn't told Tiff about losing her virginity to Harlan. No time for that, since both Tiff and she had been removed from Rocky Creek the following day and sent to different facilities. Caitlyn to Austin and Tiffany to San Antonio.

"Maybe Farris wasn't at Rocky Creek," Harlan said a moment later. "But he could have found out from the person who did see and hear us."

True. And despite the balmy night, that sent a chill through her.

Judas priest.

Farris had money from his family's hugely successful computer software business and could have hired someone to do his dirty work.

But why would Farris tell her not to talk to the Rangers?

He wouldn't.

Farris had no connection to what had gone on at Rocky Creek and Jonah Webb. At least, she was reasonably sure of that, but Caitlyn made a mental note to do more checking.

"How did you find out about Tiffany's car accident and that Sherry was missing?" Harlan did another of those glances around, and it made her consider running to his house. Thankfully, it wasn't far away, and she could see the light he'd left on in the hall.

"Tiff's fiancé called to let me know about her death. He asked me to get in touch with anyone from Rocky Creek who might want to know. I haven't stayed in touch with anyone, but I tried to track down Sherry. She runs an investment firm in Houston, and her business partner, Curtis Newell, said she left without giving him any notice."

"Maybe Sherry doesn't want to be found." Harlan shrugged. "Could be she just needs some downtime."

Caitlyn had already considered that and more. "None of her friends knows where she is. *None*. That's suspicious to me, and there doesn't appear to be any crisis going on in her life that would make her disappear. Also, she didn't actually tell anyone in person that she was leaving."

Harlan made a *hmm* sound to indicate he was thinking about that. "I'll call around, see what I can find. It could turn out to be nothing." He led her through the yard and to the porch. "Still, it's suspicious, especially when you consider everything else."

Harlan opened the front door, but then stopped and turned to face her. "For the record, if anything like this happens again, don't assume I'm out to kill you. And don't break into my house—*ever*."

The last word had hardly left his mouth when Caitlyn saw alarm go through Harlan's eyes. She shook her head, not understanding, but she didn't have time to ask what had put the alarm there.

Harlan dropped the folder, letting it slip from his arm and onto the floor, and in the same motion he spun away from her. Toward the living room.

But it was too late.

Caitlyn saw the movement behind them. Someone in the shadows. And that someone pointed a gun directly at Harlan.

But it wasn't a gun.

It was a Taser.

One hit from it, and Harlan let out a choked groan. She watched in horror as he dropped to the floor.

Caitlyn heard the scream bubble up in her throat, and she turned to grab Harlan's gun.

God. This couldn't be happening. Not again. Here she was fighting for her life, and worse. Harlan was in grave danger, too.

She didn't get a chance to grab the gun. No chance to do anything. She made it only a few steps before she felt the jolt from the Taser. It crackled through her entire body.

Just like that, she had no control. No chance to scream or get away.

Nothing.

Caitlyn couldn't even turn to see her attacker's face. But she heard the voice. It was like something from a cartoon. There was no humor in it, though, only fear that spread like ice through her veins when he whispered a warning.

"Time's up, Caitlyn."

# Chapter Three

Harlan winced at the dull throbbing ache in his head. But when he opened his eyes, the glare of sunlight turned the ache into a jolt of pain that nearly knocked the breath right out of him.

No time to adjust to the light and pain, though. He had to fight back.

He had to save Caitlyn and himself.

That reminder gave him a much-needed spike of adrenaline, and he shot to a sitting position and reached for his gun.

It wasn't there.

He blinked, focusing, and glanced around for his Glock. No shoulder holster. No Glock. In fact, the only thing he was wearing was his boxers.

Hell.

What was going on?

He dragged in a few quick breaths, hoping to clear his head. It helped. The last thing he remembered was being in the doorway of his house and someone shooting him with one of those long-range projectile Tasers. Well, he wasn't in his house now.

But he didn't know where he was.

It was a motel room from the looks of it, and he was on the bed. Not alone, though. That gave him another jolt of adrenaline, and his body went into fight mode until he realized the person beside him was Caitlyn.

She was wearing only her bra and panties. Skimpy ones at that.

And she wasn't moving.

Harlan nearly shouted out her name, but then realized it wouldn't be a smart thing to do. That was because he noticed something else—his left wrist was handcuffed to her right. He certainly didn't remember that about the attack, but he was guessing Caitlyn hadn't been the one to do this.

That meant they were not alone.

"Caitlyn?" he whispered.

No response. He put his left hand to her throat and felt her pulse. Steady and strong. That was good. But other than being alive, there wasn't much else good about this.

He tried again to wake Caitlyn while he looked around to assess their *situation*. It was a bare-bones kind of room. Bed, dresser, two nightstands and a TV. No phone, though. The adjoining bathroom door was wide-open, and while he couldn't see anyone, that didn't mean someone wasn't in the shower. Or the closet.

The someone who'd cuffed them.

But in the main part of the room there were no signs of anyone but Caitlyn and him. Heck, he didn't even see their clothes. Whatever had happened, they were clearly being held captive, and that meant they needed to get out of there. Or at least find some way to defend themselves.

Harlan gave Caitlyn's arm a hard shake, and this time he got a response. A groggy moan.

"Wake up," Harlan insisted. "We have to leave now."

Easier said than done. Because of the cuffs and the tornado going on in his head, he couldn't just bolt from the bed, but he hauled Caitlyn to a sitting position, anchoring her in place so she wouldn't topple back over. Her eyes finally eased open, and as he'd done, she looked around.

"Where are we?" she mumbled at the same moment that Harlan asked, "Any idea how we got here?"

Caitlyn groaned when she looked first at what she was wearing. Or rather what she wasn't wearing—clothes. And then at the cuffs.

"What happened after I got hit with the Taser?" he asked. Harlan got to his feet, looped his arm around her waist and helped her stand.

"I don't know." She tried to put her hand against her forehead. Probably because like him, she was in pain. But the handcuffs sent Harlan's arm brushing across her breasts.

"Sorry," she mumbled. Caitlyn blew out another breath. "I saw you get hit with the Taser, and I tried to get your gun. My gun," she corrected. "You'd put it in the back waist of your jeans."

Yeah. He remembered that part. The part about falling flat on the hardwood floor, too—emphasis on the *hard*. But that was where his memories stopped. Obviously Caitlyn had been attacked second, and that meant she might recall more than he did.

"You remember anything after he got you with the Taser?" he asked.

"No." She glanced around the room again. "I certainly don't remember being brought here. Or having my clothes taken off. Did you do that?"

He shook his head and was reasonably sure he would have remembered undressing Caitlyn. Or someone else undressing her in front of him. And that could mean only one thing.

"After the Taser hit, someone must have drugged us,"

Harlan explained. It was the only thing that made sense, and yet it didn't make sense at all.

"God," Caitlyn mumbled. She jerked her uncuffed hand to her mouth and pressed her fingers there for several seconds.

Harlan didn't like that *God* one bit. "What do you remember?"

She looked at him, blinked, and along with the grogginess, he could see fear in her eyes. "The person was using one of those voice scramblers, and he said something to me." She gulped in some air. "'Time's up, Caitlyn.'"

Tears watered her eyes, and he saw the muscles in her body tense. She was terrified. With reason.

"It's okay," Harlan tried to assure her. But it was a lie. Everything was far from *okay,* and it wouldn't get even marginally better until they were in a safe place. "You're still alive, so he obviously didn't carry through on his threat."

But why not?

It was a sickening thought, but their attacker had had plenty of time and opportunity to kill them both.

With his arm still looped around her, Harlan grabbed the lamp from the nightstand, the only semi-weapon in the room, and went to the window. He stayed to the side, keeping Caitlyn behind him, and eased back the curtain.

Yeah, they were definitely in a motel, and not a high-end one either. The window and front door faced a parking lot where there were several vehicles. However, he didn't see his truck or Caitlyn's car.

"Ever heard of the Starlight Inn?" he asked, noting the large sign at the end of the parking lot.

"No." She pressed her body against him when she peered over his shoulder. "It doesn't look familiar."

Not to him either, and they sure weren't in Maverick Springs. Harlan had lived there for sixteen years since he'd left Rocky Creek, and he knew every nook and cranny of the town.

So where were they, and who'd brought them here?

"I need to check the bathroom." With Caitlyn in tow, he started in that direction. Where their captor could be hiding.

Of course, there was no reason for the person to hide, since he was calling the shots here. But Harlan hoped he was there so he could bash the moron to bits for doing whatever the hell he'd done to them.

That gave Harlan a moment's pause.

What exactly had he done to them?

He glanced at Caitlyn again, specifically at her body, running his gaze from her face to her breasts to her belly, where he spotted a tiny black ink tattoo with letters.

And then below.

There didn't appear to be anything obvious, like love bites or bruises, but they were wearing just underwear and had woken up in a bed.

"Did we…?" she asked, clearly picking up on the reason he was gawking at her body.

"No." And that, too, could be a whopper of a lie, especially if someone had given them a drug that had caused memory loss. But Harlan wasn't going to worry about that now, particularly since they had more immediate problems.

With the lamp ready as a club, he went in ahead of Caitlyn. The shower curtain was closed. Of course. No chance that any of this would be easy. Harlan readied himself and used his foot to shove back the vinyl curtain. It slithered open, the metal rings jangling on the overhead bar and sounding far more sinister than it would have under normal circumstances.

Empty.

Well, it was empty except for their clothes and shoes, which had been neatly folded and placed in the tub.

Harlan tossed the lamp aside and rifled through the garments, looking for either his or Caitlyn's gun. They weren't there. Neither were their phones or a key for the cuffs.

"What's going on?" Caitlyn asked. She grabbed her jeans and started to put them on. Not easily because of the blasted handcuffs.

Harlan put on his jeans, too. Best not to go after their captor while he was practically butt naked. "I'm not sure. But judging from what this dirt-for-brains said to you about time being up, it's all part of the threats. That could mean we're back to someone who doesn't want you talking to the Rangers or your stalker, Farris. He could have hired someone to do this, or maybe he's out of the institution."

That sort of stuff happened all the time. Inmates were released and no one bothered to tell the victims.

"No," she said while she put on her shoes. "If Farris were out, he would have just killed me. He wouldn't have drugged us and brought us here."

She was obviously basing that conclusion on his previous attack, when he'd tried to strangle her. Something that turned Harlan's stomach. But Farris could have taken a new direction in his criminal activity, so Harlan wasn't going to rule him out. No. Just the opposite.

Farris—or the person he'd hired—was at the top of his list.

Harlan tugged on his boots and looped his shirt over his arm, since there was no way he could put it on. Caitlyn, however, ripped the right side and sleeve of her top so she could cover herself. Probably for the best. Her bra and what was beneath it were just plain distracting.

Too many memories.

Harlan headed back to the front door, but he took a moment to rifle through the nightstand drawer to find something—anything—he could use to pick the lock on the handcuffs. But there wasn't a stray paper clip. That meant going outside without being able to give Farris, or whoever had done this, a full fight.

There was a local telephone directory in the bottom drawer. Not thick or big enough. While it wouldn't stop a bullet, he grabbed it and rolled it so that it formed a nightstick of sorts. Hardly his weapon of choice when they didn't know what they were up against, but maybe he could avoid a showdown until he was in a better position to kick somebody's butt for doing this to Caitlyn and him.

"Stay behind me," Harlan warned Caitlyn, and he eased open the door and looked outside.

It was early morning, maybe seven or so, and there was no one in the parking lot, but a car did go by on the street in front of the motel. It didn't stop, and Harlan didn't call out to the driver.

That was because he had a bad feeling they were being watched.

After all, why would someone go to all the trouble of using a Taser on them, drugging them and bringing them to this place only to let them easily escape?

Harlan kept close to the building and headed for the office sign at the front. Right by the road. Once inside he could call his brothers, who were no doubt wondering where the heck he was. It was a workday, and he should have already been at the marshals' office in Maverick Springs.

He and Caitlyn were still a good twenty yards from the office when a dark blue truck turned into the parking lot. But it didn't just turn. The tires squealed as the driver whipped into the lot, and Harlan automatically pulled Caitlyn to the ground in front of one of the parked cars, an older-model red four-door sedan.

The truck slowed once it was in the lot, and the driver inched around, pausing in front of each door. Maybe checking the numbers? Maybe looking for any sign of them.

Or witnesses.

That was a strong possibility, since there appeared to be other guests staying at the motel. The driver finally came to a stop in the parking spot directly in front of the room they'd just escaped from.

Harlan stayed low, pulling Caitlyn as far behind him as he could manage. He watched. And held his breath. He didn't want to fight like this. Not where Caitlyn could be in the line of fire and also in his way. He wouldn't be able to fight while handcuffed to her.

It didn't take long, just a few seconds, before the truck door flew open and the driver stepped out. A man wearing dark clothes. He kept his back to Harlan, so he couldn't see his face, and didn't recognize the man's gait. However, he thought he might recognize the gun he held next to his right leg. It looked exactly like Harlan's standard-issue Glock.

Harlan tried to take in as many details of the man as he could, including the number of his license plate and the way he practically kicked down the door of the motel room. Whoever this guy was, he was riled to the core, and that meant there'd be no showdown between

Harlan and him. Not at this moment anyway, but once he had Caitlyn someplace safe, he was coming after this dirt wipe.

"You know that guy?" Harlan asked her.

"Hard to tell." Her breath was racing, hitting against his bare shoulder and back, and every muscle in her arm was iron hard. "But it could be Farris. We need to find out if he's out of the institution."

He would. And maybe Caitlyn would be able to confirm if it was or wasn't Farris when she got a look at his face. The trick was to let Caitlyn get that look without the guy seeing her. Harlan didn't want the man using that Glock on them.

From inside the room, Harlan heard a loud crash, as if someone had bashed something against the wall. Harlan waited with his breath held, and within seconds the man burst out of the room.

Caitlyn groaned softly, and Harlan knew why.

They couldn't see his face to determine if it was her stalker because the guy was wearing a ski mask. He jumped back into the truck and sped away. He was already a few yards past the vehicle where they were hiding when the driver of the truck slammed on his brakes.

"What's he doing?" Caitlyn asked, her voice a hoarse whisper.

Harlan didn't answer. Didn't want to make a sound, but he eased himself lower to the ground so he could watch from beneath the car.

His heart slammed against his ribs when he heard the truck door open again. And Harlan saw black combat boots when the guy stepped out. The man didn't move for what seemed to be an eternity, and it gave Harlan too much time to think of all the things that could go wrong.

"Get back in the truck," Harlan said to himself, hoping the guy would do just that.

But he didn't.

He took a step. Then another.

Oh, hell.

The armed man was walking straight toward them.

# Chapter Four

It took every bit of Caitlyn's self-control—and Harlan's bruising grip on her arm—to stay in her place. Her instincts were screaming for her to bolt. To get far away from the ski-masked man who was just a few yards away and closing in fast. But running would only get her shot.

Harlan, too.

Because she hadn't missed that the man coming toward them was also armed. And angry. Everything about his body language told her he was working on a short fuse and a hot temper, and it was too much to hope that all that fury was aimed at someone other than Harlan and her.

But why?

Soon she wanted to know the answer to that, but unfortunately they might be killed before they learned why this man was after them.

Even though she tried not to make a sound, that was just about impossible with her heart and breath galloping out of control. Unlike Harlan. He was focused only on the man's movement, and he didn't show any sign of the fear Caitlyn was feeling.

She glanced around them, looking for anything she could use as a weapon. The only things within reach were a couple of small rocks, so Caitlyn scooped them up and waited. God, she wished they had a phone so she could at least call the cops.

The man stopped, and Caitlyn pulled in her breath. Held it. Waiting and praying that he would just turn around, go back to his truck and drive away.

That didn't happen.

Because her attention was nailed to him, she saw the shift of his weight to the front of his feet, and he slowly bent his knees. Lowering himself. Stooping down. And there was only one reason for him to do that.

So he could look beneath the cars.

Caitlyn tried to hold out hope that he wouldn't see them. Or that someone would see him and send him running. After all, a man in a ski mask was bound to look suspicious.

Harlan turned his head slightly to the side. "Get ready to move," he mouthed.

That caused panic to shoot through her again. Move where? There were only two places for them to go— right or left—and either way the man would see them.

Even though she'd braced herself for the man to fire, it was still a hard jolt when the blast came. In the same second, Harlan used their handcuffed connection to jerk her to the side. Away from the bullet that slammed into the ground.

The sound was deafening, and it seemed to echo through the parking lot. No way the guests would miss that, and it would certainly prompt someone to call the cops.

She hoped.

Still, it wouldn't help them now.

The sound she didn't hear was a car alarm. Caitlyn had hoped there'd be one and that the blaring noise would send the man running back to his truck. It didn't. No alarm, just the man coming for them.

Harlan didn't stay put. He shoved her behind him as far as he could. Which wasn't far. And he dragged them to the side of the vehicle.

Even over the roar in her ears, Caitlyn had no trouble hearing the man's footsteps. Definitely not light. More like stomps. Of course, she already knew he was in a rage, so it was no surprise that he was coming at them like a madman.

But why was he trying to kill them now when he'd had plenty of time to do it while they'd been unconscious inside the motel room?

Caitlyn didn't have time to consider an answer because there was another shot. This one tore through the hood of the car and came so close to them that she could swear she felt the heat and movement of the bullet.

Shoving her along, Harlan hurried to the back of the car, and he dragged her behind the beat-up old station wagon next to them. She caught just a glimpse of the shooter before another bullet came their way. This one tore off a chunk of the car's bumper.

Still no car alarm.

Harlan kept them moving. Away from the shooter and toward the motel check-in. That didn't deter the man. She could still hear his stomps, but she also heard something else.

Shouts.

Someone was yelling out to call 911, but the shots kept away anyone who might otherwise want to help. She prayed no one inside the rooms would get hurt.

Harlan pulled her to the far side of the station wagon. Still three vehicles away from the motel office. Way too far to make a run for it, and besides, if the clerk was smart, he would have already locked the door.

"Hell," she heard Harlan mumble.

And she soon realized why. The shooter wasn't just stomping now. He'd broken into a run.

Heading right for them.

Harlan levered himself up and hurled the rolled-up phone book at the guy. From the sound it made, it smacked him somewhere on the body, but she didn't see exactly where. That was because Harlan got them moving again—this time to a small car that put them one step closer to the office.

Another shot.

Then another.

The bullets tore right through the small car and slammed into the truck parked next to it. The sound was instant. A shrill blast from the truck's security alarm. But the noise did something else that Caitlyn hadn't counted on.

It drowned out their attacker's footsteps.

She had no idea where he was, but that lasted only a few seconds. She soon saw his exact location.

The man barreled around the back of the small car, and before he even came to a stop, he was already taking aim. Harlan was moving, too. Trying to get them out of the line of fire.

Caitlyn scrambled as Harlan dragged her along, but she turned and tossed the handful of rocks right at the guy.

Pay dirt.

The rocks distracted him, and his shot was off. The bullet slammed into the ground, sending a spray of sharp chunks of concrete at them. Even with the debris, Harlan managed to get them to cover behind the next vehicle.

Their attacker made a feral sound. A sort of outraged growl, but he didn't speak.

He fired another shot, but this one didn't come anywhere near close to them. Good. Maybe he was no longer in control.

Over the shrill car alarm Caitlyn heard another sound. A welcome one. Sirens. And they already sounded close.

Harlan pulled her farther down to the concrete, and for a moment she thought he'd done that because he'd gotten a glimpse of the shooter, but he peered under the vehicle.

"He's getting away."

Because of the clamor of sirens and noise, Caitlyn didn't actually hear Harlan's words, but she saw them form on his mouth. The relief was instant, but it was quickly replaced by another feeling. Major concern. If the shooter managed to escape, they might never know who he was or why he'd launched this attack.

Harlan made a quick peek over the hood of the car, and he cursed. She soon figured out why. The truck zipped past them, flying across the parking lot.

That got Harlan and her to their feet, and she prayed the cops were there, in place and ready to stop this guy.

But they weren't.

The truck bolted out of the parking lot and onto the street that fronted the motel.

Still cursing, Harlan got them moving again toward the motel office. "Keep your hands up so everyone can see them," he warned her.

Mercy. Caitlyn hadn't considered that someone might think they'd fired those shots, but in the chaos of a situation, anything could happen. They lifted their hands just as two police cruisers braked to a stop. Not in the parking lot but on the very street where the gunman had just escaped.

With their guns drawn, the cops barreled out and used their cruisers for cover. They aimed their weapons at Harlan and her.

"I'm Marshal Harlan McKinney," he shouted over the alarm. "You need to go after the driver of a blue truck." And he rattled off the license plate.

The cops didn't move, and she couldn't blame them. Harlan and she were handcuffed together, disheveled and probably didn't look like victims of a kidnapping, even if that was exactly what they were.

Now Caitlyn cursed. It would take precious minutes, maybe longer, for the cops to sort all of this out, and the shooter could be long gone by then.

The door to the motel office opened just a fraction, and a lanky man poked his head out a few inches. "The guy that drove out of here fired shots at them," he confirmed.

But that still didn't get the cops moving. The four officers said something to each other. Something she couldn't catch because of the alarms, but Harlan started lowering himself to his knees. Caitlyn did the same, and soon she found herself facedown on the concrete.

Finally the cops came out from cover and made their way toward them. Also, the alarm stopped so she could actually hear what they were saying.

"Marshal McKinney?" one of the uniforms called out.

"Yeah," Harlan verified. "There's probably a missing persons report on me."

"There is," the cop verified. He looked at his phone and then at Harlan, probably comparing a photo to his face.

She hadn't even considered that Harlan's brothers

would be looking for him and would have alerted the
authorities, but Caitlyn was thankful they had.

"No missing report on you," the cop said to her. "But
you look familiar. Are you that reporter?"

She settled for mumbling a yes, since she and the
cops were rarely in the same corner. This was one exception, though. She was thankful beyond words to have
been rescued.

The cop reached down and helped them back to their
feet, but Harlan didn't stay put. He immediately started
toward the cruisers.

"We need to go in pursuit now," Harlan insisted, and
it sounded like an order. "And get us out of these damn
cuffs."

The cop didn't argue, and as they approached the
other officers, she heard one of them phoning in the
shooter's license plate. Maybe they'd get lucky and catch
him, but Caitlyn's heart dropped when she saw they were
on an access road. The ramp to the interstate was literally just yards away.

One look at Harlan, and she saw the frustration and
anger in his eyes, too.

"What happened to you two?" the lanky officer asked
them. His name tag identified him as Sergeant Eric Tinsley.

Harlan threw open the side door of the cruiser and
jumped in, pulling her practically into his lap, since there
wasn't much room in the passenger seat.

"I can't let you do this," Tinsley said.

Harlan met the cop's gaze. "This guy kidnapped us
and tried to kill us. He's not getting away."

And while Harlan's tone left no room for doubt about
that, they both knew the shooter was doing just that—
getting away.

"When the motel clerk called 911, he gave a description of the vehicle," Tinsley said. "Law enforcement will be on the lookout for it."

"That's not enough," Harlan insisted. "I need to find this guy."

Tinsley looked around as if figuring out what to do, but then he tipped his head to the backseat of the cruiser. "Get in and buckle up so my partner can ride with us. Can't do this without backup, and you're not exactly in any position to assist."

Harlan made an even more frustrated sound of agreement and got her moving into the backseat. There was a metal mesh divider between the front and back. Clearly for prisoner transport, but she didn't care about that. Caitlyn only wanted to go after the shooter.

Thankfully, that didn't take long.

Tinsley's partner tossed Harlan a key that he took from the glove compartment, and he jumped in. "It's a universal key," he explained as they sped away from the motel.

Harlan didn't waste any time unlocking the cuffs, and Caitlyn's hand dropped like a stone. The muscles in her hand and arm were knotted. Her head was still pounding, too, but those were minor things. At the moment no one was shooting at them, and maybe they could get a lot of answers as to why this had happened, if they could just catch up with that blue truck.

A truck she didn't see.

Tinsley drove up the ramp and onto the interstate, and while there were a few other trucks on the road, the blue one was nowhere in sight.

Mercy.

They had to find him.

"Who's this shooter?" Tinsley asked.

Harlan didn't have time to answer because Tinsley's phone rang. A few moments later he hung up and shook his head. "You're sure that was the right license plate for the blue truck?"

"Positive." Harlan didn't look at the man when he answered. He was literally on the edge of the seat, checking out the traffic while he shoved his arm through the sleeve of his shirt.

"Then it's bogus," Tinsley informed them.

She didn't know who groaned louder—Harlan or her. Now there was no way to know who owned the vehicle unless they found it, and with each passing mile, her hopes were getting lower and lower in that department.

"He's not working alone," Harlan said, glancing first at her and then briefly meeting Tinsley's gaze in the rear-view mirror. "Someone hit us with a Taser, drugged us and put us in that motel room."

"You saw more than one person?" Tinsley asked.

"No, but if the shooter had been the one to put us there, he wouldn't have had to look for the room."

Caitlyn thought back to those terrifying moments before the shooting. The man hadn't gone directly to the room, and he'd spent some time inside looking around. He probably wouldn't have had to do that if he'd known all along they were there.

That tightened the knot in her stomach.

God, how many were in on this?

"One man probably couldn't have carried me," Harlan muttered, as if he knew exactly what she was thinking.

Yeah. Harlan was a big guy, and that meant there had probably been at least two who'd carried them from his house and to the motel. Caitlyn didn't want to think of what else those men had done, but she was positive she hadn't been raped. That was something, at least. A *big* something.

"This has to be connected to Rocky Creek," she said to Harlan. All those threats couldn't be coincidence.

But then she had to shake her head.

*Time's up, Caitlyn. Tomorrow you die.* That had been the last threat she'd received, and it hadn't happened. The guy with the Taser hadn't killed her, though he would have had ample opportunity to do just that. Plus, it would have been a heck of a lot easier than drugging them and dragging them to that motel.

Almost as if they'd been bait.

Or something.

"What's the date?" she asked.

The officers seemed surprised, but Tinsley checked his watch. "The fourteenth."

"It's still *tomorrow,*" Harlan verified. "And I'm pretty sure the shooter was supposed to make that threat come true."

Yes. And he nearly had. She'd lost count of how many shots he'd fired, but any one of them could have hit Harlan and her.

"He wasn't an expert shot," Harlan continued. "And it was personal."

Caitlyn couldn't argue with either of those points. "That leads us back to Farris."

She was about to ask for a phone so she could make some calls to find out if Farris was indeed still in the institution, but she stopped when she spotted the truck just ahead. Not speeding away. Not even on the interstate.

But rather at a standstill in the emergency lane.

"That's it," Harlan told the officers.

Tinsley turned on the lights and siren, called for backup and eased to a stop behind the truck. Caitlyn

tried to look inside the vehicle, but Harlan didn't give
her a chance. He caught the back of her neck and pushed
her down on the seat.

"Stay put," Harlan insisted.

Tinsley looked back at Harlan as if he might tell him
the same thing, but he didn't stop Harlan from getting
out with him and his partner. Both cops drew their weapons, and they stayed behind the cover of their doors while
they kept their attention fastened on the truck.

Caitlyn lifted her head just a little so she could look,
too, but the back window on the truck had a heavy tint,
and she couldn't see inside the truck cab.

Tinsley called out for the driver to exit the vehicle. No
response, though. Ditto for his second attempt.

The seconds dragged by, and even though Caitlyn
tried to keep her heartbeat and breathing steady, she
failed big-time. She'd known she was in danger before
she even went to Harlan's place, but she hadn't considered that she could be bringing the danger to him.

He could be killed.

Right here, if the gunman started shooting.

Even though there was bad blood between them, the
last thing she wanted was him to be hurt. Or involved
in this. But then she rethought that, too.

Harlan was involved.

One of the threats had even mentioned what he'd said
to her that night they'd had sex. So maybe the person
behind all of this had written that knowing it would
make her suspect Harlan. Knowing that she would go
running to him.

If so, this was all her fault.

Her breath stalled again when the cops began to inch
toward the truck door, and Harlan stayed right with them
despite the fact that he wasn't armed. Each step they

took put her heart higher in her throat, but she could only sit there, watch and pray that this was all about to end. If they had the shooter, then they would know who was behind this.

And why.

Tinsley approached the driver's side. His partner, the other. But Harlan moved even closer to Tinsley when the officer peered into the window. He said something to Harlan. Something she couldn't hear, but Caitlyn didn't need to hear the words to see the frustration in Tinsley's body language.

It was Harlan who threw open the driver's door, and again she didn't need to hear what he said to know he was cursing a blue streak. That was the last straw.

Nothing could have held Caitlyn back at that point.

She bolted from the cruiser to see what had caused the profanity and frustration. And she soon saw.

The truck was empty.

She looked back to the interstate, hoping she'd catch a glimpse of the shooter—maybe on foot, maybe driving away in another vehicle. It was possible he was doing just that, but if so, he was nowhere in sight.

"He left something," Harlan said.

Caitlyn followed his gaze and soon saw what had captured Harlan's attention. A folded piece of paper was on the steering wheel.

"I want it processed for prints." But Harlan didn't touch it. No doubt because he didn't want to disturb any evidence that the shooter might have left, not just on the paper but in the truck itself.

"Something's written on it," Tinsley pointed out.

"Yeah." Harlan shook his head, repeated it. "It's a message," he said, looking at Caitlyn. "For you."

# Chapter Five

Harlan cursed the bad phone reception at the Maverick Springs Hospital, and everything else he could think of.

There was a lot on that particular list.

He could make out only half of what his brother Slade Becker was saying, but even so, Harlan wasn't hearing anything good.

His other brother Declan had brought Harlan his phone from the house because it had all his contact numbers, but what he needed was to hear some good news.

According to Slade, there was no sign of the shooter and no security cameras at the motel in Cross Creek where he and Caitlyn had been taken, cuffed and left for a killer to finish them off. If the crappy news had ended there, it might not have been so bad.

But it didn't.

Sergeant Tinsley had added to the growing heap of *bad* by telling Harlan that there didn't appear to be any prints or traces in either the truck or on the note the SOB had left with Caitlyn's name scrawled on the folded sheet of paper. A note with just a handful of words.

*This isn't over. You're a dead woman.*

Harlan wanted to disagree with that threat, but he couldn't. As long as the shooter and his accomplice were out there, this was far from over for Caitlyn. And as for the dead part—well, that's what he had to stop from happening.

"What about any info on Jay Farris?" Harlan asked his brother.

"Still trying. He was transferred to a private facility about a month ago—" And the rest was static gibberish, but Harlan thought Slade said something about the facility not giving them access to records without a court order. "You've got to call the Ranger back, Harlan."

Now, that part came through loud and clear.

*Figures.*

It was the one thing in this conversation that he didn't want relayed, because the Ranger in question was none other than Griffin Morris, who'd been assigned to investigate Jonah Webb's murder. If Harlan had thought for one second that Morris had any info about this incident, he'd be on the phone to him, but no. Morris wanted to question Harlan as a possible suspect—accessory to Webb's murder.

Harlan didn't have time for that.

The door to the examining room opened finally, and Harlan told Slade that he would call him back. Right now he needed to make sure Caitlyn was all right, and judging from the glimpse that Harlan got of her face from over the doctor's shoulder, she wasn't. She was shades too pale and looked ready to collapse.

Dr. Cheryl Landry stopped in the doorway and met Harlan's gaze. "She'll be okay. Your turn now. Want to go into the examining room next door so I can give you a checkup?"

"It can wait." Yet something else he didn't have time for—and besides, he'd already done the important part. He'd had the lab draw a blood sample to see if they could identify what had been used to drug him.

The doctor frowned, but she didn't look surprised. Probably because she'd been stitching up Harlan and his brothers for the better part of a decade. She knew cooperation wasn't their strong suit.

"At least get some rest," the doctor grumbled. "And that goes for both of you. I'll call as soon as I have the lab results from the tox screens." She walked away, still mumbling and scribbling something on a chart.

Caitlyn didn't get up from the examining table. Practically limp, she sat there wearing green scrubs that were identical to Harlan's. One of the first things on his to-do list was to get them a change of clothes, since theirs had been bagged for processing. He doubted there'd be any usable trace evidence on them, but their luck might change.

He sure as heck hoped so anyway.

Harlan walked closer, easing the door shut behind him so he could ask her a question that he wasn't sure how to ask. He played with the words in his head, but Caitlyn beat him to it.

"I wasn't sexually assaulted," she volunteered. "No signs of recent sex, consensual or otherwise."

Harlan was relieved but not surprised. Well, not surprised except for the recent-sex part. With Caitlyn's looks, he figured she must have a current lover, but maybe Farris had destroyed that part of her life, too.

Thankfully, he'd seen no indications on her body of a violent attack, and he'd gotten an up-close-and-personal look at it, since she'd been wearing only panties and a bra in bed. Besides, if they'd had sex he would have remembered.

Even drugs wouldn't have blocked that out.

Hell, bad blood and sixteen years hadn't been able to make him forget having sex with her.

"I'm guessing there are no breaks in the investigation," she mumbled, pushing her hair away from her face.

Harlan shook his head and caught her arm when she practically stumbled off the table. "There's some red tape involved in getting more info about Farris at the private facility where he was transferred. Did you know he'd been moved?"

"No." She gave a weary sigh and looked up at him with those equally weary blue eyes. "I went in the wrong direction on this. All those threats seemed to point to you."

And he wasn't too happy that she'd jumped to believe the worst about him. But then he mentally shrugged. She'd probably thought the worst because in their last conversation they'd been at each other's throats.

He'd blasted her six ways to Sunday over that article she'd written about him.

"We can go back to my place and wait," he insisted. "You need to get some rest and something to eat. And we can make a few calls to try to speed up all the wheels that are turning right now."

He'd also have to put some time in at the office, but the adrenaline crash was getting to him, too.

"Is my car still at your house?" she asked.

"Yeah." It was one of the things he'd managed to hear Slade confirm. Her car was there, and there'd been no damage to the place. "But you're not driving anywhere. It's not safe, Caitlyn."

He braced himself for a big argument. Caitlyn was even more pigheaded than he was, but it had to be a sign of exhaustion when she only shrugged. "I just want to catch this bastard."

Harlan was right there with her. Literally. She took a step but then stumbled again. And this time she fell into his arms. Except it was more than a fall. She was so weak, she didn't hit him with a thud. She melted against him.

Not good.

Because their arms went around each other. Their bodies met. And she looked up at him. At the same moment he looked down at her.

Everything seemed to freeze.

In fact, lots of weird things happened. The memories came. Not those of the attack—something that should have been occupying his thoughts—but other memories. Those that involved kisses.

And more than kisses.

The corner of her mouth lifted, and that half smile seemed as wobbly as the rest of her. She gave his arm a pat, grazing his chest in the process. The rest of her did a little grazing, too. But she didn't move away.

Neither did Harlan.

Oh, man. He didn't need this now. Not ever. The memories were bad enough, but now his asinine body was starting to act as if it was about to get lucky.

It wasn't.

And Harlan repeated that to himself.

"Even hate can't cool *that* down," Caitlyn mumbled. With that shocker of a remark, she brushed her mouth over his, opened the door and headed out.

Harlan was right behind her, but it took him a moment to get his tongue untangled over that blasted half kiss. Man, something that wussy shouldn't have packed such a wallop.

"I don't hate you," he clarified, choosing to deal with the easier part of that shocker. He didn't intend to touch the other with a ten-foot pole. "I hated what you did. I don't like it when people screw around with my badge and career."

"That article was my career," she countered. "If I hadn't written it, someone else would have."

That was probably true, but this wasn't a reasoning kind of thing here. Her article had painted him and the Marshals Service in a bad light, and he'd caught a boatload of flak over it. Flak he'd aimed right back at her when he'd called her.

"I'm not a jerk," she added, "but sometimes I have to make decisions I don't want to make." Caitlyn stopped and looked out when they reached the door.

Just as Harlan did. He didn't see anyone ready to gun them down, but his brother Declan was waiting, leaning against his truck, which was parked next to one of the standard-issue cars that Harlan had used to drive them from headquarters to the hospital.

"Declan," Caitlyn said, and she hurried to him and pulled him into her arms for a hug.

Harlan wasn't jealous of his little brother, but it was a little unnerving to see Caitlyn nestled there as if it were the most natural place on earth for her to be.

Declan smiled and lifted a strand of her hair. "Last time I saw you, it was pink, and you had a nose ring."

She returned the smile. "Last time I saw you, you weren't taller than me."

Declan put his mouth to her ear, whispered something. When he was done, Caitlyn did the same and then they finally pulled away from each other.

"Best not to stand out here in the open like this," Harlan grumbled.

He frowned, first because they were out in the open with a gunman loose and then because he was—hell's bells—jealous.

Yeah, he was.

He didn't want to be, but wanting the feelings to go away didn't make it happen. He forced himself to remember that blasted article she'd written. And the fact that Caitlyn had thought he was a would-be killer.

That gave him the attitude adjustment he needed.

Harlan took her by the arm and pulled her toward the car. "Slade told me there was a problem getting info on Farris," he said to Declan.

"There was. The facility wouldn't confirm or deny they had a patient by that name. The court order was taking too long, so Dallas threatened to close them down for harboring a fugitive."

"Good." Harlan wished he'd been the one to do the threatening even if a threat like that was little more than a bluff. For Pete's sake, this was an attempted-murder investigation, and in his book that should trump privacy issues of someone who shouldn't have been granted privacy in the first place.

"Farris is out, isn't he?" Caitlyn asked.

Harlan looked at his brother and wondered how she'd come to that conclusion. He didn't see anything in Declan's expression to indicate that particular piece of bad news.

But then Declan nodded. "He only spent a few days at the private facility before he was released to his personal shrink."

Caitlyn didn't make a sound, but she dropped onto the seat. "How did he get out?"

"Not sure yet. The court order should tell us that, but in the meantime, we have his name and his picture that we got from old articles on the internet."

Old articles probably connected to the time he'd attacked Caitlyn. Harlan was looking forward to putting this guy right back where he belonged. It took a special piece of slime to try to kill a woman.

"Every law enforcement agency in the state will be looking for Farris," Declan added.

Yeah, but according to Caitlyn, Farris was rich. That meant he had resources and could already be out of the country or at least hidden away. Well, if he didn't still want to kill them, that was. If he did, then Farris wouldn't go far. He'd continue to stalk Caitlyn.

"It might not be Farris," Declan reminded them. "That's why we need to take a harder look at all of this."

Harlan couldn't agree more. "I'll be by the office later, and I can expand the search."

"Not until tomorrow," his brother corrected. "Saul's orders. He put you on quarters for twenty-four hours and doesn't want to see you before then. Made it official and everything with some paperwork."

Great. Just great. Saul Warner, his boss, was forcing him to get some rest. Rest that Harlan needed badly. But he'd much rather be working the case, and the best place to do that was at the office.

Harlan hit the accelerator much harder than he'd planned and ended up peeling out of the parking lot.

"Is the anger for me, Farris or the fact you can't go to work today?" she asked.

Harlan didn't even try to lie. "All three."

She made a sound to indicate she wasn't surprised. "Don't worry." Caitlyn reached over and took the phone that was sticking out of his front pocket. "I'll make arrangements to stay elsewhere."

He snatched the phone back from her and headed for the ranch. "Elsewhere?"

"Yes. As in with a friend or something."

"Sheez. Are you trying to get yourself and your *friend*

killed? That last threat wasn't a joke, Caitlyn. This whack job isn't backing down."

The color drained from her face again, and she swallowed hard. Okay. So he hadn't meant to yell at her, but he also had to make it clear that the danger wasn't over just because they were no longer cuffed together and half-naked in a motel room.

"We have ranch hands who can set up security," he went on. "They can keep an eye out for this guy." And he could do a better job of securing his own house. He didn't have a burglar alarm, but he could lock all the windows and doors and keep watch.

"If I stay with you, I'll put you in danger, too," she said, her voice catching.

"I'm already in danger. The threats were meant to send you to me. The guy was waiting in my house with a Taser." Not exactly a pleasant thought that someone had gotten the jump on him and that it could have cost them both their lives.

"Besides," Harlan added, "I'm a marshal, and until we work out what's going on, you're not leaving my sight."

Her left eyebrow swung up. "Really?" she said with a massive amount of skepticism. "You want to *protect* me?"

There it was again. That irritating nails-on-a-chalkboard effect, since she was questioning his intentions as a lawman.

"I *will* protect you," he insisted. Wanting to do it was an entirely different matter. "And so will my brothers."

Declan included. Not a surprise, but that encounter in the parking lot still was.

"What'd you whisper to Declan?" And why he was wasting time on this, he didn't know. Oh, wait. Yeah, he did. Caitlyn was making him crazy, and not in a good way.

"Old joke." A smile bent her mouth just a little. But she didn't share either the reason for that smile or the joke itself.

Cursing again, he was about to shove his phone back into his pocket when it buzzed, and it wasn't one of his brothers' names on the screen. However, it was someone he recognized.

"Ranger Griffin Morris," Harlan snarled, and he let the call go to voice mail, where the Ranger would no doubt leave a message, adding to the others he'd already left.

"Morris," Caitlyn repeated. "The guy investigating Webb's murder. He's interviewed you?"

"Several times." And then it occurred to Harlan that the Ranger had almost certainly interviewed Caitlyn, too.

"Yes, I've talked to him," she confirmed. "He thinks one of us helped Sarah Webb kill her husband."

Harlan waited for more, but she didn't add anything. "What'd you tell him?" he came out and asked.

"The truth." She didn't hesitate either. "That I hated Webb just like the rest of you did, but I didn't help put a knife in him."

"Morris believed you and your alibi?"

Now there was some hesitation. "I think so. Again, I told him the truth—that I was with you. Why?"

"Because he sure as hell doesn't seem to believe me. I guess he figures I was big enough to help Sarah haul a dead body down a flight of stairs."

"You were. *Are*," she corrected. Caitlyn paused, then huffed. "And I guess because of my history, I'm not exactly reliable in the eyes of the law."

Probably not. Even though her juvie records were supposed to have been sealed, the Rangers had likely discov-

ered that Caitlyn had spent some time in reform school,
and she'd been in more than a fight or two both before
and during her stay at Rocky Creek Children's Facility,
where Webb had been murdered.

"My bad-girl past is coming back to haunt us," she
mumbled. "I'm sorry about that."

Despite the mumble, he heard the sincerity, and he
didn't want her apologizing for her past. Especially when
part of that past was a facade.

"You weren't a bad girl," he reminded her. "You just
wanted everyone to think you were." Harlan tossed her
a look, daring her to argue with that fact.

After all, she'd been a virgin when they'd had sex.

"You'll always be my first," Caitlyn said under her
breath.

Normally that wouldn't have caused a chill to snake
down his spine, but it did now because it was the exact
wording in one of the threats. He'd given it plenty of
thought, but he wasn't any closer to figuring out who
had written those threats. However, Caitlyn was right
about one thing—whoever it was either knew them or
knew someone who'd been spying on them that night at
Rocky Creek.

That was just one of the puzzling things about their
situation.

"Why me, Caitlyn? Why give yourself to me?" Harlan hadn't actually meant to say that aloud, but it just
popped out of his mouth. It figured. He'd been saying
and doing a lot of dumb things since Caitlyn had broken
into his house the night before.

She lifted her shoulder as if the answer were obvious. "I really liked you and knew you wouldn't just use
me." She glanced at him. "And for the record, I know it

wasn't your first time, but the *you'll always be my first* was a nice touch. Made it feel special."

She made *nice touch* seemed like a ploy or lip service. It hadn't been. He'd blurted it out much as he'd just done his question. And even though it grated on him to have her believe he'd used that as some line, this time Harlan kept his mouth shut.

Sometimes the memories should just stay buried. Especially since they had so many other things to work out.

He took the turn toward Blue Creek Ranch, and he tried to remember all the things he had to do. Calls he had to make. Security arrangements. Updates on all the moving wheels of this investigation. The list was growing by leaps and bounds, but he needed to add something important.

Find Sherry Summers.

The missing former Rocky Creek resident might have answers about what was happening to them now. Of course, Sherry might not be alive. The killer might have already gotten to her.

In addition to Sherry, Harlan also needed to go through the list of suspects who could have helped Sarah Webb kill her SOB of a husband.

The Rangers had Caitlyn and him on that list.

But there had to be someone else, someone who'd actually done the crime.

"Who's your best guess for Sarah's accomplice?" he asked Caitlyn.

"Rudy Simmons," she answered right off the bat.

Yeah, the caretaker was on Harlan's suspect list, too. But so far, there'd been no evidence pointing to the man. Plus, Webb and Rudy had actually been friends. Maybe Webb's only friend.

"Kirby," Caitlyn mumbled.

He hated to hear her mention his foster father's name in the context of a murder, but Kirby could have indeed done it, especially after the beatings that Webb had given Harlan and his foster brothers. Kirby knew about the abuse, had been working hard to try to stop it, but maybe his foster father had reached a boiling point.

"Rocky Creek was supposed to be closing," Caitlyn continued, "but there were rumors that Webb had found a way to keep it open. If Kirby thought he couldn't get any of you out…"

She didn't finish. Thank God. Because that was indeed a huge motive, one that made his stomach tighten and churn.

"I'm worried about Declan's alibi," Harlan confessed.

Or rather his lack of an alibi. Declan should have been in the infirmary that night, since Webb had given him a hell of a beating earlier that day. But no one had seen Declan there, and so far his foster brother wasn't volunteering any information in that department. Of course, Harlan hadn't pushed too hard either, because if Declan did confess, then Harlan would be duty bound to do something about it.

Declan knew that, too.

"There are plenty of other suspects," Caitlyn went on.

It sounded as if she were dismissing Declan as the accomplice. Maybe because of that warm and fuzzy hug. But Harlan couldn't argue with her. Declan had been barely thirteen at the time and small to boot, and there was a long list of people who would have gladly helped Sarah squash a monster.

Including her own son, Billy Webb.

"Neither the Rangers nor any of us has had any luck finding Billy. What about you?" Harlan asked.

"None. I know he tried to commit suicide, so God

knows what Webb did to him to mess up his head. I'm sure the routine beatings didn't help. Webb gave many of us enough physical and psychological scars to ruin us for life."

And Billy and Declan weren't the only ones on the receiving end of those beatings. Webb had come after most of them—including Sarah and even Caitlyn.

She made a *hmm* sound. "He had a wicked punch," Caitlyn mumbled, rubbing her jaw. "He was the first man who ever hit me, and I swore he'd be the last."

That tightness in his gut moved to his chest, and it didn't matter that all of this had gone down sixteen-plus years ago. It still stung to know what Caitlyn had gone through.

What they all had.

He hated that this attack had brought so many of those old wounds to the surface.

"I have to get some things out of my car," Caitlyn said when they passed the vehicle she'd left parked near his house.

"I'll have one of the ranch hands do it." There were plenty of trees and shrubs just across the road from her car, and he couldn't rule out that someone could hide there and take a shot at her.

He came to a stop in front of his house and was glad to see his brother Slade on his porch. Harlan was equally pleased to see the two armed ranch hands in the pasture between his place and the main house. That meant Slade had already taken some security measures.

There'd need to be more.

Seated in one of the white rocking chairs, Slade was armed with a rifle and his Glock in his waist holster. He looked like an Old West outlaw in his battered jeans, boots and black shirt.

"Harlan," Slade greeted when they got out of the car.

Then Slade's dark blue eyes landed on Caitlyn. No huggy welcome like the one Declan had given her. Slade wasn't the huggy type, and besides, like Harlan he was still pissed off about that article—which seemed close to being petty considering all the other crud that was going on now.

"Inside," Harlan instructed. And he didn't waste any time getting Caitlyn on the porch and through the already open front door. "Has the house already been processed for prints and evidence?"

Slade nodded. "Nothing so far, but it'll take the lab a while to work on everything they collected."

No doubt. Harlan was also betting they wouldn't find anything useful. He'd caught only a split-second glimpse of the man who'd used the Taser on them, but he was pretty sure the guy had been wearing gloves.

"All the ranch hands are armed," Slade continued. "And Wyatt's on his way back from the hospital with Kirby and Stella."

"The hospital?" Caitlyn and Harlan asked in unison.

"Kirby was just there for his cancer treatment, but as soon as they're back at the house, Wyatt will lock up and set the burglar alarm."

Good. Kirby was too weak to fight off a killer, and while Kirby's fiftysomething-year-old friend Stella was a decent shot, Harlan didn't want to test her marksmanship if someone managed to get onto the ranch. He considered taking Caitlyn to the main house as well, but he figured Kirby had already had enough upsets for the day.

"Stella?" Caitlyn asked. "The one who used to work at Rocky Creek?"

The very one. Harlan settled for a nod, but he saw that little flicker go through her eyes. Caitlyn had been pretty close to Stella in those days, but the bottom line was the woman was still a suspect as accessory to Webb's murder. Not in Harlan's mind. But apparently in everyone else's.

Including Caitlyn's.

"How long has Stella been here?" Caitlyn pressed.

"Not long." And this wasn't a subject he cared to discuss. Not with other things that needed to be done. "I want the road watched," Harlan told his brother, glancing back up at Caitlyn's car.

"Got two men heading out there now," Slade answered. "More will cover the back fence."

Yeah. Because that was the most vulnerable part of the ranch. The pastures had been designed to hold and feed livestock, not to ward off gunmen, and there were plenty of places where someone could climb the fence and gain access to the ranch.

"Any sign of our missing attacker?" Harlan asked, sweeping his gaze around the house and grounds.

Slade shook his head and opened his mouth, but he stopped when they saw an SUV approaching. A vehicle that Harlan recognized, thank God. It pulled to a stop in front of Harlan's house, and he spotted his brother Wyatt at the wheel. Stella was riding shotgun and a sickly-looking Kirby was slumped in the backseat.

Slade's phone rang, and he went out to the porch to take the call while Harlan went toward the SUV. So did Caitlyn, and before she even got there, Stella stepped out. The women greeted each other with open arms and squeals of delight.

"Girl, you are a sight for sore eyes," Stella declared.

"You, too. And you haven't changed a bit."

Stella touched her fingers to her graying auburn hair. "You and Wyatt could always lay on the sweet talk, but

I'm a shallow woman and bent by flattery." She smiled at the joke, but the humor didn't quite make it to her weary eyes.

Caitlyn's attention landed on Kirby.

"Marshal Granger." Caitlyn's voice was clogged with emotion, probably because it looked as if the man was critically ill.

And hell, he might be.

One of Harlan's biggest fears was that Stella and Kirby were trying to keep the bad news about Kirby's prognosis to themselves.

"Caitlyn." Kirby managed a thin smile but didn't move from his position on the backseat. "Does this mean Harlan and you are back together?"

So no one had told him about the attack. Good. Harlan wasn't opposed to holding back some bad news, too, especially since it would only worry Kirby.

"Caitlyn's just visiting," Harlan settled for saying.

Kirby studied them both. Shook his head. "That's not a just-visiting kind of look on her face. Always thought you two were more suited for each other than you were willing to let on."

Harlan wasn't sure he liked this turn in the conversation, and he wanted to remind Kirby about the article Caitlyn had written, but behind them Slade cleared his throat and tapped his cell phone.

*Oh, man.* Not more bad news.

Harlan helped Stella back into the SUV. "You best get Kirby home."

Wyatt and Harlan exchanged a glance, and even though he'd call Wyatt to remind him about taking some extra security measures, his brother and he were no doubt on the same page.

"Was that call about Jay Farris?" Caitlyn asked Slade the second the SUV drove away.

Slade shook his head. "Don't know anything about Farris yet." He looked at Harlan. Then Caitlyn. "No. This bad news is about the two of you. The Rangers have sworn out a warrant for your arrests. They're on the way here now to take you both into custody."

# Chapter Six

Caitlyn stared at Slade and mentally repeated the bombshell he'd just dropped. It didn't get any more clear the second time it went through her head.

"Arrest us?" she asked. "Why?" And that was the real question, because none of this was making sense right now. "We were the ones who were nearly killed."

Slade's eyes were already an intense steely-blue, but that darkened them even more. "This doesn't have anything to do with the attack. At least I don't think it does. Someone anonymously sent the Rangers so-called *proof* that you two are responsible for the disappearance of Sherry Summers and the murder of Tiffany Brock."

A lot more things went through her head—including a *good God* or two. It had to be a joke that anyone would think she or Harlan had anything to do with what had happened to the two women, but Slade wasn't the joking type.

"Proof?" Harlan questioned.

Slade immediately shook his head. "The Rangers haven't shared it with the marshals, so I don't know what they have. All Ranger Morris would say was that you'd both be taken into custody. I've put out a few feelers, and maybe someone will know what's going on."

Harlan scrubbed his hand over his face. "Then I guess I'll have to see what Morris has when he arrives."

"Probably not a good idea for you to be here much longer," Slade warned. "As far as the Rangers are concerned, you've gone rogue and are on your way to being a full-fledged outlaw."

Caitlyn saw the slight flinch Harlan made, but she figured that reaction was just the tip of the iceberg. This had to cut him to the core, because if there was one thing he wasn't, it was a rogue lawman. She doubted Harlan had ever even had a parking ticket.

"And since they plan to charge you both with murder, there won't be bail," Slade continued. "They'll throw both your butts in jail."

Mercy. That didn't help Caitlyn deal with this. She tried to understand everything Slade had just told them, but it didn't make sense.

"First of all, there's no proof that Tiffany was even murdered," she said, trying to latch on to anything that would shed light on this. "I talked to her fiancé, Devin Mathis, and he said she died in a car accident."

"A suspicious one," Slade supplied.

And Caitlyn couldn't argue with that. Devin had indeed believed the accident had been staged, even though at that time the police hadn't been able to find any evidence to prove foul play. Maybe they'd found something now, but Caitlyn couldn't see how it would be linked back to Harlan and her. She hadn't seen or heard from Tiffany in years.

Then there was Sherry's disappearance. It fell into the suspicious category, too. In fact, it was Caitlyn's former roommates' circumstances that had made her believe Harlan—or someone else—could be trying to off residents of the Rocky Creek Children's Facility.

She was, of course, leaning to her *someone else* theory now.

"I also talked with Sherry's business partner, Curtis Newell," she continued. "And he doesn't think Sherry's away on some impromptu vacation. The hard drive on her computer has been wiped clean, and there's no money or clothes missing. Only her. He's thinking foul play, too. In fact, he hired a P.I. to try to find her."

Caitlyn turned to Harlan to get his take on this, but he just shook his head. "Whatever the Rangers have must be fake. We'll have to talk with them and sort it out."

Slade stepped in front of Harlan when he started to go inside. "Didn't you hear me? If you stay, they'll arrest you, and God knows how long it'll take to clear your names. It'd be a heck of a lot easier if you could figure out what's going on, and that won't happen if you're in Ranger custody."

Harlan didn't seem overly concerned with that, but Caitlyn sure was. She'd spent some time in jail before being transferred to juvenile hall and then reform school, and she didn't want to go back. Especially because someone had manufactured evidence against them.

"Can you talk to the Rangers again and try to find out what they have before they get here?" she asked Slade.

Harlan and Slade exchanged glances, and even though Slade didn't look too hopeful, he took out his phone and made a call. Harlan looked around the grounds again as if searching for bogeymen, and he nudged her inside. She had no idea how much time they had before the Rangers arrived, but they needed to make every second count.

"I need a phone," she insisted. Caitlyn glanced around but didn't see a landline or a cell. "I can try to track down Farris. He's the one who probably sent false evidence to the Rangers."

"Farris wasn't at Rocky Creek," Harlan reminded her. "And so far, everything seems to connect back to that." He paused, shook his head again. "And yet it doesn't connect at all."

"Unless Sherry or Tiffany saw something to do with Webb's murder." Caitlyn hadn't tossed that out there off-the-cuff. She'd had days to go over every single scenario, and that was one of them. "If they did, then maybe Sarah's confession brought this all back to the surface, and now her accomplice is trying to tie up loose ends."

Harlan didn't disagree. Nor did he make any move to give her a phone. "Maybe Farris is behind Tiffany's car accident and Sherry's disappearance. He could have done that as a way to draw you out."

Maybe. She had practically been in hiding prior to that. Always moving and working mainly from home. And the threats and suspicious activity had indeed brought her out into the open. It sickened her to think that Farris could have used her old childhood connections to do that.

"I need a phone," she repeated. "I can find out when Farris left the private institution."

But even the timing might not give him an alibi for these crimes. With his money, he could have hired someone to kill Tiffany and stage it to look like a car accident.

But that didn't make sense.

"If Farris had killed Tiffany to draw me out, he would have wanted me to know it was murder. It's the same for Sherry. A disappearance doesn't have the same emotional punch as murder."

Harlan made a sound of agreement, and he looked at her. Their gazes connected, but she hadn't needed that connection to know he was exhausted and frustrated.

Just as she was. He forced out a long, weary breath and ran his fingers down the length of her arm.

It was far more comforting than it should have been.

So was the gentle grip he put on her wrist before his hand slipped into hers. Despite the mess they were in, she managed a weak smile.

And that was how Slade found them when he stepped into the entry with them. His expression stayed stony, but his eyebrows rose a fraction.

"Reliving the past?" he asked, and the tone of his voice wasn't friendly.

Caitlyn and Harlan moved away from each other. Not that they could go far. The entry was small, barely five feet across.

"I'm guessing you have something to tell us?" Harlan snapped at his brother.

"Yeah. Any chance either of you was near the site of Tiffany's car wreck?" Slade asked.

"No," Caitlyn and Harlan answered at the same time.

"Didn't figure you were, but someone sent the Rangers two eyewitness accounts that say otherwise."

"The eyewitnesses are lying." Which might be easy to prove if she and Harlan had solid alibis. Judging from Slade's expression, though, that wasn't all the news he had for them. "What else do the Rangers have?" she asked.

"My source says there are emails. Lots of them. From both of you to Sherry. And in those emails, you threaten her to stay quiet."

Despite the bone-weary fatigue, that sent a roar of anger through her. "Stay quiet about what?"

Slade shook his head. "Not sure, but I'm betting it has something to do with the Webb investigation."

Yeah, it almost certainly did. "But I didn't send any

emails. In fact, the only reason I tried to contact Sherry was because of the threats I'd received."

"And I haven't been in touch with her at all," Harlan confirmed. "In fact, I didn't even know she was missing until Caitlyn showed up at my house in the middle of the night."

"I'll get someone on the emails," Slade explained. "And disproving those two eyewitnesses. Still, I think you should both lie low—away from the Rangers— because someone's clearly trying to frame you, and it's my guess they're doing that to take you out of commission."

So they couldn't investigate whatever the heck was happening to them.

She looked at Harlan to see what his take was, but his phone buzzed before he could say anything. "It's Sergeant Tinsley from Cross Creek."

Caitlyn immediately shifted her attention to the call, and she hoped like the devil that it was good news. Maybe they'd even managed to catch the ski-masked guy who'd shot at them.

"Marshal McKinney," Harlan answered, and she could hear the hope in his voice, too. They so needed a break.

But it wasn't exactly relief or good news that she saw in Harlan's body language. Caitlyn couldn't hear what Tinsley had said to make Harlan's forehead bunch up, but she figured it meant their attacker was still at large.

"Thanks for letting me know," Harlan said to Tinsley. "And call me the minute you find him." He ended the call and looked at her. "They got a print off the threatening note that was left on the steering wheel of the truck."

That was the last thing Caitlyn had expected, especially since Tinsley had already told them the cab of the truck was clean—no sign of anything they could use to confirm the identity of their attacker.

"The print belonged to Billy Webb," Harlan added.

Caitlyn didn't even try to stop the sound of surprise she made. Billy—Sarah and Jonah Webb's son. And a prime suspect as his mother's accomplice in the murder. Better yet, he was the one suspect the Rangers hadn't been able to find or interview.

"Billy," Slade repeated. "This is the first time he's surfaced since his father's body was found."

"First time he's surfaced in years," Harlan agreed. "He hasn't been using a credit card or bank account. No current driver's license either. Even his own mother claims she hasn't heard from him. The guy's been off the grid for years—so long in fact that I thought he might be dead."

Yes, and that was why the attack and the threats didn't make sense. "Why would he come after Harlan and me—especially like this?"

All three of them stayed quiet a moment, obviously giving that some thought. "Maybe he wants revenge," Slade finally suggested.

Harlan's gaze connected with hers, and she saw his *bingo!* moment.

"Maybe Billy didn't want his father dead," Harlan continued. "Maybe he's going after people he thinks could have helped his mother. Sarah's in a guarded room at the hospital," he quickly added.

Probably because he saw the alarm in her eyes. If this theory about Billy was true, then he would want his mother dead—and Sarah was in a coma, unable to protect herself.

There was no love lost between Caitlyn and Sarah. The woman had never lifted a finger to stop her husband from beating the kids at Rocky Creek. Caitlyn included. But truth was, Caitlyn owed Sarah a huge favor. If she hadn't knifed her own husband to death, then Harlan, his brothers and all the rest might have had to spend even more time in that hellhole.

"Why would Billy go after Sherry and Tiffany?" Slade asked—the very question that was on Caitlyn's mind. "They both had decent alibis for the night of the murder."

Decent but maybe not enough. "Billy might know something we don't," Caitlyn concluded. "There were a lot of people moving around the facility that night, and the window for Webb's murder is wide enough that anyone could have done it."

A chilling thought. Because maybe that meant Billy could be picking them off one by one. Still, Caitlyn wanted to know why he'd started with Tiffany. Maybe Sherry, too. And then moved on to her.

"Do you have a current photo of Billy?" she asked. "Because I wasn't able to find one."

Both Harlan and Slade shook their heads, and she knew exactly what that meant. Yes, Sergeant Tinsley and plenty of other cops would be looking for Billy, but without a current photo, it would make that search a whole lot more difficult—especially since, as Harlan had already pointed out, Billy had been off the grid for a while now.

Caitlyn heard the sound of a car engine, and all three of them turned toward the road. She couldn't see the ranch hands Slade had said would stand guard there. But she did see the approaching bright red sports car.

Hardly the kind of vehicle a Texas Ranger would drive.

"Someone you know?" Caitlyn immediately asked Harlan and Slade.

They didn't answer but moved in front of her like a curtain of solid muscle. Slade already had his rifle ready, and Harlan drew his gun. Caitlyn didn't blame them. If she'd had her weapon, she would have pulled, too.

The car came to a noisy stop, the tires kicking up gravel and dust from the road, and the driver didn't waste a second before she heard the car door open. She couldn't actually see it, because both men were blocking her view.

"You know him?" Harlan asked his brother.

Slade shook his head.

Caitlyn came up on her tiptoes and looked at their visitor from over Harlan's shoulder.

God.

Her heart dropped to the floor.

"Caitlyn," the man said. Despite the wide smile stretching his mouth, he lifted his hands in the air as if surrendering. "Long time, no see."

"Who is he?" Harlan demanded.

Caitlyn opened her mouth, but it took several moments to get her throat unclamped so she could speak. "Jay Farris."

# *Chapter Seven*

Harlan aimed his gun directly at the man walking toward his porch. Slade did the same, and he took up position on the other side of Caitlyn.

"Don't come a step closer," Harlan warned their visitor.

Farris came to a dead stop, but he kept smiling. Either this guy was truly nuts—a distinct possibility—or else he enjoyed unnerving everyone around him, because that smile was downright spooky. This darn sure wasn't a smiling kind of situation.

Harlan had never seen a photo of Farris and hadn't been sure what to expect, but he hadn't expected *this*. Farris wasn't the sort of man to blend into a crowd. Not with that stark bleached-blond hair and deep tan. In his cutoff khakis and white T-shirt he looked more like a rich beach bum than a would-be stalker.

Too bad Harlan couldn't say with 100 percent certainty that it'd been Farris wearing the ski mask at the motel. And now the waters were even muddier with Billy Webb's fingerprint that had been found on the latest threatening note. Still, Harlan wasn't about to dismiss blondie here as innocent just because Billy had resurfaced.

"Caitlyn," Farris repeated as if welcoming her to come closer.

Harlan didn't budge in case she intended to do just that, but Caitlyn didn't move either. One glance at her, and Harlan realized that was because she was frozen in place. She was too pale again, and she definitely wasn't smiling. He saw every bit of the fear in her eyes.

"What do you want?" she snapped at Farris. Her gaze was frozen as well on the madman who'd not only made her life a living hell, but also had tried to strangle her.

Yet here he was. Free as a bird.

Harlan would soon figure out what he could do about remedying that. The restraining order that Caitlyn had on Farris would have likely expired, but they could get a new one.

"I needed to see you," Farris said. If he was alarmed by the two guns trained on him, he didn't show it. "It's all over the news about your kidnapping. Someone took shots at you, they said, and when I saw Marshal McKinney's name, I did an internet search and found the address of the ranch. I thought you might be here."

Hell's bells. Of course it would be on the news. Harlan had forgotten about trying to suppress the story so it wouldn't clue in people like Farris that Caitlyn might be with him or any members of his family. Of course, if Farris was the person trying to kill them, he already knew about the attack anyway.

But there was something about this that just didn't fit.

If Farris had wanted Caitlyn dead, then why hadn't he killed her after he hit her with the Taser? He would have had the perfect opportunity, since she couldn't have fought back. Of course, sometimes crazy people didn't do logical things, and maybe he wanted a fight. Maybe he wanted to prolong her fear as long as possible.

"Are you okay?" Farris asked Caitlyn. "Were you hurt?"

She made a sound, a burst of laughter, but it wasn't from humor. "That's a strange question coming from you. The last time you were within reaching distance of me, you put your hands around my neck and tried to choke the life out of me."

It made Harlan's blood boil to hear that. Caitlyn wasn't a large woman by any means, and he hated that she'd come so close to dying. Back then and again today.

Finally Farris's smile dissolved. "Yes, *that*," he mumbled. He scratched his eyebrow, then his head. "I was going through some bad stuff, but I got the help I needed, and I'm all better now."

"Forgive me if neither my neck nor I believe that," Caitlyn snapped.

Harlan wanted to cheer for her. It was hard to sound that gutsy when he could feel her trembling against his back.

"I can understand why you'd be skeptical," Farris went on as if discussing a parking ticket rather than a felony. "But, honestly, I'm just here to help."

"Help?" she repeated.

"How the hell can you help?" Harlan added. "And you'd better say it fast because you're not going to be anywhere near this ranch in a couple of minutes."

Despite his warning, Farris stayed unruffled, which only added to Harlan's opinion that this guy was crazier than a june bug. "I need to reach in my pocket and take out something. Please don't shoot me when I do it."

Harlan wasn't about to agree to that until he had more info. "What's in your pocket?"

"Something you both should see. It's a photo."

That got his attention. Apparently it got Caitlyn's, too. "What kind of photo?" she demanded.

"One of the marshal and you. Someone sent it to me early this morning."

Obviously as puzzled as he was, Caitlyn glanced at Harlan and shook her head.

"Take out the picture slowly, using just two fingers, and hold it up for us to see," Harlan ordered. "Don't come any closer."

Farris followed Harlan's orders to a tee, and he thrust the photo in their direction. Even though Farris was a good five yards away, Harlan could still make out Caitlyn and him. Her gasp let him know that she'd made it out, as well.

It was a shot of Caitlyn and him half-naked on the motel bed.

"Needless to say, I was shocked to get this," Farris went on. A muscle flickered in his jaw, and for the first time since his arrival, Harlan thought he might be seeing some real emotion on the man's face.

And that emotion was jealousy.

*Great.* Just what they needed. A jealous nut job of a stalker with homicidal tendencies.

"Who sent that to you?" Harlan asked.

"Don't know." Farris looked at the photo, and the jaw muscle got even tighter. "Someone rang my doorbell this morning, and when I answered it, no one was there. Just an envelope on the doorstep with this photo and a note inside." Farris's gaze snapped to Caitlyn. "I didn't know you were seeing your old flame."

"I'm not," she insisted.

Farris studied the picture again, made a sound of disagreement. "You're in bed with him."

"Not voluntarily," Harlan supplied. "Someone drugged us and handcuffed us together."

That caused Farris to pull back his shoulders, and without taking his attention off the photo, he shook his head again. "I don't see any handcuffs."

"They were there." Harlan held up his left hand so that Farris would see the reddish circular bruise on his wrist. "Now, what did the note say?"

It took a moment for Farris to answer, and while he could be faking, he seemed genuinely surprised with the handcuff revelation. "The note was typed, and it said you were in room 109 at the Starlight Inn in Cross Creek."

"God," Caitlyn murmured.

Harlan hadn't thought it possible, but he felt her muscles tense even more, and she put her hand on the small of his back. Probably because her legs weren't so steady. With her still fighting off the effects of the drug and the near fatal shooting, a confrontation with her stalker was the last thing she needed, but Harlan saw this from the eyes of a lawman. That photo was evidence of a setup.

Well, it was if Farris was telling the truth.

Harlan had no plans to believe him any time soon.

"I'll bet you weren't happy when you saw that picture of Caitlyn and me," Harlan remarked, and he kept a close watch on the man's reaction.

"I wasn't." His gaze rifled to Harlan. "Wait a minute. You don't think I was so enraged when I saw this that I then tried to kill you?"

Harlan shrugged, but that was exactly the direction he was going. "You tell me. Is that what happened?"

"No." Farris cursed and denied it again. "I got help for my mental problems. I'm not a violent person anymore."

"I don't believe you," Caitlyn said, and she cleared

her throat and repeated it. "Because someone did come to that motel room and try to kill us."

"Well, that someone wasn't me," Farris practically shouted. But the fit of temper went as fast as it came, and he scrubbed his hand over his face. "Look, I came here because I wanted to make sure you were okay and because I thought you should know about this photo. Caitlyn, someone obviously wants to hurt you."

"Obviously," she said with a massive amount of sarcasm dripping from her voice. "But I didn't need you or the photo to convince me of that. The bullets convinced me just fine."

"I'm sure they did. But what's this all about?" Farris pressed. "Is this happening because of one of your articles?"

Harlan wished it were that simple. Heck, for that matter he wished he could just go ahead and arrest Farris on the spot and force him to confess to setting all this up.

But Billy's fingerprint didn't fit.

In fact, it was entirely possible that Billy had been the one to set it up and that he'd merely used Farris as a pawn. As unhinged as Farris seemed to be, he'd be easy to manipulate.

"This is Marshal Slade Becker," Harlan said, tipping his head to his brother. "And he's going to escort you into town, where you'll be tested for gunshot residue."

He waited for Farris to object, but the man only shrugged. "I didn't fire a gun."

"Then you have nothing to be concerned about, do you?" Harlan answered.

Farris glanced at his car. Then the road. And Harlan braced himself for the man to make a run for it. He didn't. Farris turned back to them and nodded.

"Hope the test won't take long," Farris said. "I have a therapy appointment in two hours."

"I'll make it fast," Slade growled. "I'll follow you to the marshals' building on Main Street in town, and don't think about ditching me because I *will* chase you down."

Coming from Slade, that was a formidable threat, and Harlan mumbled a thanks to his brother.

"My advice," Slade whispered to Harlan. "Don't wait around for Ranger Morris to arrive and arrest you. We need to be able to clear your name in case this bleached-blond piece of work doesn't pan out." He went down the porch steps to his truck.

"I'll be in touch, Caitlyn," Farris called out to her as if this had been some kind of social visit. The man was an idiot.

Or else he was very smart.

And that was what worried Harlan most.

"What happens if there's gunshot residue?" Caitlyn asked. "Will that be enough to arrest him?"

Harlan watched them drive away. "Enough to hold him for a while."

He took her by the arm and led her back inside. Partly because he didn't want Farris gawking at her in his rear-view mirror. But the main reason was there could still be another attack.

Right away he noticed the open drawers on his TV cabinet. Things had been moved around but not trashed even though there was fingerprint powder on just about every visible hard surface. His brothers had no doubt sent an entire team of CSIs out to his place once they'd realized he was missing.

Caitlyn pulled in a weary breath and sank onto his sofa. "What are we going to do about those warrants for our arrest?"

Harlan wasn't sure she was going to like this. Or even if it was the right thing to do, but he was going to listen to Slade on this. "We should leave."

She'd already started to ease the back of her head onto the sofa, but that stopped her. Harlan figured she'd at least question that decision.

Caitlyn didn't.

She got up and looked down at the scrubs she was still wearing. "At least let me get my overnight bag from my car so I can change clothes."

He nodded, locked the door. "I need to do the same." He'd stick out like a sore thumb in the green scrubs because he didn't come close to looking like a medic. "I won't be long, and if you hear a car drive up, stay away from the windows."

Harlan headed to his bedroom and grabbed a pair of jeans. His bed was unmade and things had been tossed around. A reminder that whoever had shot them with a Taser had probably ransacked the place.

But looking for what?

More proof that he and Caitlyn were sleeping together? Something to do with Webb's murder?

He pulled on his jeans and was in midzip when he heard the movement, and he automatically grabbed his gun and whirled in that direction.

However, it was only Caitlyn.

"Yeah, I'm jumpy, too," she muttered. She bracketed her hands on the jamb. "But I was thinking of something. Whoever orchestrated this attack didn't make any mistakes—"

When her explanation came to a fast halt, Harlan followed her gaze to his body. To his bare chest. Maybe even his open zipper.

"Sorry," she mumbled.

"Not to worry. I think we got an eyeful of each other when we woke up in that bed this morning." An eyeful he shouldn't be remembering with everything else on his mind, but Harlan was sure he wouldn't be able to forget it any time soon.

The past sixteen years had settled nicely on her body.

She cleared her throat, anchored her attention to the floor. "As I was saying…" But it took her several more seconds to continue. During that time, Harlan zipped up and grabbed a shirt. "Our attacker drew me out, waited until we were together and used that Taser before either of us could fight."

Harlan nodded. "He wasn't sloppy. So why leave a fingerprint on the threatening note in the truck?"

She nodded, too. "Are you thinking Farris might have planted Billy's print there?"

"Yeah." That was exactly what he was thinking. Too bad it would be a bear to prove, but it all started with finding Billy and getting his side of the story.

Harlan finished dressing and yanked open his nightstand drawer. His backup Glock was still there—yet another piece of this weird puzzle. Why hadn't their attacker taken it? He grabbed both it and his badge and some extra ammo.

But not the condoms.

Too much temptation, and he and Caitlyn already had enough of that without adding condoms to the mix.

"Where are we going?" Caitlyn stepped back when he approached the door. Purposely putting some distance between them.

And he knew why.

Despite his fatigue and stress, that old attraction was still there, rearing its head. Good thing Caitlyn knew it'd be stupid and reckless for them to act on it. But not acting on it would test them to the limits.

Because they were going to be attached at the hip, so to speak.

He opened his mouth to tell her they were heading to a place that Declan owned, but then he stopped and glanced around the room. Their attacker had clearly had some time to look for whatever he'd been looking for, but he'd also had time to plant a listening device. That was a long shot, of course, since the person probably thought he and Caitlyn wouldn't live long enough to return to his house, but it was a chance Harlan didn't want to take.

"I'll tell you when we're out of here," he whispered.

Caitlyn's eyes widened, and she, too, made a sweeping glance around the room. That also got her moving pretty darn fast, and they made it to the door before his phone buzzed.

"Please tell me there's not a problem with Farris," Caitlyn mumbled.

Harlan shook his head and stared at the caller's name on the screen. It was a name he recognized, but barely. "It's Curtis Newell."

The business partner of the missing woman, Sherry Summers.

"I didn't know you knew him," Caitlyn said, looking at the screen.

"I don't." Harlan hit the answer button. "Marshal McKinney."

"Marshal." The man sounded relieved or something. "I got your number from the Marshals Service because I'm trying to get in touch with Caitlyn Barnes. I heard about the shooting."

Harlan groaned. God knew how many people had

heard and how many welfare-check calls like this there'd be. He didn't have time for them.

"Caitlyn's okay," Harlan assured the man.

"That's good, but it's not why I'm calling." Curtis said it so quickly that his words ran together. "I really need to speak with her."

Okay. Not a welfare check. In fact, this guy sounded frantic.

Harlan glanced at her, and she motioned for him to put the call on speaker. He did.

"I'm here, Curtis," Caitlyn said. "What's wrong? Have you found Sherry?"

"No, we haven't found her. But there's plenty wrong. God, Caitlyn, what the hell's going on?"

Harlan didn't like the sound of that, and judging from the way Caitlyn pulled in her breath, neither did she. "What happened?" she asked.

"I went over to Sherry's condo to check her mail and see if there were any messages on her answering machine. I've been doing that since she went missing. Someone had trashed the place and left her a threatening note."

Great day in the morning. If these were connected, then their attacker had been very busy. "What did the threat say?"

He heard Curtis's hard, quick breaths. "'This isn't over. You're a dead woman.'"

Caitlyn pressed her fingers to her mouth, but it didn't stop the soft gasp she made. That was because it was the identical threat that had been left for her in the truck.

"But that's not all," Curtis went on. "I just got a call from Devin Mathis. You know who he is?"

Yet another name that was familiar to Harlan, but he didn't know why.

"He was engaged to Tiffany Brock, a former resident at Rocky Creek who died in a car accident."

"Devin says she was murdered," Curtis corrected. "And he got a note, too. Someone left it on his car this morning. Not a threat exactly—the note was just one word. *Dead.*"

As a lawman, Harlan forced himself to look at the logistics of this. He and Caitlyn had been in Cross Creek, but if he remembered correctly, Sherry's condo and business were in Houston. So that meant their attacker likely had an accomplice. Or else had hired someone to do his dirty work. Because that was too much ground for one person to cover in that short period of time.

"Did the cops get any prints?" Caitlyn asked Curtis. Her voice was shaking as much as her hands were.

"Two—they were both on the notes that were sent to Devin and the one left in Sherry's condo. That's why I had to talk to you. I have to know what's going on."

"I don't know what's happening," she answered. "Was it Billy Webb's prints on the threat?"

"No." His breath seemed to shudder. "Caitlyn, it was yours and Marshal McKinney's. Did you two do something to Sherry? Are you trying to silence her?"

Oh, man. That hit him hard.

"No," Harlan and Caitlyn answered in unison. She looked at him, shook her head. "How could that have happened?"

Harlan didn't have any more answers for her than he did Curtis Newell. That was bad enough, but then he heard the sound of an approaching vehicle. One glance out the window, and he saw it was Ranger Morris. Not alone either. There were two other Rangers with him— and they'd likely come to arrest Caitlyn and him.

This was all a setup, of course, and the evidence was

growing. Harlan seriously doubted that the cops who'd found the prints on those notes had withheld that evidence. If the Rangers hadn't heard it, they soon would.

"We'll call you back," Harlan said to Curtis.

"No—" Curtis insisted.

But Harlan ended the call anyway. "Come on." Harlan took Caitlyn by the arm and headed for the back door. "We have to leave now."

# *Chapter Eight*

Caitlyn didn't even ask Harlan where they were going as he maneuvered the truck along the sharp curves on the rural road. But she hoped and prayed it was somewhere safe. Away from the person trying to kill them.

Away from the Rangers, too.

With everything else going on, it could be downright dangerous for them to be arrested, since it was clear now that someone was playing a cat-and-mouse game. Why, she didn't know. But here were notes left for both Devin and Curtis with Harlan's and her fingerprints and the so-called evidence someone had sent to the Rangers. No matter how many times she tossed it around in her head, she kept coming back to one place.

Rocky Creek.

And one specific event: Jonah Webb's murder.

Harlan had grabbed a laptop and some supplies from his family's main ranch house while they were making their *escape,* and she hoped she got a chance to use the computer to do some research.

"Never been a fugitive from justice before," Harlan grumbled. He finished off the last bite of the fast-food burger they'd stopped for along the way after they'd gotten out of Maverick Springs.

Caitlyn shrugged. "I have. When I was fourteen, I

got into a car with some friends. Didn't know the car was stolen until the cops spotted us, and we ran. Don't worry—you'll do better with your fugitive status once you get past the sick-to-your-stomach stage."

He looked at her from the corner of his eye. She certainly wasn't making light of it—she was scared, tired and frustrated. But in the grand scheme of things, the Rangers seemed like the least of their worries.

And complicating things even more was the old attraction between them.

But for some reason, it was both of those things that felt like dead weight on her shoulders. The Rangers—that was understandable. The attraction not so much. Well, except for Harlan's hot body and the way that hot body filled out his jeans and T-shirt. He wasn't a bad boy, but he looked the part. She knew just how gentle he could be.

Even for a girl's first time.

She'd had a few lovers since then, but Caitlyn had never had a man treat her like priceless crystal while taking her breath away with pleasure. Ironic. That her first time had been her best, and she hadn't even known what she was doing. Thank goodness Harlan had.

"What you thinking about?" Harlan asked.

Her gaze slashed to his as she wondered what had prompted that question. Oh. Her fast breathing. Flushed cheeks. And though those things were nonverbal, judging from the heated, puzzled look in Harlan's eyes, he was picking up on it.

His breath kicked up the pace, too. No flushed cheeks, but the pulse on his throat did a little gallop. His lips parted. Probably to say something to her. But it was a reminder that the man's kisses were orgasmic.

Mercy.

Enough of this.

"Um, I keep thinking that I'm responsible for nearly getting us killed." It wasn't exactly a lie. She *had* thought this over and over again in the past few hours.

He blinked. Frowned. But didn't challenge her.

She crammed most of her burger into the bag. No appetite. "If I hadn't suspected you, I wouldn't have come to your house—"

"He would have found another way to get us together."

That was probably true, but if she hadn't come to Harlan, she suspected they wouldn't be dealing with the Rangers and definitely not the heat.

Harlan checked the rearview mirror again. Something they'd both been doing during the entire drive, but there was no one behind or ahead of them. He turned onto another road, more rugged than the previous one, and drove another mile. He brought the truck to a stop in front of a log house. This wasn't a cabin. It looked more like a vacation home nestled in the woods.

"Declan owns it." Harlan got out and grabbed the bags that they'd hastily packed at the ranch.

Talk about a surprise—for several reasons. For one thing, she'd always thought of Declan as a rolling stone. Not really the home-owner type. But that was just an observation, not her real concern.

Her real concern was security.

Harlan had already switched phones to a prepaid cell and had left word with his brothers to transfer any calls to the number. He'd also made sure they weren't followed. Still, there was the obvious five-hundred-pound gorilla in the room.

"What if the Rangers look for us here?" she asked. "Declan is, after all, your foster brother."

"They won't look here. The place isn't actually in his

name. About two years ago, a distant relative of his from Ireland left it to him in his estate."

During their many chats, Declan had told her he was from Ireland. He still had a trace of the brogue, but it seemed odd that an Irish relative would buy a place like this in the middle of Nowhere, Texas, and then leave it to Declan.

"Why didn't this relative come forward when Declan was placed in Rocky Creek?" Because she knew his time there had been hell for him, and almost any family would have been better than what he'd had to face at the orphanage.

"Don't know," Harlan replied. He pressed in some numbers on the keypad by the door to unlock it. "Let's just say Declan has some secrets and leave it at that."

That only made her uneasy feeling even more uneasy. "Not secrets about Rocky Creek?" And more specifically, about Webb's murder?

But Harlan only shrugged, opened the door and punched in yet more numbers to disarm the security system before it started to beep. Obviously he wasn't planning to spill anything else about his kid brother, but that didn't mean Caitlyn couldn't do some digging. Right now, everyone was a suspect.

Well, except Harlan.

She seriously doubted he'd screw himself over like this if he was trying to hide his guilt about anything. Of course, he seemed genuinely close to his brothers, so they probably wouldn't put him through this either.

Now, she was a different story.

With the exception of Declan and maybe Stella, Harlan, his foster brothers and foster father might love to see her squirming on the end of a hook. That was why Kirby's words back at the ranch had surprised her. Something about her and Harlan being suited for each other. Well, he was wrong about that.

Despite the attraction, of course.

In that one area, she and Harlan seemed way too suited, and that didn't please either of them.

Harlan reset the alarm when he closed the door, and they put the bags on a foyer table and looked around. It looked like a place out of a glossy magazine, with its wood floors, leather furniture and massive stone fireplace. Even a work desk with a computer in the corner.

"There's a stocked freezer," Harlan said, leading her into the kitchen. "And canned goods. Just in case we're here longer than tonight. The bedrooms are upstairs."

"Two of them?" She hadn't intended to sound so concerned, but she did.

"Two," he verified, giving her a flat look. It would have worked—she might have believed the offended/uninterested act—if she hadn't seen the pulse at his throat begin to throb.

Jeez Louise.

It was bad enough that she was battling her hormones, but Harlan needed to stay sane. And unaroused.

"Why don't you go ahead and get some rest?" he mumbled.

She took a deep breath, hoping for a clear head. Didn't happen. "I'd rather get a little work done. And change my clothes," she said, looking down at the scrubs she was still wearing.

Harlan looked about to argue, but his phone buzzed. "It's Slade."

Which likely meant this might be news of the investigation. However, Harlan didn't put the call on speaker. Maybe because he wanted to buffer any more bad news they might get.

While he was occupied with that, Caitlyn went to the computer in the corner desk and turned it on. The perfect thing to get kisses and arousing thoughts out of her mind was to work. She logged on to her email account to the dozens of unanswered emails, including several from her boss, Jeb Parker, asking about the two articles she was supposed to be writing.

That caused her stomach to knot.

She hadn't forgotten about the articles, but nearly being killed had put them way on the back burner.

The first was a piece she needed to do about a captured fugitive who'd murdered his entire family and then fled. Caitlyn had managed to be in the news station's helicopter during the chase, and even though she'd already given Jeb several eyewitness articles, he wanted a follow-up. Not just a written one, but a TV appearance so they could run the footage of the helicopter chase. It would be an easy paycheck for her once she got around to it.

There was nothing easy about the second one.

Caitlyn opened the latest version of the second story that she'd put in secure cyber storage, and the headline she'd given it caused the knot in her stomach to get significantly worse.

"Trouble?" she heard someone ask.

Her own gasp echoed through the room. She'd been so caught up in what was on the screen, she hadn't heard anyone come up behind her, and she whirled around, automatically bringing up her hands to defend herself. But no defense was necessary. Because it was Harlan.

"Wired up much?" he murmured. "You really need to rest." Then he tipped his head to the screen. "Bad news?"

Caitlyn shook her head and stepped in front of it. "I'm just getting behind at work." Then she noticed his expression. "Did you get bad news?" she repeated.

Harlan lifted his shoulder. "Disappointing news," he corrected. "Slade tested Farris, but there was no gunshot residue on him."

She groaned. "So no arrest."

"No arrest," he confirmed. "But that doesn't mean he's innocent. It could mean he had on latex gloves when he fired those shots."

Caitlyn couldn't remember seeing gloves, but their attacker could have been wearing them. "What about an alibi for the shooting? Does Farris even have one?"

"Says he was alone at his parents' house, but claims one of the maids might be able to verify it."

"Or lie about it," Caitlyn muttered. If Farris had tested positive, it would have at least gotten him off the streets so Harlan and she could try to build a case against him.

"Farris turned over the photo and the note to Slade," Harlan went on. "The lab might be able to get some prints."

"Our prints," she supplied. "Like the ones on the threats that Devin and Curtis got."

Another shrug. "I figure when we were knocked out cold, it would have been easy to put our fingerprints on just about anything."

That sent a chill through her. Heaven knew what other *evidence* was going to surface. "But why is the person doing this? Why try to set us up?"

"Maybe to take the fall for Webb's murder." He paused, huffed. "But I'm pretty sure we were supposed to die in that motel room."

Caitlyn had already come to the same conclusion, but it was a whole new level of fear to hear it spoken aloud. Now the thoughts came at her nonstop. Billy had perhaps set them up and then sent Farris that photo, figuring the crazed stalker would do the killing for him.

And he'd come darn close to succeeding.

"Yeah," Caitlyn mumbled.

He was examining her face. Her eyes. And he no doubt knew what this was doing to her, because it was doing the same thing to him. Maybe worse. He had family to protect, and it didn't matter that his brothers were marshals and could take care of themselves. He never wanted to put them in danger, period.

"What about the motel?" she asked. "Were there any eyewitnesses who can help get us a better description of the shooter?"

"None. There was a traffic camera on the interstate, but it wasn't aimed in the direction of the motel."

And it was probably why their attacker had chosen to put them there.

"No sign of Billy yet," Harlan went on. "But the initial lab results are back, and it appears you and I were drugged with etorphine hydrochloride."

"The drug used on animals," she immediately supplied. "I did an article on it a while back." She snapped her fingers, trying to recall some details. "Only veterinarians have access to it, so maybe that's a way to trace our attacker."

Harlan was already shaking his head before she finished. "A large supply of it went missing a couple of months ago, and it's been showing up in black markets all over the country. Anyone with enough cash could have bought it, and I doubt we'll find a drug dealer willing to rat out a customer."

No. And besides, if it was Billy or Farris, they probably would have just hired someone to buy the drug for them so they could stay a step removed from any possible evidence.

"Do you have *any* good news?" she asked. And yes, there was frustration in her voice.

"Maybe. Slade is setting up meetings with both Curtis Newell and Devin Mathis. We'll see them in the morning."

Sherry's business partner and Tiffany's fiancé. Both had received threats and both might have information about who was behind the attacks. *Might*.

"Please tell me we're not meeting them here?" Caitlyn asked.

"No. And we obviously can't go to the marshals' building. Slade's making arrangements for someplace safe." He took her by the arm again. "Now rest."

God, she needed it. Every one of her muscles was stiff and sore. And rest would give her stupid body a chance to cool down from Harlan fantasies. She might have gotten her feet moving toward the stairs if Harlan hadn't flexed the grip on her forearm, sliding his fingers down, down, down. To her wrist. Then to her hand.

There was nothing sexual about it. Hand-holding. But he might as well have touched her in the most intimate of places, because her body turned warm and melty.

Harlan had started it with the hand-holding foreplay, but Caitlyn escalated things. Couldn't stop herself. That mouth was right there in front her. Mesmerizing. Filled with the hottest memories. So she leaned in. Pressed her lips to his.

Oh, mercy.

Big mistake. The contact hit her like a lightning bolt. All the heat, fire and intensity zapped her. Not just her either. Harlan made a sound. That male rumble in his chest and throat, and he dragged her to him. The press of their lips became a full-fledged kiss. French and everything.

Especially *everything*.

His arms were strong. She knew that. But knowing and experiencing it were two different things. Those strong arms drew her in until she was against his body. Not that she needed a punch of heat, but it made the kisses even better.

Mercy, he was good at this.

Gentle and rough at the same time. His hand went into her hair, to the back of her head so he could control the movement, angle and pressure. He already controlled everything else, so Caitlyn didn't even try to resist.

He tasted good. Like something familiar but forbidden. That was Harlan. A contradiction. Their bodies pressed closer. Until she could feel all those muscles on his chest.

His zipper, too.

No cooldown for her. Just the opposite. While her head yelled for her to back away, Caitlyn let her fingers and mouth play with fire. She slid her hand between them and touched. That incredible chest. His stomach— hard and tight.

She wanted to go lower. Actually, she wanted sex, and clearly Harlan wanted that, too, because his stomach wasn't the only part of him that was hard.

Without breaking the kiss, he moved her, turned her, until her bottom was pressed against the edge of the desk. A good angle for sex. Not so good for cashing in on some willpower. The new position put him right between her legs.

Everything aligned.

Only the blasted clothes were in the way. And as hot as the kisses had made her, clothing removal was just one touch away.

Or not.

Harlan stepped back.

Not easily. And she wasn't sure he wouldn't just dive right back at her again.

Harlan stood there. Breathing hard. Smelling like the sex she wanted to have with him. His hands tightened into fists. Finally one of them had acted like a responsible adult, but Caitlyn was having a hard time remembering why that was important.

Oh, because they had other things to do. Like clear their names and catch a killer.

So why did *this* suddenly seem more important than anything else?

"We need to agree that was a mistake," he insisted.

She glanced at the erection straining the zipper of his jeans. Then at her own nipples, puckered and very visible since she wasn't wearing a bra.

"A compromise," she murmured. "Let's just agree that it was mutual…and really, really good."

He laughed. The sound was so unexpected that it took Caitlyn a moment to shake off the tension and smile. Not because there was anything to smile about, but it was impossible to stay in sex-land with that laugh. And that smile. Mercy, the man had some big weapons in his male arsenal, and that smile was one of them. Except the smile didn't last. It dissolved in the blink of an eye, and the look on his face definitely wasn't that of a happy man.

"What the hell is that?" he snapped.

A jolt of fear went through her. God, she couldn't take any more bad news.

Afraid of what she might see, Caitlyn followed his gaze to the laptop screen. The scalding kiss had numbed her brain, because she'd forgotten *that* was on the screen. The working headline said it all.

U.S. Marshals' Cover-Up of Jonah Webb's Murder?

The question mark was there for a reason, because

she wasn't at all sure there'd been a cover-up, but Harlan likely wouldn't even notice it. That was because his attention was nailed to the first paragraph and the other question she'd posed.

*With his foster sons' help, did retired marshal Kirby Granger get away with murder?*

"I can explain." But she couldn't. There was no explanation she could give Harlan that would undo the fury she now saw in his eyes.

"Save it," Harlan growled. He grabbed his bag and stormed upstairs.

## Chapter Nine

"Really?" Caitlyn grumbled. "You couldn't come up with a better meeting place?"

For once in the past fourteen hours or so, Harlan agreed with her, but he didn't mimic the huff she made when Slade turned onto the road at the weathered sign.

Rocky Creek Children's Facility.

Apparently they were headed back for another trip down memory lane. Harlan was more than a little fed up with those—especially the ones that involved Caitlyn. And her apparent need to screw over his family any chance she got.

"I figured this is the last place the Rangers would look for you," Slade explained. Except he always sounded as if he were picking a fight when he spoke. "Besides, it's vacant, and Joelle gave me the keys."

Joelle, their sister-in-law who'd once honchoed the investigation when it was still in the inquiry stage. That was why Joelle had the keys in the first place. Well, it sure as heck was past that inquiry stage now with the Rangers trying to arrest Caitlyn and him.

"Rudy Simmons, the caretaker, is away on a trip," Slade added. "So we'll have the place to ourselves."

"Jeez." Caitlyn forced out several breaths and pressed

her hand over her heart. "If I'd known we were coming here, I would have had a shot of tequila or something."

Again Harlan agreed. The redbrick building was practically pristine. Grounds, too. Ironic that it looked so welcoming, but if someone had asked him to paint a picture of hell, it'd be Rocky Creek.

"It doesn't exactly have good memories for any of us," Harlan mumbled. Slade added a grunt of agreement.

Caitlyn mimicked that grunt. "You never did tell me how you ended up here," she added, glancing at Harlan.

"Bad luck." That was Harlan's usual answer when it came up in conversation. Which wasn't very often. But Caitlyn already knew that bad luck had played into everyone's stay at the hellhole. "My mom cut out when I was three, and I lived with my grandmother until she passed away."

"How old were you?" She sounded truly interested or maybe she just wanted the distraction. Harlan wouldn't have minded one either, but he also didn't want conversation to distract him from keeping them safe.

"Twelve." He looked around, trying to see if there were any threats. "By then I was a big kid, and I think that intimidated any potential foster parents. Guess they figured I'd beat them to a pulp or something."

"Yeah." She hesitated, nibbled some more on her bottom lip. "I got the same attitude. The piercings and hair color didn't help."

"All those fights probably didn't either," Slade growled, and Caitlyn mumbled an agreement. His phone dinged, and he glanced at the screen before he passed it to Harlan.

"The background checks on Curtis and Devin," Harlan relayed.

That got the worried look off Caitlyn's face, and she

scooted closer to him so she could see. Not that she had
to scoot far. They were all sharing the single seat in
Slade's truck and were already way too close. The maneuver put them hip to hip.

Harlan ignored it.

Okay, he tried.

And he focused on the summary that his brother Clayton had done on Curtis Newell. The basics were all there.
Age thirty-seven, no criminal history. He had an MBA,
and from the looks of it, he'd sunk nearly every penny
of his inheritance from his grandmother into the private
equity business that he and Sherry had started three
years earlier.

No red flags.

The business wasn't exactly thriving, but there were
no signs that it was about to go bust either. The only
thing that seemed marginally suspect was that even before Sherry's disappearance, Curtis had been making the
bulk of the business decisions despite the fact that she
was the majority owner. That could be explained simply because Sherry had delegated that responsibility to
him. Of course, it could also mean that Curtis had a lot
to gain if Sherry died. He would become the sole owner
of their company. People had murdered for a lot less.

Harlan moved on to the next report, for Devin Mathis.

"Whoa," Caitlyn said just seconds into the record.

Definitely a whoa. "According to the San Antonio
cops, Devin initially was a suspect in Tiffany's car *accident*," Harlan said so that Slade would be in on this.
"Several of Tiffany's friends have come forward to say
the relationship had soured and that she was about to
break off the engagement."

He mulled that over, and yes, it was a possible motive
for Tiffany's murder. Love gone wrong always was. But

that didn't explain Sherry's disappearance and the other things happening to Caitlyn and him.

"Wait." Caitlyn pointed toward the next line of the report. "Devin *was* a suspect, but he has a decent alibi. He was out of town for two days prior to the accident, and witnesses report that Tiffany drove the vehicle during that time."

"That only means Devin didn't tamper with the brakes or anything," Harlan pointed out. "He could have hired someone to do it for him."

Her sound of agreement was laced with frustration, and Harlan knew why. They still didn't have the answers they needed to make an arrest, and essentially both men had motive. What was missing was any kind of proof.

Slade pulled his truck to a stop in front of the building, and if he was having any kind of reaction to the place, he didn't show it.

"Curtis should be here any minute." Slade checked his watch and tossed Harlan the key for the front door. "He's bringing a P.I. friend with him. More like a bodyguard if you ask me. The guy's scared."

Yeah, because of the fingerprints found on the threatening notes. Harlan's and Caitlyn's. He didn't blame the man for not trusting them.

"I'll drive back down and wait at the end of the road so I can keep watch," Slade continued. "Devin Mathis is supposed to be checking into a hotel in town soon. When he arrives, he's to give me a call, and I'll let you know. Didn't figure you'd want to talk to Curtis and Devin together."

He didn't. Harlan wanted to hear what each man had to say about the threats and this entire mess of a situation. Of course, that might be harder because of the whole distrust issue.

"Thanks, Slade. For everything," Harlan added. Yeah, he wasn't exactly comfortable being here, but he was grateful that his brother had been able to set it all up.

Slade drove away, leaving both Caitlyn and him looking up at the building. "Let's get in there," she said under her breath, "and exorcize a few demons and ghosts."

Maybe because their kissing session was still hot on his mind, that comment didn't sound as shaky as her reaction when she'd first realized this was their meeting place. The building had the demons, all right. Probably ghosts, too, and not all bad. After all, this was also where he and Caitlyn had done the deed sixteen years ago.

They'd been the least likely couple to get together—ever. Her with her reform-school background, goth-girl attitude, piercings and weekly hair-color change. He'd been the Boy Scout. Not literally. No opportunity for that, but he'd never considered himself a bad boy. Still, he and Caitlyn had found their way together.

And they'd found each other again with that mistake of a kissing session.

*Opposites attract, right?*

But in their case, opposites had to stop attracting. If he could just figure out how.

"I'm sorry about the article," she said out of the blue.

Harlan didn't look at her. He unlocked the door and pushed it open. "Sorry I found out or sorry you wrote it?"

"Both." She paused. "It was a knee-jerk reaction to those threats. I figured if you were sending them to me, I wanted some kind of insurance. You know, something for the world to read if I ended up dead in a suspicious car accident?"

Now he looked at her. "When are you going to send it to your boss?"

"I won't. I deleted it this morning before we left to come here."

It wasn't the answer he'd expected. "That won't hurt your *career?*" And yeah, it was a jab at her earlier excuse for writing the article that had burned him. Except to her it probably wasn't an excuse.

And he hated that he could see it from her side.

"My boss owes me a boatload of favors," she answered. "So no, pulling one article won't burn too many bridges."

*Too many,* but it would burn some.

"Why'd you kill the article?" he asked, not sure he wanted to hear this.

"The kiss," she readily admitted.

Harlan cursed. Yeah, that kiss was pretty darn potent, but he didn't think for one minute that it had changed her mind.

Had it?

"Look, you're not trying to kill me, and I'm not trying to screw you." She winced at her word choice. "Correction—I'm not trying to get you or your family in judicial hot water."

Good to hear. Not sure he totally believed it. "So, you think Kirby's innocent?"

"No." Not a second of hesitation either. "But if he's guilty, if he did help kill Webb, then I'd rather give him a medal than write one word that might put him behind bars."

Harlan figured that was probably the truth, or close enough to it, but he wasn't about to let go of his anger just yet. The point was—she had written the article. Maybe just days ago. And it was still too recent to have him forgive and forget.

His phone buzzed, and when he answered it, Harlan

heard Slade's voice. "Curtis Newell's driving up to the building now."

Showtime. Or rather interview time. Harlan put his phone away and popped the snap holder over his gun in his holster. "Just a precaution," he mumbled when Caitlyn made a sound of surprise.

Maybe it hadn't occurred to her that someone could have followed Curtis. Someone who could try to get past Slade. Plus, Harlan didn't know this man, and he wasn't going to blindly trust him. Curtis would be in the same mind-set.

Both he and Caitlyn drew in long breaths at the same time, and they looked out at the car that came to a stop directly in front of the steps. Earlier, Harlan had seen photos of Curtis, so he instantly recognized the stocky ginger-haired man who got out. He was wearing a dark blue suit more appropriate for a business meeting than an abandoned orphanage.

The second man was tall and bulky, and the jacket he was wearing no doubt concealed a weapon. He didn't come inside but rather stood in the doorway after his employer entered.

"Thanks for coming," Harlan greeted Curtis.

He gave an uneasy nod, barely sparing Harlan a glance before his gaze settled on Caitlyn. "I need to hear you say you didn't have anything to do with Sherry's disappearance."

"I didn't," she answered without hesitation. "And we didn't send her any threatening emails to warn her to shut up."

"The authorities think otherwise," Curtis reminded her.

"It doesn't mean it happened. Someone drugged and

kidnapped Harlan and me, and we think the person got our prints on those notes when we were out cold."

Curtis kept staring at her. There were dark circles under his eyes—which were bloodshot. He looked like a man in need of sleep. "Then who's doing this?" he pressed.

"We don't know. But the person tried to kill us."

"Did he kill Sherry, too?" His voice cracked.

Now it was Harlan's turn to say, "We don't know."

Curtis made an unmanly-sounding moan. "I'm in love with her. And no, she didn't feel the same way about me, but I couldn't turn it off. The heart wants what it wants, you know?"

Harlan glanced at Caitlyn at the same moment she glanced at him. He frowned. She lifted her shoulder. The heart wasn't in on his attraction—well, hopefully not anyway—but Harlan could substitute heart for body, and it would describe the feeling he was trying to fight.

"I'm doing everything to find Sherry," Curtis went on. "But the cops have no leads. It's like she just vanished."

Harlan wanted to give the man some hope, but he didn't intend to lie. "I think everything that's happening is linked to this place and Jonah Webb's murder. Did Sherry ever say she'd seen anything the night Webb disappeared?"

Curtis started shaking his head but stopped, paused. "She let something slip about four months ago, on the day that Webb's remains were discovered."

A day that Harlan remembered well. A crew working on the power lines had found what was left of Webb's body in a shallow grave about a mile from the Rocky Creek facility. Harlan had always figured the man was dead, but it hadn't been confirmed until that day.

"Sherry seemed worried," Curtis went on, "and when

I asked why, she said she might have been in the wrong place at the wrong time that night."

Harlan and Caitlyn exchanged another puzzled glance. "I called Sherry just days after that, and she didn't mention anything to me. Any idea what she meant?" Caitlyn asked.

"No. But I can tell you that she was scared." His gaze went to Harlan. "Of you and your family. But others, too. She said she didn't think she could trust anyone from Rocky Creek."

Judging from the slight sound Caitlyn made, that was news to her. To Harlan, too. And he was reasonably sure that Sherry hadn't said anything to the Rangers investigating the case. Certainly not to Joelle either when she'd been interviewing possible witnesses and suspects.

"Once when Sherry was on the phone, I heard her talking about Rocky Creek," Curtis continued. "She was scribbling down something, and later when I looked, I saw it was five names." He reached into his pocket, extracted a piece of paper. "I kept it."

Harlan took the paper that Curtis thrust at him, and Caitlyn moved closer. The names had indeed been scrawled along with some doodles, but they were still legible: Tiffany Brock, Caitlyn Barnes, Kirby Granger and Harlan McKinney. There was one other name on the list.

Billy Webb.

"I looked him up on the internet," Curtis said, "and I know it was his father who was murdered. I also found out he attempted suicide. I think Sherry was actually talking to him when she wrote down those names."

"What makes you say that?" Caitlyn asked.

"Just a gut feel." He shook his head. "I know you want more. I want more, too, because we need information to find Sherry. What if this crazy man is holding her captive somewhere?" Curtis grimaced. "What if he's torturing her?"

Harlan's stomach twisted, but that wasn't the worst-case scenario. No. The torturing could already be over, and Sherry could be dead.

Harlan's phone buzzed. Slade again. "Devin Mathis made it into town," his brother informed him. "Should I tell him where we are and have him drive out here?"

Curtis glanced behind him at the end of the road where the sleek car had come to a stop. "You have other people to see. I'll be going."

"You can go ahead and tell him to come out," Harlan said to his brother, and he purposely didn't mention Devin's name.

On the surface there didn't seem to be a direct connection between Devin and Curtis, and Harlan wanted to keep it that way. He didn't want the two teaming up to try to find the culprit for their loved ones' ill fates. Especially since they'd probably team up against Caitlyn and him.

Curtis looked at the note. "Could I please have that back? I want to keep it."

Harlan returned it and started to insist that the man give it to the authorities. That would be the legal thing to do, but it would be yet even more dirt against Caitlyn, Kirby and him. And besides, it might not even be important. Maybe Sherry was just jotting down names from her past.

Or setting them up.

"What?" Caitlyn whispered to him.

But Harlan didn't answer until Curtis had walked away and was out of earshot. "Curtis didn't mention one possibility—what if Sherry's alive and behind all of this?"

Caitlyn looked ready to dismiss that, but she didn't. "Maybe she helped Sarah kill Webb, and now she's trying to eliminate anyone who could prove it."

It was a stretch, and it only complicated things to add another suspect, but Harlan wanted to consider all the angles. Farris could be doing this to get his version of revenge against Caitlyn. Or Farris could be Billy's pawn.

And then there was Curtis.

He could have killed Sherry simply because she'd rejected him or because of a disagreement with their business—especially since Sherry was technically his boss since she owned the majority of their company. Of course, that didn't make all the other pieces fit, but that only meant Harlan had to look harder in case that connection was there.

His phone buzzed, and Harlan answered it, figuring it was Slade, who'd tell them that Devin would be arriving soon.

"Harlan?" With just that one word, he could hear the trouble in his brother's voice. "I'm coming your way. We need to get the heck out of here fast."

"Why? What happened?" Harlan didn't wait. He took Caitlyn by the arm and got them out the door, running toward Slade's truck barreling up the road toward them.

"Someone alerted the Rangers that you're here. Don't know who, but I just got a call from a friend who's also a dispatcher."

Even though the call wasn't on speaker, Caitlyn must have heard anyway because she cursed. Slade braked to a stop in front of them, and he and Caitlyn jumped inside. Slade didn't wait even a second before he sped away.

"Who made the call?" Caitlyn fumbled with her seat belt and finally got it on.

"Don't know, but you gotta figure it was Curtis," Slade answered. "The call was made just seconds after he walked out of the meeting."

Hell, Harlan should have seen this one coming, but he'd figured that Curtis just wanted answers, too.

But maybe not.

"Curtis might have set us up," Harlan speculated. But he had to rethink that. If Curtis had simply wanted them arrested, he could have made the call before the meeting. In fact, he could have made it the moment he knew their location.

"Maybe Curtis wanted to find out what we knew." Caitlyn tossed out the words. "So he could either find Sherry or try to cover his tracks."

It was downright spooky how often they seemed to be on the same wavelength.

"So if Curtis is behind the attacks, then how does Tiffany's accident fit into all of this?" Slade asked.

"Maybe it doesn't fit, but Curtis could have used it," Harlan said and Caitlyn murmured an agreement. "Curtis would have known about the accident, and manufactured the threats and such to make it seem as if the two are connected."

In his experience people were often willing to do any- and everything to cover their tracks when a death was involved. But Harlan didn't want to start pointing the finger at Curtis simply because he'd called the authorities on them. And besides, maybe he hadn't.

Maybe it was Devin.

Before Harlan could even voice that, Slade's phone buzzed again. "Devin Mathis," he announced, and handed the phone to Harlan. Probably because Slade was practically flying down the country road.

"Marshal McKinney," Harlan answered, and he put it on speaker so Slade and Caitlyn could hear. "We're going to have to reschedule our meeting—"

"Maybe not," Devin answered. "In fact, I don't think we can reschedule. I'm still in town at the hotel and was on my way out the door for our meeting when I got a visitor."

Probably the Texas Rangers. It wouldn't be that much of a stretch for them to put a tail on Devin on the off chance that he could lead them to Caitlyn and him.

"He says it's important," Devin went on, "that he needs to talk to you right away. And he doesn't want to go out to Rocky Creek to do it."

Surprise went through Caitlyn's eyes. "Is the guy's name Ranger Griffin Morris?"

"No," Devin immediately answered. "This guy's not a lawman. Says his name is Billy Webb."

Of all the names Harlan had expected Devin to say, that wasn't one of them. Half the state seemed to be looking for Billy, and here he'd shown up on Devin's doorstep.

"Why is he there, and what does he want?" Harlan asked.

"He won't tell me, but he says if you get here within thirty minutes, he can tell you everything he knows about what happened to his father."

# Chapter Ten

Caitlyn braced herself for Harlan to nix this meeting with Devin and Billy. He was operating on adrenaline now, making nonstop calls to set everything up. He clearly had a need to get whatever information Billy might have, but she figured any second Harlan would remember that she was in the truck with them and that it might not be *safe* for her to go face-to-face with Billy. And then Harlan would backtrack.

She hoped he didn't.

Because she was as anxious as Harlan and Slade to figure out what was going on. Maybe the info that Billy wanted to share with them wouldn't come with a huge price tag.

Harlan finished his latest call to Dallas, made a sweeping glance on both sides of the road leading into Rocky Creek. No one was following them, but the town was just ahead. Rocky Creek wasn't a big town, but there'd be people and traffic, both of which would make this trip hard on the nerves. Still, it had to be done.

"Dallas is on the way," he relayed to them. "I'll call the sheriff if things don't look right at the hotel."

"If you call him, he'll have to arrest us." The reminder wasn't necessary, but she said it anyway. Caitlyn didn't want to end up behind bars—that would put an end to this meeting in the worst way possible.

Well, one of the worst.

If Billy was a killer, then an arrest might be the least of their worries.

"Why the hell would Billy go to Devin?" Slade asked. He took the turn onto Main Street and drove toward the town center.

Caitlyn had already asked herself that question. Harlan, no doubt, too. "It only makes sense if he's connected to Tiffany or her car accident."

Harlan looked at her then, and she saw the trouble brewing in his eyes. "You'll wait in the truck with Slade. I'll go in and talk to Devin and Billy." And it wasn't exactly a suggestion.

"Billy might say things to me that he won't tell you," she fired back.

"Then those are things I won't get to hear, because you're not going anywhere near him."

So, this was the nixing that she'd braced herself for. Caitlyn tried to figure out a way around it—she really wanted to confront Billy face-to-face. But Harlan wasn't going to budge, and considering that Slade's expression was even steelier than usual, he was backing up Harlan on this.

"At least use your cell to call Slade, and then keep the phone on so I can listen that way."

If Harlan heard her suggestion, he didn't acknowledge it. He had his attention nailed to the hotel. During her days at the orphanage, the building had once been a private residence, but now it had been converted into a cozy bed-and-breakfast called the Bluebonnet Inn.

Slade came to a stop, not directly in front of the place but yards away. No sign of either Devin or Billy, but there were other vehicles parked on the street and two in the small heavily treed area on the far side of the inn. There was also a trickle of traffic in front of and behind them.

Too many places for someone to hide and wait to attack.

"Get down on the seat," Harlan warned her, and he eased his hand over his Glock before he opened the door.

"Be careful," she warned him right back.

But Harlan barely made it a step when the front door to the inn flew open, and Caitlyn saw a man run onto the porch. Not Billy, but Devin. She'd never actually met the man, but she'd seen plenty of photos, and he lived up to his rich preppy image in his khakis and white shirt. However, his expression wasn't preppy or rich but rather that of a concerned man.

"Billy left out back." Devin's voice wasn't a shout exactly, but it was close, and he pointed in the direction of the two vehicles beneath the sprawling oaks in the inn's parking lot. "That's his car."

Not exactly the economy vehicle she'd expected, but rather a Mercedes. Maybe Billy had come up in the world.

With his gun drawn, Slade stepped from the truck. "I'll go after him," he said to Harlan. "You wait here with Caitlyn."

Slade jumped the picket fence and hurried across the perfectly manicured lawn toward the cars, but Devin didn't follow him. He came down the steps and made a beeline for Harlan and her.

"Why did Billy leave?" Harlan asked. His tone wasn't friendly, and he, too, had his gun drawn.

Devin shook his head. His breath was gusting, and his forehead was bunched up. "He got a call, and it must have spooked him or something. He didn't even say anything. He just started running."

Maybe a phone call from the person he was working with—or trying to set Billy up. Maybe even Farris.

Harlan volleyed his attention between Devin and Slade, all the while maneuvering himself so that he was in front of her. Protecting her. Caitlyn wasn't much of a damsel in distress, and she especially didn't like it when Harlan put himself in even more danger for her. She opened the glove compartment and found exactly what she expected to find there.

Slade's backup weapon.

She took it and got out, but she didn't move into the open. She might not be a damsel in distress, but she wasn't stupid either.

Harlan shot her a *get back in* glare, but she ignored it. "What did Billy plan to tell us?" she asked Devin.

She figured Devin would just shake his head, but he didn't. "He said he was being set up," Devin answered without taking his attention off the parking lot where Slade had now disappeared from sight. "He said someone planted his fingerprints on the threatening note left for you."

Caitlyn knew what that felt like, since someone had done the same to Harlan and her, but that didn't make Billy innocent. "How'd the person get his prints so he could do that?"

"He told me it could have even been something he actually touched. He remembers a waiter at a restaurant handing him a menu that had a piece of paper on the back of it to cover up some dishes that the waiter claimed were no longer available."

"Someone posed as a waiter to get his fingerprints?" Harlan didn't sound any more convinced than she was.

Devin nodded. "Billy said he took the menu, but after the waiter took his order, he didn't come back. He figured it was just lousy service and left, but now he's not so sure. He thinks it was a setup."

"Who did he say set him up?" Harlan asked.

Now Devin's gaze shifted to them. "You two. He thinks one of you helped his mother kill his father and now you're trying to cover your tracks."

Harlan mumbled the exact profanity that Caitlyn was thinking. "We're not the ones doing the setting up. We're on the receiving end of a scheme to make us look guilty as sin. We're not."

"Well, someone's behind this," Devin insisted. "And that someone likely murdered Tiffany."

Devin made it clear with his glare that he thought that the *someone* was Harlan and/or her. And Harlan made it clear with his glare that he was tired of being accused of something they hadn't done.

"I understand Tiffany and you didn't have an ideal engagement?" Harlan tossed out the words.

That put some starch in Devin's posture. "Are you accusing me of something?"

"Just asking a simple question. Generally I like simple answers to them."

"No, what you're looking for is a scapegoat." Devin stabbed his index finger toward Harlan's chest. "If you tie me to Tiffany's accident, then you can try and tie me to everything else that's happening. But I have no motive."

"Sure you do," Caitlyn challenged. "Tiffany was about to break off the engagement. It would have humiliated you in front of your friends and family." That was a stretch of the truth, but judging from the way Devin's eyes narrowed, it hit a nerve.

His breath was gusting even harder now, and it took Devin a moment to speak. "Let's just say for the sake of argument that I did it. How the hell could that possibly connect to Billy Webb or the disappearance of this other woman?"

Harlan shrugged. "Maybe you want to muddy the waters."

"That doesn't make sense."

"It does if you manage to get suspicion off yourself and onto someone else."

Devin opened his mouth, no doubt to return verbal fire or at least deny it, but Slade came back into view. He touched his hand to the hood of the Mercedes, said something and hurried toward them.

"No sign of Billy," Slade grumbled, and he turned to Devin. "How long ago did you say he arrived?"

"Right before I called you."

Slade shook his head. "Then something's not right, because if Billy arrived fifteen minutes ago like you said, the hood of his car should be hotter from the engine running."

That narrowed Devin's eyes again. "I'm sick and tired of being accused of lying. For all I know Billy could have been sitting out there for a while before he came inside."

Harlan took a step closer to Devin. "And why would he do that?"

"I don't know and I don't care. I came here to try to help, but all of this has just convinced me that you or one of your lawmen brothers left that threatening message." Devin turned and headed for the inn. "If you want to speak to me about anything else, you can call my lawyer." He went inside and slammed the door behind him.

"That went well," Caitlyn mumbled. She glanced at Harlan and Slade. Then at the silver Mercedes. "You think Devin set all of this up, that maybe Billy was never even here?"

"It's possible." Harlan answered so quickly that he'd probably already come to the same conclusion. "It's also possible that Devin's calling the Rangers if he hasn't already. We need to leave now."

Harlan didn't wait. He took her by the arm, pushing her back into the truck. "If Devin is still here when Dallas arrives, he'll take him in for questioning."

That was something at least, but it didn't seem nearly enough.

Harlan had already started to get in when Caitlyn caught a movement by the Mercedes. A blur of motion.

"Is it Billy?" she asked.

Harlan didn't have time to answer because the blur of motion became a lot clearer. Someone wearing a ski mask. And that someone was armed.

He took aim at them and fired.

HARLAN'S HEART SLAMMED against his chest, and he threw himself onto the seat and in front of Caitlyn. It wasn't a second too soon, because the bullet blasted into the passenger's side window where he'd just been standing.

"Get us out of here!" Harlan told Slade.

His brother started the truck and threw it into gear just as a spray of bullets crashed through the front windshield. Slade had no choice but to get down. Harlan had to as well, and then a jolt knocked him forward, slamming his shoulder and head hard into the dash.

"What the heck was that?" Caitlyn hadn't collided with just the dash, but with Harlan, too.

Harlan's head was spinning from the impact, but from what he could tell, someone had crashed into their rear bumper. "Is it a second gunman?"

Slade sat up enough to look in his side mirror. "Don't think so. Looks like the driver got shot and lost control of the vehicle."

Hell. Just what they didn't need. An innocent by-stander in this dangerous mix. It was bad enough that Caitlyn was here, but God knew how many people could be hurt. One way or another, Harlan had to stop the shooter.

Whoever he was.

From the glimpse he'd gotten of the man—and it was definitely a man—it could be any of their suspects: Curtis, Farris, Billy. Even Devin. He'd definitely had time to go back inside the inn, don a ski mask and head to the parking lot to fire those shots. Yeah, it'd be risky because someone inside could have seen him, but maybe Devin was desperate enough to try to cover his tracks.

With bullets, and lots of them.

Some of those bullets tore through the car on the street behind them again, and each shot echoed through him. Mercy. He hated that Caitlyn, he and now Slade were right in the middle of danger again.

"The sheriff will be here any second." Caitlyn was shaking and had a death grip on the gun she was holding.

But Harlan knew the fear wasn't just for the shooter. It was also for the sheriff's arrival. Once he was on the scene, he'd have to arrest them.

The sound of sirens pierced through the gunfire. So did the shouts and screams of people nearby. People who'd hopefully taken cover. He didn't want anyone else hurt today, and the best way to make sure that happened for them was to get out of there. Without them, the shooter would have no targets. No reason to fire.

"Hold on," Slade warned them a split second before he hit the accelerator.

His brother stayed low in the seat, probably barely able to see over the dash. The truck lurched forward and plowed through the white picket fence that surrounded the inn, but it jarred to a stop because the tires bogged down in the soft ground and grass.

Oh, hell.

Now they were sitting ducks.

The shots didn't stop. In fact, they seemed to come at them even faster, each of them tearing through into the truck. Any one of the bullets could be lethal, and the only thing Harlan could do was keep his body over Caitlyn's to protect her as much as possible. If he lifted his head to return fire, he'd be shot and that would leave Slade to fight this battle on his own.

The sirens got closer, but Slade ignored them and kept pumping the gas to get them out of the bog. He gave the steering wheel a sharp turn to the left. The truck tore through yet more of the fence. Gate, too. But he managed to get even clearance from the vehicle that had collided with them. Slade peeled out onto the street and floored it.

The shooter gave them one last parting shot. A bullet slammed through the back window and sent a spray of safety glass onto them. Then, nothing. The rain of bullets finally stopped.

Harlan lifted his head enough to look out the side mirror. Thankfully, it was still intact, and he saw the swirling lights of a police cruiser headed right for the scene.

But he also saw something else.

A man running up the sidewalk away from the inn. Not a jog either. A full out-and-out run. Away from the truck and directly toward the police cruiser. The guy wasn't wearing a ski mask and wasn't carrying a gun, so Harlan couldn't tell if this was their shooter or not.

The shooter could have easily ditched both ski mask and weapon to make himself look innocent.

Harlan wanted to turn around and go back to haul this guy in for questioning, but the sheriff must have had the same idea. The cruiser braked to a loud stop, the tires kicking up smoke on the asphalt, and Harlan caught just a glimpse of the two officers spilling out of the car and heading for the runner.

Slade didn't stop. Didn't slow down. He sped away. Of course, that didn't mean they were out of the woods. The sheriff had probably seen them leaving the scene. And if not, Devin or some other eyewitness would give him enough details so that he'd know exactly whom to arrest.

That ate away at Harlan.

He'd hoped this meeting would give them information to help their cause, but now it was just another note in their fugitive status. Worse, he'd entangled Slade in this now.

"We'll have to ditch the truck as soon as we can," Slade reminded them.

Just hearing the words hurt, too. Worse than any gunshot wound he'd ever had. Heck, they were acting like criminals, and even though an arrest would be bad, it couldn't be as bad as this.

Harlan glanced back in the mirror. "Turn around."

Caitlyn lifted her head, stared at him. "Have you lost your mind?"

"No. I've regained it. We'll just have to conduct the rest of this investigation behind bars. I want to go back, tell the sheriff what happened and check on the bystander who might have been shot.

"Turn around," Harlan repeated when Slade kept staring at him, too.

Cursing, mumbling and sounding generally displeased with this notion, Slade hit the brakes and did a screeching U-turn in the road. "You'd better know what the hell you're doing," he added.

He did. It was the right thing. And no, it wouldn't be justice, since he and Caitlyn had been framed, but it was the only way he could live with himself.

Caitlyn huffed, sat up and pushed her hair from her face. "Always knew you were a Boy Scout." And it didn't sound like a compliment. Except after another huff, she leaned over, kissed his cheek. "I never was good at this running-from-the-law stuff either. Last time I did it, I ended up in reform school."

"Ditto," Slade growled. But unlike Caitlyn, he didn't seem nearly convinced that this was what they should be doing.

Harlan's phone buzzed, and he put the call on speaker when he saw Dallas's name on the screen. "We have a problem." Harlan greeted his brother.

"Yeah, I just heard. Someone tried to kill you. Wyatt's monitoring everything on the police radio, and I'm listening to it as it's happening," Dallas added. "I'm on my way to Rocky Creek now, not far out, so I should have some more details in the next half hour."

Good. They would need someone on their side at the police station. "We're on our way back, too."

Dallas didn't say anything for several moments. "Hold off on that and let me handle this. Caitlyn and you should go somewhere and wait."

"I don't want Slade in trouble for this," Harlan protested.

"He won't be. If someone sees the shot-up truck and reports it, I'll just tell the sheriff that I ordered Slade to get Caitlyn away from the scene. She's a civilian and doesn't need to be in the middle of a gunfight. I'll also

convince the sheriff you went with them so Slade would
have some backup in case Caitlyn was attacked again."

Harlan could hear the chatter from the police radio
in the background. "Ranger Morris is calling in as we
speak," Dallas continued, "and I want to find out what
he has to say."

"But someone was shot at the scene," Harlan argued.

More radio chatter. "Yeah, and the sheriff is taking
someone into custody."

The guy running from the scene, no doubt.

Caitlyn pulled in a hard breath. "Is it Devin Mathis?"

"No," Dallas answered. "According to the man's ID,
it's Billy Webb."

# Chapter Eleven

Caitlyn sank onto the far end of the sofa at Declan's cabin and tried to focus on the lanky dark-haired man on the laptop screen.

Billy Webb.

Maybe he had the answers that would help them clear all of this up. Of course, he might only give them more questions, and that didn't help steady her any.

The cup of tea she'd just made herself was too strong and bitter, but she drank it anyway for the caffeine hit. She needed to be alert.

The wait and watch could go on for hours.

Maybe she wouldn't fall apart during that wait, but the odds weren't good. She already felt like one big raw nerve, and the images of the shooting just wouldn't stop. Hopefully, those images would end with their wait, and she could find some way to keep herself from losing it.

Some way that didn't involve leaning on Harlan's shoulders.

He hadn't offered his shoulder, and Caitlyn hadn't pushed. It would have been nice to be able to come unglued in his strong arms—even if that would only make things worse in the long run. Harlan didn't need her boo-hooing all over the place, and she didn't need to think of his arms as anything other than off-limits.

Despite the mental pep talk and her attempts to stop it, Caitlyn felt tears burn her eyes, and she blinked them back, praying they didn't spill onto her cheeks. But they did, and when she went to swipe them away, Harlan looked at her.

"I'm okay," she quickly lied. He knew it was a lie, too, but he stayed put on his end of the sofa and fastened his attention back on the computer screen.

Thanks to Dallas, who was at the Rocky Creek sheriff's office, she and Harlan had not only visual but audio, as well. Ditto for his brothers back at the Maverick County marshals' office. All of them, including Slade, were tuned to it to see what Billy Webb had to say.

Or rather not say.

Because the only talking Billy had done was to ask for a lawyer.

Dallas hadn't mentioned to Sheriff Bruce Sheldon that the computer feed was also going to the cabin for Harlan and her to view. Probably for the best, since there was still a warrant out for their arrests. Though Harlan obviously didn't agree with her *for the best.*

His mood had been past the surly stage since Slade had dropped them off so he could head back to Rocky Creek and see if he could help. Like Harlan, Slade was a lawman to the core, and it was eating away at Harlan that the only thing he could do was sit, watch and stew. The only thing she could do was sit, watch and fight back tears.

"If we'd stayed, the gunman probably would have started firing more shots," she reminded him—again. "More people could have been hurt."

Or dead. They'd gotten lucky. According to Dallas, there was only one wounded bystander, and he'd already been treated and released.

Harlan made a sound, sort of a grunt of disagreement.

He glanced at his phone. No messages or calls since the last time he'd checked a few minutes earlier, and he got up and went to the front window.

"If Billy moves, let me know," he grumbled.

But Billy didn't move. He sat at the table in the interview room, not looking especially concerned about anything. In fact, nothing about him was what Caitlyn had expected. The boy she remembered had been scared of his own shadow, but this Billy was, well, poised. The expensive-looking gray suit helped. So did the fashionable haircut. Definitely not the appearance of a man with mental issues or someone who'd been in hiding and off the grid.

And that in itself posed yet more questions.

Maybe Dallas would soon have some answers for them when he got back the results of the background check. Answers to questions like where had Billy been all this time. Why was he dressed like a business executive?

And had he been the one to shoot them?

He'd already submitted to a gunshot-residue test, and it had come back negative. That wasn't the only thing working in his favor of innocence. Dallas had already relayed to them that Billy had had no weapon on him when the sheriff had taken him into custody. Plus, there'd been no evidence in his car to prove he'd been the shooter or even part of the attack.

Maybe he wasn't. It was possible someone had set him up just as they'd done to Harlan and her.

Harlan did another phone check, huffed and leaned against the window frame. He was no doubt as exhausted as she was, but he didn't have the same weary look that Caitlyn was sure she had. He just looked, well, rumpled in his jeans and shirt. Of course, Harlan had a way of taking rumpled to a whole new level.

What the devil was she going to do about him?

They couldn't get within five feet of each other without touching or kissing. Good kissing, too. The kind that reminded her that she only wanted more from him, and more was something she was reasonably sure Harlan couldn't and wouldn't give her. Beneath all the rumpled hotness was still a nice guy who probably thought it best not to start something with her that he couldn't finish.

"I don't suppose it'd do any good if you tried to rest?" she suggested. "Might be a while before Billy's lawyer shows."

"Rest?" His left eyebrow rose.

Uh-oh. Did he think she meant *that* kind of rest? Maybe. Despite her teary red eyes, she was probably giving off weird vibes that his very male body had no trouble detecting.

"Could you rest?" And it sounded like a challenge coming from him. So, not *that* after all. He was just pointing out that neither of them would get much resting done until Billy did some talking.

Yes, it was going to be a long wait.

Or maybe not.

Harlan's phone finally buzzed, and he answered it so fast that it bobbled in his hand. "Dallas," he answered, and put the call on speaker.

Caitlyn set her tea aside and turned the laptop monitor in Harlan's direction so they wouldn't miss anything if Billy's lawyer showed. However, she also didn't want to miss any of this phone conversation, so she hurried closer to Harlan.

"Got the initial background check on Billy," Dallas started. "The clothes and car aren't an act. About ten years ago his paternal grandparents let him tap into a huge trust fund they'd set up for him, and he's been paying with cash this whole time. He's also been living in a house that's still in his grandmother's maiden name."

"Why didn't Billy's mother know any of this?" Harlan immediately asked. But he didn't wait for an answer. "Maybe she did and just didn't say."

Bingo. Of course, they couldn't ask her now because Sarah Webb was in a coma and might never wake up.

"Sarah could have lied about his whereabouts because she didn't want him to have to answer questions about that night," Dallas went on, "especially if he had anything to do with his father's murder."

Caitlyn tried not to huff, but she'd wanted more. Something that pointed the finger at Billy or else excluded him as a suspect. "Is there anything in Billy's background to indicate why he'd go after Harlan, me, Tiffany or Sherry?"

"Nothing." Dallas's sigh was louder than hers had been. "The fingerprint could have been gotten without his knowledge, as you two well know. And with no GSR on his hands and no solid evidence to point to him, I doubt the sheriff can hold Billy long. Heck, even Devin is saying he doesn't think Billy's the shooter, and he probably got the best look at the guy."

Interesting. Devin didn't seem like the good-hearted type to remove suspicion from a man he hardly knew.

Unless he did know him.

"Is it possible Devin and Billy were working together?" Caitlyn asked. "Because there was something... private in the threats I received."

She looked at Harlan at the same moment he looked at her. *You'll always be my first, Caitlyn.* Yes, definitely private and intimate. Too bad just the reminder brought back other recollections. Of that night. Of the recent kisses. Memories of everything she shouldn't be remembering.

Great. Her body reacted. The heat swirled through her. Slow and easy.

"Private?" Dallas questioned.

No way would she spell it out for him, so Caitlyn settled for an explanation that wouldn't make Harlan and her squirm. "Something that could have possibly been overheard by someone at Rocky Creek and then told to the person who's trying to kill us."

Dallas made a sound of agreement. "Someone like Billy. I'll look into that, but again, I doubt it'll be enough to hold him. I'll call you as soon as I have anything."

Harlan clicked the end-call button, and even though he didn't say anything, Caitlyn felt his frustration. It helped her a little because it kept her tears at bay. Tears and crying would only add to his frustration. Hers, too.

He made another of those sounds, part huff and part groan, and his gaze met hers. Her gaze of him was a little distorted, however, because she was literally seeing him through tear-speckled lashes. She didn't dare wipe her eyes again because it would only draw attention to something she didn't want him to notice.

"You should really think about getting some rest," he said. "You heard what Dallas said. Even when Billy's lawyer shows, it'll probably be just to get him released."

"And maybe a rightful release," she muttered.

He lifted his shoulder but didn't break the stare they had locked on each other. He did move, though. He reached up and brushed the pad of his thumb over those tears. "All those bad times at Rocky Creek, I never saw you cry."

"I'd rather have eaten glass. Tears are a sign of weakness."

Another shrug. "They're normal in situations like these."

"You aren't crying," she pointed out.

The corner of his mouth lifted just a fraction. "Wouldn't go with my image."

The corner of her mouth rose, too. Not a smile exactly. The fear and emotion from the shooting were too close to the surface for that, but it felt good to share a moment like this with Harlan. A moment that didn't involve her crying on his shoulder.

But the moment changed when he didn't pull back his hand. He kept it there. His fingers rested on her cheek while his heavy-lidded gaze melted all over her. Okay, the melting was her interpretation. Harlan certainly didn't look on the verge of kissing her again.

"Why me?" he asked.

Caitlyn blinked, shook her head.

"Why did you really give yourself to me at Rocky Creek?"

Oh. *That.* She didn't miss the *really* part of his question. After all, she'd already told him she had offered up her virginity because he was a good guy. That was true, but it was more than that.

"Why not Wyatt?" Harlan pushed. "He had the hots for you."

Caitlyn couldn't pretend that she hadn't noticed Wyatt's attention. She had. "Wyatt certainly had the looks," she confessed. "But you were the total package."

Ouch. That seemed way too relationship-y, and Harlan got that deer-caught-in-the-headlights look. Time to put this right back on him.

"Why me?" she fired back.

His hand moved from her cheek to her chin. So near her mouth. And his touch felt so good that she wanted to move into it. And maybe would have, but coming on the heels of her *total package* slip, the timing sucked.

He shook his head. "Doesn't work that way for a guy. You offered, and I accepted."

Now it was her turn to give him the skeptical eye. "Plenty of girls offered, not just at Rocky Creek but at the high school, too. The gossip mill worked pretty well in those days, so if you took up anyone else's offer other than Amy Simpson and that cute cross-country runner with the big boobs, I didn't hear about it."

And Caitlyn would almost certainly have heard, because she hadn't exactly hidden her feelings for Harlan. Also, since she was somewhat of a pariah, people would have loved to have thrown in her face the fact that Harlan was into someone else.

This time, the sound he made was of agreement. "Old water," he mumbled. "Old bridge."

"Yes, except this old water still feels…a little warm," she settled for saying.

The corner of his mouth lifted even higher, and while they truly had nothing to smile about, that helped with her raw nerves, too.

She figured that would do it. No way would Harlan keep touching her and staring at her after that comment. Things were no doubt getting too *trip down memory lane* for him. But he surprised her—and judging from the profanity he mumbled, surprised himself—when he leaned in and put his mouth to hers.

That brief jolt of surprise vanished. Tears, too. In fact, it was as if his mouth took her on a supersonic ride to another place, another time.

Of course, it didn't stay just a kiss. They were stupid

and weak when it came to each other. Caitlyn wrapped her arms around him, moved in closer and bam! She got what she'd been fantasying about but knowing it shouldn't happen. She got Harlan's shoulder, arms and chest.

Oh, and pretty much everything else, too.

Now body to body, they deepened the kiss, and the ache it created felt just as necessary as air.

The feeling only got worse when Harlan ran his hand between them, touching parts of her that were begging for attention. She remembered this touch. This raging insane need that he could create inside her.

Thank goodness oxygen soon became an issue, because they had to break the kiss and gulp in deep breaths. During those brief seconds their gazes met again, and Caitlyn was sure Harlan would realize the mistake they were making.

But nope.

They went right back to each other, the kiss even more intense. The touching harder and crazier. They grappled to get closer and knocked each other off balance. Harlan's shoulder slammed into the wall, but that still didn't loosen the grip they had on each other.

Or the precise alignment.

Harlan's beefcake chest gave her breasts some mind-blowing pressure. Ditto for the rest of him. Every part of them aligned so that his sex was against her. Yes, there were clothes between them, but she could still feel every last inch of him.

There was a serious problem with their being former lovers. Her body was trying to convince the rest of her that a round of quick sex with Harlan would be good for both of them.

*Very* good.

But afterward…well, afterward would be awkward and would likely put some distance between them. She didn't need distance when they were essentially fighting for their lives.

Caitlyn reminded herself of all that. Three times. And even though it took every ounce of willpower, she gripped him by the shoulders and pushed herself away from him.

Oh, mercy.

She instantly felt the loss, and regret of a different kind. The realization, too, that she was just as attracted to Harlan now as she had been sixteen years ago.

Caitlyn groaned. Stepped back even farther.

"I need to apologize," he mumbled.

She shook her head. "It's not that. I'm just trying to keep myself from going back for another round. Because we both know where this will lead if we keep kissing."

He stayed quiet a moment, giving that some thought, and giving her the look. The one that had melted her too many times to count. Caitlyn felt the tug, as if they were connected by a big rubber band that might snap her back to him at any second. And it probably would have.

If Harlan's phone hadn't buzzed.

Neither of them seemed relieved by the sound, but Caitlyn thought that later—when her body had cooled down some—they might be thankful for the interruption.

*Might.*

Harlan took out the phone. "It's Slade." And like the other call, he put this one on speaker.

"Hope you're sitting down," Slade immediately said, "because you're not going to believe what's just happened."

Caitlyn automatically groaned. Slade's tone always

sounded the same to her—drenched in a gallon of gloom and doom—so she braced herself for more bad news.

"The Rangers killed the warrants for your arrest," Slade announced.

Harlan and she stared at each other, and even though it wasn't much to process, just one sentence, it didn't seem to make sense.

"Why?" they asked in unison.

"Still digging for the details, but whatever evidence they thought they had, it was discredited."

She shook her head. "How?"

"By someone unexpected. Farris."

That was the last name on earth she'd expected Slade to say. "How?" she repeated.

"Don't know all the facts there either, but what I do know is that Farris claims he sent those threatening emails to Sherry."

The surprise caused her stomach to flip-flop. Not that she'd thought for one second that Farris was innocent in all of this. Nope. But the surprise was that he would admit any wrongdoing.

And why would he?

"What does Farris want?" Caitlyn had meant the question more for herself than Slade.

"Who knows, but he's here at the Rocky Creek sheriff's office, and he's talking," Slade told her. "My advice? Since the law's not after you, both of you should get down here now and hear what this little viper has to say."

# Chapter Twelve

Even though Caitlyn and he were walking into the Rocky Creek sheriff's office, Harlan didn't exactly feel safe.

For a darn good reason.

They'd been shot at less than two miles from here.

Plus, they were about to face down two of the men who could be responsible for the shooting. Harlan wanted Caitlyn far from here, tucked away someplace safe. But someplace safe might not exist, and right now his best bet was to keep her by his side. He hoped like the devil that his decision didn't have anything to do with their recent kissing session.

But it probably did. And that riled him to the core. Attraction and kisses shouldn't be playing into any decision about her safety.

He got Caitlyn inside the building and immediately came face-to-face with not just Sheriff Sheldon but three uniformed deputies. Normally the uniforms wouldn't have made Harlan uneasy, but it had been less than a half hour since the Rangers had dropped the charges against Caitlyn and him. It might be a while before he trusted anyone with a badge unless it was one of his brothers.

And speaking of family, both Slade and Declan came up the side hall toward the reception area. Slade greeted them with his usual no-greeting that included zero change in his expression, but Declan's forehead bunched up, showing his concern.

"You two okay?" Declan asked, but his question seemed more for Caitlyn than Harlan.

Or maybe that was just Harlan's overactive imagination. He was still nursing a twinge of jealousy over the whispered conversation that Declan and she had had back at the hospital.

"Fine," Caitlyn lied, and she repeated it, sounding less of a lie when Declan gave her arm a gentle pat.

Harlan felt a rumble of jealousy over that, too, and wondered if he should just hit himself in the head with a big rock. It might knock some sense into him.

"Billy Webb's in the first room down the hall," Sheriff Sheldon informed them. "With his lawyer. That's my way of saying he's probably not gonna be talking much, but it doesn't matter, I guess, since we got nothing to hold him. He said he'd be leaving as soon as he spoke to you."

Well, at least Billy had waited around. Harlan didn't know if that proved his innocence or if he just didn't want to look guilty. "And what about Farris?"

The sheriff tipped his head toward the hall again. "He's in the room next to Billy Webb. No lawyer yet, but he's got a couple on the way. I figure he won't be leaving any time soon. It's gonna take us a while to sort through all of this, and the Rangers want to talk to him, too."

No surprise there. "I want to question Farris. You got any problems with that?"

Sheldon shook his head. "If you get him to confess to firing those shots, I want to know about it. Rocky Creek ain't the wild, wild West, and I don't want anybody thinking they can come in here and start shooting up the place."

Harlan doubted Farris would confess to anything that

serious. In fact, this could all be part of the cat-and-mouse game he was playing with Caitlyn. Still, sometimes people spilled things they didn't intend.

"There's a camera in the interview room," the sheriff added. "Already turned on. I read Farris his rights, told him everything was on the record, so whatever he says I can and will use against him."

Harlan thanked Sheldon and considered asking Caitlyn to wait with Slade or Declan. It would save her from facing down Farris again, but before Harlan could even make the suggestion, she was already walking in the direction of the interview rooms.

Harlan caught up with her, and they stopped in the doorway of the first room. The moment Billy spotted them he got to his feet.

"Caitlyn, Harlan," Billy greeted, and he came to them and shook their hands. His lawyer, a bald bulky man, got up, too, and stood behind him. "Wish this was under better circumstances," Billy added.

There was no trace of the stutter that Billy had once had. No trace of the painfully shy kid who'd kept to himself. Heck, he was wearing a Rolex, for heaven's sake, and from the looks of it, he'd had a recent manicure.

Yeah, he'd come up in the world, all right.

But Harlan knew that money didn't make a man innocent.

"You think Devin Mathis set up the shooting?" Billy came right out and asked.

Harlan had to shrug. "Who set up the meeting—you or Devin?"

"I did, but he'd been trying to find me for weeks. Even hired a P.I. So did Sherry's business partner, Curtis Newell." Billy looked at Caitlyn then. "And you."

She confirmed that with a nod. "A lot of people have

been looking for you, especially me. Any reason you didn't want to be found?"

"I have a new life now," he said without hesitation. "I didn't want to get caught up in the old memories and a past I'd rather just forget."

"But something changed your mind," Harlan pointed out.

"Yes." He gave a weary sigh. "I started reading about the investigation of my father's death. About Tiffany's car accident and Sherry's disappearance. I didn't think it was a coincidence that those things were happening so soon after my mother's…incident at your family's ranch."

The *incident* had nearly killed Harlan's brother Dallas and Dallas's wife, Joelle. Sarah Webb had hired armed men to make sure no one uncovered the fact that she'd murdered her husband. Sarah had been seriously injured in the attack that she'd orchestrated and had lapsed into a coma before she could name her accomplice.

Was Harlan now looking at that accomplice?

"Who helped your mother kill your father?" Harlan asked.

"I honestly don't know, but it wasn't me." Again Billy didn't hesitate. "If you remember correctly, I didn't have much of a backbone in those days."

Caitlyn stared at him. "Or maybe you did. Webb was beating your mother nearly every time his temper blew, and from what I remember, it happened often. You must have wanted to see him get his due."

Billy shrugged. "I didn't say I didn't have motive. I did. Just like the rest of you. My father had gotten approval to keep Rocky Creek open, and none of you wanted that—especially Kirby. Plus, Declan had been on the receiving end of Dad's fists that day. Joelle, too, if I remember correctly. All of that is motive for wanting him dead."

Harlan couldn't argue with any of it. Joelle had been a resident at Rocky Creek, and Webb had slapped her for some piddly infraction. Dallas and Joelle were just teenagers then, like the rest of his foster brothers, but they'd also been lovers. And Dallas was beyond protective of her, giving him a big reason to go after Webb.

But Harlan figured someone beat Dallas to it and put that knife in Webb.

The only thing Harlan was certain of was he hadn't killed the headmaster, and he was sure Caitlyn hadn't been involved either. For argument's sake, if he ruled out members of his family—and he intended to do that whether he should or not—that left Billy, Devin and Curtis.

Maybe Sherry, too, if she'd faked her disappearance.

Harlan took a business card from his wallet and wrote down the number for the prepaid cell he was still using. "Call me if you find out anything."

"I will." Billy took out a card, too. "And I ask you to do the same for me." He pulled in a long breath. "My father was a despicable man and deserved to die, but I've spent a decade and a half getting away from the muck that he caused in my life and others'. I don't want to be pulled back into it. That's why it's important that *I* find whoever's behind these attacks so my name will be cleared."

*"I?"* Harlan challenged. He didn't like the sound of that. "What are you planning to do?"

"Something that should have been done years ago. I intend to find the person responsible for my father's death."

Billy didn't wait for Harlan to respond to that. He

eased past them, barely sparing them a glance, and he and his lawyer walked away.

"You believe him?" Caitlyn asked before they were even out of earshot.

Harlan had to shake his head. Billy was the obvious suspect in his father's death, and that made him the obvious suspect in any cover-up.

If that was what was going on.

But Billy wasn't the one who'd confessed to any wrongdoing. That honor fell to Jay Farris.

"I'm going in there," Caitlyn said before Harlan could offer to do the interview alone. She leaned in, lowered her voice to a whisper. "I can't let him know how much he still scares me."

Oh, man. Harlan gave her arm a rub as Declan had done, but when that didn't work, he dropped a kiss on her cheek. The fear was in her eyes again, probably because she hadn't had time to recover from the last attack. Now here she was about to face down someone who'd tried to kill her.

Maybe more than once.

"Besides," she added, "if Farris tries to strangle me again, I fully expect you to beat the living daylights out of him. Yes, I know that sounds sexist, but you're bigger than I am and can do a lot more damage. Promise me, if it comes down to it, you'll do *damage*."

He couldn't help it. He smiled. "I promise." In fact, Harlan almost welcomed it. He had a lot of dangerous energy boiling inside him, and he figured Farris better not push any of his buttons or he'd be on the receiving end of that energy.

Harlan opened the interview-room door, and unlike Billy, Farris didn't jump to his feet. He sat there, his face buried in his hands. "I'm so sorry, Caitlyn."

Harlan wasn't interested in an apology, and apparently neither was Caitlyn. She folded her arms over her chest. "Start talking, and explain the threatening notes and how you were able to discredit that so-called evidence."

Taking his time, Farris lowered his hands. "You should probably sit down."

"Start talking," she repeated. It wasn't a suggestion either.

Farris reached inside his pants pocket and pulled out a handful of paper. Not neatly folded—it looked as if he'd crammed it in there.

"My instructions," Farris explained, which didn't explain anything.

Harlan went closer and looked at the first note, which was handwritten in block letters. *Leave this for Caitlyn to find.*

"There was a note attached to it," Farris went on, "the one that warned her if she talked to the Rangers she'd be sorry." He fished out another note. "This one was attached to the one that said she'd die if she talked to them."

Harlan riffled through the others. If he followed Farris's explanation, then one of them would have been attached to the note that included the very private sentence—*you'll always be my first.*

"I didn't know where Caitlyn was, but this person knew—one of the notes had her address. Still, I didn't want to leave those threats for her to find," Farris went on. "I knew they'd upset her."

Caitlyn gave him a flat look. "And you expect me to believe that my being upset would bother you?"

Farris opened his mouth, but then his attention landed on Harlan, specifically how close he was standing to Caitlyn. Farris's gaze darted away but not before he swallowed hard. "It would have bothered me. Whether you believe it or not, I didn't want to torment you."

"But you did," she fired back.

"Only because I got that note." Farris jabbed his index finger at the papers.

Harlan didn't need to ask for clarification as to which note Farris meant, because it had already caught Harlan's attention. "'Do as I say, or you and Caitlyn will both die.'"

Farris nodded. "And with everything else going on, I didn't think it was a bluff."

"Who sent these to you?" Harlan didn't bother to sound as if he believed Farris. Because he didn't. Farris could have written all the notes himself and could have hired someone to find Caitlyn.

"I don't know who sent them, but whoever it was killed my dog, slashed my tires and vandalized my place. Then I got this note." He plucked another one from the stash. "It said if I didn't do as I was told, then the order releasing me from the institution would be revoked and I'd have to go back in. He—or she—said that's where they'd kill me."

Harlan studied his body language. It was right for someone who was genuinely upset, but Farris was likely a nutcase, which meant he could probably lie and not have any of the telltale signs.

"Ranger Morris will want to see all those notes," Harlan reminded Farris. If the man objected to that, he didn't show it either. "For now, talk to us about the evidence that you supposedly refuted."

"I disproved it," Farris corrected. Another gaze dodge. In Harlan's experience, that wasn't a good sign. "One of the notes said to hack into Sherry's computer and make it appear that Caitlyn and you had done it."

Caitlyn made a sound of surprise. "How'd you do that?"

"I'm good with computers." Farris's tone was somewhat defensive now, but he still didn't make direct eye contact. "Good at hacking," he mumbled. "My family owns a software business, and I've always helped. And as for setting you up, I just used your own personal computers."

"How?" Harlan demanded. "And if you say you broke into my house—"

"I didn't. Not yours anyway, but I did break into Caitlyn's once I had her address, and I used her computer so it could be traced back to her."

Harlan saw the goose bumps riffled over her arms. Yeah, that was a major creep factor to have her stalker, the SOB who'd tried to strangle her, break into her home.

"I didn't think it'd be easy or wise to get into your place." Farris glanced at Harlan. "So I made it look as if I'd used your computer. It was good enough to fool the Rangers anyway."

Caitlyn muttered some profanity and shifted her position so that she was even closer to him. Harlan figured it would just rile Farris even further or set him off, but after all the violations Farris had just confessed to, that seemed like a plus. So Harlan slid his arm around Caitlyn's waist and eased her to him. Until they were side by side, facing down this SOB who'd made their lives miserable.

"If I hadn't told the Rangers what I'd done, they'd still be after you." And Farris's eyes narrowed when he said that.

"If you hadn't lied in the first place, the Rangers would have had no reason to suspect us." Harlan didn't intend to give this guy any credit for clearing up something he'd helped set up.

"Did this note writer ever contact you personally?" Harlan asked.

"No. Just through the notes." Farris hesitated. "But I figured it was one of you. Or maybe Devin or Curtis. I don't have a motive to kill Tiffany in a fake car accident."

"You didn't have a motive to set me up," Harlan reminded him. "Other than the so-called threats you received. But you did it anyway."

"Wait a minute." Farris jumped to his feet. "You think I killed Tiffany? I didn't," he insisted before Harlan could answer. "I figure she was a pawn, just like I was."

Harlan gave that pawn theory some thought. Not Farris as a pawn but Tiffany as one. Maybe she had been if her fiancé, Devin, had murdered her and then tried to fix it so that it appeared connected to Rocky Creek.

"What about Sherry?" Caitlyn pressed. "Is she a pawn, too?"

"I don't know." With his mini fit of temper apparently exhausted, Farris sank back onto the chair. "But I found some strange things when I hacked into her computer."

"Like what?" And Harlan hoped whatever it was, Farris had kept copies, because Curtis had already told them that Sherry's hard drive had been wiped clean.

"She had notes, like a computer diary or something." Eyes still narrowed, he looked at Caitlyn. "Sherry wrote that she'd overheard you and Harlan that night in the basement."

Harlan felt the muscles in her body jerk. His probably did, too. *"That night?"* But he already knew what Farris meant.

"She said she was looking for a place to have a smoke,

and she heard what you said to Caitlyn. Afterward. The line you said about her being your first."

Not a line, but Harlan had no intention of correcting him. At least now they knew who at Rocky Creek had overheard them. So did that mean Sherry had written those threatening notes? Harlan glanced at Caitlyn and saw the same question in her eyes.

"What else was in Sherry's files?" Caitlyn asked.

"That's just it—nothing that I would expect to find there. No files about her business or anyone else personal in her life. It was all about Tiffany's car accident and how she wondered if it was connected to Webb's murder."

Yeah, that was suspicious. Unless Sherry really was guilty and had done that to cover her tracks.

Harlan heard the rapidly approaching footsteps and automatically stepped in front of Caitlyn. He also put his hand over his weapon. But it was a false alarm of sorts.

"We're Jay Farris's attorneys," the man in the lead said. "And this interview ends now."

Farris only shrugged and tipped his head to the camera mounted in the corner. "That'll need to be turned off, too." His eyes were certainly no longer narrowed, and he seemed in complete control. In fact, he had the smug look of a man who'd accomplished his mission.

Whatever the hell that was.

Had all of this been some kind of act?

"Harlan can't protect you, you know." Farris had his attention pinned to Caitlyn now. "That's why I told you all about the notes and everything this person has made me do. I believe him when he says he'll kill you. And if you stay with Harlan, you'll both end up dead."

Harlan walked closer, stared down at Farris. "Is that a threat?"

"A warning." Farris lowered his voice to a whisper.

"Whoever's behind this is smart, and if he or she can't use me to deliver threats and hack into computers, then they'll find someone else. Probably already has."

Harlan would have liked to dispute that, but he was afraid it was the truth. And that meant he had to get to the bottom of this fast—especially if Farris couldn't be connected to any of the violent things that had happened. If the Rangers could tie him only to the notes and the computer hacking, then he'd be released on bond. *Soon.*

One of the lawyers made an impatient sound and motioned for Caitlyn and him to leave. Harlan obliged. Caitlyn was trembling, and the sooner he got her away from Farris, the better. He didn't want her to have to face the sheriff and the others while she was still composing herself, so Harlan led her into the now empty interview room where they'd talked with Billy.

"I'm a mess." Caitlyn swiped away a tear that slid down her cheek. "I'm scared. I can't think straight." Her gaze whipped to his. "And I really wanted an excuse for you to beat Farris to a pulp."

"The day's not over." He meant that to try to move things in a lighter direction, but it didn't work.

Harlan made a mental note to pick a fight with Farris first chance he got. No, it wasn't very lawman-like, but he hated seeing Caitlyn like this and wanted to do whatever it took to ease that tension from her body and face.

That caused him to freeze.

Oh, hell. He wasn't thinking straight either, and he knew exactly what was to blame. "Maybe we should just have sex and get it over with."

Okay. He clearly hadn't thought that through and should have kept that little suggestion to himself. Caitlyn stared at him. Blinked.

Then she smiled.

So maybe it had been worth sticking his foot in his mouth after all.

"We should have sex here?" Her mouth quivered again, and she slipped into his arms.

He made a show of looking at the hard tiled floor and table. It was to be part of the joke, but Harlan felt his body tense. Oh, man. Sexual jokes were never a good idea when it came to Caitlyn.

"Sorry, didn't mean to interrupt…anything," Declan said.

Harlan and she practically flew apart, and both cursed. No doubt because neither of them had heard anyone step into the doorway of the room. A big reminder that he should be thinking with his head.

"What do you want?" Harlan snapped.

"Probably not the same thing you do." Declan winked at Caitlyn. "Just have to tell you that I'm heading back to Maverick Springs." He tipped his fingers to the brim of his Stetson in a mock salute and strolled away.

That dangerous energy inside him hadn't lessened much, and for reasons he didn't want to explore, this whole winking and whispering with Declan was getting to him.

Okay, he did want to explore it.

"What's going on between Declan and you?" Yet another thing he should have thought through before opening his mouth.

"What do you mean?" And it sounded like a genuine question.

Too bad, because Harlan figured it'd make him sound like a jealous fool when he clarified it. "The whispering in the hospital parking lot."

"Oh, that." She shrugged but generally looked uncomfortable. "It's just an old bad joke."

And again she didn't offer to share it.

Probably for the best, especially since his phone buzzed. He didn't want to talk to anyone right now. Not until he saw the name on the screen.

Billy.

Harlan immediately got a bad feeling about this. "Anything wrong?" he greeted Billy. He didn't put the call on speaker, but Caitlyn moved her ear close enough to hear.

"Plenty. You need to get out to the Rocky Creek facility now." Billy's words raced together. "There's been another murder."

# Chapter Thirteen

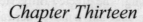

Caitlyn hadn't thought this day could possibly get any worse, but she'd obviously been wrong.

"Who's been murdered?" Harlan asked Billy.

No answer.

Harlan got the same result when he tried again. Either Billy had hung up or the call had dropped. Of course, there was a third possibility. The worst of the scenarios.

Maybe Billy wasn't in any shape to answer.

Harlan hung up and jabbed the redial button. Caitlyn moved even closer to him, until they were breath to breath, but there was nothing to hear except for the call going to voice mail.

Mercy. She hoped Billy was okay, and while she was hoping, she added the hope that the man wasn't lying. She didn't know why he would, but with all the other crazy things happening, anything was possible.

Harlan hurried back into the main area of the sheriff's office. "Billy Webb just called and said someone was murdered out at Rocky Creek."

"You can ride out with me," Slade offered, and then headed outside, toward his truck that was parked just ahead of Harlan's. This one didn't have any bullet damage, so Slade must have traded out vehicles after the attack.

Declan had already left, but the sheriff and one of the deputies grabbed their hats and hurried to a cruiser in the side parking lot.

Harlan opened the passenger door of Slade's truck, but then stopped and looked at her. "This could be dangerous."

"I know." She climbed onto the seat anyway. "But I'd rather risk going to Rocky Creek with you than stay here at the sheriff's office with Farris."

No way could he argue with that. Besides, from what she could tell, there was only one deputy left to keep watch over Farris.

Yeah, the odds were much better with Harlan.

She slid over, and Harlan got in so that Slade could start the engine and speed away. Harlan tried Billy's number again but still no answer.

The sun had already started to dip low in the sky, and the twilight and darkness wouldn't make this trip easier—especially if the lawmen had to chase down a killer.

Slade sped over the country road, the sheriff's cruiser with the lights and siren going right behind them. Caitlyn was so caught up in the tenseness of the moment that she nearly jumped out of her skin when she felt someone touch her.

But it was Harlan.

A reassuring touch, too. He slid his hand over hers. It instantly made things better. And worse. Because this attraction going on between them was getting just as complicated as the investigation.

Caitlyn groaned. "You asked what the whispering between Declan and me was about. Well, I told you it was nothing, and it was. But I don't think you believed me."

Harlan looked at her if she'd lost it. Heck, maybe she

had, but telling him that embarrassing inside joke was better than thinking about all the other things that were making her crazy. Like wondering who'd been murdered and why Billy wasn't answering his phone.

"Declan knew how I felt about you and used to tease me," she continued before Harlan said anything. "He'd come up to me at random places and times and whisper in my ear, 'Are you still crushing on Harlan?' My answer was always the same—'Am I still breathing?'"

Harlan's wide eyes took on a poleaxed expression that even the meager light couldn't cover.

Slade cleared his throat. "I can't exactly step out while you two talk," he complained. "And I really don't want to hear this."

Fair enough. It was on the personal side, even if it happened to be the silly musings of a teenage girl. It was right up there with the boy-band magazines she'd read so many times she'd memorized them.

"Why are you telling me this now?" Harlan demanded. "Do you think we're about to die or something?"

"Maybe," she admitted. That wasn't something they could totally dismiss. After all, someone had already tried to kill them twice, and as Harlan had pointed out, the day wasn't quite over yet. "But I also didn't want you to think I was keeping secrets."

"Like the article you were writing on Kirby," Slade challenged.

"Caitlyn axed that article," Harlan tossed out just as fast.

It had cost him to defend her and Caitlyn appreciated it. However, she knew it was motivated by the attraction. But even a strong attraction wasn't going to smooth over the differences between Harlan and her.

Would that stop them from landing in bed?

No.

But it would basically ensure that she'd get a broken heart out of this. In the grand scheme of things that was better than dying, but it was a sad day in a woman's life when it came down to those two options.

Slade turned onto the road toward Rocky Creek. Not cloaked in darkness, thank goodness. There were plenty of security lights blazing, and when the building came into view, Caitlyn immediately spotted not one car but two. One of them belonged to Billy, and she recognized another as Curtis's.

"What the hell is going on?" Harlan mumbled, and he tried Billy's phone again. Still no answer.

Before Slade and the cruiser even pulled to a stop, Curtis got out. Not alone either. He had his bodyguard with him—the same man who'd been with him when he'd visited Harlan and her.

But Billy wasn't in his vehicle.

It was empty, and the driver's door was wide-open. Worse, the repeated beeping sound let her know that the key was still in the ignition. Headlights on, too. Whatever had gone on here, it appeared that Billy had made a hasty exit.

And not a voluntary one.

"What happened?" Harlan asked Curtis the moment he got out. He drew his gun just as the sheriff and deputy did when they hurried from the cruiser. "Where's Billy Webb? And who was murdered?"

"Murdered?" Curtis repeated. The shock in his voice made it seem as if he was hearing this for the first time. And maybe he was.

"Billy didn't say anything about anyone being murdered." Curtis was trying to catch his breath, and he motioned for his bodyguard to move closer to him. "Billy called me about a half hour ago and asked me to meet him here."

Caitlyn got out of the truck as well, but when she tried to go closer to the men, Harlan blocked her path. He scanned the area and positioned himself in front of her like a sentry.

"And you came because Billy asked?" Caitlyn didn't know if he was lying or just plain stupid. "There's a killer on the loose." Heck, maybe Curtis himself, and if so that would explain why he hadn't been afraid that he might die out here.

Of course, the same could be said for Billy.

"Where's Billy?" Harlan demanded.

"Don't know. We just got here a few minutes ago, and we found his car like this. He's not answering his phone either."

"How in the name of heaven did Billy convince you to come out here?" she asked.

Curtis cursed, but not at them. He cursed himself. "Billy said he was meeting someone who had answers about Sherry's disappearance. I need answers, and he sounded as if he had them. Besides, Sherry always said she liked Billy, that he was a good kid. I thought I could trust him."

"My advice? Don't trust anyone," Harlan warned. He looked back at her. "Stay put, and if anything goes wrong, get inside the truck."

She nodded, only because she didn't want an argument to distract him from finding the person Billy claimed had been murdered. Still, she didn't want Harlan headed into those woods.

But that was exactly the direction he went.

Slade stayed with her, taking over protection detail,

but Harlan looked at the ground around Billy's car and started walking toward a thick cluster of trees on the east side of the property. Thankfully, he didn't go alone. Both Sheriff Sheldon and the deputy followed.

"I want a gun," she whispered to Slade. She figured he had some kind of backup on him. He stared at her, debating what to do, and finally reached into the back waist of his jeans and pulled out a small pistol.

"I was wrong to trust Billy, wasn't I?" But Curtis didn't wait for an answer. "Is he a killer? Is he the one behind all these bad things that have been happening?"

"I don't know." But considering that Billy wasn't answering his phone and was nowhere in sight, it was just as likely that Billy had been the victim of foul play.

Curtis hitched his thumb to the building. "Can we at least go inside and wait? I feel like a sitting duck out here."

"The door's got a lock on it," his bodyguard observed.

Harlan had a key, or at least he'd had one for their earlier visit. But then Caitlyn remembered that he hadn't locked it when they'd run out of there after someone— maybe Curtis—had called the Rangers on them.

"So who locked it?" She glanced back at Slade.

But Slade just lifted his shoulder. "Not me. Maybe the groundskeeper, Rudy Simmons, is back from his trip."

Caitlyn remembered the man, but he hadn't been there during their earlier visit. However, he could be the one Billy had called about. Maybe Billy had found the man's body, but that didn't answer the question of where Billy had gone.

And had he been forced to make a hasty exit from his vehicle?

Her heart began to bang against her chest when Harlan and the other lawmen disappeared into the woods.

After the past two days of nothing but danger and chaos, she should have been numb to it by now, but Harlan and numb didn't go together.

There was no sound, no warning, but the security lights suddenly went out. Before Caitlyn could even react, Slade latched on to her, swinging her between him and the truck seat, and raised his gun.

"Harlan?" she shouted.

No answer. She braced herself for the sound of shots. For anything. But nothing happened.

Her heart was past the pounding stage now, and everything inside her screamed for her to run and help Harlan, but Slade kept her pinned in place.

Her eyes adjusted to the pitchy darkness, and thanks to the lights from Billy's car, she had no trouble seeing Curtis and his bodyguard. Both had weapons drawn, too. But the one person she couldn't see was Harlan.

"He could be ambushed." Her voice didn't have much sound, but Slade must have heard it.

"Harlan?" Slade called.

The moments crawled by, and Caitlyn hadn't thought that silence could terrify her any more than she already was, but it did. She couldn't just stand there if Harlan was in some kind of danger.

"I have to go," she told Slade, and she made sure it didn't sound like a suggestion.

That earned her another glare from him. Some profanity, too. But he started moving along with her. "Stay behind me and try not to get killed."

Not exactly a friendly invitation, but she'd take what she could get. Caitlyn stayed right with Slade as he made his way to the woods. Not a speedy trip, though, because he kept looking back at Curtis and his bodyguard. Caitlyn did, too, but neither man made an attempt to follow them. In fact, they got back inside their car.

Each step seemed to take a lifetime, but Slade didn't run. He inched along, his gaze snapping all around them. Caitlyn kept watch, too, but by the time she made it to the trees, the worst-case scenarios were starting to smother her.

Until she heard Harlan.

He whispered something she didn't understand, and before she actually saw him, his hand snaked out from the tree and he jerked her toward him. It was too dark for her to see his expression, but he put his mouth to her ear.

"Shhh." And Harlan tipped his head toward their right.

Caitlyn followed his gaze and saw a faint light in the distance. Maybe a flashlight, but if so, it was on the ground, and if someone was holding it, the person didn't seem to be moving.

Was it Billy?

And if he wasn't moving, did that mean he'd been hurt or even killed?

Harlan motioned for Slade to move behind her. He did, and along with the sheriff and deputy, they began to make their way toward the light. Above them a breeze was rattling the leaves just enough that it made it harder for Caitlyn to hear. Maybe those leaves and the breeze wouldn't mask the footsteps of anyone trying to sneak up on them.

They were still a good ten yards away from the light when Harlan's phone buzzed. Mumbling some profanity about the bad timing, he took out his cell, the screen like a beacon in the darkness.

"It's Billy," Harlan relayed to them in a whisper. He

didn't put the call on speaker but Caitlyn stayed close enough to hear.

"Someone tried to kill me," Billy blurted out.

Mercy. That was not what she wanted to hear. It meant the killer was still out here in these woods.

"Where are you?" Harlan asked. He got them moving again.

"By the creek. Right after I talked to you, someone fired a shot at me. That's when I ran."

Caitlyn couldn't be sure, but she thought she actually heard the rushing creek water in the background. She certainly heard the fear in Billy's voice.

"I dropped my flashlight in the woods." Billy moaned. "By the body."

"Whose body?" Harlan demanded.

Billy made another sound as if he'd sucked in his breath. "I hear footsteps."

And with that, the call ended.

"Head to the creek," Harlan told Slade. "Take the deputy with you."

Slade didn't question his brother's order and neither did the deputy. As she watched them hurry away, however, Caitlyn had a sickening thought.

What if Billy had set all of this up?

What if he'd done this to separate them so he could pick them off one by one?

Maybe there'd been no murder—only the ones that Billy was planning now. Their murders. But Caitlyn wouldn't just let Billy or anyone else kill them without a fight. Thank God she'd gotten the gun from Slade.

Harlan pushed aside a low-hanging tree branch, and from over his shoulder Caitlyn spotted the flashlight on the ground amid some weeds. The lines of light sprayed out like fingers and moved with each new brush from the breeze.

Then Caitlyn saw the body.

There went her theory about no murder. The person was in a heap facedown.

The three of them moved forward in unison. Not much they could tell, though, because the person was wearing a raincoat and slicker-style hat.

"Keep watch," Harlan reminded them, and he stooped to touch his fingers to the person's neck.

Almost immediately he drew back his hand. "Dead."

Caitlyn's breath swooshed out. She'd hoped this was a false alarm, but no such luck. And she seriously doubted that it was the killer dead on the ground.

No.

This was another victim.

Harlan didn't touch the rest of the body or the flashlight, but he pushed the button on his phone to illuminate the screen so he could lower it to the face.

Even with the angle and the hat, Caitlyn could see the person's features, and she staggered back.

God.

Sherry Summers was no longer missing. She was dead.

# *Chapter Fourteen*

Harlan was glad it was close to midnight, because that meant this hellish day would soon be over.

Finally.

There was no way of knowing if tomorrow would be equally hellish, but anything short of death and serious injury would be an improvement.

"Anything new?" Caitlyn asked. She stood in the doorway of his home office sipping a longneck beer that she'd snagged from his fridge.

Nothing new that he wanted to relay to her, so he settled for a grunt that could have meant anything.

She'd showered. He caught a whiff of his soap. Shampoo, too. But they seemed to smell a lot better on her than they'd ever smelled on him.

"It's my last change of clothes," she mumbled, glancing down at her jeans and white camisole.

It took Harlan a moment to realize why she'd volunteered that. Because he was looking her over from head to toe. Actually, he was past the looking stage and had progressed to gawking, so he forced himself to glance away. Not that it would help. Her image was branded in his head. Her taste, too.

Heck, plain and simple, he was just branded all over when it came to Caitlyn.

That wasn't a news flash to either of them. She had yet to step into his office since they'd arrived back at his house. In fact, she'd pretty much avoided getting anywhere near him.

Maybe because she felt as he did. If they touched, the hellish day might come crashing down on them.

Harlan wasn't sure what the result of the crashing might be—maybe sex or a good falling apart—but the latter seemed a lot to risk with the exhaustion already closing in.

Even though every bone and muscle in his body was yelling for him to get some sleep, he continued to scroll through the reports and emails he was getting about the investigation. Everyone seemed to be in on it. The marshals. Rangers. The locals from Rocky Creek. The governor was even asking questions, because Sherry's body had been found on state-owned property. So Harlan read them all, not liking much of what he was reading.

Farris was already out of jail on bond. Lots of money and good lawyers could manage that even for a man who should be locked away for life.

Billy was in hospital being treated for a gunshot wound to the arm. It wasn't serious, but the man had been so shaken up that he'd required some sedation. However, he'd be released soon.

Devin was nowhere to be found, and Curtis had had a major meltdown when he'd seen Sherry's body. According to his lawyer, Curtis was so distraught, he wouldn't be able to answer questions for a while.

Caitlyn cleared her throat, grabbing his attention again. "How'd Sherry die?"

Oh, it was going to hurt to say this and hurt even more for her to hear it. "She'd been strangled."

Caitlyn clamped her teeth over her bottom lip, but

not before she made a helpless little sound. Harlan could almost see the memories of Farris's attack zooming through her head.

"Farris could have done it," she choked out.

Yeah, Farris could have indeed killed Sherry, and his motive might be all mixed together with his obsession with Caitlyn. "We won't know for a while, but the ME thinks Sherry could have been dead for days."

Hell, maybe even weeks, because when Harlan had touched her, she'd felt ice-cold, as if her body had been frozen and then partially thawed. That meant any of their suspects could have killed her at any time, and their alibis were out the window.

"Did Billy happen to say how he knew the body was there?" Still holding the nearly full bottle of beer in her hand, Caitlyn reached down, pulled off her shoes and rubbed her feet. It seemed, well, normal except her hands were trembling.

"He said, but it didn't make a lot of sense." Harlan was hoping he could blame that on the sedative Billy had been given. "He claims he was out at Rocky Creek just to look around and maybe talk to the groundskeeper, and then he heard something in the woods and went to have a look. That's when he found the body."

"*Claims?* You don't believe him."

Harlan had to shrug. "As far as I'm concerned, he's still a suspect."

"Along with Devin, Curtis and Farris." The next sound she made was one of pure frustration.

She bobbled, nearly lost her footing and Harlan stood to catch her. However, Caitlyn waved him off and slid down to a sitting position on the floor. "I'd love to lean on you tonight, but we both know it'd lead straight to the bed."

Since it had already crossed his mind—many times— he hadn't expected her *stating the obvious* comment to hit him like a sucker punch. But he actually lost his breath for a moment. Not a very manly reaction, which was weird, because everything else about his reaction was manly times a thousand. His body sure wasn't going to let him forget that if he pushed this, just a little, he could have Caitlyn in his bed.

Or on his office floor.

The corner of her mouth lifted. "Face it, we're too tired for sex anyway."

"No such thing."

She laughed. It was smoky and thick and laced with the fatigue that had obviously made them both punchy. "What we need is to catch the killer, get some rest and then…go out to dinner or something."

"I'd prefer the sex. But dinner's a good start."

He stood there, watching her and wondering how long it was going to take him to get on the floor with her. But a thought stopped him, and he mentally repeated what she'd just said.

*Catch the killer.*

The only way that was going to happen was to flush him out.

Caitlyn tilted her head, studied him. "That doesn't seem like a foreplay kind of look in your eyes."

"It's not." And while it hurt to say that, he saw a glimmer of hope. A way of maybe ending the danger so that he and Caitlyn could, well, *have dinner*.

"What are you doing?" she asked when he took out his phone.

"Putting out some bait."

He called the marshals' office, and Slade answered.

Obviously, Caitlyn and he weren't the only ones not getting any sleep tonight.

"Nothing to update," Slade immediately volunteered. "How about you?"

"No, and that's why I want to shake things up. I need something leaked, but I want it to come from the marshals so it looks official."

"I can send it from my work computer. What you want leaked?"

"A lie," Harlan readily admitted. "You okay with that?"

Slade just grunted. "What's the lie?"

"That the ME found something on Sherry's body. A partial fingerprint on the back of her neck that's consistent with the ligature marks from the strangulation that caused her death. And I want you to say that the Rangers are sending someone to the morgue first thing in the morning so the print can be retrieved and processed."

Slade stayed quiet a moment. "Most people know that it's hard as hell to retrieve a fingerprint from a body."

"Hard but not impossible. All I need is for Sherry's killer to have enough concern that he'll try to do something to cover up that print."

And not something that involved Caitlyn and him either. Nor anyone in his family.

"Guess this means you'll want someone watching the morgue?" Slade clarified.

"Oh, yeah. And I don't want the ME or anyone else in the building."

"No one's over there anyway this time of night. Not even a security guard, but they do have an alarm."

"Keep it on and have someone in place to watch all entrances and exits before you send out the leak. You got the manpower for that?"

"I can find it." Slade didn't hesitate. "I'll call you when I have something."

Caitlyn got to her feet and scrubbed her hand down the side of her jeans. "If it's Farris, he'll hire someone to destroy the evidence."

Harlan agreed. Billy likely would, too. And that left Devin and Curtis. He didn't know them well, but if they were behind these deaths, he doubted either would want evidence to convict them.

Of course, even if they managed to make an arrest, it still meant unraveling all the threatening notes, Farris's computer-hacking adventures, Tiffany's car accident, their own kidnapping and the shootings.

"What now?" Caitlyn asked.

"Now we wait." Harlan checked the time. "You should get some rest," he reminded her again. Reminded himself, too.

But he didn't move. Couldn't. And he swore that someone had cemented his feet to the floor.

"Do we really want to do this?" she asked, her voice all warm and breathy.

Since he was a guy, his body wasn't going to let him think long and hard about a question like that. So he just jumped right into the mistake they'd be making no matter how much thought he gave it.

Harlan reached out, hooked his arm around her waist and pulled her to him. The problem was she didn't even put up a token resistance or offer any other questions that might force him to think. Then he kissed her and forgot all about questions and common sense. Forgot all about the other things he should be doing.

Hell, he forgot how to breathe.

Everything hit him at once. The feel of her in his arms. The way she fit against his body. Her taste. Yeah, especially that. Some women just tasted good, and Caitlyn tasted better than good.

She made a little purring sound deep in her throat that stalled his breath, and she coiled her arms around him. Soon they were plastered against each other. Until his body started to remind him just how much better this kiss would be if he stripped off Caitlyn's clothes and kissed every inch of her body.

Caitlyn clearly had the same idea, because she went after his shirt. And she wasn't very good at it. She tugged, pulled, catching his chest hair. It didn't cool him down one bit, and he finally let go of her for just a second so he could shuck the shirt off over his head.

Her eyes lit up, she smiled and she looked at his chest as if she planned to have him for dinner. Harlan figured he was looking at her the same darn way.

While she kissed his chest, touched him and generally made him hot and crazy, Harlan rid her of her own top. Her bra was lace and white. Barely there. But it was too much between them, so he quickly rid her of it and did some payback. He dropped lower and kissed her breasts.

A lot.

"Yes," she mumbled. "And so help me, you'd better not call this off when your conscience kicks in."

He lifted his head so he could give her a flat look, took her hand and pressed it to the front of his jeans. "Does it feel like I'll call it off?"

Her next smile had a touch of the devil in it. "No." She shoved down his zipper and put her hand inside. Not just inside his jeans either. She might have fumbled with the shirt, but she found her way into his boxers without a problem and latched on to his erection.

Harlan was sure his eyes crossed.

"Hell," he muttered. And while he could still walk, he scooped her up and headed for his bedroom.

"Not up for sex on the floor?" she teased. Tormented, too, because while his hands were occupied with carrying her, she kept touching him. Kept driving him crazy. Until he dropped her onto the bed, yanked off his boots and settled on top of her.

Harlan grabbed her jeans and pulled them off. Panties, too. He saw the tiny white scars on her belly and some letters tattooed on her left hip.

She followed his gaze to what had snagged his attention. "I had navel rings. Relics from my wild-child days."

Now all hidden away for him to rediscover. That sent a rush of fire through him, but he stopped when he looked at the letters again.

*H. M.*

"Harlan McKinney," she provided.

"You had my initials tattooed on your body?" He felt his mouth drop open.

"Hey, a girl's first time is a big deal, and I didn't have enough money to put your whole name there."

He was touched. And sad that she'd obviously thought so much of him.

"No trips down memory lane," she insisted, and kissed him so hard and deep that memory lane vanished.

Harlan kissed her right back. Not just her mouth either. But her breasts again. Her belly. Yeah, the tat. Before he went even lower and kissed her in the hottest, wettest part of her body.

"We didn't do this at Rocky Creek." She made a sound of pleasure and wound one hand into his hair. Her other hand clamped onto the bedding as if she was trying to anchor herself.

"We didn't do a lot of things."

Like go back for seconds, something that Harlan thought he might like to do tonight, especially since it was clear that this wasn't going to last nearly as long as he wanted.

"I want you naked," he heard her say a split second before she gave his hair a yank.

That got him moving up her body again. Caitlyn used her hands and feet to slide off his jeans and boxers, and even with all that moving around and adjusting, she still managed to get in some pretty potent kisses. She also pulled him on top of her.

Exactly where he wanted to be.

But thankfully all his common sense wasn't gone, because he fumbled in the nightstand drawer, located a condom and somehow managed to get the darn thing on even with Caitlyn pulling and tugging at him.

"No virgin surprises this time," he heard her whisper.

But the jolt was still there when he pushed inside her. Pure pleasure. There went his breath again, and he didn't care if he ever got it back. The only thing that mattered now was moving inside her and finding the release for the powder keg of pressure roaring through every inch of him.

Caitlyn was clearly on the same page when it came to pressure and release. She lifted her hips. Dug her fingers into his back. And met him thrust for thrust.

He felt the climax ripple through her body. Saw it, too, in the depths of her crystal-blue eyes. Heard it in her uneven breath. She mumbled something.

His name, he realized.

With his name still shaping her lips, she pulled him down to her. And kissed him.

Harlan returned the kiss. Hard and deep. And with Caitlyn's taste in his mouth, he let her take him to the only place he wanted to go.

CAITLYN WONDERED WHY she was still so wide-awake when she desperately needed sleep. She'd dozed on and off, but that was about it.

Her body was slack from the great sex, and she had a nice little sexual buzz still going on. Plus, she was in Harlan's bed snuggled in his arms while he snoozed away.

It should have been a perfect recipe for sleep.

If she could only turn off her mind.

For the first time in days, it wasn't the investigation that was weighing her down. Nor was it the sex or the anticipation of it. It was the consequences of sex that troubled her now. Harlan would regret it. Not the act itself, but he would likely feel as if he owed her something.

Like dinner.

Or dates.

He knew that she wouldn't expect anything from him. After all, she hadn't so much as whimpered when they'd parted company sixteen years ago.

Well, she hadn't whimpered in front of him anyway.

But she had spent plenty of nights sobbing her eyes out for a boy she thought was so far above her that she would only pull him down into the gutter with her. But now there was no bad-girl gutter, just the massive differences in their chosen careers.

But after sex, even that didn't feel like an obstacle.

And that was why even if Harlan knew he didn't owe her, he would feel as if he did. Because he was a good man to the very core. She'd known that sixteen years ago, and she certainly knew it now.

"Don't you ever stop thinking?" he mumbled.

She looked down at him as he peeked out at her from one partially opened eye. "You can hear me think?"

"Pretty much." He hauled her closer, chest to chest, and tucked her head beneath his chin. "Other than your navel, what else did you have pierced?"

Caitlyn couldn't help it—she smiled. "You don't want to know."

Harlan pulled back, met her gaze. "Now I really want to know."

Mercy, he was even hotter post-sex with that rumpled black hair and sleepy gray bedroom eyes.

"I had my nose pierced." Caitlyn touched the spot that had long since healed. "My eyebrow." Also healed. "And my earlobes." She still had double sets of those, but once there had been a quadruple line of piercings.

He stared at her, obviously waiting. "Nothing else?"

"Sorry to ruin your erotic fantasies."

"Nothing's ruined." He ran his thumb over her bottom lip. "So, what were you thinking so hard about?"

Uh-oh.

Here it came. The dreaded relationship conversation. Caitlyn figured Harlan wasn't any better at this than she was. She also figured it was a conversation he didn't even want to have. She sure didn't.

"I was planning our wedding." And she didn't crack a smile when she said it.

That got his eyes wide-open.

Now she smiled. "Wait. Did I say wedding? I meant our next round of this." She slid her hand between them and touched, touched, touched. "Actually, I was thinking you've gotten really good at sex."

"So have you." Harlan pulled her back to him for a kiss, and just like that she was all hot again.

Sheez.

She wasn't a teenager, but she was acting and feeling like one.

The kissing continued. Not fast and frantic like before. But slow and lazy. Oh, yes. This time there'd be foreplay, and even though she'd just had Harlan, she wanted him and the foreplay all over again.

"Do I owe you an apology? A heart-to-heart talk?" Even with his mouth on hers, she could feel his smile. "Or an engagement ring?"

She smiled, too. "I'll settle for what you're doing right now."

But the last word had barely left her mouth when Harlan's phone buzzed.

He cursed, got up and located his jeans on the floor. Not easy to do, since every item of their clothing was scattered around. Still naked, he took out the phone and jabbed the button to answer it.

Harlan's back was to her, but Caitlyn could see the anger over the interruption drain from his body. He turned and met her gaze, and she saw that the anger had been replaced by serious concern.

"Who?" Harlan snapped. But he obviously didn't get an answer, because he repeated it until he was practically shouting into the phone.

That got Caitlyn moving, and while she tried to hear what was going on, she snatched up her clothes and started dressing. "What happened?" she asked the second Harlan ended the call. He, too, put on his jeans.

"That was Billy. He said someone's kidnapped him. The person dragged him from his car and took him to Rocky Creek."

Her stomach went to her knees. Not only because she

was concerned for Billy but because she knew this meant Harlan had to respond.

"Who did this?" she asked.

But Harlan shook his head and tugged on his boots. "Billy said it was someone wearing a ski mask."

Which told them nothing, because it could be any of their suspects.

Including Billy himself.

"Billy said if I brought anyone else to Rocky Creek, the kidnapper warned him that he'd start shooting." Harlan pressed a button on his phone, sandwiched the cell between his shoulder and ear and kept dressing at a frantic pace. As if every second counted.

And it probably did.

"It could be a trap." But she knew Harlan had no doubt already considered that.

"I'm sure of it, but I have no choice. I have to go."

It was his job, yes, but Caitlyn wanted to grab him and make him stay put.

"Slade," Harlan said when his brother came on the line. "We got a huge problem. Someone's kidnapped Billy. And Declan."

"Declan?" Caitlyn said on a gasp. Oh, God.

"Yeah, Declan," Harlan verified and went back to his phone conversation with Slade. "We have to get out to Rocky Creek right away."

*Chapter Fifteen*

Everything inside Harlan was racing—the bad thoughts and the fear for his brother's life. But he forced himself to think. He couldn't go off half-cocked when all of this could be a trap. One that could get Caitlyn, Declan, Billy, him and God knew who else killed.

First things first. He tried to call Declan, hanging on to the hope that this was all a hoax, that Declan would answer and assure him that he hadn't been kidnapped.

But the call went straight to voice mail.

Next up, he tried the number Billy had just used to call him. No answer there either.

That got Harlan moving even faster, and he grabbed some extra ammunition from the top shelf of his closet. An extra weapon, too, so he'd have a backup.

"Declan's really been taken?" Caitlyn asked. There was little color in her face now, and her hands were trembling.

"Probably." And Harlan could blame himself for that. "I shouldn't have planted the lie about the fingerprint."

Her shoulders went back. "You had no idea this monster would go after Declan."

No, but he should have anticipated it. He'd counted heavily on the guy trying to destroy the so-called fingerprint evidence. And maybe that was still the plan. The killer could be using Declan as a distraction.

Harlan made another call—this time to Slade. "Make sure you keep someone at the morgue."

Slade assured him that he would, and Harlan quickly ended the call so he could head out. "I'll take you to stay with Kirby and Stella—"

"I can help."

He took her by the arm and got her moving. "You can also get killed. Don't argue, because this isn't up for discussion. You'll stay with Stella, Kirby and Wyatt. The ranch hands will be around, too, and all of them know how to shoot."

"You really think the killer would come here?"

No. He didn't. And that was why Harlan had come up with this plan to leave her here. There were a dozen ranch hands plus Wyatt. The main house had a brand-new security system, something that just about everyone in town was talking about. The killer would know this wasn't the place for a showdown. Besides, killing them wouldn't destroy the evidence.

Unless the killer knew the fingerprint was fake.

That put a hard knot in his gut, but Harlan didn't back down on his plan. He led Caitlyn through his house and to the front door. His truck was parked just on the other side of the fence. Just a few yards away. But he didn't go barreling out into the darkness. He took a few precious seconds to look around. He didn't see anyone lurking in the shadows, but that didn't mean someone wasn't there.

"Wait here," he ordered and hurried out the door.

He braced himself for shots. For anything. But nothing happened, thank God.

Harlan jumped into his truck, started it and backed up enough so he could drive through the fence. The wood pickets went flying, and he stopped directly in front of the steps. He threw open the passenger door.

Even though Caitlyn was visibly shaken, she got moving when he motioned for her to get in. The second she was on the seat, she slammed the door, and he sped away. Toward the main house that was about a quarter of a mile away.

He took out his phone again to call Stella and tell her what was going on, but before he could press in her number, his cell buzzed, and he saw Billy's number on the screen. That didn't help the knot in his stomach. Yeah, he needed to talk to Billy, but he hoped like the devil that the man wasn't about to deliver some bad news.

"The kidnapper gave me a written message to pass on to you," Billy said.

"Who is he, and why the hell doesn't he tell me himself?" Harlan fired back.

"I don't know who he is, but I think he wants me to talk to you so you won't hear his voice. He says you have to bring Caitlyn with you."

Harlan didn't even have to think about it. "No way."

"If you don't, he'll kill Declan."

It was a good thing he'd reached the ranch house and could come to a stop. "Tell the kidnapper to let me talk to Declan," Harlan insisted. Because even though it wasn't something he could accept, he had to know if his brother was still alive. "Now!" he added when he didn't get an immediate response.

There were some sounds of the phone being moved around, and the seconds crawled by. Caitlyn sucked in her breath and scrambled across the seat until her ear was pressed right to his.

"Harlan," he finally heard Declan say.

Relief flooded through him. Fear, too. His brother

was alive, and now he had to figure out how to keep it that way. "What happened?"

"I'm sorry. So sorry." Declan sounded drunk. Or rather drugged. "I was in the parking lot at work and someone hit me with a Taser."

Just as the killer had done to Caitlyn and him. "Are you okay?" And now it was Harlan's turn to hold his breath.

"He gave me something, some kind of drug, and I don't even think I can stand up."

Harlan knew the exact feeling. "Who took you?"

"None of our suspects. This guy's a hired gun, and the person who hired him is staying out of the picture."

Or maybe was elsewhere so he could attack. After all, Declan wasn't the primary target. Now the question was—had the killer used Declan to draw them out to Rocky Creek, or was this some kind of distraction to launch another attack? Or maybe a break-in at the morgue?

"I'll kill him." From the other end of the line, the voice tore through the silence, and it wasn't Declan or Billy. In fact, Harlan didn't think he'd ever heard that voice before.

"Who are you?" Harlan demanded.

"Someone who's going to kill your kid brother if you don't do as I say. And I'll keep killing until Caitlyn and you are out here. You've got forty-five minutes."

His heart dropped. "Not enough time." And Harlan didn't mean just distancewise either. It wasn't enough time for him to think up a way around this.

"Then you'll have to hurry, won't you?" the man taunted. "And remember, don't bring anyone with you or the bullets start flying. Just Caitlyn and you."

"Wait." Harlan tried to think. "It'd be suicide for me

to take Caitlyn in there. What kind of assurance do I have that you won't just kill us all?"

"None," the man readily answered. "But if you don't come, people are going to start dying."

Harlan had no trouble recognizing the next sound. The blast of a gunshot. Even though the sound came through the phone, it was still deafening, and it rocketed through him.

"Declan?" he shouted.

But Harlan was talking to himself, because the line went dead.

CAITLYN HAD TO make Harlan understand what needed to happen here. "There's no way I'll let you sacrifice Declan for me."

Even though her voice was shaking like the rest of her, she left no room for argument. Still, she saw the argument in Harlan's eyes.

"Declan's a lawman." He sounded as if he was trying to convince himself along with her. "I can figure a way out of this."

"And if you show up without me, you could all be dead before you have time to think of it." In fact, someone might already be dead.

That possibility twisted everything inside her.

She tried to reassure herself that the kidnapper wouldn't kill Declan, because he was the bait. The bargaining tool, as well. But it was possible that Billy had been shot or was already dead.

Unless, of course, Billy was behind this.

"We're wasting precious time," Caitlyn reminded him. "Start driving to Rocky Creek."

But he didn't. Harlan sat there, his attention volleying

between her and the ranch house, where he'd intended to leave her.

"Look, we'll work out the details as we drive," she added. "And if by the time we get there you don't think you can make it safe, then you can drop me off at the sheriff's office in Rocky Creek."

That caused him to belt out some really bad profanity, but he threw the truck into gear and started driving. Thank God. Caitlyn certainly wasn't eager to rush to a showdown with this monster who'd made their lives hell, but she couldn't live with herself if she got Declan killed.

Harlan took out his phone and sped down the dark country road away from the ranch. "Slade," he said when his brother answered. "There's been a change of plans. Caitlyn and I are driving to the Rocky Creek Children's Facility."

She couldn't hear Slade's response.

"No, it's probably not a good idea," Harlan added to whatever Slade said, "but if I leave Caitlyn at the ranch, she'll try to follow."

She would, no doubt about it, and it was scary that Harlan knew her so well.

"Keep someone on the morgue," Harlan continued, "but we'll need backup. *Quiet* backup," he amended. "You remember how to get to Rocky Creek from that old ranch road?" He paused. "Good. Take that route and try to come up from behind. I don't know where they're holding Declan, but it's probably either inside the main building or close to it."

He finished that call and immediately made another to Dallas so he could ask about how tight the security was at the ranch. "Just a precaution," Harlan said to her when he no doubt saw the renewed concern in her eyes.

The next call was to his brother Clayton. After Harlan

gave him a quick update, he asked him to do a quiet approach to the facility using the east side of the property. The woods where Sherry's body had been found. Harlan also reminded Clayton that Slade would be nearby, probably so they wouldn't accidentally shoot each other.

There was a lot of potential for things to go wrong.

"What about me? What do you need me to do?" she asked the moment he ended the call with Clayton.

But Harlan didn't answer. He kept driving and punched in another number. This time he put the call on speaker. However, the person who answered didn't say anything either.

"Billy?" Harlan greeted. "Are you there?" Nothing. But Caitlyn thought she could hear someone breathing on the other end of the line. "Billy, I need to talk to the man who kidnapped Declan."

"What the hell do you want?" The man's voice was so loud that Caitlyn jumped before she could stop herself. And it wasn't Billy. It was Declan's kidnapper.

"I need to work out some kind of deal," Harlan said.

"The only deal you're going to get is the one I already gave you. You and Caitlyn need to get out here and come alone. Nothing about that needs to be worked out."

"But it does." Harlan glanced at her, and even though he didn't say anything to her, he shook his head. "Caitlyn's sick, throwing up all over the place. I don't even think she can stand up."

That explained the headshake. He didn't want her jumping to say that she'd be there. Still, Caitlyn doubted the lie would work, especially since this guy likely had plans to kill them.

"She's pregnant," Harlan added. "We started seeing each other a couple of months ago. In secret. I didn't want to tell my family or anyone else because of this Webb investigation hanging over us. Talk to your boss, because I don't think he'd want to put a pregnant woman in the middle of a mess like this."

She figured the guy would just laugh that off, but he stayed quiet for several moments. "I'll get back to you on that."

Harlan punched the end-call button. "If he agrees, you're going to the sheriff's office." He mumbled something she didn't catch. "And if he doesn't agree, then it's probably Farris who's behind this."

Oh, yes. Because a pregnancy would only make Farris want to kill her even more. But if it was Billy, Devin or Curtis, why did they even want Harlan and her?

"Why would the killer want us dead if he still believes there's an incriminating fingerprint on Sherry's body?" she asked.

Harlan shook his head. "I'm not sure how any of this fits. Or if it fits at all. It could be just Farris playing a sick game."

For a moment Caitlyn thought she might indeed throw up. Her stomach was churning. "And if so, then you just made yourself a target, because Farris will think you fathered this make-believe baby. He'll be so enraged that he'll want to tear you apart."

"Hopefully. Anything to make him come after me and not Declan and you."

That turned her blood to ice. No way did she want Harlan to take the brunt of this, but how could she stop it?

*How?*

Maybe if she had a chance to speak to Farris, she could bargain with him. Maybe even make him believe that she'd go with him if he'd just call off this stupid plan. Of course, she couldn't go with him because he'd likely just kill her the first chance he got. But she might be able to buy them some time so that Harlan could rescue Declan, and maybe even Billy.

Harlan swore and looked at the phone screen as if trying to will the kidnapper to call back. The minutes and miles were just dissolving, and Harlan's mood got worse when the headlights landed on the sign ahead of them.

Rocky Creek Children's Facility.

He took the turn, but he switched off his headlights.

"I want a gun," Caitlyn insisted.

Harlan tipped his head to the glove compartment. "There's one in there."

Caitlyn opened it and pushed aside some plastic handcuffs and papers so she could grab the .38. She prayed she wouldn't have to use it, especially since she wasn't that good a shot. If it came down to her having to take out the killer and the kidnapper, then she and Harlan would be in deeper trouble than they already were.

Harlan pressed the redial button on his phone and again put the call on speaker.

"No deal," the kidnapper said the moment he answered. "You bring Caitlyn here with you."

Thanks to the moonlight, she got a glimpse of Harlan's jaw muscles that had turned to steel. "I want to talk to your boss, and I'm not taking no for an answer."

Harlan took the final turn, and ahead Caitlyn could see the silhouette of the sprawling facility. It looked even more menacing in the dark, and even though she didn't have second thoughts about coming here, Harlan apparently did.

He stopped the truck.

"You'll have to take no for an answer," the kidnapper insisted. "My boss is, well, indisposed right now."

Maybe because he was at the morgue trying to de-

stroy evidence that didn't exist. If so, it was possible
that whoever Slade had watching the place would capture him. And if not, that meant someone had to nab
this kidnapper and get him to confess the name of the
person who'd hired him.

Not exactly an easy night's work.

"Call him," Harlan insisted. "Tell him I'm not bringing Caitlyn unless he speaks to me." With that line drawn
in the sand, Harlan hung up.

And the waiting began.

So did Caitlyn's renewed attempts to get Harlan to
budge. "Stating the obvious here, but I don't want you to
risk Declan's life for me. Besides, Farris won't just kill
me once I step from the truck. He'll want…some time
with me," Caitlyn settled for saying.

There went her stomach again. Another lurch. Mercy,
she didn't want Farris within a hundred miles of her,
but using herself as bait was the only way to reason
with him.

"And if it's not Farris?" Harlan's question hung in
the air, and he turned his head so their gazes met. "This
person could want us dead simply because he thinks
we've uncovered something that'll incriminate him as
Webb's killer."

Yes, she'd considered that, but she could almost feel
Farris nearby. It didn't make sense, and she wasn't the
sort to rely on gut feelings or intuition, but she couldn't
dismiss the feeling that Farris had some part in this.

She checked the time on the dash clock. Time was
almost up. Well, it was if they were to believe the kidnapper's ultimatum that they had to arrive within forty-
five minutes.

"What happens if he doesn't call back?" she asked.

Harlan opened his mouth to answer, but then he

stopped. His gaze slashed to her side of the truck. Except his attention didn't land on her, but outside the window.

"Get down!" he shouted, and he drew his gun.

He didn't wait for her to move. Harlan caught the back of her neck and shoved her down onto the seat.

# Chapter Sixteen

Harlan braced himself for an attack, for bullets to come bashing through the truck. He kept his gun aimed and ready while he pinned Caitlyn beneath him.

But nothing happened.

It was hard to hear over his own pulse pounding in his ears and Caitlyn's ragged breathing, but he damn sure didn't hear any bullets. He lifted his head so he could try to get a better look at the shadowy figure that he'd seen just seconds earlier.

"Stay down." Caitlyn latched on to him and tried to pull him back onto the seat with her.

"I think he's gone," Harlan let her know.

"Who was it?"

He had to shake his head, but it wouldn't have been Slade or Clayton. If they'd somehow managed to get out here ahead of him, they wouldn't be in this area of the grounds. Maybe it hadn't been the kidnapper either, because there was a huge possibility that the killer had hired more than one henchman. God knew how many hired guns Caitlyn and he would have to face, and that was the biggest reason of all for him to throw the truck into gear and haul her butt to the sheriff's office. It had been a huge mistake bringing her here.

"Declan," she reminded him.

He wasn't about to let his kid brother die, but he was pretty sure Declan and he were of a like mind on this. Neither would want to sacrifice Caitlyn to save themselves. Of course, Caitlyn was insisting the same thing about them.

Harlan waited, and the seconds seemed to be flying by. He took out his phone again to call the kidnapper, but he also moved off Caitlyn so he could put the truck in gear. He spared her a glance to see how she was holding up—not well—but then he kept his attention pinned to their surroundings. Hard to do with the moon creating some eerie shadows over the trees and shrubs.

He pushed the redial button. And waited. Waited some more. Until he thought his heart might beat out of his chest. Everything inside him yelled for him to get Caitlyn out of there, so he threw the truck into Reverse. Maybe the kidnapper would see that he was leaving and answer the damn call.

Or not.

Harlan had barely touched his foot to the accelerator when the blast came. He didn't see the shooter, but he felt the impact, all right. The bullet slammed into the front windshield, taking out the safety glass and zinging past his head.

Caitlyn screamed for him to get down, and he did. Harlan also gunned the engine and tried to put some distance between them and the shooter.

More shots came.

Not just one either, but bullets began to pelt the truck. Whoever was shooting at them was almost directly ahead, maybe behind one of the trees that was close to the road.

Since Harlan couldn't lift his head enough to see where he was going, he tried to do the best he could to keep the truck on the road. He also fired a blind shot in the direction of the shooter in the hopes that he'd get lucky. Or at least get the guy to duck behind cover.

It didn't work.

The shots didn't slow down one bit, and it didn't take long before the truck jolted. And Harlan knew why. The gunman had shot out the front tire. Maybe both of them. Harlan lost what little control he had of the steering wheel, and they slammed into the ditch.

With the impact, both Caitlyn and he flew into the dash. His shoulder hit the steering wheel, and by some miracle he managed to hang on to his gun. However, Caitlyn wasn't so lucky. He heard the heavy jolt her body took, and even though she immediately tried to scramble to get her gun, Harlan didn't think it would be easy to find in the darkness and with all hell breaking loose.

More bullets came, and even though he tried to steer the truck, things went from bad to worse when he realized they couldn't move. They'd landed in a ditch filled with several inches of water. Just enough to bog down the tires on the driver's side of the truck.

A bullet crashed through the passenger's window, and even though Caitlyn was still searching for her gun, the sheet of safety glass crashed against her head.

Hell. The shooter had moved, maybe closing in on them from the right. He couldn't just sit there while they were gunned down. The metal exterior of the truck wouldn't keep them safe much longer. Maybe his brothers would arrive soon, hear the shots and give him some backup.

Harlan fired a shot in the direction of the shooter, and in the same motion he threw open his door. Not easy, because he had to push the bottom of the door through the boggy ditch. However, he finally got it open wide enough that he could get Caitlyn out of there.

"This way." He reached across the seat and hauled her closer.

Caitlyn continued to fumble for the gun and grabbed it just before Harlan dragged her out with him. Both of them stepped into the ditch. Definitely not dry. It was filled with stagnant water and clotted mud, and he sank all the way to his knees.

He used the door for cover and kept track of the angle of the bullets. They were still coming from the other side of the truck. Good. Maybe they'd stay that way at least for a few more seconds.

"Move fast," Harlan warned her, and he stepped out of the ditch, pulling her along with him.

He didn't even try to stay on his feet, because it would make them too easy a target. With Caitlyn in tow, Harlan dove behind the nearest tree. They hit the ground hard, and he landed right on the same shoulder that had slammed into the dash. The pain shot through him, but he ignored it and came up ready to fire.

Harlan pulled the trigger, the bullet landing somewhere in the direction of the shooter. He waited to see if the guy would move and come after them.

But nothing.

No more shots.

Harlan drew Caitlyn even closer until he had her pressed against the tree. She, too, had her gun aimed across the road where the shooter had fired his last shot, but all that either of them could do was keep their aim ready and listen for any sound of movement.

Nothing.

Where the devil was this guy?

Harlan glanced up the road at the building. Still no sign of anyone there, not even any vehicles. Not that he'd expected the kidnapper to have Declan in plain sight, but he hoped that his brother wasn't anywhere in the line of fire.

Caitlyn was trembling now, and her breath was gusting to the point that he was worried she might hyperventilate. He didn't want to say anything out loud for fear it would help the shooter pinpoint them, but Harlan did brush his lips on her temple. It wasn't much, but it was the best he could offer for now. Once he got her out of this, though, he'd owe her a huge apology for nearly getting her killed.

That thought had no sooner crossed his mind when he finally heard something. Definitely not a shot.

But footsteps.

Not coming from the front of the truck either, but from the back.

Harlan moved again, pushing Caitlyn behind him so he could face the person making those footsteps. The person wasn't exactly skulking and was coming at them fast. Maybe it was one of his brothers trying to make enough noise so that Harlan wouldn't shoot first.

Even though Harlan couldn't actually see Caitlyn, he felt her adjust, and she moved her gun into position, too. They waited, breaths held.

They didn't have to wait long.

The person came out from the back of the truck. Running. Harlan couldn't make out who the guy was before he launched himself at Caitlyn and him.

BEFORE CAITLYN COULD get out of the way, the man plowed into them, knocking Harlan, her and himself to the ground. Once again she lost the grip on the gun and it went flying. Too bad she couldn't have flown with it, because both men crashed right down onto her.

Suddenly she was fighting for her breath. She couldn't

move, but mercy, she could feel. She felt as if she'd been
hit by a couple of Mack trucks.

Harlan latched on to the guy and shoved both himself
and the man off her. Thank God. Still fighting for breath,
Caitlyn rolled to the side and tried to pick through the
darkness to see who'd done this. She seriously doubted
it was Clayton or Slade, because they probably would
have said something before launching an attack.

And there was no doubt about it—this was an attack.

The man threw a punch at Harlan, and it connected,
but it glanced right off his jaw as if he hadn't even felt it.
Maybe because the blow hadn't been that hard, but also
because Harlan had to be operating on pure adrenaline.

Caitlyn certainly was.

Despite the crushing pain in her chest, she groped
around on the ground, searching for the gun she'd
dropped. Harlan might need her as backup if something
went wrong with this fight.

A shot blasted through the air.

Sending her heart to her knees.

Despite the other shots, the sound was still unexpected, and deafening. And it robbed her of her breath
again.

"Harlan?" she shouted. But she couldn't tell if he'd
been hit or if he'd even been the one to fire that shot.

The scuffle continued with fists flying and with the
men tangled around each other in the fight. They stumbled backward and would have crashed into her again
if Caitlyn hadn't scrambled out of the way just in the
nick of time.

Harlan's back bashed into the tree. She heard the
sound of pain he made. His profanity, too. And despite
that pain he came up fighting. He drew back his gun and
knocked the guy upside the head.

Still the man didn't stop.

Caitlyn saw the weapon he had clutched in his hand. He made a feral sound. More animal than human. And though she didn't recognize his voice, there was something about that sound, some raw emotion in it that she did recognize.

"Farris?" she called out.

The man stopped. For just a fraction of a second. And he turned toward her as if he were trying to launch himself at her.

Harlan didn't let that happen.

He grabbed Farris by the throat and slung him to the ground. Unlike her, however, Farris held on to his gun, and even though he was on the ground, he pointed the weapon directly at her.

Caitlyn froze.

"Marshal, if you pull the trigger, I'll pull mine," Farris warned. "And Caitlyn will die."

God. This was exactly what she'd spent months trying to avoid. Yes, Harlan was armed, and he had his gun pointed at Farris, but Farris could get off a shot, kill her and then turn that gun on Harlan.

She had to do something to stop this.

"You have no reason to kill Harlan." She tried to keep her voice level. Hard to do, since she was shaking from head to toe.

"Yeah, I do." Farris was shaking, too, and she prayed he didn't pull that trigger before she could talk him out of it. "I know you're pregnant, and I know it's his kid."

She shook her head. "No. I'm not pregnant."

"You're lying. I heard Harlan when he said it, and he was practically gloating."

So Farris had been listening in on that call. No surprise there, since it was his hired gun they'd been talking to. The person had likely kidnapped Declan and Billy, too, because Farris wouldn't have wanted to get his hands dirty like that.

But he'd saved his fight to come after her.

"How could you have gone to his bed?" Farris spat out the words, and without taking his eyes or gun off her, he got to his feet. Less than a yard away from Harlan.

"I didn't," she lied. She shook her head when Harlan inched closer to Farris. Probably because he was planning to knock that gun from his hand.

Or try.

But Caitlyn was hoping it wouldn't come to that.

"Harlan hates me," Caitlyn said, "because I'm writing an article about his foster father. I'm spilling all the details of how the marshals are covering up his involvement in Jonah Webb's murder."

Farris glanced at Harlan. Maybe to see if he could tell if that was true. Harlan didn't jump to defend her, thank God, but there must have been something about Harlan's expression that made Farris's mouth twist into a snarl.

"Don't you know that I see you've been with him?" Farris fired back.

Yeah, she could see that, and she could argue it until she was blue in the face, but Farris wasn't going to believe her. It was time to go with plan two.

"I'll go with you," she told Farris.

Now Harlan protested. First with some vicious profanity. And while he didn't exactly look at her, she could feel every muscle in his body reacting to that. "You're not going anywhere with this nutcase."

"That's not your decision to make," Farris fired back. Though he still didn't sound convinced that she was telling the truth.

And she wasn't.

No way would she leave with him. Heaven knew what kind of sick ways he could come up with to torture her before he killed her. And he would kill her. His obsession and rage wouldn't allow him to keep her alive. But Caitlyn was counting heavily on Harlan being able to stop a getaway. All she needed to do was give Farris enough distraction for Harlan to get the jump on him.

She took a step closer to Farris, hoping that it was distraction enough.

It snagged Farris's attention, all right. His split-second glances turned just slightly longer each time his gaze swung in her direction. He was obviously trying to figure out if he could trust her. Or at least trying to figure out how to get her out of there while neutralizing Harlan.

"I'll go with him," she said to Harlan.

Like Farris, Harlan gave her only a quick glance, but in that simple glance something passed between them. She saw his silent assurance that he was not going to let her die.

Too bad that Farris must have seen it, too.

A strangled groan tore from Farris's throat. "You're in love with him. You bitch!"

And that was the only warning she got before Farris launched himself at her. He didn't reach her.

Thanks to Harlan.

Before Farris could get to her, Harlan tackled him, and again both men crashed to the ground. This time, though, she saw Farris's gun go flying, and Caitlyn knew this fight was pretty much over. Harlan not only outsized him, he'd been trained how to fight.

Still, Farris fought like a wildcat, all the while yelling and flailing his arms around. One punch from Harlan, however, and Farris's head flopped back.

Caitlyn reached for Farris's gun so that he wouldn't

be able to snatch it up, but reaching for it was as far as she got.

Someone hooked an arm around her neck, and her body snapped back. She landed right against his chest. And before she could make a sound, someone shoved a gun to her head.

*Chapter Seventeen*

Harlan had to restrain himself, but part of him wished that Farris was dead so the man could no longer torment Caitlyn.

But he wasn't about to murder an unarmed man.

Especially one he could restrain. He grabbed Farris and hauled him to his feet so he could drag him to the truck and get a pair of plastic handcuffs from the glove compartment.

Harlan stopped when he caught a movement from the corner of his eye, and without loosening his grip on Farris, he whirled in Caitlyn's direction.

Everything inside him came crashing down.

No, hell, no. This couldn't be happening. But it was. Caitlyn was standing there, white as a ghost in the pale moonlight, and someone had a gun on her.

"I didn't see him in time," she whispered.

That felt like a fist around his heart. She was apologizing for being put in another life-and-death situation. One not of her own making. It was Farris's making.

Or maybe not.

Harlan had to amend that theory when he caught a glimpse of the man's face. Not some hired gun. He knew this man.

Curtis.

"You said I could have Caitlyn," Farris practically shouted. "You said you wouldn't hurt her."

"There's been a change of plans." Curtis's voice was eerily calm, and unlike Farris, his hand wasn't shaking.

The mark of a cold-blooded killer.

"Marshal McKinney, you need to put down your gun and step away from Farris," Curtis ordered.

Harlan didn't budge, but Farris struggled, fighting to get away from him. However, Harlan held on. He didn't want Farris going after Caitlyn. Not with that gun right at her head. Even if Curtis didn't have plans to shoot her, the gun might accidentally go off.

"This guy isn't dealing with a full deck," Harlan said, tipping his head to Farris. "If I let him go, he might try to kill all of us."

"He won't." And there didn't appear to be a shred of doubt in Curtis's tone, which meant they'd worked out some kind of sick deal.

Caitlyn didn't say a word. Didn't take her gaze off Harlan, and he cursed when he realized that she was still giving him an apologetic look.

"Your gun," Curtis reminded Harlan. "And let go of Farris so he can leave."

Farris made another of those outraged sounds. "I'm not leaving without her." Again he tried to tear himself away from Harlan, but Curtis shifted the gun toward Harlan and him.

"My advice—cooperate." And coming from Curtis, it didn't sound like a suggestion. "If things work out as planned, you might be able to have Caitlyn after all." Curtis's mouth tightened. "Though why you'd want a woman in love with another man, I don't know."

It was twice in one night that someone had accused her of being in love with him, and if Harlan hadn't been between this rock and a hard place, he might have given it some thought. However, the only thoughts he had right now were how to get out of this.

Caitlyn muttered something and shifted her body weight as if she might drop to the ground. Curtis hooked his arm around her neck, snapped her to him and pointed the gun at her again.

As bad as it was to see that gun right on her—and it was bad—Harlan had to look at the bigger picture here. He had to keep Curtis's mind off the fact that Harlan was still armed. The longer he could hang on to his gun, the better.

"Where's Declan?" Harlan wanted to know the answer to that, but he wasn't sure he'd get the truth from Curtis. Still, the conversation might distract him until Harlan could figure out a way to get that gun from his hand.

"He'll join us soon. At gunpoint, of course."

Harlan didn't doubt the gunpoint part. In fact, there might be several hired guns in on this. But why was he bringing Declan here?

"You plan to use Declan for more leverage?" Harlan asked. But he already had the ultimate leverage with Caitlyn.

"You don't need Declan or Harlan down here if you have me," Caitlyn volunteered. "You can let them go."

Curtis made a sound of disagreement. "I need you both, actually. You and Harlan," he clarified, aiming a glare at Farris. "Temporarily. Just hold on to your sanity a moment or two longer, and you might get what you want from this."

Because Harlan still had a grip on Farris, he felt the man's muscle tense. "I paid big money to get her," Farris shouted. "Hell, I funded this entire operation for one reason. *Her.*"

So that explained, well, pretty much nothing. Farris had the money to pay for an attack like this, but Harlan still didn't know the reason Curtis would plan their capture and murder.

But he could guess why.

"It's your fingerprint they'll find on Sherry's neck," Harlan challenged.

Curtis didn't jump to deny it. "There'll be no fingerprint to find, because right about now someone's blowing up the morgue."

Harlan had no idea if that was true, but at that exact moment his phone buzzed. He couldn't take his attention off Curtis to see who was calling and why. But maybe if someone had tried to set an explosive at the morgue, then the person watching the place had managed to stop it.

He could hope anyway.

Curtis obviously hoped the opposite because he smiled. For a moment or two anyway. Then he glanced down at his watch and cursed.

Was this profanity for Declan because he hadn't arrived yet? Or was something else going on? Either way, Harlan hoped he had his own backup in the area. Certainly by now Slade and/or Clayton should be nearby, and he hoped like the devil it didn't take them too long to get here.

"This is the third time I've asked you to put down that gun," Curtis warned Harlan. "If I have to ask again, I start shooting, and Caitlyn will get the first bullet."

Now Harlan cursed. Because he knew time for distraction was over. He couldn't risk Caitlyn's life, so he dropped his gun on the ground. Right by his feet. Maybe he'd be able to get to it in a hurry if things turned bad.

And he was afraid *bad* was just getting started.

"You murdered Sherry," Caitlyn concluded, obviously trying to make her own distraction. "And now you're trying to cover it up by using us." Despite the gun at her head, she tossed Curtis a glare. "Did you kill Tiffany, too?"

"I had to. I'd already killed Sherry and needed a way to cover it up." Curtis lifted his shoulder. "I figured if the Rangers would try to link Tiffany's death to Webb's murder, then they'd try to link Sherry's, too."

"And you wanted Sherry dead because she was asking questions about some of your shady business investments." Plain and simple, it was a guess, but judging from the way Curtis's eyes narrowed, Harlan had hit pay dirt. "So you sent out those threatening notes to make everyone believe her disappearance was connected to Rocky Creek."

"I sent those notes," Farris piped up.

Curtis huffed as if dealing with an annoying insect. "Because I told him to do it. Farris isn't much of a self-starter when it comes to detailed plans like this one. All that psychosis gets in the way."

Taunting a crazy man wasn't how Harlan would have gone about this. However, it was obvious Curtis wasn't pleased with the man who'd paid to cover up a murder, all so he could get his hands on Caitlyn.

"I'm guessing that Curtis promised he'd draw out Caitlyn for you," Harlan asked Farris.

"He promised more than that," Farris confirmed. "He contacted me out of the blue and said he could draw her out. He told me I could do whatever I wanted and that I wouldn't have to go back to that place."

To the institution, no doubt.

Curtis checked his watch again. Cursed some more.

The man was obviously unaware or just didn't care that Farris was about to snap.

"Henry?" Curtis called out. Probably to the man who'd kidnapped Declan.

No answer.

And that only made Curtis's profanity even worse.

"You think Curtis will keep his promise to you?" Caitlyn asked, her attention nailed to Farris now. "You really believe he'll let you out of this alive? Not a chance. No way would he let a loon like you go so you could spill to every lawman in the state."

Farris stopped struggling, his gaze locked with Caitlyn's. Hell. She was baiting him. The very thing Harlan didn't want her to do, even if she was trying to get Farris to go after Curtis and not her.

"Don't listen to her," Curtis snapped.

"He doesn't want you to listen because he knows I'll tell you that you've been duped. All that money you spent, and he has no intention of following through on his promises." She paused, managed a syrupy smile. "Because he intends to keep me for himself."

Farris froze. Unlike Caitlyn, Harlan couldn't see the man's expression, but he didn't need to see it to feel the rage roar through Farris's body.

Before Harlan could stop him, Farris ripped out of Harlan's grip and, screaming, lunged for Caitlyn.

Just as a shot blasted the night air.

THE SHOT CAME so close to Caitlyn's right ear that she felt the heat from the bullet. And the deafening noise. God, it was awful. The pain stabbed through her head, and she would have fallen to her knees if Curtis hadn't kept a death grip choke hold around her neck.

But Farris was the one who dropped to his knees.

With his gaze frozen on her, he slipped to the ground. "I'll always love you," Farris said.

Even though the pain made everything sound like a roar, she somehow managed to hear the words. Sickening words from a sick man.

Farris reached out as if he might try to touch her, but Curtis kicked at him, his boot connecting with Farris's hand. Grunting in pain, Farris pulled back his hand and clutched it to his chest.

Where the bullet had slammed into him.

"Goodbye, Caitlyn," Farris mumbled, and he slumped into a heap.

Caitlyn didn't have to feel his pulse to know he was dead. She could see it on his now lifeless face. There was no way she could feel sorry for him. Not after everything he'd done, but she was also painfully aware that the biggest threat wasn't Farris.

But rather Curtis.

Now that he'd killed Farris and confessed to Sherry's murder, there was no way he'd let them walk out of there alive. Of course, there was no way she and Harlan would just stand by while he shot them either. But Curtis was the one with the gun.

There was a rustling sound to her left, and while keeping her firmly in his grip, Curtis pivoted in that direction. Harlan moved, too. Toward his gun on the ground next to Farris.

"If you pick it up, she dies," Curtis warned him.

Harlan stopped, but the rustling sound didn't.

"Henry?" Curtis called out.

"Not Henry," the person answered.

Slade.

Caitlyn felt instant relief followed by instant fear. Slade sounded close. Very close. And that meant he could be hurt. It was bad enough that she and Harlan were in danger—Declan, too—but she didn't want to add any more of Harlan's family members to the mix.

"Who are you?" Curtis demanded.

"Marshal Slade Becker. And I'm guessing you're about to be dead."

That didn't help with her fear. Yes, Slade was likely a good shot, but Curtis's gun was still pressed right to her head. Worse, at any second he could turn that gun on Harlan.

Curtis dragged her toward a tree until his back was right up against it. That would make it much harder for Slade to get off a shot.

And that meant this was likely a standoff.

"Where's Declan?" Harlan called out to his brother. He didn't take his attention off her, and his body was in a position as if he was primed and ready for a fight.

"Safe and with Clayton. He's a little groggy from being drugged, but he'll be okay. We've cuffed the kidnapper."

Caitlyn had no idea if that was true, but prayed it was, because it meant Curtis had no backup.

Curtis reacted to what Slade had said by cursing and digging the gun barrel into the side of her head. She felt the skin break and the sting of pain. Felt the warm blood, too.

But the worst was seeing Harlan's reaction.

Anger seemed to jolt through his entire body, and she shook her head, praying he wouldn't do anything that would get him killed.

"They found a guy at the morgue, and he had a bag of explosives with him," Slade continued, his voice calm as if discussing the weather. "I'm guessing so he could blow up the place with Sherry's body inside. The sheriff called in a SWAT team and they have him surrounded."

"Shut up!" Curtis yelled. He cursed and shoved her forward. "Caitlyn's coming with me, and you'll both back off because if you don't, she dies."

This couldn't play out in her favor. Either Harlan would get shot trying to stop Curtis, or if Curtis did manage to take her, she wouldn't live long. She, Harlan and now Slade were the ultimate loose ends.

Maybe even Declan, too.

She had to do something to stop this from becoming worse than it already was. But what? Hard to do much of anything when she didn't have a weapon and Curtis was bigger and stronger than she was.

"I'll go with him." She kept her gaze pinned to Harlan when she said that and hoped he would get out of the way when Curtis started shooting.

And he *would* shoot.

Maybe in the next second or two. He was probably counting on the shots to draw out Slade, since Harlan's brother wouldn't be able to return fire as long as she was Curtis's human shield.

"I'm going to hold you to that dinner date," Caitlyn added.

She saw surprise flash through Harlan's eyes, and she also felt Curtis move the gun away from her head.

Mercy.

He was taking aim at Harlan.

Harlan reacted, already moving down and to the side. Or rather trying to do that so he could scoop up his gun. But she knew there wasn't enough time, because Curtis already had him in his sights.

Caitlyn screamed at the top of her lungs and twisted her body so that she could shove her side against Curtis. It didn't knock him down, but it did cause his hand to move at the exact moment that he pulled the trigger.

The bullet flew past Harlan and smacked into the tree next to him.

Harlan didn't waste any time, and he didn't stoop to pick up his gun. He came right at them, looking very much like a linebacker going after an opposing player. Caitlyn tried to grab Curtis's hand to stop him from firing again.

But she failed.

Curtis pulled the trigger not once but twice, both shots blasting so close to her ear that it drowned out all other sounds. Including whatever Harlan said to her. While he ran toward them, she saw his mouth moving, almost as if he were speaking in slow motion, but she couldn't make out a word.

But she sure felt the impact of Harlan tackling Curtis.

Harlan was a big man, and all those solid muscles plowed right into them. All three went to the ground so hard that Caitlyn could have sworn she saw stars. The pain would have been well worth it.

If Curtis hadn't managed to get off another shot.

Caitlyn couldn't see where the bullet landed, but she prayed it hadn't hit Harlan.

She rammed her elbow into Curtis's stomach and felt the small victory when he yelped in pain. But her victory was short-lived, because he fired again.

And then he bashed the gun against the side of her head.

It was as if her brain exploded, and Caitlyn had no choice but to quit fighting. The only thing she could do was try to get out of the mix so she'd have a better chance of grabbing that gun from Curtis.

She twisted and turned. Tried to maneuver her body

to the side. But she was pinned between them, and she caught the blows coming from both men's fists. It was obvious that Harlan was trying to fight around her, but Curtis kept shoving her right at Harlan's fist.

Caitlyn felt a hard jolt, and for a moment she thought she'd been punched again. But this was no punch. Someone took her by the shoulder, his grip hard and bruising, and he yanked her from the middle of the fight. She caught a glimpse of Slade's face before he slung her on the ground behind him and went after Curtis.

Not that Harlan needed his help.

With her out of the way, Harlan clamped on to Curtis's right wrist and slammed his hand against the tree. The gun finally went flying. But before it even fell, Harlan landed a crushing blow to Curtis's jaw. His head flopped back and his body went limp.

Caitlyn's vision was still blurred from the punches she'd taken. Her hearing sucked, too, because of the bullets fired so close to her ear. But she could see and hear enough to know that this fight was over. Farris was dead and Harlan hauled Curtis to his feet and bashed him into the tree.

Slade pulled a pair of plastic cuffs from his pocket and used them to restrain the man.

"I'll transport him in my vehicle and call the sheriff to see if they have the situation at the morgue contained," Slade volunteered. He looked back at her. "You okay?"

"Fine," she lied. She tried to get up, but her legs were just too wobbly. Caitlyn decided to sit there for a few seconds and catch her breath.

The danger had passed, yes, but it would take a lifetime or two to forget how close they'd all come to dying tonight.

"You should probably run her by the hospital," Slade suggested to Harlan.

Harlan's gaze snapped to her, and she could have sworn the color drained from his face. She must have looked pretty bad for him to have that reaction, and he hurried to help her to her feet.

"Were you shot?" But he didn't wait for her to answer. He shoved her hair from her face and looked her over.

"Not shot," she assured him. However, her panic soon mimicked his when she saw the blood trickling down the side of his head. "Were you?"

He shook his head, snapped her to him and hugged her. It was a little too hard, considering that every part of her was hurting, but Caitlyn didn't pull away. That hug was exactly what she needed.

"This isn't over," Curtis snarled. The look he gave them all could have frozen Hades.

"Sure looks like it's over to me," Harlan snarled right back.

Slade grabbed Curtis and got him moving.

"If you arrest me, he dies," Curtis shouted over his shoulder.

That stopped Slade in his tracks, and he turned and stared at the man. "What the hell does that mean?"

Harlan moved closer, and because he still had her in his grip, Caitlyn got her legs working so she could move, too. This was probably some last-ditch ploy from Curtis to get them to release him, but Caitlyn was positive that wasn't going to happen. Curtis had killed at least two people and had attempted to kill them. The only place he was going was to jail.

But still Curtis smiled.

Definitely not the expression she'd expected, and an icy chill went through her that was bone deep.

"I have an insurance policy." Curtis's smile widened. "If you arrest me, he dies."

*No.* That icy chill got significantly worse. "Who dies?" Caitlyn managed to ask.

"Kirby, of course. Must have forgotten to mention that I sent a hired gun to the ranch." Curtis met Harlan's stare head-on. "And if he doesn't get a call from me in the next few minutes, his orders are to start shooting."

# *Chapter Eighteen*

Harlan couldn't get his body to move fast enough. He whipped out his phone and punched in the number of the ranch office. The chief hand, Cutter, should have answered the landline, but it rang several times before the answering machine kicked in.

Hell.

He tried Wyatt's cell next because his brother was supposed to be inside the ranch house with Kirby and Stella. But again it rang only once and then went to voice mail.

There could have been a dozen reasons for Wyatt and Cutter not to answer, but Harlan could think of only one very bad one.

The ranch was under attack. His family could need immediate help, and here he was a good forty-five minutes out.

"I'll phone Sheriff Geary," Slade volunteered. He kept a firm grip on Curtis and made the call so he could get some backup out to the ranch. Still, it would take the sheriff at least twenty minutes to arrive.

"My hired gun will be mighty hard to see in the dark," Curtis bragged. "No telling how many places he could hide on a ranch and wait to ambush any- and everyone. You can get all the lawmen you know out there on foot, and it won't save Kirby because you can't kill what you can't see."

It took every ounce of Harlan's restraint not to knock this guy's teeth down his throat. "Call off your man," Harlan demanded.

"Not a chance." Any sign of gloating disappeared, and the eyes of a killer stared back at Harlan. "If I have to rot in a jail cell, then it'll help knowing that you've lost someone you love."

That did it. Harlan caught Curtis's shoulder and bashed him into a tree. "Call off your man," he repeated, and to get his point across he gave Curtis another hard knock.

Curtis laughed. "You think I can file charges for brutality? Heck, might even get the case thrown out because you beat a confession out of me."

Not a chance, and while he would like to add more bruises and maybe a broken bone or two to Curtis's injuries, it was clear this conversation was getting them nowhere fast.

"The sheriff's on his way out to the ranch," Slade relayed to Harlan. "He'll try to contact Wyatt and the others, too."

It was a good start, but not nearly good enough. Harlan needed a vehicle, and unfortunately his truck was literally in a bog.

"What about a chopper?" Caitlyn asked. "Do the marshals have one?"

Harlan shook his head. "The nearest one is in San Antonio, and the sheriff doesn't have one either." They were looking at an hour, maybe longer because it would take an approval higher than Saul to get a chopper in the air.

Kirby, Stella and God knew who else could be dead by then.

Caitlyn snapped her fingers, took his phone and started punching in numbers. "I'm calling my old boss" was all she said.

Harlan wasn't sure she'd get anywhere with this call, but one thing good came out of it. For the first time since his arrest, Curtis actually looked concerned that his plan might not work.

"No time to explain," Caitlyn said the moment her boss answered. She was talking so fast that her words ran together. "But you know all those favors you owe me— well, I'm cashing in. I need the news chopper in the air *now*. Get it out to the Blue Creek Ranch near Maverick Springs." She paused. "Yes, that's the place. Put on the search-and-find lights. There's a gunman on the loose out there, and people are in danger."

Harlan hadn't realized he was holding his breath until she hit the end-call button and handed him back his phone. "He's on the way out there."

Good. Though a reporter probably wouldn't have a way to take out the gunman, at least the lights might help pinpoint the guy's location.

"My truck's that way, parked just up the road," Slade said, tipping his head in that direction and tossing Harlan his keys. "Take Caitlyn with you and leave now. Clayton, Declan and I will take this piece of slime and catch up with you."

Harlan didn't refuse his brother's offer, and even though Caitlyn didn't appear to be in any shape to run, he didn't want to leave her alone there with Farris's body. And he damn sure didn't want her having to ride back to Maverick Springs with the man who'd just tried to murder her.

"Curtis could be lying," Caitlyn said when he caught her hand and got them moving.

Yeah. And Harlan had to remind himself that a lone hired gun would be seriously outnumbered by Wyatt and the other ranch hands. Plus, the security system would have alerted them that they had an intruder trying to break into the house.

Well, unless Curtis had somehow managed to take that out, too.

But Harlan didn't allow himself to go there. He just ran, and when it was clear that Caitlyn wasn't going to be able to keep up with him, he scooped her up in his arms and ran as fast as he could.

His lungs were burning when he finally reached Slade's truck, and he practically shoved Caitlyn inside. She clearly had injuries on her face and arms, and he prayed he wasn't making things worse with his rough treatment.

"Give me your phone," she insisted. "I'll keep calling while you drive." But she didn't wait for him to hand her the phone—she yanked it from his pocket.

"Try Dallas first. His number should be in there because I called him earlier." He started the engine and drove out of there fast.

Thank God there was no traffic at this hour. No rain or fog either. Of course, he'd be driving like a crazy man, so that created more than enough obstacles in their path.

Every passing second seemed to take hours, and with each of those seconds, his worries skyrocketed. Even if Caitlyn and he got there before the gunman could start shooting, that would only put her right back in danger. He couldn't do that to her, but he had to help his family.

Caitlyn scrolled through the recently called numbers, located Dallas's and pressed the button. Harlan heard the call go to voice mail. His nerves were already shot, and that sure didn't help.

"Who should I try next?" she asked.

Harlan mentally went through the possibilities. "Try the house's landline," he finally said, and he rattled off the number.

He heard the rings from the other end of the line. And he prayed and waited. He stopped counting at five rings and was ready to tell her to hang up and call someone else. But then Harlan heard a voice.

Stella.

"Who's there?" Stella demanded.

Caitlyn hit the button to put the call on speaker. "It's me, Harlan. What's going on?"

"Maybe some trouble," the woman immediately answered. Her voice was a whisper. "Somebody set off that new security alarm, and Cutter, Dallas and Wyatt are out there trying to figure who it is."

So unless this was a horrible coincidence, Curtis hadn't been bluffing. He had indeed sent someone. Even though he was already speeding, Harlan went even faster, and prayed the miles would disappear between him and the ranch.

"It's a gunman hired by Curtis Newell," Harlan told her, "and he has orders to shoot up the place."

"Great day in the morning." Stella also mumbled something he didn't catch. "I doubt Wyatt and the others will answer their phones. Probably got the ringers off. What should I do, Harlan? It's dark out there, and trying to find a gunman would be like looking for a needle in a haystack."

Yeah, and the guy could just hide until he had an easy kill shot. "A helicopter's on the way. It might help. In the meantime stay down and stay quiet. Kirby, too," Harlan added. "I don't want either of you taking any chances."

"But if someone could get hurt—"

"Wyatt and Dallas know how to handle this," he said, cutting off any protest. No way did he want Stella out there facing down a hired killer. "Sheriff Geary should be out there any minute now. Call him and tell him what's going on so he doesn't walk into an ambush."

"I will, but get here as fast as you can."

Oh, he would do that. He damn sure didn't want Curtis claiming any more victims. It was bad enough that he'd gotten his hands on Caitlyn.

Harlan glanced at her, but it took more than several glances to take it all in, and what he saw turned his stomach. Even in the thin moonlight, he could see the blood. Not just one spot either but multiple places, including a line running from her eyebrow to her chin.

He'd lost count of how many punches she'd taken while in the middle of his fight with Curtis. Too many, that was for sure.

Harlan cursed, shook his head. "Look what that SOB did to you."

"That bad, huh?" She leaned over and looked in the rearview mirror. "Yeah, that bad."

Caitlyn used the back of her hand to swipe at the blood. Since there was blood on her hand, that didn't work very well, so she grabbed some tissues from his glove compartment. But she didn't dab at her face. She dabbed at his, and even though Harlan tried not to react, he winced when she hit a sore spot.

"Look what that SOB did to you," she repeated.

Harlan didn't want to do a mirror check, but he could

feel some of his injuries. Maybe even a cracked rib or two. Still, he'd gotten off lucky.

Because Caitlyn was alive.

The realization of that miracle hit him so hard that he hooked his arm around her and pulled her closer to him. He needed to feel her next to him. Needed to know that she was somehow going to forgive him for not doing a better job of protecting her.

"I'm sorry." He kept his eyes on the road, but he brushed a very gentle kiss on her injured cheek.

She pulled back, looked at him. "For what?"

"For not living up to that complete-package notion you had about me."

That earned him a scowl. "I would give you an elbow jab for that, but I don't want to add to the bruises." She settled against him as if that was exactly where she belonged. "You lived up to the *notion* just fine."

Harlan kept his attention fastened on the road, but he couldn't push the other thoughts out of his head. Thoughts of Caitlyn. Not just of all the bad things that had gone wrong since she'd come back into his life. But of the things that had gone right, too.

Like this moment with her next to him. Making love to her. Hell, just being with her.

"Look." Her head whipped up from his shoulder, and she pointed to the night sky.

Even with just a quick glance, Harlan saw the light in the distance. The helicopter had arrived and had a giant spotlight aimed at the ranch.

He hadn't thought it possible, but time seemed to go even slower, and he could have sworn it took him an hour to drive those last two miles. However, the closer he got, the brighter the light was from the helicopter.

Harlan flew past his place and drove the last leg to

the main house. When he took the final curve, he saw
someone. And not just someone but a man holding a
rifle. His heart went to his knees until he realized that
someone was Wyatt.

And he wasn't alone.

Dallas and Cutter were there. The sheriff, too, and
they all had weapons pointed at a man kneeling on the
ground.

Harlan slammed on the brakes and jumped out. Caitlyn did, too, and she hurried to his side. Just in case
things weren't as under control as he thought, Harlan
stepped in front of her.

"You're a little late," Wyatt greeted him. "Thanks to
the chopper, we found this moron about two minutes ago.
Don't worry. Everyone's okay. He didn't get off a shot."

The relief was instant. A lot of prayers had been answered tonight. "You can thank Caitlyn for the chopper,"
Harlan let his brother know.

"Well, thank you, darlin'." It was Wyatt's usual charm-
ing tone, and he aimed that rock-star grin at Caitlyn. A
grin that dissolved right away when his gaze landed on
them.

"Sheez, you two look like hell," Wyatt mumbled at
the same time Dallas said, "How many fights did you
lose tonight?" Dallas didn't wait for an answer, because
his phone buzzed.

"We won the important one," Harlan insisted.

Well, the important one against Curtis anyway. Harlan figured there was another battle he had left to fight,
and this one was just as important as life and death. He
put his arm around Caitlyn and pulled her closer to him.

"I'll get this guy into town," the sheriff volunteered.

"I want a plea deal," the man grumbled as Sheriff
Geary led him to the cruiser parked just a few yards

away. "I'll tell you whatever you want to know. I've got proof that Sherry found out Curtis was laundering money. I stashed away some emails and notes. I'll give 'em to you for a plea deal."

"The only way that deal will happen is if you also have proof that Curtis killed her," Harlan argued.

"Got that, too. He killed her himself. Strangled her right there in her office and then he had me help him cram the body into a freezer at my hunting cabin. I'll show you where it all happened if I get that plea deal."

Harlan wasn't about to refuse the information, but it wouldn't be needed to convict Curtis. Not only did they have his confession, he'd murdered Farris in front of them.

"Clayton, Slade and Declan are on their way to the jail with Curtis," Dallas relayed when he ended his call. "And I just let the chopper crew know the threat was over so they could leave."

Good. One less thing to worry about. Next on his list was getting Caitlyn checked out by the doctor. Well, the next to the next thing. He had something he had to get off his mind first, and it wouldn't wait.

"I don't want just a dinner date with you," Harlan told her.

Caitlyn blinked, and thanks to the chopper he had no trouble seeing her surprised expression. He braced himself for some comeback that would dismiss everything they'd found together.

She shook her head. "And I don't want just sex with you."

Dallas cleared his throat and muttered something about needing to check on Kirby and Stella. Wyatt mumbled something about them finding a bed—soon.

Harlan ignored them both and kissed her. He tried

to keep it gentle because they were cut in all the wrong places, but he wanted it to be hot and deep enough to cloud her head a little. Or maybe just to make her remember that they had something special here.

The sheriff's cruiser drove past them. The chopper turned and whirled away, taking the clopping noise with it. But Harlan didn't break the kiss until breathing became an issue.

He pulled back, gathered his breath so he could say what he needed to say.

"I'm in love with you."

Except he wasn't the one to say it. Caitlyn did. She took the words right out of his mouth.

"Run for cover if you feel the need," she continued. "But I've been in love with you since I was sixteen. And though I'm sure you'd like me to feel differently, I'm still in love with you."

He smiled. Winced. Smiled again. "I want you in love with me because I'm in love with you."

Now she smiled. Slow and easy. She grabbed a handful of his shirt and snapped him to her. Yeah, they both winced, but Harlan was sure the heat and love overpowered the pain.

"Marry me," he said. Harlan made sure it wasn't exactly a question. Because he couldn't take no for an answer.

Caitlyn had been in his life for a long time, and now he wanted her in his heart for even longer.

For a lifetime.

She nodded. "Yes, and if I could say it any faster, I would, because I don't want you to change your mind."

He had no intention of changing his mind and showed her with another kiss.

"Caitlyn, you'll always be my first," he said with his lips touching hers. "And my last."

She smiled. "Even better." Caitlyn kissed him to show him how much she meant it.

\* \* \* \* \*

# Rachel caught his arm.

Seth turned back to her, his gaze first settling where her fingers circled his rain-slick forearm, then rising to meet hers. His eyes were forest-green in the low light, as deep and mysterious as the rainy woods outside the car.

"You saved my life last night, and you've asked for nothing in return. You didn't even try to use it against me just now, when you could have. Any con man worth his salt would have."

He grimaced. "I'm no saint."

"I'm not saying you are. I'm just saying I believe you."

The interior of the car seemed to contract, the space between their bodies suddenly infinitesimal. She could feel heat radiating from his body, answered by her own. Despite his battered condition, despite the million and one reasons she shouldn't feel this aching magnetism toward him, she couldn't pretend she didn't find him attractive.

# THE SMOKY MOUNTAIN MIST

## BY
## PAULA GRAVES

MILLS &
BOON

First published in Great Britain 2013
by Mills & Boon, an imprint of Harlequin (UK) Limited,
Eton House, 18-24 Paradise Road, Richmond, Surrey TW9 1SR

© Paula Graves 2013

ISBN: 978 0 263 90365 2
ebook ISBN: 978 1 472 00730 8

46-0713

Harlequin (UK) policy is to use papers that are natural, renewable and recyclable products and made from wood grown in sustainable forests. The logging and manufacturing processes conform to the legal environmental regulations of the country of origin.

Printed and bound in Spain
by Blackprint CPI, Barcelona

Alabama native **Paula Graves** wrote her first book, a mystery starring herself and her neighborhood friends, at the age of six. A voracious reader, Paula loves books that pair tantalizing mystery with compelling romance. When she's not reading or writing, she works as a creative director for a Birmingham advertising agency and spends time with her family and friends. She is a member of Southern Magic Romance Writers, Heart of Dixie Romance Writers and Romance Writers of America.

Paula invites readers to visit her website, www. paulagraves.com.

For the old Lakewood gang,
those still with us and those gone,
who made trips to the Smokies so much fun.

# *Chapter One*

Rachel Davenport knew she was being watched, and she hated it, though the gazes directed her way that cool October morning appeared kind and full of sympathy. Only a few of her fellow mourners knew the full truth about why she'd disappeared for almost a year after her mother's sudden death fifteen years ago, but that didn't change the self-consciousness descending over her like a pall.

She locked her spine and lifted her head, refusing to give anyone reason to doubt her strength. She'd survived so far and didn't intend to fall apart now. She wasn't going to give anyone a show.

"It's a lovely gathering, isn't it?" Diane, her father's wife of the past eight years, dabbed her eyes with a delicate lace-rimmed handkerchief. "So many people."

"Yes," Rachel agreed, feeling a stab of shame. She wasn't the only person who'd lost someone she loved. Diane might be flighty and benignly self-absorbed, but she'd made George Davenport's last days happy ones. He'd loved Diane dearly and indulged her happily, and she'd been nothing but a caring, cheerful and devoted wife in his dying days. Even if Rachel had resented the other woman in her father's life—and she hadn't—she would have loved Diane for giving her father joy for the past eight years.

"I sometimes forget that he touched so many lives. With me he was just Georgie. Not the businessman, you know? Just a sweet, sweet man who liked to garden and sing to me at night." Fresh tears trickled from Diane's eyes. She blotted them away with the handkerchief, saved from a streaky face by good waterproof mascara. She lifted her red-rimmed eyes to Rachel. "I'm going to miss the hell out of that man."

Rachel gave her a swift, fierce hug. "So am I."

The preacher took his place at the side of the casket and spoke the scripture verses her father had chosen, hopeful words from the book of Ephesians, her father's favorite. Rachel wanted to find comfort in them, but a shroud of loss seemed to smother her whole.

She couldn't remember ever feeling quite so alone. Her father had been her rock for as long as she could remember, and now he was gone. There was her uncle Rafe, of course, but he lived two hours away and spent much of his time on the road looking for new acts for his music hall.

And as much as she liked and appreciated Diane, they had too little in common to be true friends, much less family. Nor did she really consider her stepbrother, Diane's son, Paul, anything more than a casual friend, though they'd become closer since she'd quit her job with the Maryville Public Library to take over as office manager for her father's trucking company.

She sometimes wondered why her father hadn't ceded control of the business to Paul instead of her. He'd worked at Davenport Trucking for over a decade. Her father had met Diane through her son, not the other way around. He had been assistant operations manager for several years now and knew the business about as well as anyone else.

Far better than she did, even though she'd learned a lot in the past year.

She watched her stepbrother edge closer to the casket. As his lips began moving, as if he was speaking to the man encased in shiny oak and satin, a dark-clad figure a few yards behind him snagged Rachel's attention. He was lean and composed, dressed in a suit that fit him well enough but seemed completely at odds with his slightly spiky dark hair and feral looks. A pair of dark sunglasses obscured his eyes but not the belligerently square jaw and high cheekbones.

It was Seth Hammond, one of the mechanics from the trucking company. Other Davenport Trucking employees had attended the funeral, of course, so she wasn't sure why she was surprised to see Seth here. Except he'd never been close to her father, or to anyone else at the company for that matter. She'd always figured him for a loner.

As her gaze started to slide away from him, he lifted the glasses up on his head, and his eyes snapped up to meet hers.

A zapping sensation jolted through her chest, stopping her cold. His gaze locked with hers, daring her to look away. The air in her lungs froze, then burned until she forced it out in a deep, shaky sigh.

He looked away, and she felt as if someone had cut all the strings holding her upright. Her knees wobbled, and she gripped Diane's arm.

"What is it?" Diane asked softly.

Rachel closed her eyes for a moment to regain her sense of equilibrium, then looked up at the man again.

But he was gone.

"I DON'T KNOW. She looks okay, I guess." From his parking spot near the edge of the cemetery, Seth Hammond kept an eye on Rachel Davenport. The cemetery workers had lowered the oak casket into the gaping grave nearly twenty minutes ago, and most of the gathered mourners had dispersed, leaving the immediate family to say their final private goodbyes to George Davenport.

"It's not a coincidence that everyone around her is gone." The deep voice rumbling through the cell phone receiver like an annoying fly in Seth's ear belonged to Adam Brand, FBI special agent in charge. Seth had no idea why the D.C.-based federal agent was so interested in a trucking company heiress from the Smoky Mountains of Tennessee, but Brand paid well, and Seth wasn't in a position to say no to an honest job.

The only alternative was a dishonest job, and while he'd once been damned good at dishonesty, he'd found little satisfaction in those endeavors. It was a curse, he supposed, when the thing you could do the best was something that sucked the soul right out of you.

"I agree. It's not a coincidence." Seth's viewpoint from the car several yards away wasn't ideal, but the last thing a man with his reputation needed was to be spotted watching a woman through binoculars. So he had to make do with body language rather than facial expressions to get a sense of what Rachel Davenport was thinking and feeling. Grief, obviously. It covered her like morning fog in the Smokies, deceptively ephemeral. She stood straight, her chin high, her movements composed and measured. But he had a strong feeling that the slightest nudge would send her crumbling into ruins.

Everyone was gone now. Her mother by her own hand fifteen years ago, her father by cancer three days ago. No brothers or sisters, save for her stepbrother, Paul, and it wasn't like they'd grown up together as real siblings the way Seth and his sister had.

"Have you seen Delilah recently?" Brand asked with

his usual uncanny way of knowing the paths Seth's mind was traveling at any given moment.

"Ran into her at Ledbetter's Café over the weekend," Seth answered. He left it at that. He wasn't going to gossip about his sister.

Brand had never said, and Seth had never asked, why he didn't just call up Delilah himself if he wanted to know how she was doing. Seth assumed things had gone sideways between them at some point. Probably why Dee had left the FBI years ago and eventually gone to work for Cooper Security. At the time, Seth had felt relieved by his sister's choice, well aware of the risk that, sooner or later, his sister's job and his own less savory choice of occupations might collide.

Of course, now that he'd found his way onto the straight and narrow, she was having trouble believing in the new, improved Seth Hammond.

"I got some good snaps of the funeral-goers, I think. I'll check them out when I get a chance." A hard thud on the passenger window made him jerk. He looked up to find Delilah's sharp brown eyes burning holes into the glass window separating them. "Gotta go," he said to Brand and hung up, shoving the cell phone into his pocket. He slanted a quick look at the backseat to make sure he'd concealed the surveillance glasses he'd been using to take images of the funeral. They were safely hidden in his gym bag on the floorboard.

With a silent sigh, he lowered the passenger window. "Hey, Dee."

"What are you doin' here?" His sister had been back in Tennessee for two weeks and already she'd shed her citified accent for the hard Appalachian twang of her childhood. "Up to somethin'?"

Her suspicious tone poked at his defensive side. "I was attending my boss's funeral."

"Funeral's over, and yet here you are." Delilah looked over the top of the car toward the Davenport family. "You thinking of conning a poor, grieving heiress out of her daddy's money?"

"Funny."

"I'm serious as a heart attack." Her voice rose slightly, making him wince.

He glanced at the Davenport family, wondering if they had heard. "You're making a scene, Dee."

"Hammonds are good at making scenes, Seth. You know that." Delilah reached into the open window, unlatched the car door and pulled it open, sliding into the passenger seat. "Better?"

"You ran into Mama, did you?" he asked drily, not missing the bleak expression in her dark eyes.

"The Bitterwood P.D. called me to come pick her up or they were throwing her in the drunk tank." Delilah grimaced. "Who the hell told them I was back in town, anyway?"

"Sugar, there ain't no lyin' low in Bitterwood. Too damned small and too damned nosy." Unlike his sister, he'd never really left the hills, though he'd kept clear of Bitterwood for a few years to let the dust settle. If not for Cleve Calhoun's stroke five years ago, he might never have come back. But Cleve had needed him, and Seth had found a bittersweet sort of satisfaction in trying to live clean in the place where he'd first learned the taste of iniquity.

He sneaked a glance at George Davenport's grave. The family had dispersed, Paul Bailey and his mother, Diane, walking arm in arm toward Paul's car, while Rachel headed slowly across the cemetery toward another grave nearby. Marjorie Kenner's, if he remembered correctly. Mark Bramlett's last victim.

"I know vulnerable marks are your catnip," Delilah drawled, "but can't you let the girl have a few days of un-molested grief before you bilk her out of her millions?"

"You have such a high opinion of me," he murmured, dragging his gaze away from Rachel's stiffened spine.

"Well-earned, darlin'," she answered, just as quietly.

"I don't suppose it would do any good to tell you I don't do that sort of thing anymore?"

"Yeah, and Mama swore she'd drunk her last, too, as I was puttin' her ginned-up backside to bed." Bitter resignation edged her voice.

*Oh, Dee,* he thought. *People keep lettin' you down, don't they?*

"Tell me you're not up to something."

"I'm done with that life, Dee. I've been done with it a few years now."

Her wary but hopeful look made his heart hurt. "I left the truck over on the other side of the cemetery. Why don't you drive me over there?"

He spared one more glance at Rachel Davenport, wondering how much longer she'd be able to remain upright. Someone had been working overtime the past few weeks, making sure she'd come tumbling down sooner or later.

The question was, why?

"I DIDN'T GET to talk to you at the service."

Rachel's nervous system jolted at the sound of a familiar voice a few feet away. She turned from Marjorie's grave to look into a pair of concerned brown eyes.

Davis Rogers hadn't changed a bit since their breakup five years ago. With his clean-cut good looks and effortless poise, he'd always come across as a confident, successful lawyer, even when he was still in law school at the University of Virginia.

She'd been sucked in by that easy self-composure, such a contrast to her own lack of confidence. It had been so easy to bask in his reflected successes.

For a while at least.

Then she'd found her own feet and realized his all-encompassing influence over her life had become less a shelter and more a shackle.

Easy lesson to forget on a day like today, she thought, battered by the familiar urge to enclose herself in his arms and let him make the rest of the world go away. She straightened her spine and resisted the temptation. "I didn't realize you'd even heard about my father."

"It made the papers in Raleigh. I wanted to pay my respects and see how you were holding up." He brushed a piece of hair away from her face. "How *are* you holding up?"

"I'm fine." His touch left her feeling little more than mild comfort. "I'm sad," she added at his skeptical look. "And I'll be sad for a while. But I'm okay."

It wasn't a lie. She *was* going to be okay. Despite her crushing sense of grief, she felt confident she wasn't in danger of losing herself.

"Maybe what you need is to get out and get your mind off things." Davis cupped her elbow with his large hand. "The clerk at the bed-and-breakfast where I'm staying suggested a great bar near the university in Knoxville where we can listen to college bands and relive our misspent youth. What do you say, Rach? It'll be like Charlottesville all over again."

She grimaced. "I never really liked those bars, you know. I just went because you liked them."

His expression of surprise was almost comical. "You didn't?"

"I'm a Tennessee girl. I liked country music and blue-grass," she said with a smile.

He looked mildly horrified, but he managed to smile. "I'm sure we can find a honky-tonk in Knoxville."

"There's a little place here in Bitterwood we could go. They have a house bluegrass band and really good loaded potato skins." After the past few months of watching her father dying one painful inch at a time, maybe what she needed was to indulge herself. Get her mind off her losses, if only for a little while.

And why not go with Davis? She wasn't still in love with him, but she'd always liked and trusted him. It was safer than going alone. The man who'd killed four of her friends might be dead and gone, but the world was still full of danger. A woman alone had to be careful.

And she *was* alone, she knew, bleakness seeping into her momentary optimism.

So very alone.

FOR THE FIRST time in years, Seth Hammond had a place to himself. It wasn't much to talk about, a ramshackle bungalow halfway up Smoky Ridge, but for the next few weeks, he wouldn't have to share it with anyone else. The house's owner, Cleve Calhoun, was in Knoxville for therapy to help him regain some of the faculties he'd lost to a stroke five years ago.

By seven o'clock, Seth had decided that alone time wasn't all it was cracked up to be. Even if the satellite reception wasn't terrible, there wasn't much on TV worth watching these days. The Vols game wasn't until Saturday, and with the Braves out of play-off contention, there wasn't much point in watching baseball, either.

He'd already gone through the photos from the funeral he'd taken with his high-tech camera glasses, but as far as he could tell, there was nobody stalking Rachel Davenport at the funeral except himself. He supposed he could go through the photos one more time, but he'd seen enough of Rachel's grief for one day. He'd uploaded the images to the FTP site Adam Brand had given him. Maybe the FBI agent would have better luck than he had. Brand, after all, at least knew what it was he was looking for.

He certainly hadn't bothered to let Seth in on the secret.

*You have turned into a dull old coot,* Seth told himself, eyeing the frozen dinner he'd just pulled from Cleve's freezer with a look of dismay. *There was a time when you could've walked into any bar in Maryville and gone home with a beautiful woman. What the hell happened to you?*

The straight and narrow, he thought. He'd given up more than just the con game, it appeared.

"To hell with that." He shoved the frozen dinner back into the frost-lined freezer compartment. He was thirty-two years old, not sixty. Playing nursemaid to a crippled old man had, ironically, kept him lean and strong, since he'd had to haul Cleve Calhoun around like a baby. And while he wasn't going to win any beauty pageants, he'd never had trouble catching a woman's eye.

An image of Rachel Davenport's cool blue eyes meeting his that morning at the funeral punched him in the gut. He couldn't remember if she'd ever looked him in the eye before that moment.

Probably not. At the trucking company, he was more a part of the scenery than a person. A chair or a desk or one of the trucks he repaired, maybe. He'd become good at blending in. It had been his best asset as a con artist, enabling him to learn a mark's vulnerabilities without drawing attention to himself. Cleve had nicknamed him Chameleon because of his skill at becoming part of the background.

That same skill had served him well as a paid FBI informant, though there had been a few times, most recently in a dangerous backwoods enclave of meth dealers, when he'd come close to breaking cover.

But looking into Rachel Davenport's eyes that morning, he'd felt the full weight of being invisible. For a second, she'd seen him. Her blue eyes had widened and her soft pink lips had parted in surprise, as if she'd felt the same electric zing that had shot through his body when their gazes connected.

Maybe that was the longing driving him now, propelling him out of the shack and into Cleve's old red Charger in search of another connection. It was a night to stand out from the crowd, not blend in, and he knew just the honky-tonk to do it in.

The road into Bitterwood proper from the mountains was a winding series of switchbacks and straightaways called Old Purgatory Road. Back in the day, when they were just kids, Delilah, a couple of years older and eons wiser, had told Seth that it was named so because hell was located in a deep, dark cavern in the heart of Smoky Ridge, their mountain home, and the only way to get in or out was Purgatory Road.

Of course, later he'd learned that Purgatory was actually a town about ten miles to the northeast, and the road had once been the only road between there and Bitterwood, but Delilah's story had stuck with him anyway. Even now, there were times when he thought she'd been right all along. Hell *did* reside in the black heart of

Smoky Ridge, and it was all too easy for a person to find himself on a fast track there.

Purgatory Road flattened out as it crossed Vesper Road and wound gently through the valley, where Bitterwood's small, four-block downtown lay. There was little there of note—the two-story brick building that housed the town administrative offices, including the Bitterwood Police Department, a tiny postage stamp of a post office and a few old shops and boutiques that stubbornly resisted the destructive sands of time.

Bitterwood closed shop at five in the evening. Everything was dark and shuttered as Seth drove through. All the nighttime action happened in the outskirts. Bitterwood had years ago voted to allow liquor sales by the drink as well as package sales, hoping to keep up with the nearby tourist traps. While the tourist boom had bypassed the little mountain town despite the effort, the gin-guzzling horse was out of the barn, and the occasional attempts by civic-minded folks to rescind the liquor ordinances never garnered enough votes to pass.

Seth had never been much of a drinker himself. Cleve had taught him that lesson. A man who lived by his instincts couldn't afford to let anything impair them. Plus, he'd grown up dodging the blows of his mean, drug-addled father. And all liquor had done for his mother was dull the pain of her husband's abuse and leave her a shell of a woman long after the old bastard had blown himself up in a meth lab accident.

He'd never have gone to Smoky Joe's Saloon for the drinks anyway. They watered down the stuff too much, as much to limit the drunken brawls as to make an extra buck. But they had a great house band that played old-style Tennessee bluegrass, and some of the prettiest girls in the county went there for the music.

He saw the neon lights of Smoky Joe's ahead across Purgatory Bridge, the steel-and-concrete truss bridge spanning Bitterwood Creek, which meandered through a narrow gorge thirty feet below. The lights distracted him for only a second, but that was almost all it took. He slammed on the brakes as the darkened form of a car loomed in his headlights, dead ahead.

The Charger's brakes squealed but held, and the muscle car shuddered to a stop with inches to spare.

"Son of a bitch!" he growled as he found his breath again. Who the hell had parked a car in the middle of the bridge without even turning on emergency signals?

With a start, he recognized the vehicle, a silver Honda Accord. He'd seen Rachel Davenport drive that car in and out of the employee parking lot at Davenport Trucking every day for the past year.

His chest tightening with alarm, he put on his own emergency flashers and got out of the car, approaching the Honda with caution.

Out of the corner of his eye, he detected movement in the darkness. He whipped his gaze in that direction.

She stood atop the narrow steel railing, her small hands curled in the decorative lacework of the old truss bridge. She swayed a little, like a tree limb buffeted by the light breeze blowing through the girders. The air ruffled her skirt and fluttered her long hair.

"Ms. Davenport?" Seth's heart squeezed as one of her feet slid along the thin metal support and she sagged toward the thirty-foot drop below.

"Ms. Davenport is dead," she said in a faint, mournful tone. "Killed herself, you know."

Seth edged toward her, careful not to move too quickly for fear of spooking her. "Rachel, that girder's not real steady. Don't you want to come down here to the nice, solid ground?"

She laughed softly. "Solid. Solid." She said the word with comical gusto. "'She's solid.' What does that mean? It makes you sound stiff and heavy, doesn't it? Solid."

*Okay, not suicidal,* he decided as he took a couple more steps toward her. *Drunk?*

"Do you think I'm cursed?" There was none of her earlier amusement in that question.

"I don't think so, no." He was almost close enough to touch her. But he had to be careful. If he grabbed at her and missed, she could go over the side in a heartbeat.

"I think I am," she said. Her voice had taken on a definite slurring cadence. But he decided she didn't sound drunk so much as drugged. Had someone given her a sedative after the funeral? Maybe she'd had a bad reaction to it.

"I don't think you're cursed," Seth disagreed, easing his hand toward her in the dark. "I think you're tired and sad. And, you know, that's okay. It means you're human."

Her eyes glittered in the reflected light of the Charger's flashers. "I wish I were a bird," she said plaintively. "Then I could fly away over the mountains and never have to land again." She took a sudden turn outward, teetering atop the rail as if preparing to take flight. "She said I should fly."

Then, in heart-stopping slow motion, she began to fall forward, off the bridge.

# *Chapter Two*

He wasn't going to reach her in time.

A nightmare played out in his head as he threw himself toward her. His hands clawing at the air where she'd been a split second earlier. His body slamming into the rail that stopped him just short of throwing himself after her over the side of the bridge. He could see her plummeting, her slender body dancing like a feather in the cold October breeze until it shattered on the rocks below.

Then his fingers met flesh; his arms snaked around her hips, anchoring her to him. Though she was tall and thin, she was heavy enough to fill the next few seconds of Seth's life with sheer terror as he struggled to keep her from tumbling into the gorge and taking him with her.

He finally brought her down to the ground and crushed her close, his heart pounding a thunderous rhythm in his ears. She pressed closer to him, her nose nuzzling against the side of his neck.

"This is nice," she said, her fingers playing over the muscles of his chest. "You smell nice."

His body's reaction was quick and fierce. He struggled to regain control, but she wasn't helping him a bit. Her exploring hands slid downward to rest against his hips. His heart gave a jolt as her mouth brushed over the tendon at the side of his neck, the tip of her tongue flicking against the flesh.

"Taste good, too."

He dragged her away, holding her at arm's length in a gentle but firm grip. "I need to get you home."

She smiled at him, but he could see in the dim light that her eyes were glassy. Clearly she had no idea where she was or maybe even who she was. Whatever chemical had driven her up on the girder was still in control.

"Rachel, do you have the key to your car?" He didn't want to leave her car there to be a hazard to other drivers trying to cross the bridge.

She shook her head drunkenly.

Keeping a grip on one of her arms, he crossed and checked the vehicle. The key was in the ignition. At least she hadn't locked the door, so he could move it off the bridge. But did he dare let Rachel go long enough to do so?

"Rachel, let's take a ride, okay?"

"'Kay." She got into the passenger seat willingly enough when he directed her there, and she was fumbling with the radio dials when he slid in behind the steering wheel. "Where's the music?"

"Just a minute, sugar." He started the car. A second later, hard-edged bluegrass poured through the CD speakers—Kasey Chambers and Shane Nicholson. He had that album in his own car.

She started singing along with no-holds gusto, her voice a raspy alto, and complained when he parked the car off the road and cut the engine.

"Just a minute and we'll make the music come back," he promised, keeping an eye on the road. There had been no traffic so far, but his luck wouldn't hold much longer.

He needed to get her out of there before anyone else saw the condition she was in.

He almost laughed at himself as he realized what he was thinking. He'd been a cover-up artist from way back, trying to hide the ugly face of his home life from the people around them. He'd gotten good at telling lies.

Then he'd gotten good at running cons.

Still, he thought it was smart to protect Rachel Davenport from prying eyes until she was in some sort of condition to defend herself. He didn't know what had happened to her tonight, or how big a part she'd played in her own troubles, but he didn't care. Everybody made mistakes, and she'd been under a hell of a lot more pressure than most folks these past few weeks.

She could sort things out with her conscience when she was sober. He wasn't going to add to her problems by parading her in front of other people.

He buckled her safely into the passenger seat of the Charger and slid behind the wheel, pulling the bluegrass CD from a holder attached to his sun visor. He put the CD in the player and punched the skip button until the song she'd been singing earlier came on. She picked up the tune happily, and he let her serenade him while he thought through what to do next.

Delivering her to her family was the most obvious answer, but Seth didn't like that idea. Someone had gone to deadly lengths in the past few weeks to rip away her emotional underpinnings, and Seth didn't know enough about her relationship with her stepmother and stepbrother to risk taking her home in this condition. She seemed friendly enough with them, but they didn't appear particularly close. In fact, there was some speculation at work whether Paul Bailey was annoyed at being bypassed as acting CEO. He might not have Rachel's best interests at heart.

The particulars of George Davenport's will had become an open secret around the office ever since he'd changed it shortly after his terminal liver cancer diagnosis a year ago. Everybody at the trucking company knew he'd specified that his daughter, Rachel, should be the company's CEO. It had been a bit of a scandal, since until that point in her life, Rachel Davenport had been happy working as a librarian in Maryville. What did she know about running a business?

She'd done okay, taking over more and more of her father's duties until his death, but would Paul Bailey have seen it that way?

The song ended, and the next cut on the album began, a plaintive ballad that Rachel didn't seem to know. She hummed along, swaying gently against the constraints of the seat belt. She was beginning to wind down, he noticed with a glance her way. Her eyes were starting to droop closed.

Maybe he should have taken her straight to the hospital in Maryville to get checked out, he realized. What if she'd overdosed on whatever she'd taken? What if she needed treatment?

He bypassed the turnoff that would take him to the Edgewood area, where Bitterwood's small but influential moneyed class lived, and headed instead to Vesper Road. Delilah was housesitting there for Ivy Hawkins, a girl they'd grown up with on Smoky Ridge.

A detective with the Bitterwood Police Department, Ivy was on administrative leave following a shooting that had left a hired killer dead and a whole lot of questions unanswered. Ivy had taken advantage of the enforced time off to visit with her mother, who'd recently moved to Birmingham, and had offered Delilah a place to stay while she was in town.

"Rachel, you still with me?" he asked with alarm as he noticed her head lolling to one side.

She didn't answer.

He drove faster than he should down twisty Vesper Road, hoping the deer, coyotes and black bears stayed in the woods where they belonged instead of straying into the path of his speeding car. He almost missed his turn and ended up whipping down Ivy Hawkins's driveway with an impressive clatter of gravel that brought Delilah out to confront him before he even had a chance to cut the engine.

"What the hell?" she asked as she circled around to the passenger door.

"You did some medic training at that fancy place you work, right?"

Delilah's eyebrows lifted at the sight of Rachel Davenport in the passenger seat. "What's wrong with her?"

"That's what I'd like to know." He gave Rachel's shoulder a light shake. She didn't respond.

"What are you doing with her?"

"It's a long story. I'll tell you about it inside." He nodded toward the door she'd left wide-open.

Inside the house, he laid Rachel on the sofa and pressed his fingers against her slender wrist. Her pulse was slow but steady. She seemed to be breathing steadily.

She was asleep.

He stood up and turned to look at his sister. She stared back at him, her hands on her hips and a look of suspicion, liberally tinged with fear, creasing her pretty face.

"What the hell happened? Did you do something to her?"

Anger churned in his gut, tempered only by the bitter

knowledge that Delilah had every reason to suspect him of doing something wrong. God knew she'd dug him out of a whole lot of holes of his own digging over the years until she'd finally tired of saving him from himself.

"I found her in this condition," he explained as he pulled a crocheted throw from the back of the sofa and covered Rachel with it. "On Purgatory Bridge."

"On the bridge?"

"*On* the bridge," he answered. "Up on the girders, about to practice her high-dive routine."

"My God. She was trying to kill herself?"

"No. She's on something. I thought maybe you could take a look, see if you could tell from her condition—"

"Not without a tox screen." Delilah crossed to the sofa and crouched beside Rachel. "How was she behaving when you found her?"

"Drunk, but I didn't really smell any liquor on her." The memory of her body, warm and soft against his, roared back with a vengeance. She'd smelled good, he remembered. Clean and sweet, as if she'd just stepped out of a bath. "She was out of it, though. I'm not sure she even knew who *she* was, much less who I was."

"Was she hallucinating?" Delilah checked Rachel's eyes.

"Not hallucinating exactly," Seth answered, leaning over his sister's shoulder.

She shot him a "back off" look, and he stepped away. "What, then, exactly?"

"She seemed really happy. As if she were having the time of her life."

"Standing on a girder over a thirty-foot drop?"

"Technically, she was swaying on a girder over a thirty-foot drop." Even the memory gave him a chill. "Scared the hell outta me."

"You should've taken her to a hospital."

Worry ate at his gut. "Should we call nine-one-one?"

Delilah sat back on her heels, her brow furrowed. "Her vitals look pretty good. I could call a doctor friend of mine back in Alabama and get his take on her condition."

"You have a theory," Seth said, reading his sister's body language.

"It could be gamma hydroxybutyrate—GHB."

Seth's chest tightened with dread. "The date rape drug?"

"Well, it's also a club drug—lower doses create a sense of euphoria. You said you found her near Smoky Joe's, right? She might have taken the GHB to get high."

He shook his head swiftly. "No. She wouldn't do that."

Delilah turned her head to look at him, her eyes narrowed. "And you would know this how?"

"We work in the same place. If she had any kind of track record with drugs, I'd have heard about it."

Delilah cocked her head. "Really. You think you know all there is to know about Rachel Davenport?"

He could tell from his sister's tone that he'd tweaked her suspicious side again. What would she think if he told her he was working for her old boss, Adam Brand?

As tempted as he was to know the answer, he looked back at Rachel. "If it's GHB, would it have made her climb up on a bridge and try to fly?"

"It might, if she's the fanciful sort. GHB loosens inhibitions."

Which might explain her drunken attempt at seduction in the middle of Purgatory Bridge, he thought. "How can we be sure?"

"A urine test might tell us," Delilah answered, rising to her feet and pulling her cell phone out of the pocket of her jeans. "But it's expensive to test for it, and it's almost impossible to detect after twenty-four hours." She shot her brother a pointed look. "Do you really want it on record that she's got an illegal drug in her system?"

Delilah might look soft and pretty, but she was sharper than a briar patch. "No, I don't," he conceded.

"We can't assume someone did this to her," she said, punching in a phone number. "After all, she just buried her father. That might make some folks want to forget the world for a while."

As she started speaking to the person on the other end of the call, Seth turned back to the sofa and crouched next to Rachel. She looked as if she was sleeping peacefully, her lips slightly parted and her features soft and relaxed. The calm expression on her face struck him hard as he realized he had never seen her that way, her features unlined with worry. The past year had been hell for her, watching her father slowly die in front of her while she struggled to learn the ropes of running his business.

He smoothed the hair away from her forehead. Most of the time when he'd seen her at the office, she had looked like a pillar of steel, stiff-spined and regal as she went about the trucking business. But every once in a while, when she didn't know anyone else was looking, she had shed the tough facade and revealed her vulnerability. At those times, she'd looked breakable, as if the slightest push would send her crumbling to pieces.

Had her father's death been the blow to finally shatter her?

Behind him, Delilah hung up the phone. "Eric says we just have to keep an eye on her vitals, make sure she's not going into shock or organ failure," she said tonelessly.

"Piece of cake," he murmured drily.

"We could take shifts," she suggested.

He shook his head. "Go on to bed. I'll watch after her."

He certainly wouldn't be getting any sleep until she was awake and back to her normal self again.

There was a long pause before Delilah spoke. "What's your angle here, Seth? Why do you give a damn what happens to her?"

"She's my boss," he said, his tone flippant.

"Tell me you're not planning to scam her in some way."

He slanted a look at his sister. "I'm not."

Once again, he saw contradictory emotions cross his sister's expressive face. Part hope, part fear. He tamped down frustration. He'd spent years losing the trust of the people who loved him. He couldn't expect them to trust him again just like that.

However much he might want it to be so.

BLACKNESS MELTED INTO featureless gray. Gray into misty blobs of shape and muted colors and, finally, as her eyes began to focus, the shapes firmed into solid forms. Windows with green muslin curtains blocking all but a few fragments of watery light. A tall, narrow chest of drawers standing against a nearby wall, a bowl-shaped torchiere lamp in the corner, currently dark. And across from her, sprawling loose-limbed in a low-slung armchair, sat Seth Hammond, his green eyes watching her.

She'd seen him at her father's funeral, she remembered, fresh grief hitting her with a sharp blow. She'd looked up and seen him watching her, felt an electric pulse of awareness that had caught her by surprise.

And then what? Why couldn't she remember what had happened next?

Her head felt thick and heavy as she tried to lift it. In her chest, her heart beat a frantic cadence of panic.

Where was this place? How had she gotten here?

Why couldn't she remember anything beyond her father's graveside funeral service?

She knew time must have passed. The light seeping into the small room was faint and rosy-hued, suggesting either sunrise or sunset. The funeral had taken place late in the morning.

How had she gotten here?

Why was *he* here?

"What is this?" she asked. Her voice sounded shaky, frightening her further. Why couldn't she muster the energy to move?

She needed to get out of here. She needed to go home, find something familiar and grounding, to purge herself of the panic rising like floodwaters in her brain.

"Shh." Seth spoke softly. "It's okay, Ms. Davenport. You're okay."

She pushed past her strange lethargy and sat up, her head swimming. "What did you do to me?"

His expression shifted, as if a hardened mask covered his features. "What can you remember?"

She shoved at the crocheted throw tangled around her legs. "That's not for me to answer!" she growled at him, flailing a little as the throw twisted itself further around her limbs, trapping her in place.

Seth unfolded himself slowly from the chair, rising to his full height. He wasn't the tallest man she'd ever met, but he was tall enough and imposing without much effort. It was those eyes, she thought. Sharp and focused, as if nothing could ever slip past him without notice. Full of mystery, as well, as if he knew things no one else did or possibly could.

Her fear shifted into something just as dangerous. Fascination.

*Snake and bird,* she thought as he walked closer, his pace unhurried and deceptively unthreatening.

"What's the last thing you remember?" He plucked at the crocheted blanket until it slithered harmlessly away from her body. He never touched her once, but somehow she felt his hands on her anyway, strong and warm. A flush washed over her, heating her from deep inside until she thought she was going to spontaneously combust.

What the hell was wrong with her?

*He asked you a question,* the rational part of her brain reminded her. *Answer the question. Maybe he knows something you need to know.*

Instead, she tried to make a run for the door she spotted just beyond his broad shoulders. She made it a few steps before her wobbling legs gave out on her. She plunged forward, landing heavily against the man's body.

His arms whipped around her, holding her upright and pinning her against his hard, lean body. The faint scent of aftershave filled her brain with a fragment of a memory—strong arms, a gentle masculine murmur in her ear, the salty-sweet taste of flesh beneath her tongue—

She tore herself out of his grasp and stumbled sideways until she came up hard against the wall. Her hair spilled into her face, blinding her. She shook it away. "What did you do to me?"

She had meant the question to be strong. Confrontational. But to her ears, it sounded weak and plaintive, like a brokenhearted child coming face-to-face with a world gone mad.

*Or maybe it's not the world that's gone mad,* a mean little voice in the back of her head taunted.

*Maybe it's you.*

# *Chapter Three*

Seth met Rachel Davenport's terrified gaze and felt sick. It didn't help that he knew he'd done nothing wrong. She clearly believed he had. And he would find few defenders if she made her accusation public.

Cleve Calhoun had always told him it never paid to help people. "They hate you for it."

What if Cleve was right?

"You're awake." The sound of Delilah's voice behind him, calm and emotionless, sent a jolt down his nervous system.

Rachel's attention shifted toward Delilah in confusion. "Who are you?"

"Delilah Hammond," Delilah answered. She took the crocheted throw Seth was still holding and started folding it as she walked past him toward the sofa. "How are you feeling?"

"I don't know," Rachel admitted. Her wary gaze shifted back and forth from Delilah to Seth. "I don't remember what happened."

Delilah slanted a quick look at Seth. "That's one of the symptoms."

"Symptoms of what?" Rachel asked, looking more and more panicky.

"GHB use," Delilah answered. "Apparently you did a little partying last night."

"What?" Rachel's panic elided straight into indignation. "What are you suggesting, that I did drugs or something?"

"Considering my brother found you about to do a double gainer off Purgatory Bridge—"

"I don't think you planned to jump off," Seth said quickly, shooting his sister a hard look. "But you were not entirely in control of yourself."

Delilah's eyebrows arched delicately. Rachel just looked at him as if he'd grown a second head.

"I was not on Purgatory Bridge last night," she said flatly. "I would never, ever…" She looked nauseated by the idea.

"You were on the bridge," he said quietly. "Apparently whatever you took last night has affected your memory."

"I don't…take drugs." Her anger faded again, and the fear returned, shining coldly in her blue eyes.

"Maybe someone gave something to you without your knowledge."

Seth's suggestion only made her look more afraid. "I don't remember going anywhere last night. I don't—" She stopped short, pressing her fingertips against her lips. "I don't remember anything."

"If you took GHB—"

Seth shot his sister a warning look.

She made a slight face at him and rephrased. "If someone slipped you GHB or something like it, it's not uncommon for you to experience amnesia about the hours before and after the dosage."

"What's the last thing you remember?" Seth asked.

Rachel stared at him. "I want to go home."

"Okay," he said. "I can take you home."

She shook her head quickly. "Her. She can take me."

Damn, that hurt more than he expected. "Okay. But what do you plan to tell your family?"

Her eyes narrowed. "Why?"

"I didn't know if you'd want people to ask uncomfortable questions."

Her expression shifted again, and her gaze rose to Seth's face. "My father would know what to do."

He nodded. "I'm sorry he's not here for you."

Her eyes darkened with pain. "Did you know my father asked if I thought he should hire you?" she said slowly. "He told me your record. Admitted it would be a risk. I don't know why he asked me. At the time, I didn't have much to do with the company. I guess now I know why."

"He trusted your instincts," Seth said.

She looked down at her hands. "Maybe he shouldn't have."

"What did you tell him?" Delilah asked, her tone curious. "About Seth?"

Rachel's gaze snapped up to meet Seth's. "I told him to give the man a second chance."

"Thank you," Seth said.

"I've been known to be wrong."

*Ouch again.*

Her eyes narrowed for a moment before she looked away, her profile cool and distant. To Delilah, she said, "I would appreciate a ride home. Do you think I should go to a doctor? To get tested for—" She stopped short, agony in her expression.

"Probably," Delilah said. "I could drive you to Knoxville if you don't want to see anyone local."

She shot Delilah a look of gratitude, the first positive

expression Seth had seen from her since she'd awoken. "Yes. Please."

As Delilah directed her out to the truck, she looked over her shoulder at her brother. "I'll take care of her." She followed Rachel out into the misty morning drizzle falling outside.

He nodded his gratitude and watched them from the open doorway until the truck disappeared around the bend, swallowed by the swirling fog. Then he grabbed his keys and headed out to the Charger, ignoring the urge to go back inside and catch some sleep.

He had to talk to a man about a girl.

NO SIGN OF recent sexual activity. The doctor's words continued ringing in her ears long after he'd left her to dress for departure. He'd said other things as well—preliminary tox screen was negative, but if she'd consumed GHB or another similar drug, it might not be easily detectible on a standard test. And depending on how long it had been since the drug was administered, it might not show up on a more specific analysis. He'd seemed indifferent to her decision not to test for it.

She supposed he had patients who needed him more than she did.

"How are you doing?" Delilah Hammond looked around the closed curtain, her expression neutral. There was an uncanny stillness about the other woman, an ability to remain calm and focused despite having a drug-addled woman dumped in her lap to take care of. She had a vague memory that there had been a Hammond girl from the Bitterwood area who'd become an FBI agent.

"I'm fine," Rachel lied. "Are you an FBI agent?"

Delilah's dark eyebrows lifted. "Um, not anymore. I

left the FBI years ago. I work for a private security company now."

"Oh."

"What did the doctor tell you?" she asked gently.

"No sign of sexual activity, but they also couldn't find a toxicological explanation for my memory loss. Something about the tests not being good at spotting GHB or drugs like it."

"You don't have any memory of where you might have gone last night?" Delilah picked up Rachel's discarded clothes from the chair next to the exam table and handed them to her.

"None. The last thing I remember is being at the cemetery."

Delilah left the exam area without being asked, giving Rachel a chance to change back into her own clothes in private. When Rachel called her name once she'd finished dressing, Delilah came back around the curtain.

"Look, I'm going to be straight with you," Delilah said. "Because I'd want someone to be straight with me. I know about Mark Bramlett and the murders. I know that they all seemed to be connected to Davenport Trucking in some way. Or, more accurately, connected to you."

Rachel put her fingertips against her throbbing temples. "Why do I feel as if everybody knows more about what's going on in my life than I do?"

"If someone's targeting you, up to this point it's been pretty oblique. But drugging you up and leaving you to fend for yourself outside on a cold October night while you're high as a kite?" Delilah shook her head. "That's awfully direct, if you ask me. You really need to figure out why someone would want you out of the way."

"You think I should go to the police."

The other woman's brow furrowed. "Normally, I'd say yes."

"But?"

"But is there any reason why it might not be in your best interest for the police to be involved?"

Rachel's head was pounding. "I don't know. I can't think."

"Okay, okay." Delilah laid her hands on Rachel's shoulders, her touch soothing. "You don't have to make that decision right now. Let's get you home and settled in. Is there someone there who can keep an eye on you until you're feeling more like yourself?"

"No," Rachel said, remembering that her stepmother had made plans to leave for Wilmington after the funeral. Diane's sister had invited Diane to visit for a few days. Paul had his own place, and while she and her stepbrother were friendly enough, she wouldn't feel comfortable asking him to play nursemaid. She already suspected he thought she was in over her head at the trucking company. He might even be right.

She didn't want to give him more reasons to doubt her.

"I'd offer to watch after you myself, but I have to drive to Alabama as soon as I can get away. I have a meeting with my boss, and it's a long drive. But you're welcome to stay at the house while I'm gone."

She wondered if Seth was staying there, too. She didn't let herself ask. "I'm okay. I'll be fine at home by myself."

"Are you sure?"

Rachel nodded, even though she wasn't sure about anything anymore.

"Smoky Joe" Breslin wasn't exactly thrilled when Seth roused him from bed on a rainy morning to answer a few questions, and his responses were laced liberally with profanities and lubricated by a few shots of good Tennessee whiskey. Seth had never been much of a drinker, so he nursed a single shot while Breslin knocked back three without blinking.

"Yeah, she was in here last night. Looked like a hothouse flower in a weed patch, but she seemed to be enjoying the music. And there were a few fellows who enjoyed lookin' at her, so who was I to judge?"

"Was she alone?" Seth asked.

"No, came in with some frat boy type. He tried a little something with her and she gave him a whack in the face, and some of the boys escorted him out. Not long after that, she headed out of here."

"What kind of condition was she in?"

"I don't know. I wasn't really watchin' when she left. I know she wasn't fallin'-down drunk or nothin'."

"You didn't check to make sure she wasn't driving?"

"Hell, you know how it can get around here on a busy night! I can't babysit everybody who comes here for the show. I do know she didn't have much to drink, so I didn't worry too much about it."

Which meant that unless she'd gone somewhere else to drink, it hadn't been alcohol alone that had put her up on that bridge.

"What can you tell me about the frat boy?" he asked Joe.

The older man grimaced. "Just some slicked-down city fellow. You know the type, comes in here with his nose in the air givin' everyone the stink-eye like he was better than them. I was glad to see the girl give him what for, if you want my opinion." Joe poured another glass of whiskey and motioned to top off Seth's.

Seth waved him off. "Did he pay for the drinks?"

"Yeah."

"Cash or credit?"

"Credit. One of them gold-type cards for big spenders. Flashed it like it was a Rolex watch or something."

"Would you have the receipt?"

Joe cut his eyes at Seth. "You pullin' another scam? I don't put up with that around here. You know that."

"No, no scam." He took no offense. "The woman he hit on is a friend of mine, see. I'd like to talk to the man about his behavior toward her."

"I see." Joe shot him an approving look. "Well, tell you the truth, she seemed to handle him pretty good all by her lonesome. But I'll see what I can dig up for you. Just promise me you're not gonna beat him up or shoot him or anything like that. I don't want the cops trackin' you back here and giving me any trouble."

"Just want to talk," Seth assured him, although if he found out that Frat Boy had anything to do with drugging Rachel Davenport, he couldn't promise he'd keep his fists to himself. She'd come way too close to going off the bridge the night before. She wouldn't have been likely to survive that fall.

Maybe the guy had slipped her something hoping it would make it easy to get lucky with her rather than to make her go off the deep end and hurt herself, but that distinction sure as hell didn't make drugging her any less heinous a crime.

And there was still the matter of the murders. Over the past two months, four women connected to Rachel Davenport had been murdered in what had initially seemed like random killings. Until investigators found the perpetrator and learned he'd been hired to kill those women and make the deaths look random. With his dying words, he'd admitted that it was "all about the girl."

All about Rachel Davenport.

Joe came back from the cluttered office just off the bar bearing a slip of paper. "Guy signed his name 'Davis Rogers.'"

The name wasn't familiar. Could have been someone Rachel knew from Maryville or even an old friend in town for her father's funeral. He'd ask her about him when she got back from the hospital.

The thought of her trip to Knoxville made his chest tighten as he left Smoky Joe's Saloon and headed toward the road to Maryville. He'd taken the past two days off work, but he was scheduled to work the next four. He had some vacation time coming to him, and he figured this might be the right time to take it.

He was surprised to find Paul Bailey in the office when he asked to see whoever was in charge while Rachel was out. Bailey had the account books open and looked up reluctantly when Seth stepped inside.

"Mr. Bailey, I've had a family situation come up. I know it's short notice, but I have a couple of weeks of vacation built up, and I'd like to take them now if possible."

Bailey's gaze was a little unfocused, as if his mind was still on whatever he'd been doing before Seth interrupted. "Yeah, sure. Nobody else has any days off scheduled, and they'll be happy to have the extra hours this time of year, with the holidays coming up. Just let Sharon at the front desk know what days you're taking, and she'll put it on the schedule."

"Thank you." Seth started to turn away, then paused. "I'm real sorry about Mr. Davenport."

"Thank you," Bailey answered with a regretful half smile.

On impulse, Seth added, "By the way, do you know a Davis Rogers?"

Bailey's gaze focused completely. "Why do you ask?"

"I just ran into a guy with that name last night at a bar," Seth lied. "He mentioned he knew the family. We drank a toast to Mr. Davenport."

"Last night?"

Seth kept his expression neutral. "Yeah. He mentioned he was thinking about selling his car, and I know someone in the market. I should've gotten his phone number, but I didn't think about it until afterward."

"He's not from here," Bailey said with a dismissive wave. "Probably couldn't work out a sale anyway before he heads back to Virginia."

Seth had a vague memory that Rachel had gone to college somewhere in Virginia. So, maybe an old college friend.

Maybe even an old boyfriend.

A sliver of dismay cut a path through the center of his chest. He tried to ignore it. "Thanks anyway." He left the office before Paul Bailey started to wonder why one of his fleet mechanics was suddenly asking a lot of nosy questions.

He stopped in the fleet garage, where he and the other mechanics shared a small break room. The three mechanics working in the garage today were out in the main room, so he had the place to himself.

Grabbing the phone book they kept in a desk drawer, he searched the hotel listings, bypassing the cheaper places. Joe Breslin had described Davis Rogers as a slicked-back frat boy, which suggested he'd stay at a nice hotel.

Was that Rachel's type? Preppy college boys with their trust funds and their country club golf games?

*Drop it, Hammond. Not your concern.*

She wasn't exactly what he considered his type, either. She was attractive, clearly, but quiet and reserved. And maybe if he hadn't begun to put clues together that suggested the recent Bitterwood murders were connected to Davenport Trucking, he might never have allowed himself to think about Rachel Davenport as a person and not just a company figurehead.

But ever since he'd given up the con game for the straight and narrow, he'd shown an alarming tendency to take other people's troubles to heart. And Rachel Davenport's life was eaten up with trouble these days.

An old twelve-step guy he knew had told him overcompensation was a common trait among people who felt the need to make amends for what they'd done. They tended to go overboard, wanting to save the whole damned world instead of fix the one or two things they could actually fix.

And here he was, proving the guy right.

Using his cell phone, he called Maryville hotels with no luck. He was about to start calling Knoxville hotels when he remembered there was a bed-and-breakfast in Bitterwood that offered the sort of services a guy like Davis Rogers would probably expect from his lodgings. The odds were better that he was staying in Knoxville, but Sequoyah House was a local call, so what would it hurt?

The proprietor at Sequoyah House put him right through to Davis Rogers's room when he asked. Nobody answered the phone, even after several rings, but Seth had the information he needed.

He had a few tough questions for Davis Rogers, and now he knew where to find him.

# Chapter Four

On the ride back to Bitterwood, Rachel realized she had no idea where her car was parked. Seth had said he'd found her on Purgatory Bridge, so it made sense that she'd left her car somewhere in the area. Delilah agreed to detour to the bridge to take a look.

Sure enough, as soon as they neared the bridge, Delilah had spotted the Honda Accord parked off the road near the bridge entrance, just as Seth had said.

"Do you have your keys?" Delilah asked as she pulled the truck up next to Rachel's car.

"Yeah. I found them in my pocket." God, she wished she could erase the last twenty-four hours and start fresh. But then, she'd have to face her father's funeral all over again. Feel the pain of saying goodbye all over again. The stress of staying strong and not breaking. Not letting anyone see her crumble.

What would those mourners at the funeral have thought, she wondered, if they'd seen her acrobatics on the steel girders of Purgatory Bridge last night?

She shuddered at the thought, not just the idea of making a spectacle of herself in front of those people, but also the idea of Purgatory Bridge itself. Crossing the delicate-looking truss bridge in a car was nerve-racking enough. Standing on the railings with land a terrifying thirty feet below?

Unimaginable.

The morning rain had gone from a soft drizzle to sporadic showers. Currently it wasn't raining, but fog swirled around them like lowering clouds. As Rachel crunched her way across the wet gravel on the shoulder of the road, Delilah rolled down the passenger window. "You sure you feel up to driving?"

"I'm fine," she said automatically.

"Take care of yourself, okay?" Delilah smiled gently as she rolled the window back up, shutting out the damp coolness of the day. Rachel watched until the truck disappeared around the bend before she slid behind the wheel of the Honda.

The car's interior seemed oppressively silent, her sudden sense of isolation exacerbated by the tendrils of fog wrapping around the car. Outside, the world looked increasingly gray and alien, so she turned her attention to the car itself, hoping something would jog her missing memory.

What had she done the last time she was in her car? Why couldn't she remember anything between standing at her father's gravesite and waking up in a strange room with Seth Hammond watching her with those intense green eyes?

A trilling sound split the air, making her jump. She found the offending noisemaker—her cell phone, which lay on the passenger floorboard. Grinning sheepishly, she grabbed it and checked the display. She didn't recognize the number.

"Hello?"

"Rach! Thank God, I've been trying to reach you for hours."

"Davis?" The voice on the other end of the line belonged to her grad school boyfriend, Davis Rogers. She hadn't heard from him in years.

"I thought maybe you regretted giving me your number and were screening my calls. Did you get home okay?" Before she could answer, he continued, "Of course you did, or you wouldn't be answering the phone. Look, about last night—"

Suddenly, there was a thud on the other end of the line, and the connection went dead.

Rachel pulled the phone away from her face, startled. She looked at the display again. The number had a Virginia area code, but Davis had spoken as if he was here in Tennessee.

She tried calling the number on the display, but it went to voice mail.

He'd said he'd been trying to call her. She checked her own voice mail and discovered three messages, all from Davis. The first informed her where he was staying—the Sequoyah House, a bed-and-breakfast inn out near Cutter Horse Farm. She entered the information in her phone's notepad and checked the other messages.

In the last message, Davis sounded upset. "Rachel, it's Davis again. Look, I'm sorry about last night, but he seemed to think you might be receptive. I've really missed you. I didn't like leaving you in that place. Please call me back so I can apologize."

She stared at the phone. What place? Surely not Smoky Joe's. Why was her ex in town in the first place—for her father's funeral? Had she seen him yesterday?

And why had his call cut off?

SEQUOYAH HOUSE WAS a sprawling two-story farmhouse nestled in a clearing at the base of Copperhead Ridge.

Behind the house, the mountain loomed like a guardian over the rain-washed valley below. It was the kind of place that lent itself more to romantic getaways than lodgings for a man alone.

But maybe Davis Rogers hadn't planned to be alone for long.

Most of the lobby furnishings looked to be rustic antiques, the bounty of a rich and varied Smoky Mountain tradition of craftsmanship. But despite its hominess, Sequoyah House couldn't hide a definite air of money, and plenty of it.

The woman behind the large mahogany front desk smiled at him politely, her cool gray eyes taking in his cotton golf shirt, timeworn jeans and barbershop haircut. No doubt wondering if he could afford the hotel's rates.

"May I help you?" she asked in a neutral tone.

"I'm here to see one of your guests, Davis Rogers."

"Mr. Rogers is not in his room. May I give him a message?"

"Yes. Would you tell him Seth Hammond stopped by to see him about a matter concerning Rachel Davenport?"

He could tell by the flicker in her eyes that she recognized his name. His reputation preceded him.

"Where can he reach you?"

Seth pulled one of the business cards sitting in a silver holder on the desk. "May I?" At her nod of assent, he flipped the card over and wrote his cell phone number on the back.

The woman took the card. "I'll give him the message."

He walked slowly down the front porch steps and headed back to where he'd parked in a section of the clearing leveled off and covered with interlocked pavers to form a parking lot. Among the other cars parked there he spotted a shiny blue Mercedes with Virginia license plates.

Seth looked through the driver's window. The car's interior looked spotless, with nothing to identify the owner. If Ivy Hawkins weren't on administrative leave for another week, Seth might have risked calling her to see if she could run down the plate number. She'd investigated the murders that had started this whole mess, after all. She'd damned near fallen victim to the killer herself. She might be persuaded.

But her partner, Antoine Parsons, had no reason to listen to anything Seth had to say. And what would it matter, really? Seth already knew Davis was staying at Sequoyah House. Though if the car with the Virginia plates was his, it did raise the question—if he wasn't in his room, and he wasn't in his car, where exactly was he?

As he headed back toward the Charger through the cold rain, a ringing sound stopped him midstep. It seemed faint, as if it was coming from a small distance away, but he didn't see anyone around.

He followed the sound to a patch of dense oak leaf hydrangea bushes growing wild at the edge of the tree line. The cream-colored blossoms had started to fade with the onset of colder weather, but the leaves were thick enough to force Seth to crouch to locate the phone by the fourth ring. It lay faceup on the ground.

Seth picked up the phone and pressed the answer button. "Hello?" he said, expecting the voice on the other end to belong to the phone's owner, calling to locate his missing phone.

The last thing he expected was to hear Rachel Davenport's voice. "Davis?"

Seth's gaze slid across the parking lot to the car with the Virginia plates. His chest tightened.

"Davis?" Rachel repeated.

"It's not Davis," he answered slowly. "It's Seth Hammond."

She was silent for a moment. "This is the number Davis Rogers left on my cell phone. Where is he? What's going on?"

"I don't know. I heard the phone ringing and answered, figuring the owner might be looking for his phone."

"Where are you?"

"Outside Sequoyah House." He pushed to his feet and started moving slowly down the line of bushes, looking through the thick foliage for something he desperately hoped he wouldn't find.

"What are you doing there?" She couldn't keep the suspicion from her tone, and he couldn't exactly blame her.

"I went and talked to Joe Breslin at Smoky Joe's Saloon. He remembered seeing you there with a man last night. So he looked up the man's credit card receipt and got a name for me."

"I was at Smoky Joe's with Davis?" She sounded skeptical. "That is definitely not his kind of place."

"Maybe it's yours," he suggested, remembering her sing-along with the bluegrass CD.

"Did you talk to Davis?"

"The clerk said he wasn't in his room, so I left him a message to call me." He paused as he caught sight of something dark behind one of the bushes. "I used your name. Hope you don't mind." He hunkered down next to the bush and carefully pushed aside the leaves to see what lay behind.

His heart sank to his toes.

Curled up in the fetal position, covered in blood and

bruises, lay a man. Seth couldn't tell if he was breathing. "Rachel, I have to go. I'll call you back as soon as I can."

He disconnected the call and put the cell phone in his jacket pocket. The tightly packed underbrush forced him to crawl through the narrow spaces between the bushes to get back to where the man lay with his back against the trunk of a birch tree. He'd been beaten, and badly. His face was misshapen with broken bones, his eyes purple and swollen shut. Blood drenched the front of his shirt, making it hard to tell what color it had been originally. One of his legs lay at an unnatural angle, suggesting a break or a dislocation.

Seth touched the man's throat and found a faint pulse. He didn't know what Davis Rogers looked like, but the proximity of the battered man and the discarded cell phone suggested a connection. He backed out of the bushes, reaching into his pocket for his own cell phone to dial 911.

But before his fingers cleared his pocket, something hit him hard against the back of the neck, slamming him forward into the bushes. His forehead cracked against the trunk of the birch tree, the blow filling his vision with dozens of exploding, colorful spots.

A second blow caught him near the small of his back, over his left kidney, shooting fire through his side. That was a kick, he realized with the last vestige of sense remaining in his aching head.

Then a hard knock to the back of his head turned out the lights.

AFTER TEN MINUTES had passed without a call back from Seth, Rachel's worry level hit the stratosphere. There had been something in his tone when he'd rung off that had kept her stomach in knots ever since.

He'd sounded…grim. As if he'd just made a grue-some discovery.

Given the fact that he'd answered Davis's phone a few seconds earlier, Rachel wasn't sure she wanted to hear what he'd found.

What if something bad had happened to Davis? He'd been her first real boyfriend, the first man she'd ever slept with. The first man she'd ever loved, even if it had ultimately been a doomed sort of love.

She might not be in love with him anymore, but she still cared. And if Seth's tone of voice meant anything—

Forget waiting. She was tired of waiting. Seth had said he was at Sequoyah House. The bed-and-breakfast was five minutes away.

She grabbed her car keys and headed for the door. If she wanted to know what was going on, she could damned well find out for herself.

EVERYTHING ON SETH'S body seemed to hurt, but not enough to suggest he was on the verge of dying. He opened his eyes carefully and found himself gazing up into a rain-dark sky. He was drenched and cold, and his head felt as if he'd spent the past few hours banging it against a wall.

He lifted his legs one at a time and decided they were still in decent working order, though he felt a mild shoot-ing pain in his side when he moved. Both arms appeared intact, though there was fresh blood on one arm. No sign of a cut beneath the red drops, so he guessed the blood had come from another part of his body.

He couldn't breathe through his nose. When he lifted his hand to his face, he learned why. Blood stained his fingers, and his nose felt sore to the touch. He forced himself to sit up, groaning softly at the effort, and looked around him.

He was in the woods, though there was a break in the trees to his right, revealing the corner of a large clapboard house. Sequoyah House, he thought, the memory accompanied by no small amount of pain.

Some of his memories seemed to be missing. He knew who he was. He knew what day it was, unless he'd been out longer than he thought. He knew what he'd been doing earlier that day—he'd been hoping to talk to Rachel Davenport's old friend Davis Rogers. But Rogers hadn't been in his room, so Seth had given the desk clerk a message for Rachel's friend and left the bed-and-breakfast.

He remembered walking back to the parking area where he'd left the Charger.

What then?

His cell phone rang, barely audible. He pulled it out from the back pocket of his sodden jeans and saw Adam Brand's name on the display. Perfect. Just perfect.

Then an image flashed through his aching head. A cell phone—but not this cell phone. Another one. He'd heard it ringing and come here into the woods to find it.

But where was the cell phone now?

He answered his phone to stop the noise. "Yeah?" The greeting came out surly. Seth didn't give a damn—surly was exactly how he felt.

"You were supposed to check in this morning," Brand said.

"Yeah, well, I was detained." He winced as he tried to push to his feet. "And the case has gone to hell in a handbasket, thanks for asking."

"What's happened?"

"Too much to tell you over the phone. I'll type you up a report. Okay?"

"Is something wrong? You sound like hell."

Seth spotted a rusty patch in the leaves nearby. His brow furrowed, sending a fresh ache through his brain. "I'll put that in the report, too." He hung up and crossed to the dark spot in the leaves.

The rain had washed away all but a few remnants of red. Seth picked up one of the stained leaves and took a closer look.

Blood. There was blood here on the ground. Was this where he'd been attacked?

No. Not him. There had been someone else. An image flitted through his pain-addled mind, moving so fast he almost didn't catch it.

But he saw enough. He saw the body of a man, curled into a ball, as if he'd passed out trying to protect his body from the blows. And passed out he had, because Seth had a sudden, distinct memory of checking the man's pulse and finding it barely there.

So where was the man now? Had whoever left this throbbing bump on the back of Seth's head taken the body away from here and dumped it elsewhere?

If so, they'd apparently taken the discarded cell phone, as well, because it was no longer in the pocket of his jacket.

He trudged through the rainy woods, heading for the clearing ahead. His vision kept shifting on him, making him stagger a little, and it was a relief to reach the Charger after what seemed like the longest fifty-yard walk of his life. He sagged against the side of the car, pressing his cheek against the cold metal frame of the chassis for a moment. It seemed to ease the pain in his skull, so he stood there awhile longer.

Only the sound of a vehicle approaching spurred him to move. He pushed away from the car and started to unlock to door when he realized the Charger was listing drastically to one side. Looking down, he saw why—both of the driver's-side tires were flat.

He groaned with dismay.

The vehicle turned off the road and into the parking lot. Seth forced his drooping gaze upward and was surprised to see Rachel Davenport staring back at him through the swishing windshield wipers of her car. She parked behind him and got out, her expression horrified.

"My God, what happened to you?"

He caught a glimpse of his reflection in the Charger's front window and winced at the sight. His nose was bloody and starting to bruise. An oozing scrape marred the skin over his left eye, as well.

"Should've seen the other guy," he said with a cocky grin, hoping to wipe that look of concern off her face. The last thing he could deal with in his weakened condition was a Rachel Davenport who felt sorry for him. He needed her angry and spitting fire so she'd go away and leave him to safely lick his wounds in private.

But she seemed unfazed by his show of bravado, moving forward with her hand outstretched.

*Don't touch me,* he willed, trying to duck away.

But she finally caught his chin in her hand and forced him to look at her. Her blue eyes searched his, and he found himself utterly incapable of shaking her off.

Her touch burned. Branded. He found himself struggling just to take another breath as her gaze swept over him, surveying his wounds with surprising calm for a woman who'd been swinging from the girders of Purgatory Bridge just the night before.

"Did you lose consciousness?" she asked.

"A few seconds." Maybe minutes. He couldn't be sure.

She looked skeptical. "Do you remember what happened?"

"I remember coming here to talk to your friend. He wasn't in his room."

"Right, but you found his cell phone."

He felt relieved to know his memory was real and not some injury-induced confabulation. "Right."

"But you cut me off. Said you had to go."

He caught her hand, pulling it gently from his chin and closing it between his own fingers. "Rachel, it's fuzzy, and I may be remembering things incorrectly—"

"Just say it," she pleaded.

He tightened his grip on her hand. "I think your friend Davis may have been murdered."

# Chapter Five

The cold numbness that had settled in the center of Rachel's chest from the time she'd gotten Davis Rogers's call began spreading to her limbs at Seth's words. "Why do you think that?"

He told her.

She tugged her hand away from his and started walking toward the edge of the mist-shrouded woods. Seth followed, his gait unsteady.

"I can't prove any of it," he warned. "If you call the Bitterwood P.D., they won't believe a word of it. I'm not high on their list of reliable witnesses."

"I need to know for myself. Where was the blood?" Her feet slipped on wet leaves as she entered the woods.

Seth's hand closed around her elbow, helping her stay upright, despite the fact that he was swaying on his feet. "Over here." He nudged her over until they came to a stop near a large stand of wild hydrangea bushes. A fading patch of rusting red was trickling away in the rain, but it definitely looked like blood.

Rachel picked up one of the red-stained leaves and lifted it to her nose. A faint metallic odor rose from the stain. "It's definitely blood."

"I don't know what happened to him. I swear."

She turned to look at him. He really did look terrible,

blood still seeping from a scrape on the right side of his forehead and his nose crusted with more of the same. "You don't remember who did this to you?"

"No. Everything's a blur." He looked pale beneath his normally olive-toned skin. As he swayed toward her, she put out her hands to keep him from crashing into her.

"You're in no condition to drive."

He shot her a lopsided grin. "Neither is my car."

When they got back to the parking lot, she saw what he meant. Both of the driver's side tires were flat. She couldn't tell if they'd been punctured or if the air had just been let out of them. Didn't really matter, she supposed.

"Get in my car," she said, ignoring the wobble in her own legs. She didn't have time to fall apart. There was too much that needed to be done. She'd think about Davis later.

"Bossy. I like it." Seth shot her a look that was as hot as a southern summer. An answering quiver rippled through her belly, but she ignored it. He sounded woozy—probably didn't know what he was saying. And even if he did, neither of them was in any position to do much about it.

"I'm going to call the police and report Davis missing," she told him as she slid behind the wheel. "I'm going to have to include you in my statement."

He shook his head, then went stock-still, wincing. "Ow."

She turned to face him. He tried to do the same, but she could tell the movement was painful for him. Just how badly had he been beaten? "Seth, I can't leave you out of it, because you've left a trail that leads to you. You gave your name to the clerk. Your car is sitting here in the parking lot with flat tires, and if we call a wrecker to come get it, that's just another trail that leads to you."

His expression darkened. "You don't know what it's like to be everyone's number one suspect."

"You're right. I don't. But I can tell the police what I do know. I was talking to Davis when the line went dead. Then when I called Davis's phone, you answered—" She stopped short, realizing how that would sound to the police.

Seth's eyes met hers. "Exactly."

"If Davis is dead, I can't just do nothing."

"Just don't tell them I answered the phone."

He wanted her to lie to the police? "I can't leave something like that out of my statement."

He looked as if he wanted to argue, but finally he slumped against the seat. "Do what you have to."

She leaned back against her own seat, frustrated. What was she supposed to do now? Ignore his fears? Tell him he was overreacting?

She couldn't do that. Because she didn't plan on telling the police everything, did she? She certainly wasn't going to tell them she'd spent most of the previous evening apparently so drugged out of her head that she'd thought a balance beam routine on the girders of Purgatory Bridge was a good idea.

"I know what it's like to have people judging your every move," she said quietly.

He slanted a curious look her way.

"I don't want the police to know what happened to me last night. And you haven't pushed me at all to tell anyone the truth."

"I figured if you wanted it known, you'd tell it yourself."

She nodded. "I won't tell them you answered Davis's phone."

He released a long, slow breath. "Rachel, you know I didn't do anything to him. Right?"

She wondered if she was crazy to believe him. What did she know about him, really? He kept to himself at work, making few friends. She'd heard stories about his years as a con man, though she and her father had decided to judge him on his current work, not his checkered past. And he'd been a good worker, hadn't he? Showed up on time or early, did what he was asked, never caused any trouble.

But was that reason enough to trust what he said?

"I guess not." He reached for the door handle.

She caught his arm. He turned back to her, his gaze first settling where her fingers circled his rain-slick forearm, then rising to meet hers. In the low light, his eyes were as deep and mysterious as the rainy woods outside the car.

"You saved my life last night, and you've asked for nothing in return. You didn't even try to use it against me just now, when you could have. Any con man worth his salt would have."

He grimaced. "I'm no saint."

"I'm not saying you are. I'm just saying I believe you."

The interior of the car seemed to contract, the space between their bodies suddenly infinitesimal. She could feel heat radiating from his body, answered by her own. Despite his battered condition, despite the million and one reasons she shouldn't feel this aching magnetism toward him, she couldn't pretend she didn't find him attractive.

He wasn't movie-star handsome, especially now with his nose bloody and purple shadows starting to darken the skin beneath his eyes, but he was all man, raw masculinity in every angle of his body, every sinewy muscle and broad expanse.

He had big, strong hands, and even with a dozen conflicting and distracting thoughts flitting through her head at the moment, she could imagine the feel of them moving over her body in a slow, thorough seduction. The sensation was fierce and primal, intensely sexual, and she had never felt anything quite like it before.

"What now?" he asked, breaking the tense silence.

Her body's response came, quick and eager.

*Take me home with you.*

Aloud, she said, "I guess I call the police so they can start looking for Davis." She pulled out her phone and made the call to 911.

"I need to clean up," Seth murmured.

"Here." She reached across to the glove compartment, removed a package of wet wipes and handed them to him. "Best I can do."

He looked at the wet wipes and back at her, one eyebrow notching upward.

"Habit. I was a librarian," she said with a smile. "I dealt with a lot of sticky hands all day."

He pulled a wipe from the package and started cleaning off the blood, using the mirror on the sun visor to check his progress. When he finally snapped the wet wipe package closed, he looked almost normal. His nose wasn't as swollen as it had appeared with all the blood crusted on it, and the scrape on his forehead, once cleaned up, wasn't nearly as large as it had looked. Only the slight darkening of the skin around his eyes gave away his battered condition, and the rusty splotches where the blood from his face had dripped onto the front of his dark blue shirt.

"Better?" he asked.

She nodded. "You're going to have to answer questions regardless."

"I know." He slanted another wry grin in her direction, making her belly squirm. "I'd just like to look my best when I talk to the cops."

Uniformed officers arrived first to take their statements, but within half an hour, a detective arrived, a tall, slim black man with sharp brown eyes and a friendly demeanor. He'd come around the trucking company asking questions last month after a couple of their employees had been murdered, Rachel remembered. Antoine Parsons. Nice guy.

He didn't look particularly nice as his gaze swept the scene and locked, inevitably, on Seth's battered face. "Seth Hammond. You do have a funny way of showing up at all my crime scenes lately."

Seth's smile was close to a smirk. Rachel felt the urge to punch him in the shoulder and tell him to stop making things worse. But apparently he just couldn't help it. "Antoine, Antoine, Antoine. Still sucking up to the Man, I see. How's that working out for you?"

Antoine barely stopped an eye roll. "We have a missing person?"

Rachel stepped in front of Seth to address the detective. "His name is Davis Rogers. I was talking to him on the phone when I heard a thud and the phone went dead."

"You came here to look for him?"

"He'd left an earlier message on my voice mail, telling me where he was staying. It seemed the obvious place to look. I got here and found his car parked in the lot. But he's not in his room. And I found a patch of blood in the leaves nearby." She waved toward the woods.

Antoine's gaze slid back to Seth's face. "Who gave you a pounding, Hammond?"

"Not sure," he answered.

"What are you doing here? You with Ms. Davenport?"

"I came looking for Rogers. He wasn't in his room, so I was about to leave when I thought I saw something in the woods."

"Just happened to see something in the woods?" Antoine was clearly skeptical. Rachel was beginning to understand why Seth hadn't wanted her to include him in this police investigation at all. Maybe he'd earned the distrust, but clearly nobody in the Bitterwood Police Department was going to give him any benefit of the doubt.

"I heard something, actually." Seth slanted a look her way. She saw fear in his eyes but also rock-hard determination in the set of his jaw. "I heard a cell phone ringing. I found it on the ground beneath those bushes." He pointed toward the hydrangeas.

He was telling the truth about the phone, she realized with a thrill of surprise.

"It was Ms. Davenport, calling Rogers."

Antoine's brows lifted. "You said you were looking for Rogers. Why?"

She saw the hesitation in Seth's face. The truth, she realized, could be a scary thing. And not just for Seth. For her, too.

But it was better than the alternative.

She took a deep breath and answered the detective's question for Seth. "He was trying to find out what happened to me last night."

It took almost two hours to work through all the questions Antoine had for both of them. His attitude toward Seth had settled into guarded belief, though Seth knew it would last only as long as it took to get in trouble again.

At least Antoine had asked good, probing questions.

Unfortunately, neither Seth nor Rachel had any good answers. She still couldn't remember most of what had happened the night before, and Seth's memory of the attack that had left him bruised and half-conscious was similarly spotty.

He'd refused a trip to the hospital, though the paramedics thought he'd sustained a concussion. His mind was clearing nicely, and most of the aches and pains in his body had faded to bearable. He probably did have a mild concussion, but he didn't think it was any worse than that. He'd go spend the night at Delilah's and let her play nursemaid.

Except apparently Delilah was out of town for the night. "She said she was driving down to Alabama for a business meeting," Rachel told Seth after he'd assured the paramedics he'd have his sister keep an eye on him.

Well, hell. He'd just have to keep an eye on himself.

"You could stay with me tonight." Rachel's blue eyes locked with his, but her expression was impossible to read.

"That's kind of you—"

"I'm not sure it's kind," she said, the left corner of her mouth quirking upward. "I could use another set of eyes and ears in the house. I'm not inclined to stay there alone after all of this."

So when Antoine finally agreed to let them leave, Seth called a wrecker service to take the Charger to the local garage and got into the passenger seat of Rachel's car.

"You don't have to do this," he told her as she buckled herself in behind the steering wheel. "I'll be okay."

"I was serious. I don't want to be alone. I'm not sure I'm safe alone with everything that's going on."

She probably wasn't, he realized. "I'm sorry about Davis. I hope I'm wrong about what happened to him."

Her lips tightened. "I wish I believed you were."

"Do you know why he was here?"

"He must have come to the funeral." She looked close to collapse, he realized, so he didn't ask anything else until they reached the sprawling two-story farmhouse on the eastern edge of Bitterwood, a few miles south of Copperhead Ridge and light years away from the hard-scrabble life Seth had lived growing up on Smoky Ridge.

Until her father's cancer diagnosis, Rachel had kept her own apartment in Maryville, living off her earnings as a public librarian. But everything had changed when a series of doctors confirmed the initial diagnosis—inoperable, terminal liver cancer. Too late for a transplant to help. They'd given him four months to live. Chemo, radiation and a series of holistic treatments had prolonged his life by a few more months, but shortly before his death, George had said, "No more," and spent the remainder of his time on earth preparing his daughter to run the trucking company he'd built.

Seth knew all these intimate details about Rachel's life because Davenport Trucking was like any business that maintained a family atmosphere—everybody knew everybody else's business. Few secrets lasted long in such a place.

But he didn't know what Rachel thought about the drastic change in her life. Did she regret leaving the library behind? From what he knew of her work at Davenport, she had a deft hand with personnel management and seemed to have a natural affinity for the finance end of the business. People who'd grumbled about her selection as her father's successor had stopped complaining when it became clear that the company wouldn't suffer under her guidance.

But nobody seemed to know what Rachel herself

thought about the job. Did the benefit of fulfilling her father's dying wish outweigh the loss of a career she'd chosen for herself?

"This house is too big for just one person," Rachel commented as she unlocked the front door and let them inside. "I don't think Diane plans to come back here. Too much of my mother here for her tastes."

The front door opened into a narrow hallway that stretched all the way to a door in the back. Off the hallway, either archways or doors led into rooms on either side. To the immediate right, a set of stairs rose to the second floor, flanked by an oak banister polished smooth from years of wear. "Did you ever slide down that banister?" he asked Rachel.

"Maybe." A whisper of a smile touched her lips. "Think you can make it up the stairs? The bedrooms are on the second floor."

He dragged himself up the steps behind her, glad he was feeling less light-headed than he had back at the bed-and-breakfast. Rachel showed him into a simple, homey room on the left nearest the stairs. "I'll make up the bed for you. Why don't you go take a shower? The bathroom's the next door down on the right. There's a robe in the closet that should fit you. I'll see if Paul's left any clothes around you can borrow for the night."

When he emerged from the shower fifteen minutes later, he returned to the bedroom to find the bedcovers folded back and a pair of sweatpants and a mismatched T-shirt draped across the bed. A slip of paper lay on top of them. "Sorry, couldn't find any underwear. Or anything that matched. After I shower, we'll find something to eat."

She had finished her shower first and was already downstairs in the cozy country kitchen at the back of the house. "Something to eat" turned out to be tomato soup and grilled cheese sandwiches.

Rachel had finally shed the dress she'd worn to Smoky Joe's the night before, replacing it with a pair of slim-fitting yoga pants and a long-sleeved T-shirt that revealed her long legs and slender arms. She was thinner than Seth normally liked in a woman, but he couldn't find a damned thing wrong with the flare of her hips or the curve of her small, firm breasts.

"Is tomato soup okay? I should have asked—"

"It's fine. I can grill the sandwiches if you want."

She turned to look at him, smiling a little as she took in his mismatched clothes. Her stepbrother, Paul, was a little slimmer than he was, so the clothes fit snugly on his legs and shoulders. "Are you sure you're feeling up to it?"

"The shower worked wonders," he assured her, bellying up to the kitchen counter beside the stove, where she'd already prepared the sandwiches and set out a stick of butter for the griddle pan heating up over the closest eye. He dipped to get a better look at the stove top, relieved that it was a flat-top electric with no open-flame burners.

She gave him a sidelong glance as he moved closer to where she stood stirring the soup. "I'm not used to cooking with company."

"Me, either." He dropped a pat of butter on the griddle pan. It sizzled and snapped, and they both had to jump back to avoid the splatter.

Rachel laughed. "I see why. You're dangerous."

"We could switch," he suggested. "Surely I can manage stirring soup."

Switching positions, they brushed intimately close. As Seth's body stirred to life, he realized the cut of the sweatpants wasn't quite loose enough to hide his reaction if he didn't get his libido under control, and soon.

*Just stir the soup. Clockwise, clockwise, switch it up
to counterclockwise—*

"Why are you so interested in what happened to me
last night?" Rachel broke the tense silence.

He glanced at her and found she was looking intently
at the griddle, where she'd laid both of the sandwiches
in a puddle of sizzling butter, her profile deceptively
serene. Only the quick flutter of her pulse in her throat
gave away her tension.

"What is it they say? Save a person's life and they're
your slave forever after? Maybe I'm just waiting for you
to pay up."

She cut her eyes at him as if to make sure he was teasing. "Yeah, that'll happen."

He grinned. "Maybe I'm sucking up to the new boss."

*Wrong thing to say.* Her slight smile faded immediately. "New boss. I haven't even let myself think about
that yet."

"Is that going to be a problem? Me being an employee,
I mean. And being here like this. Because I'm feeling a
lot better, really. I don't have to stick around so you can
watch out for my mental state."

"That's not what I meant," she said. "I was thinking
about being the boss, period. All those people depending on what I do and say now."

He had stopped stirring while they were talking, and
a thin skin was forming on top of the soup. He started
stirring again, quickly whisking the film away. "Hasn't
that been the case for a while now?"

She was quiet a moment. "I guess so. It just didn't feel
real as long as my father was around to be my safety net."

To his dismay, he saw tears glisten in her eyes, threatening to spill. The urge to pull her into his arms and hold
her close was almost more than he could resist. He set-

tled for laying one hand on her shoulder and giving it a comforting squeeze.

She wiped her eyes with the heel of one hand and flipped the sandwiches over. "I had a long time to prepare for my father's death. And it was a relief by the end to see him finally out of pain. But now that I'm past that numb stage—"

"Your dad was a good man. Not many people would've taken a chance on someone like me. This world's a worse place with him gone."

His words had summoned tears again, but also a smile, which she turned on him like a ray of pure sunshine that brightened the room, even as the drizzle outside darkened the day.

He smiled back briefly, then forced his attention back to the soup before he got any deeper into trouble.

# Chapter Six

After lunch, Rachel made a pot of coffee and they took their cups into the den on the eastern side of the house, where a large picture window offered a glimpse of Copperhead Ridge shrouded with mist. The rain had picked up again, casting the trees in hues of blue and gray. When she turned on the floor lamps that flanked the room, the scene outside faded into reflections of the warm, comfortably furnished den and the two slightly bedraggled people who occupied it.

Seth found his own reflection depressing, given how quickly his bruises were darkening, making him look like the loser of a cage match. He turned his attention instead to Rachel, whose honey-brown hair lay in damp waves around her face. Scrubbed clean and pink, she looked about a decade younger and prettier than she had any right to be.

"How's your head feeling?" she asked.

*Light,* he thought. But it didn't have much to do with his mild concussion. "Better. Not really hurting anymore."

Her brief smile faded quickly. "I don't know what to think about Davis."

"You mean whether or not he's still alive?"

She sank into an armchair across from the sofa, curling her legs under her. She waved for Seth to sit across from her on the sofa. "I mean if he's dead. How am I supposed to feel about it?"

"I don't know that you're *supposed* to feel any particular way," Seth offered. "You just feel what you feel."

"I did love him once. He was the first man—" She stopped short, a delicate blush rising in her cheeks. She slanted a quick look at Seth. "It didn't last. We wanted such different things out of life."

Whatever it had been that Davis Rogers had wanted out of life, it was surely closer to Rachel's desires than anything Seth had done or wanted to do in his own life. If she and Davis had been miles apart, she and Seth were separated by whole galaxies.

*But it doesn't matter, does it? That's not why you're here.*

"I haven't even seen him in years. We ran into each other a while back at a football game in Charlottesville. Said hi, promised to call but never did—" She closed her eyes. "Why did he come here?"

"Probably to attend your father's funeral and see how you were."

"And now he might be dead because of me."

Seth reached across the space between them, covering her hands with one of his. "If he's dead, it's because someone beat the hell out of him."

"Because of me."

He crouched in front of her, closing his fingers around her wrists. "Look at me."

Her troubled blue eyes met his.

"I know someone's been methodically removing people from your life to isolate you. I know whoever's pulling the strings hired Mark Bramlett to kill four women who were close to you. And now, maybe, he's killed your old boyfriend, who came to town to make sure you were okay. I think he may have been behind drugging you last night, too."

Rachel's eyes darkened with suspicion. "How do you know this?"

"I started to suspect something was going on when I realized three of the four Bitterwood murders involved women who'd worked at Davenport Trucking. That was strange enough. Then I asked around and found out that Marjorie Kenner had been your friend and mentor—another librarian, right?"

"Right." She looked stricken by his words, as if the mere reminders of all she'd lost had hit her all over again. He wished he'd found some way to soften his words, but he doubted anything he could have said would have made her feel the pain any less keenly.

"What I don't know," he added more gently, "is why. If someone wanted to get you out of his way—"

"His?"

"His, her—whichever. If someone wanted you out of the way, why not just kill you?"

She blanched. "I don't know."

"I think you do. You just can't say it out loud for some reason."

She slanted a troubled look at him. "How do you know so much about me?"

He ran his thumb lightly over her knuckles, gentling her with the movement. He saw her start to relax a little, soothed by the repetitive movement of his thumb. "I know because I observe. I used to be a con man, you know. That's what con men do. Observe, compile, formulate and exploit."

Her nostrils flared with a hint of distaste. "You're approaching my trouble like you would approach a potential mark?"

"Might as well use those skills for good."

Her eyes narrowed a little, but she gave a slight nod. "So what have you observed?"

"You're scared of something. Not everyone can see it, because you hide it really well. But I see it, because that used to be my job. Finding a person's vulnerable spots and figuring out how to use them."

"But you haven't found out what it is."

"Not yet."

Her lips twisted in a mirthless smile. "And I'm supposed to spill what it is to you, make it easier?"

"I'm not the one trying to hurt you."

"How do I know that?" She pulled her hands free of his grip and pushed him out of her way, rising and pacing the hardwood floor until she reached the picture window. She met his gaze in the window reflection. "I don't really know you. And what I do know scares me."

He couldn't blame her. What he knew about himself would scare anyone. "I don't want to see you get hurt, and whether you like my skill set or not, I can use it to help you out. So whatever you can tell me, whatever you're comfortable sharing—I'll listen. I'll keep your confidence, and I won't use it against you."

She turned around to look at him. "I'm taking a huge risk just letting you stay here, aren't I?"

She wasn't going to tell him what scared her so much, he realized. It was disappointing. Frustrating. But he didn't blame her.

"Okay." He nodded. "I can leave if you want me to."

She licked her lips and held his gaze, searching his expression as if trying to see what was going on inside his mind. "No. I know you're feeling better, but head injuries can be quirky. I'd rather you stay here where I can look in on you every few hours to make sure you haven't gone into a coma."

He grimaced. "What, you're planning to wake me up every couple of hours or something?" He added a touch of humor to his voice, hoping to lighten the mood.

It worked. Her lips quirked slightly, and there was a glitter of amusement in her blue eyes when she answered, "That's exactly what I'm planning to do."

Behind the humor, however, he heard a steely determination that caught him by surprise. She apparently took the job of keeping an eye on him seriously, and he suspected it was as much for her own sake as his. Maybe it gave her a welcome distraction from the strain and grief of her life these days.

He nodded toward the picture window. "Do you always leave these windows open like this?"

Her brow furrowed. "Most of the time. It's such a beautiful view."

"It is," he agreed. "But it gives people a pretty good view of you, too."

Her eyes darkened, and she wrapped her arms around herself as if she felt a sudden chill. "I never thought about that."

She wouldn't have. She wasn't used to being a target, and Seth wished like hell she could continue living her life without precautions. But there was too much danger out there, focused directly on her, for her to let her guard down that way anymore.

The windows were curtain-free, but he thought he saw levers on each double-paned window that suggested between-the-glass blinds. "Whenever it's dark enough outside to see your reflection in the windows, you should close the blinds."

She pressed her lips in a tight line, as if it annoyed her to have to make even that small accommodation to the dangerous world around her. A sign of a charmed life, he thought, remembering how early in his own life he'd learned to take precautions against the dangers always lurking, both outside and in.

Another way he and Rachel Davenport were worlds apart.

Starting at the opposite end of the room, he helped her close the blinds until they met in the middle. She paused at the last window, gazing out at the darkness barely visible beyond their reflections.

"You think I'm spoiled," she said quietly.

He didn't answer. He'd more or less been thinking exactly that, although not with any disapproval. He envied her, frankly.

"There's a lot about my life you don't know." She closed the blinds, shutting out the rainy afternoon, and turned to look at him, her expression softening. "You look terrible. I think you may have a broken nose."

It certainly hurt like hell, but he'd examined the bones himself while taking his shower, where he could throw out a stream of profanities without offending anyone. Cracked or not, the bones and cartilage were all in the right places. "It'll heal on its own."

"Said in the tone of a man who's had a broken bone or two."

"Or ten." He made a face. "I'm fine."

She looked skeptical but didn't press him on it. She crossed back to the armchair and curled up on its over-stuffed cushions, pulling her knees up to her chest.

He didn't feel like sitting, so he wandered around the den, taking in the good furniture—some antiques, most not—and the eclectic collection of knickknacks dotting the flat surfaces around the large, airy room. Tiny animals sculpted from colored quartz formed a menagerie on a round side table near the sofa. On the fireplace mantel sat a small collection of Russian nesting dolls, painted in bright colors.

The fireplace itself was, thankfully, cold and unlit, though the extra heat might have helped to drive away the afternoon chill still shivering in his bones. He'd live without it, thank you very much.

He didn't care for fire.

The house he'd grown up in would have fit in this room, he thought, or close to it. He, Dee and his parents had lived there in grim strife for nearly fourteen years, until his father had blown the whole damned thing up, and himself with it.

He wondered what Rachel Davenport had been doing around the time of that explosion. Probably up to her eyeballs in homework from Brandywine Academy, the expensive private school she'd attended to keep her away from the Appalachian hillbillies who filled Bitterwood's public schools.

*Envy is an unattractive trait.* Cleve Calhoun's voice rumbled in his ear, full of wry humor. Hilarious advice coming from the man who'd used envy, greed, pride and vanity with great expertise against all his hapless marks. But however bad his motives for teaching Seth a few practical life lessons, Cleve had been right most of the time. Envy *was* an unattractive trait. And unfair to the envied, in Rachel's case.

It wasn't her fault she'd been loved and protected. Every child should be so blessed.

"Shouldn't you be resting?" Rachel asked.

He turned to look at her. "I'm not tired."

Her eyes narrowed slightly. "This isn't your first beating." It wasn't a question.

He didn't know whether to laugh or grimace. He managed something in between, his lips curving in a wry grin. "No, ma'am. It's not."

"Did you deserve them?"

That time, he did laugh. "Some of the time."

"Why did you choose the life you did?"

He wandered back over to the sofa, thinking about how to answer. When he'd been younger, he might have told her he didn't choose to become a con man. That life had chosen for him. He'd spent a lot of time blaming everyone in the world but himself for his troubles.

But everyone had choices, even people who didn't think they did. Delilah's childhood had been the same as his, but she'd chosen a different path, one that had made her a hero, not a criminal. He could have chosen such a path if he hadn't let hate and anger do him in.

That had been his choice. Nothing that happened before excused it.

"When I was young," he said finally, sitting on the sofa across from her, "I had a choice between two paths. One looked hard. The other looked easy. I chose easy."

A little furrow formed in her brow as she considered his words. "That simple?"

He nodded. "That simple. I was angry and tired of struggling. I was eaten up with envy and mad at the whole damned world. So when a man offered me a chance to get everything I wanted and stick it to people who stood in my way, I took it. I reckon you could even say I relished it. I was good at it, and in a twisted way, I think it gave me a sense of self-worth I'd never had before."

"So why aren't you still doing it?"

"Because nothing good, nothing real, gets built on lies."

Her solemn blue eyes held his gaze thoughtfully. "Or you could be lying to me now. Maybe this act of repentance is all for show."

"I guess that's for you to figure out."

She buried her face in her hands, rubbing her eyes with the heels of her hands. "I'm so tired."

He knew she wasn't just talking about physical tiredness. The past few months must have been hell on her emotionally, losing so many people who mattered to her, including her own father. "Why don't you go lie down? Take a nap."

"I'm supposed to be keeping an eye on you, remember?"

"I'm fine. Really. The ol' noggin's not even hurting anymore." *Well, not more than a slight ache,* he amended silently. And it was mostly at the site at the back of his head where he'd taken the knockout blow.

After a long, thoughtful pause, she rose to her feet with easy grace. He wondered idly if she'd taken ballet lessons as a child. She had the long limbs and elegant lines of a dancer.

Delilah had always wanted to take dance lessons, he remembered. He wondered if his sister had made up for lost time once she'd gotten away from Smoky Ridge. He'd have to remember to ask her.

"There's food in the fridge if you get hungry." She waved her arm toward the cases full of books that lined the walls of the den. "Lots to read, if your head's up to it. There's a television and a sound system in that cabinet if you'd rather watch TV or listen to music."

"In other words, make myself at home?"

Her lips quirked. "I'm not sure it's safe to give you that much rope."

He grinned back at her, unoffended. "Smart girl."

She headed for the stairs, but not before Seth saw her smile widen with pleasure.

RACHEL HADN'T PLANNED to take a nap. She had felt tired but not particularly sleepy when she'd climbed the stairs to her room on the second floor, but the whisper of rain against the windows and the long and stressful day colluded to lull her to sleep within minutes of settling on the chaise lounge in the corner of her bedroom.

When she next opened her eyes, the gloom outside had gone from gray to inky black, and the room was cold enough to give her a chill. She rose from the chaise, stretching her stiffened muscles, and started toward the bathroom when she heard it.

Music.

Seth must have taken her at her word and turned on the stereo system, she thought, surprised by his choice of music. She hadn't figured him for a Chopin fan.

Then she recognized the tune. Nocturne Opus 9, Number 2. It had been her mother's favorite.

It had been playing the night she'd died.

Rachel walked slowly toward the bedroom door, her gut tightening with dread. There were no Chopin CDs in the house. What the police hadn't taken as evidence, her father had gotten rid of shortly after her mother's death.

How had Seth found anything to play?

Did he know about how her mother had died? He might know the mode of her death, of course—the suicide had made the papers—but the gory details had never showed up in the news or even in small-town gossip. The police and the coroner had been scrupulously discreet, from everything her father had told her of the aftermath of her mother's death.

So how could he know about the music?

She pushed open the door. And stopped suddenly in the center of the hall as she realized the music wasn't coming from the den below.

It was coming from the attic above.

Acid fear bubbled in her throat, forcing her to swallow convulsively. Was she imagining the slow, plaintive strains of piano music floating down from above?

Was she reliving the night of her mother's death, the way she had relived it in a thousand nightmares?

She had heard music that night as well, swelling through the otherwise silent house. It had awakened her from a dead sleep, loud enough to rip through the fabric of her tearstained dreams.

She'd felt nothing but anger at the sound. Anger at her mother's harsh words, at the stubborn refusal to see things her way. She'd been fifteen and pushing against the fences of her childhood. Her father had been the more reasonable of her parents, in her eyes at least. He'd recognized her need to unfurl her wings and fly now and then.

Her mother had just wanted her to stay in the safe nest she'd built for her only child.

A nest that was smothering her to death.

She'd hated the sound of that music, the piercing trills and the waltz cadence. She'd hated how loud it was, seeming to shake the walls and shatter her brain cells.

Or maybe that had just been how it had seemed afterward. After she'd climbed the ladder up to the attic and seen her mother swaying to the music, her gaze lifted toward the unseen heavens, one hand waving in rhythm and the other closed around the butt of George Davenport's Colt .45 pistol.

Terror stealing her breath, Rachel stared up at the ladder. The very thought of climbing into the attic was enough to make beads of sweat break out across her forehead and slither down her neck like liquid fear.

But she had to know. Not knowing was worse, somehow.

Biting her lip so hard she feared she'd made it bleed, Rachel reached up and pulled the cord that lowered the ladder to the attic. Music spilled out along with the ladder, louder than before. Not the rafter-rattling decibels of her memories but loud enough.

Swallowing hard, she started to climb the ladder, clinging to the wooden rungs as if her life depended on it.

She'd had no warning of what she'd find that night. There were things she'd gotten used to about her mother—her obsession with cleanliness, her moodiness, her occasional outbursts of anger—but none of those things had seemed more than the normal foibles of life.

Maybe her father had sheltered her from the worst of it. Or maybe it wasn't as bad when her father was around. But he'd gone on a business trip, one that had eventually led to his securing the capital to start his own trucking business after working in truck fleet sales for most of his adult life. He was due back that night, but he'd been gone for almost a week.

Maybe a week had been all it had taken for her father's palliative influence to wear off.

Rachel tried to put the memories out of her head as she forced herself up the final few rungs and stepped into the attic. But the memories rose to slap her in the face.

A plastic drop cloth lay on the hard plank floor of the

attic, just as it had that night. And across the drop cloth, blood splashed in crimson streaks and puddles.

Fresh blood.

SETH HAD FOUND an old Dick Francis novel in one of the bookshelves and settled down to read, but his weariness and the rain's relentless cadence made it hard to stay awake. He'd closed his eyes for just a moment and suddenly he was back on the road to Smoky Joe's Saloon, the steel girders of Purgatory Bridge gleaming in his headlights.

He parked behind Rachel's Honda and got out, deeply aware of the brisk, cool wind whipping his hair and his clothes. It was strong. Too strong. It would fling Rachel right off the bridge if he didn't get to her.

But no matter how far he walked, she was still a few steps farther away, dancing gracefully along the narrow girder as if she were walking a tightwire. Her arms were out, her face raised to the sky, and she was humming a tune, something slow and vaguely familiar, like one of the classical pieces his sister had learned in her music class at school and tried to pick out on the old, out-of-tune upright piano that had belonged to his grandmother.

Suddenly, Rachel turned to look straight at him, her eyes wide and glittering in the faint light coming from the honky-tonk down the road.

"You can't save us all," she said.

A gust of wind slammed into his back, knocking him off balance and catching Rachel's clothes up in its swirling wake, flapping them like a sail. She lost her balance slowly, almost gracefully, and even though he threw himself forward, he couldn't stop her fall.

He crashed into the girder rail in time to hear her scream. It seemed to grow louder and louder, even as she fell farther and farther away. The thirty-foot gorge became a bottomless chasm, and the scream went on and on....

He woke with a start, just in time to hear a scream cut off, followed by dreadful silence.

# Chapter Seven

Taking the stairs two at a time, Seth reached the second-floor landing in seconds. Down the hall, Rachel lay in a crumpled heap at the bottom of a ladder dropped down from an opening in the ceiling.

"Rachel!" Ignoring the aches and pains playing chase through his joints and muscles, he hurried to her side, nearly wilting with relief when she sat up immediately, staring at him with wide, scared eyes. "Are you okay? Are you hurt?"

"I don't know." She sounded winded. "I don't know if I'm okay."

She looked terrified, as if she'd been chased down the ladder by a monster. Tremors rolled through her slim body like a dozen small earthquakes going on inside her, making her teeth rattle. Her fingers dug into his arms.

He wrapped her in a bear hug, cocooning her against his body. She melted into him, clinging like a child.

What the hell had she seen?

"I need to go downstairs," she moaned. "Please, I can't be up here."

He helped her to her feet and led her down to the den, looking around desperately for a bar service. "Do you have any brandy?"

She shook her head as she sat on the sofa. "Dad had liver cancer. We all stopped drinking after the diagnosis."

*Of course.* "Okay, well, maybe some hot tea."

As he started to get up from where he crouched in front of her, she grabbed his hands and held him in place. "Don't go."

"Okay." He settled back into his crouch, stroking her cold fingers between his. "Can you at least tell me what happened?"

"I don't know."

But he could see she did know. She just didn't want to tell him.

A hank of hair had fallen into her face, hiding half her expression from him. He pushed it gently back behind her ear. "Maybe you had a bad dream?"

She shook her head.

"Not a dream?"

She looked less certain this time when she shook her head. "I don't think it was. I've never sleepwalked before."

"Then it probably wasn't a dream," he agreed. The concession didn't seem to give her much comfort. "Do you remember why you went up the ladder? Does it lead to the attic?"

She nodded. "I was dozing. And then I heard the music."

A snippet of memory flashed in his head. Rachel, gliding precariously along the girder rail, humming a song to herself.

"Was it this song?" he asked, humming a few notes.

Her head whipped up, her eyes locking with his. "How did you know?"

The anger in her tone caught him off guard, and he

had to put one hand on the sofa to keep from toppling over. "I dreamed it. Just a minute ago."

Her eyes narrowed. "It's Chopin," she said tightly. "A nocturne. I heard it coming from the attic."

"So you went up to the attic to see where the music was coming from?"

Her lips trembled, and the bracing anger he'd seen in her blue eyes melted into dread. "I went up because I already knew where it was coming from."

He didn't know what she meant. "What did you find?"

"Everything but the body." Her gaze wandered, settling on some point far away.

He stared at her with alarm. "What body?"

Her gaze snapped back to his. "My mother's."

Letting her words sink in, he tried to remember what he knew about her mother's death. It had happened when she was young. He'd been a teenager himself, on the cusp of learning an exciting if larcenous new life at the feet of Cleve Calhoun. The death of some rich woman on the east side of town hadn't registered.

She'd killed herself, he knew. No other details had ever come out, so he'd figured she'd taken pills or slit her wrists or something.

If she'd killed herself in the attic, maybe she'd hung herself. "When you say everything was there but the body—"

"I mean everything," she said flatly. Her voice had gained strength, and her trembling had eased. "There was a plastic drop sheet, just like that night. She hated messes, so she was determined not to make one, even when—" Rachel stopped short, her throat bobbing as she swallowed hard. "The music playing was Chopin's nocturne. And afterward—the blood—"

*Oh my God,* he thought. *She saw it.*

"Did you find her?" he asked gently, hoping that was the extent of what she'd experienced that night, as bad as it must have been.

She looked up at him with haunted eyes. "I saw it happen."

He stared back at her a moment, finally understanding her reaction to whatever she'd witnessed up in the attic. "Oh, Rachel."

She looked away from him. "I saw it again. I know I saw it."

But she wasn't sure, he realized. She was doubting herself. Why?

"Do you want me to go take a look?" he offered.

Her gaze whipped back around to his. "You think I've lost my mind."

He didn't think that, although given her experience in the attic years ago and the stresses of the past few days, he had to wonder if she'd misinterpreted whatever it was she'd seen. "I just think I should take a look. Maybe there's an intruder in the house."

The idea of a third party in the house seemed not to have occurred to her, which made Seth wonder if she suspected him of trying to trick her. The wary looks she was sending his way weren't exactly reassuring. "I'll go with you."

He frowned. "Are you sure?"

She nodded quickly, her eyes narrowing.

It was a test, he realized. He'd been with her ever since she'd fallen out of the attic, so if he were the culprit, everything would be as she'd left it.

It was a chance he'd take. If someone was trying to gaslight her, he might still be in the house. They might still be in danger.

He climbed the ladder first. She waited until he'd

stepped into the attic to start up after him, clutching the rungs with whitened knuckles. She moved slowly, with care, giving him a few seconds to view the room without any comment from her.

It was a small space, rectangular, with a steeply peaked ceiling of exposed rafters. The floor was hardwood planks, unpolished and mostly unfinished, though in the center of the room, large splotches and splashes of dark red wood stain marred the planks.

He looked doubtfully at the stain. In the dim light from the single bare overhead bulb, the splotches of red *did* look like blood. But what about the drop cloth? That was a pretty significant detail for her to have conjured up with her imagination.

Except she hadn't, had she? She'd told him the drop cloth had existed. In the past, on the night of her mother's suicide.

"No." Behind him, Rachel let out a low moan.

He turned to find her staring at the wood stain, her head shaking from side to side.

"I saw the drop cloth," she said. "I did. And there was blood. Wet blood."

Seth looked back at the stain. It was clearly dry. No one would ever mistake it for wet blood. So either Rachel had imagined everything—

Or someone had been here in the attic with her, hiding, and removed the evidence after she'd run away from the terrifying sight.

"You don't believe me," she accused, color rising in her cheeks. "You think I'm crazy."

"No, I don't," he said firmly, hiding his doubts. Until this moment, except when she was clearly under the influence of some sort of drug, Rachel had seemed completely sane and lucid. Plus, he'd worked for her company for over a year now and watched her tackle the tasks of learning her father's lifework with determination and tenacity.

She deserved the benefit of the doubt.

"Where was the drop cloth?" he asked.

She waved toward the stained area. "Right there. Over that stain. It was stretched out flat, covered with blood. Splotches and puddles. Still wet."

She walked slowly to the center of the floor, gazing down at the stain. Her troubled expression made his chest tighten. "I didn't imagine it. I know I didn't."

*Okay, Hammond, think. If you were trying to con her into believing she'd lost her mind, how would you go about it?*

"Who has access to the house?"

She relaxed a little at his pragmatic question. "I do, of course. My stepmother, but she's in North Carolina. Her sister lives in Wilmington, and Diane went to spend a couple of weeks with her. I think my stepbrother, Paul, probably has a key. And my father used to keep a key in his office at the trucking company in case one of us locked ourselves out and there wasn't anyone else around."

"Do you know if it's still there?"

"I don't know. I was planning to go through my dad's office next week and see if there was anything else that needed to be handled." Grief darkened her eyes.

Impulsively, he pulled her into his arms.

She came willingly, pressing her face against the side of his throat. When she drew away from him, she seemed steadier on her feet. "You think someone set me up?"

"I've been asking myself what steps I'd take to try to convince you that you were losing your mind."

"You think that's what's going on?"

"Look at you just a few minutes ago. Shaking like a leaf and not sure you could trust your own eyes."

She looked stricken. Her reaction piqued his curiosity, but he kept his questions to himself. If it was something he needed to know, she'd tell him soon enough.

"Remember how I told you I thought those murders were part of trying to target you?"

She nodded, her expression guarded.

"What if the goal was to make you appear crazy?"

She didn't answer, but her eyes flickered with comprehension. It made sense to her, he realized. Maybe even seemed inevitable.

"Your mother was already dead, and your father was dying. If I were ruthless and wanted to make you doubt your sanity, I'd take steps to isolate you even further. I'd take away your support system. Amelia Sanderson had been your friend since you were both in college, right?" He had learned that much while nosing around town about the murders.

She nodded, a bleak look in her wintry eyes.

"April Billings was your first hire, and you saw a lot of yourself in her, didn't you?" He could tell by the shift in her expression that he'd gotten it right. He usually did, he thought with a hint of shame. It had been one of his most useful talents, his ability to read people, relationships and situations. "And you'd made Coral Vines your own personal rehabilitation project. You'd helped her find a grief counselor to deal with her pain about her husband's death. I bet you'd even given her information about a twelve-step program for her alcohol addiction."

"How do you know this?" she asked in a strangled voice.

"I used to do this for a living. Reading people. Finding out their secrets and figuring out their relationships so I could use the knowledge to my advantage."

She couldn't stop her lip from curling with distaste, though she schooled her expression quickly. It didn't matter. He felt enough disgust for his past for the both of them. "And Marjorie was like a mom to me," she added, filling in the next obvious blank. "My mentor."

"But you still didn't break, did you?" He touched her face before he realized he was going to. He dropped his hand quickly, bracing himself for her rebuke.

But all she did was smile a shaky smile. "No, I didn't break."

"I don't think it's a coincidence you were drugged the night of your father's funeral. You were as vulnerable as you'd ever been at that moment, I would guess. He couldn't let the opportunity pass."

"This doesn't make any sense. It never has. Your sister said she thought these murders were about me, and you said it, too, but why? Why would you think it? Just because I knew them?" She shook her head, clearly not wanting to believe it. "I saw the stories in the papers— Mark Bramlett was connected to serial murders in Nashville, too. What makes you think he was anything more than a sick freak who got off on killing women? Why does everyone think someone hired him?"

She didn't know about Mark Bramlett's last words, he realized. The police hadn't told her.

"I was there when Mark Bramlett died," he said.

"What? Why?"

"I'd tracked down the truck Bramlett used for the murders to help Sutton Calhoun find Ivy Hawkins. You remember Sutton, right? The guy who was investigating April Billings's murder?"

She nodded. "Yeah, he and Ivy came to me for a list of

the trucks we rented out. That's how they found Bramlett."

"I wanted to know why Bramlett killed those women. I knew them all, you know. Amelia was always kind to me, and she didn't have to be. April Billings was full of life and so much potential. I grew up with Coral Vines on Smoky Ridge. She was the sweetest kid there ever was, and after her husband died, I tried to help her out with things around her house she couldn't do herself."

"I didn't know."

"Marjorie Kenner tried to steer me right, back in school. I didn't listen, but I never forgot that she tried." He thought about the kindhearted high school librarian who'd fought for his soul and lost. "I wanted justice for them, too. I wanted to see Bramlett pay."

"Did you?"

He nodded slowly. "I watched him die. But before he went, he said something."

She closed her hand around his wrist, her fingers digging urgently into his flesh. "What?"

"I'd told Ivy Hawkins I thought you were his real target. And as he died, he told her I was right. He said, 'It's all about the girl.'"

Rachel looked horrified. "He said that? Why did no one tell me?"

"I don't know. But I can probably get in touch with Ivy Hawkins if you want confirmation."

Rachel turned away from him, her gaze moving over the attic, settling finally on a darkened corner. "I wonder—" She walked toward the corner, leaving Seth to catch up. "Do you have a light?"

He pulled his keys from his pocket and engaged the small flashlight he kept on the keychain. The narrow beam of light drove shadows out of the dark corner, revealing another trapdoor in the attic floor.

And wedged in the narrow seam of the door was a thin piece of torn plastic.

As Rachel reached out for it, Seth caught her hand. "Fingerprints."

She looked up at him, a gleam of relief in her eyes. "It's from the drop cloth. It was really here." She tried to tug the door open, but it didn't budge.

Seth reached into another pocket and pulled out his Swiss Army knife. Tucked into one compartment in the case was a small pair of tweezers. He used them to pluck the piece of plastic out of the trapdoor seam.

The flimsy plastic was shaped like a triangle, smooth on two sides and ragged on the third, where it had apparently ripped away from the bigger sheet of plastic. In one corner of the plastic, a drop of red liquid was almost dry. Seth caught a quick whiff of a sharp iron odor.

"Is that—"

He nodded. "Blood."

She put her hand over her mouth.

"Rachel, whoever did this could still be in the house."

Her eyes went wide. "Oh my God."

"Where does this trapdoor lead?"

"A mudroom off the kitchen, I think. I've never used this exit, but there's a trapdoor in the ceiling of that room."

"Are there any weapons in this house?"

She swallowed hard. "My dad had a Glock. He kept it in his bedroom drawer. I guess it's still there."

"Do you know how to use it?"

She looked sick. "Yes."

"Let's get you downstairs and locked in that room. Then I'll take a look around."

"Don't you need the gun, then?"

He shook his head. "With my record, a gun is more trouble than it's worth." He had the Swiss Army knife, and he was pretty good at fighting with whatever weapons he could find. Unless their intruder was carrying a gun himself—and Seth had a feeling he wasn't—Seth would be safe enough. He wasn't the target. Rachel was.

Rachel appeared unnerved until they reached the second-floor hallway, clear of the ladder. She seemed to calm down once she was on solid ground.

She unlocked her father's gun from its case and, with more or less steady hands, went about the task of loading ammunition into the magazine while Seth watched. She met his gaze with scared but determined eyes. "Done."

"I'll be right back." He closed the door behind him, waiting until he heard her engage the lock before he went in search of the intruder.

The stairs creaked as he descended to the first floor, making him wince. He paused at the bottom and listened carefully for any sound of movement. He heard rain battering the windows and siding. Electricity humming in the walls. His own quickened breathing.

But no other sounds.

He crossed the main hallway, checking room by room until he was satisfied they were empty. Reaching the kitchen, he stood in the center of the warm room, struck unexpectedly by the memory of his body brushing against Rachel's here earlier that afternoon, back when his worst worry was whether or not his body betrayed his unanticipated arousal.

He'd give anything to go back to that moment right about now.

The mudroom was off the kitchen, she'd said. He went to the small door on the other side of the refrigerator and listened through the wood for any sound on the other side. He heard nothing but silence.

Backtracking to the kitchen counter, he went to the knife block by the sink and selected a long fillet knife. He crossed back to the mudroom, gripped the knife tightly in his right hand and opened the door.

Nobody jumped him as he entered. The room was empty.

He looked for signs of recent occupation. At first glance, the room appeared undisturbed. No mud on the floor, no telltale drops of blood from the drop cloth the intruder must have taken with him.

But there wouldn't be, would there? That had been the point of the drop cloth, to keep the evidence contained for easy, complete removal. Rachel's tormenter wanted her to doubt her own mind, which meant he couldn't leave any clues behind.

Maybe he'd heard Seth's voice earlier, outside the attic when he'd first responded to Rachel's cries. That might have pushed him to make a hasty exit at the first opportunity, which had come when Seth had taken Rachel to the den to recover from the shock of what she'd seen.

The intruder had moved fast, rolling up the drop cloth and the evidence it contained, and made a quick escape through the mudroom hatch. But in his haste, he hadn't realized one corner of the drop cloth had snagged in the trapdoor seam.

Had he taken the time to fold the drop cloth into a more manageable square before he left the attic? Possibly not. Which meant he'd have been moving at a clip, trying to get out of the house before he was discovered. Maybe he'd left other evidence behind besides the torn piece of plastic sheeting.

The back door was locked when Seth tried the handle,

but anyone with a key could have locked it behind him as he left. Using the hem of his borrowed T-shirt, Seth turned the dead bolt and opened the door to the backyard. Beyond the mudroom door, he found a flagstone patio, not the muddy ground as he'd hoped. Not that it would have mattered, he supposed. With the rain coming down in torrents, any footprints the intruder might have left would have been obliterated in seconds.

He closed the door against the driving rain and turned, looking at the mudroom from a different angle. The room was essentially bare of furnishings save for a low, built-in bench with storage space beneath. There was nothing in any of the storage bins, suggesting the room was rarely used.

He looked at the trapdoor in the mudroom ceiling. It was two floors down from the attic. What lay between the attic trap door and the one in the mudroom?

Only one way to find out.

He caught the latch and pulled the trapdoor open. A wooden ladder unfolded and dropped to the ground.

Tightening his grip on the knife, he stepped onto the ladder and started to climb.

# *Chapter Eight*

Seth had been gone forever, hadn't he? Rachel checked her watch and saw that only a few minutes had passed.

*Time crawls when you're scared witless.*

She had settled on the cedar chest at the foot of her father's bed, trying not to think about his final moments here, as he breathed his last, labored breaths and finally let go.

Someone had changed the sheets and neatened the room after the coroner's visit. She and Diane had both been far too shattered to have thought of such a thing, so it must have been Paul. He'd been a rock for them both, a steady hand here at home and at the trucking company, as well.

He hadn't always been a big fan of his mother's second marriage—he'd worried that their relationship would make things awkward between him and her father at work, for one thing—but for the past few months, as her father fought the cancer that had ultimately taken him, Paul had put in a lot of long hours at work, helping take up the slack.

She wasn't sure what she'd have done without him. So why hadn't she called him to help her this morning instead of depending on strangers? Why did she feel certain, even now, that a man as enigmatic and unpredictable as Seth Hammond was the best person to help her?

A noise coming from the other side of the room froze her midthought. She picked up the gun from where she'd set it on the cedar chest beside her and turned toward the sound.

There. It came again. It sounded like footsteps coming from just inside her father's closet.

Then came the rattle of the doorknob turning.

Her chest tightening, Rachel lifted the small pistol, trying to remember what she knew about a good shooting stance. She hadn't done enough shooting to internalize these rules, damn it! Why hadn't she practiced more? What was the point of learning to shoot if you couldn't remember the lessons when it counted?

*Fighter's stance,* her sluggish brain shouted. Weak foot forward, strong foot back and slightly out, lean into the shot.

The door opened slowly, and Rachel's heart skipped a beat.

Seth Hammond emerged from the darkened closet, spotted the barrel of the gun aimed squarely at his chest and immediately ducked and rolled.

He hissed a profanity from behind the bed. "I think I just lost ten years of my life!"

She laid the gun on the chest and hurried around to where he crouched, his head down and his chest heaving. "How did you get into that closet?"

"That's where the trapdoor in the mudroom leads," he told her, lifting his head to look at her. "There's a hatch in the top of the closet that leads up to the attic. It has a pin lock hasp—that's why you couldn't open it from the attic."

*Of course,* she thought. There was a whole level between the attic and the mudroom. Why hadn't she thought of that?

He pushed to his feet. "I didn't find any evidence downstairs in the mudroom, but I couldn't find a light in the closet for a look around."

"There's a light switch, but it's in a weird place." She opened the closet door and reached inside, feeling for the switch positioned inside one of the built-in shoe hutches. The overhead light came on, revealing the roomy walk-in closet her father and Diane had shared during their marriage.

Diane's belongings took up most of the room, with her father's clothes and shoes filling only a quarter of the space. The area was neat and organized, Rachel knew, because while Diane could be flighty about many things, she was dead serious about her clothes and accessories, and she kept her things where she could locate them with a quick glance.

Which made the shoe box jutting at an odd angle from one of the shelves seem all the more out of place.

Rachel crossed to the box and saw that the top was slightly displaced, as well. And on the corner of the bright yellow box, a dark crimson smear was still glistening, not quite dry.

"More blood," she murmured, feeling ill.

Seth came up behind her, a solid wall of reassuring heat. She squelched the urge to lean back against him, aware that she was already leaning on him more than was probably wise.

He seemed remarkably steady for a man who'd sustained a head injury just a few hours earlier, showing few signs of pain or disorientation since he'd come here with her. On the contrary, he'd been a rock just as she'd had her feet knocked out from beneath her.

*What if that's not a coincidence?*

She shook off the thought. Seth had earned a little trust from her, hadn't he? A little benefit of the doubt.

"There was a lot of blood on that drop cloth," she said aloud. "Too much."

"May not be human, though." Seth's voice was reassuring. "It wouldn't have to be. Easy enough to get animal blood to set this up, and you could do it without breaking any laws."

She turned to look at him. "He's worried about breaking the law?"

"Never break the law if you don't have to. First rule of the con game."

"I thought the first rule of the con game was that you couldn't con an honest man." She wasn't sure where she'd heard that, but she'd always considered it to be a reasonable assumption. Honest men didn't fall for deals that were too good to be true.

Seth shook his head. "Honest men can be conned. Everyone has a price, even if the price is honorable." He grimaced. "I guess never breaking the law if you don't have to isn't necessarily the first rule of the con game, but it was the first rule Cleve Calhoun taught me."

She didn't miss the hint of affection in his voice when he spoke of his old mentor. He may have walked away from the life Calhoun had taught him, but clearly he hadn't stopped caring about the old man.

"Whoever's behind this isn't used to skirting the law," he added.

"How can you say that? He's already hired someone to kill four women. He's drugged me and probably killed Davis Rogers—oh God." Her voice cracked. "Davis. I wonder if the police have found him yet."

"I think we'd have already heard from them if they had."

She closed her eyes, fighting off her growing despair. She needed to stay strong. Not let this mess destroy her.

Not again.

"What I meant about this guy not being used to breaking the law is he's hired other people to do it so far," Seth added quietly.

"What makes you think he didn't beat up Davis himself?"

"If he was a practiced killer, he'd have killed those women himself. But he didn't. He hired someone else to do it. He doesn't want his hands dirty if he can avoid it."

Rachel heard something in Seth's voice that pinged her radar, but he spoke again before she could pin it down.

"What do you want to do now?" he asked.

"I think we need to call the police."

He nodded, though he clearly found the idea unappealing. "Okay. But call Antoine Parsons directly, not nine-one-one."

That made sense—Antoine already knew the details of the case. He seemed fair and honest, too. "You don't have to be here for it," she offered, aware that he still looked uncomfortable.

He shot her a sheepish grin. "Yeah, I do. I'm a material witness."

She started toward the phone but stopped halfway, turning back to look at him. "Seth, do you have any idea who's doing this?"

"Who's doing it? No." He shook his head firmly. "But I have an idea *why* he's doing it."

To Antoine Parson's credit, he didn't automatically start grilling Seth about why he'd been there with Rachel when the craziness started. First, he caught them up on the search for Davis Rogers. "We've searched the woods behind the bed-and-breakfast, but there's a lot of wilderness to cover in that area, and if the point of knocking out Mr. Hammond was to keep him from calling the paramedics to help Rogers, it's unlikely they'd hide the body anywhere near those woods."

Rachel flinched at his use of the word *body.* Seth's chest ached in sympathy, and he barely kept himself from giving her a comforting hug.

"We've also contacted the police in Virginia to let them know we have a report that Rogers is missing," Antoine added. "If he contacts his family or any of his friends back home, they've been asked to let us know."

Antoine had brought along a uniformed police officer to help him with the interviews. The two of them separated Seth and Rachel to get their independent statements.

Antoine took Seth's, naturally. But to Seth's relief, he approached his questions in a straightforward way and seemed to believe Seth's answers. "Bold, just walking in here and setting something up that way," the detective remarked. "Especially with you both right here in the house."

"I'm not sure whoever did this knew I was here," Seth said. "My car's in the shop having the tires fixed. The only car here is Rachel's. He might have assumed she was alone."

Antoine gave a slow nod. "And you didn't see anything of what Ms. Davenport saw in the attic?"

"Just the piece of drop cloth plastic I gave you and a stain on a shoe box in the closet that might be blood. But I think I did hear the music that Rachel heard playing." He told Antoine about his dream, leaving out the part about Rachel on the bridge girder. "I know it was just a dream, but how did I dream that particular song at that particular time?"

"Would be a hell of a coincidence," Antoine agreed. "Do you think this is connected to the previous murders?"

"Of course."

"Of course." Antoine looked thoughtful. "What's in this for you, Hammond?"

*Ah,* Seth thought. *Now we get to the grilling part.* "I knew the murder victims. I liked them, and I like Rachel Davenport, too. Her father took a chance on me when he hired me at the trucking company when most people around here wouldn't spit on me if I was on fire."

Antoine smiled a little. "I wish I could feel sorry for you, but…"

"I'm not the bad guy here."

"No, I don't think you are," Antoine agreed.

The other policeman, Gavin McElroy, joined Antoine in a huddle near the doorway of the den, leaving Seth and Rachel alone across the room.

Seth crossed to where she stood near the windows, rubbing her arms as if she was cold. "You okay?"

"Yeah." She managed a smile. "I'm sure I sounded crazy to poor Officer McElroy."

He heard a faint undertone to her words that was beginning to make a bleak sort of sense to him. She was very concerned about appearing sane, understandably. After all, her mother had committed suicide.

"You're not crazy," he told her firmly. The look of gratitude she sent his way made his stomach hurt.

Did she fear her mother's instability was hereditary? She wasn't much younger than her mother had been when she'd died. It was probably something she worried about now and then.

Maybe more often than now and then.

Did the person now tormenting her know that she harbored such a fear? The two direct attacks on her so far seemed aimed less at hurting her than convincing her she was losing her mind—first the drugging incident, inducing a state of near psychosis, then the gaslighting attempt in the attic, designed to make her believe she was seeing things that didn't exist.

Going back even further, the murders of people who'd been important to her seemed ominously significant now, too. If he'd wanted to drive Rachel to mental instability, he could think of no better way to prepare the ground than to brutally eliminate all of her emotional underpinnings. Every one of those murders had been a powerful blow to Rachel Davenport. Could that effect have been their entire purpose?

"You said you thought you knew why someone is targeting me," Rachel murmured, keeping her voice too low for Antoine and Gavin to hear. "Did you tell Detective Parsons?"

"Not yet. I wanted to run it by you first."

"You could have told me before they got here." She sounded a little annoyed. He'd kept his thoughts to himself while they'd waited because he needed to think through his suspicions before he committed to them. If he was wrong, he might be pushing the investigation in the wrong direction, putting Rachel in graver danger.

But after talking to Antoine, and realizing the police didn't have a clue what was driving the attacks surrounding Rachel, he was growing more certain he was right.

Someone wanted Rachel out of the way, and he was pretty sure it had everything to do with Davenport Trucking.

"If you were to resign as CEO of Davenport Trucking tomorrow, who becomes CEO?" he asked quietly.

She shot him a puzzled look. "There's a trustee board my father set up before he died. If something happened to me, they would make the decision, I think. I don't know. My father knew I was committed to running his company. I gave him my word."

"But accidents happen. People get high and fall off bridges, right?"

Her gaze snapped up again. "You think all of this is about getting me out of the way at Davenport?"

"What if you were deemed mentally unstable? Would that get you out of the way?"

She looked horrified. "Probably."

Antoine and Officer McElroy walked back to where they stood, ending the conversation for the moment. "We'll get a lab crew here later as soon as we can to process the access points to the attic," Antoine told them. "Meanwhile, Officer McElroy is going to stay here to preserve the chain of evidence until they arrive."

"Do we have to stay here?" Rachel asked bluntly.

Antoine looked surprised. "No, I don't suppose so, but I'm not sure you should be out on the roads in this weather."

"I don't plan to go far." She gave Seth an imperious look that did more to relieve his worries about her mental state than anything he'd seen so far. She looked like a pissed-off warrior princess, one he had a feeling he'd follow to the end of the universe if that's what she desired.

He was in serious, serious trouble.

THE CABIN NEAR the base of Copperhead Ridge had been in her father's family since her great-grandfather had built it with his own hands in the late twenties. Or so the story went. Rachel looked at the slightly shabby facade with a fond smile as she pulled the Honda into the gravel driveway near the front door.

"What is this place?" Seth had been quiet for most of the short drive, but once she killed the engine, his low drawl broke the silence.

"According to family lore, my great-grandfather built this place to cover a family moonshining operation during Prohibition." She slanted a look his way. "I'm not sure that's entirely true."

He met her look with a hint of a smile. "Good stories rarely are."

"I think it might have been embellished to give the Davenports a little hillbilly cred." She smiled. "We were damned Yankees, you see. My great-grandfather was the third son of a shipbuilding family in Maryland that had only enough money to support two sons. So he was left to find his own way in the cold, cruel world."

"And chose Bitterwood, Tennessee?" Seth gave her a skeptical look.

"There's beauty here, you know. It's not all harsh."

"Guess it depends on what part of Bitterwood you come from."

She conceded the point. "My grandfather told me his daddy knew from the moment he set eyes on Bitterwood that it was home."

Seth's expression softened. "I guess I can't argue with that. I always end up back here no matter how far I roam."

"I love this place." She nodded toward the cabin. "My grandmother was a Bitterwood native. Her roots go back to the first settlers. She and my grandfather would bring me here during summer vacations from school and we'd rough it." She laughed. "Well, I considered it roughing it."

In fact, for a primitive log cabin, the place was relatively luxurious. A removable window unit air conditioner cooled the place in the heat of summer, and a woodstove kept it cozy on all but the coldest of winter days. It had been wired with electricity a couple of decades ago, when the town borders extended close enough to the cabin to make it feasible. And with a nearby cell tower, she never had much trouble getting a phone signal.

Seth climbed the porch steps behind her, carrying their bags. She'd packed a few things before leaving her house, and they'd stopped by the bungalow on Smoky Ridge where Seth lived in order to pick up clothes for him, as well.

The shabby old house belonged to Cleve Calhoun, the con man who'd brought Seth into that lifestyle, Seth had told her, his expression defensive. He'd moved in with Cleve again a few years back, after the older man had suffered a debilitating stroke. Now that Cleve was at a rehab center in Knoxville for the next few weeks, Seth was thinking about looking for a place of his own.

Rachel wondered what sort of place a man like Seth would like, watching with curiosity as his sharp green eyes took in the decor of the cabin. She'd decorated it herself several years ago, when her grandfather had left it to her in his will. She'd been twenty-two, fresh out of college and torn between sadness at one part of her life passing and a whole vista of opportunity spreading out before her.

As a permanent place of residence, the cabin posed too many problems to be practical, but she had always treated it as an escape when life started to become overwhelming.

Was that why she'd come here now?

"Nice digs," he said with a faint smile.

"I love this place," she admitted.

"I can see why." He looked at her. "Do you come here often?"

"When I need to."

He nodded as if he understood. "Why did you bring me here? You don't bring people here normally, do you?"

She looked at him through narrowed eyes, a little spooked by how easily he could read her. "No, I don't."

"Because it's a refuge."

"Yes." She felt naked.

Suddenly, he looked vulnerable, as well. "Thank you. For trusting me enough to bring me here."

His rapid change of demeanor caught her by surprise. She hadn't realized, until that moment, that she had any sort of power over him. He'd seemed so sure, so in charge, that she hadn't given any thought to being able to influence him in any way.

It was an unexpectedly heady feeling, one that made her feel reckless.

And alive.

He was beautiful, she thought, standing there in the middle of her haven. Beautiful and feral, constantly on the edge of flight. Despite the facade of civilization, despite his obvious attempts to fight his own wild instincts, he would never be fully tame. He would never be genteel or domesticated. He'd always be a wild card.

And she'd never wanted a man more than she wanted him, in spite of that unpredictability.

Or maybe because of it.

"I wanted you here with me," she said aloud, unsure that he would understand what she meant by it. Not sure she wanted him to.

But she should have known better. He had a wild thing's instinct for reading another creature's motives.

*Fight or flight,* she thought. Which would he choose? To run?

Or to engage?

When he moved, it was swift and fierce, the decisive action of a predator with a singular purpose. He came to an abrupt stop in front of her, his gaze so intense it set off tremors low in her belly. "Do you know what you're getting into?"

Probably not, but she had no intention of retreating. "Do you?"

His mouth curved in response. She imagined the feel of those lips on hers, and the tremors inside her spread in waves until she felt as if she were going to crumble apart.

Then he touched her, a light brush of fingertips against her jaw, sparking fire in her blood.

She rose, closing the space between them until her breasts flattened against his chest. His wiry arms ensnared her, crushing her even closer, until his breath heated her cheeks. "I'm dangerous," he whispered.

She met his gaze. "I know."

Threading her fingers through his crisp, dark hair, she kissed him.

# *Chapter Nine*

Her mouth was hot and sweet, the fierce thrust of her tongue against his pouring gasoline on the fire in his belly until he thought he'd explode. He wanted her more than anything he'd ever wanted his whole life, a realization that scared the hell out of him even as it drove him to walk her backward until they ran up against the cabin wall.

She made a low, explosive sound against his mouth as her back flattened against the polished logs. Her legs parted, making room for his hips to settle flush to hers, and any hope of hiding the effect she had on his body was gone as he thrust helplessly against her hips. Neither the borrowed sweatpants nor her thin cotton yoga pants offered much of a barrier between their bodies, making it all too easy to take what they both seemed desperately to want.

*Stop,* his mind begged him. *Think.*

There was a reason he was still alone, a reason why he hadn't coaxed one of the pretty Tennessee mountain girls to take a chance on a man like him. Even reformed, he wasn't much of a catch. He was rough around the edges and wild at heart. A girl willing to settle for less than perfect could still do better.

Rachel Davenport didn't have to settle. If all she

wanted was a quick roll in the hay with a hard-bodied redneck, maybe he'd give it a go, but not when she was this vulnerable. Not the day after her father's funeral, the day she'd lost another man who was important to her.

Not the day she'd had a nerve-shattering scare and probably wanted nothing more than to feel something besides fear.

As he started to pull back, her hands moved with sureness over his body, sliding down his back to cup his buttocks, pulling him closer. For a second, everything resembling lucid thought rushed out of his head, driven away by raw male hunger for completion. He drove his hips against hers again, making her whimper. The sound was maddening, fueling his lust to the edge of control.

She tugged his shirt upward, baring his belly to the light caress of her fingertips. She dragged her mouth away from his and pressed a hot kiss against the center of his chest, her tongue dancing lightly over the curve of his pectoral muscle.

She looked up at him, her blue eyes drunk with desire. "Is that good?" she asked, her thumb tracing a circle around his left nipple. "Did you like that?"

"Yes," he breathed.

She bent her head and dropped a soft kiss along the ridge of his rib cage. "And that?"

He knew where she was headed. He knew if he let her keep going, he wouldn't be able to make any sort of coherent decision about right and wrong.

There had been a time, he realized, when the question of right and wrong wouldn't have occurred to him at all.

Did he really want to be that man again?

With a groan, he threaded his fingers through her hair and urged her to look up at him. She appeared confused but also wildly aroused, her cheeks flushed and dewy, her lips dark from his kisses.

He kissed her again, a long, slow kiss that had an oddly fortifying effect on his resolve. Rachel Davenport deserved to be wooed, with kisses that went somewhere besides straight to sex.

Even if he wasn't the man who could give her that.

When he let her go, she slumped back against the wall, staring at him through half-closed eyes. Her breath was swift and ragged, her hair a tangled curtain around her face. "Seth?"

"This isn't really what you want," he said, keeping a careful distance.

Her brow furrowed. "You don't get to make that decision."

"Okay. It isn't what *I* want."

Her gaze dropped pointedly to his sweatpants, where his body betrayed exactly what he wanted. When her blue eyes rose to meet his again, there was triumph in them. "Really."

"Rachel, please." He turned his back on her, pacing toward the front window, where night had fallen early due to the rain. His reflection stared back at him, the wild-eyed gaze of a man on the edge.

"If you think you're being noble—"

"I don't think I'm capable of being noble. I just want to be fair."

She let out an exasperated sigh. "You think I'm not in my right mind."

He shook his head, even though it was what he thought, in a way. "I think we both want to forget the past couple of days, however we can make that happen. And maybe that seems like a good idea right now, but it won't once we've crossed a line we can't uncross."

He waited for her to respond, but she remained silent. Finally, he dared a quick look at her. She still leaned against the wall, her gaze on him. Some of the heat in her eyes had died, however, as if his words had sunk in and extinguished the fire inside her.

"I don't do one-night stands," she admitted after another long, silent moment. "I don't think that's how I was looking at this."

He didn't know if her confession made him feel better or worse. Maybe a little of both, he decided, though her admission that she saw him as more than a body on which to slake her lust certainly complicated matters.

"I'm not good for you," he said simply.

"You're not bad for me."

He laughed a little. "There are hundreds of people out there who'd beg to differ."

"You've done bad things. But you're not bad. Bad people don't try to change. They don't see the need."

He felt enough in control to face her completely. He pressed his back against the hardwood frame around the panes, concentrating on the discomfort and giving his body a chance to cool down and regain control. "There's a difference between wanting to be good and being good."

"Only in degrees."

She was stubborn, he thought. And naive. "In a few days, once we figure all this out, you're going to look back at this moment and thank me for keeping my head."

Her eyes rolled upward. "You give me any more of that paternalistic hogwash and it won't take a few days."

*Fair enough,* he thought. "I don't want regrets, either."

The look she shot his way was utterly wicked, catching him by surprise. "You wouldn't have regretted it."

He laughed. "Maybe not."

She lifted her chin, her expression shifting back to

cool neutral. "Okay. I get that this is a volatile situation with really rotten timing. And I know we're not what anyone would consider a suitable match. So, you win. We don't let this happen again, not while we're trying to figure out what's happening to me and why."

He felt a squirm of disappointment that she'd conceded so quickly, but he pushed that unhelpful thought aside. "I do think someone should be with you at all times, though. You've already had two strange incidents on top of whatever happened to your friend Davis, plus the previous murders. I don't think it's safe for you to be alone right now."

"Should I hire a bodyguard?" She sounded reluctant.

Seth thought about his orders from Adam Brand. Brand, for reasons Seth didn't quite understand, had hired Seth to keep an eye on Rachel. So far, he hadn't shared that fact with her, since Brand hadn't given him permission to approach her on an official level.

But maybe it was time to talk to Brand again. He was overdue to give the man an update. He'd try to make the FBI agent see that Rachel deserved to know everything that was going on.

"I can do it," he said in answer to her question. "I can protect you."

Her dark eyebrows notched up. "I thought we decided to keep our distance from each other."

"We agreed not to…get busy with each other," he said with a wry grin. "Not quite the same thing."

"One would certainly make the other harder to resist."

True, but letting Rachel Davenport out of his sight for long was not something he was willing to contemplate. He might not understand Brand's interest in Rachel, but he understood his own. He wasn't going to let her become a casualty in whatever game her tormenter was playing.

Especially now that he had a pretty good idea why she'd been targeted.

But before he told her his theory, he needed to talk to Brand. The FBI agent could pull some strings and see if the local cops were making any progress in finding Davis Rogers, for one thing. Antoine had claimed to be forthcoming, but Seth didn't kid himself. The cops would never trust him, not really, and nothing guaranteed Antoine would keep him in the loop.

Seth had a feeling what happened to Rogers might be more than just collateral damage aimed at weakening Rachel's hold on reality. Rogers had seen her the night before, at Smoky Joe's. What if he'd seen or heard something that could incriminate the person who was really behind these attacks on her?

"Rachel, this morning at Sequoyah House, you said you talked to Davis Rogers before you heard the thud and his phone cut off, right?"

She looked puzzled by the change of topic. "I didn't really understand what he meant by what he was saying, but I guess he must have met me last night at some point. He said something about being sorry about what he did."

Joe Breslin had said the man Rachel was with had made a pass at her. Could that have been why Davis Rogers had felt the need to apologize? "Can you remember what he said exactly?"

Her brow furrowed. "He said he'd been trying to reach me—I guess that makes sense. My phone was locked in my car. Then he said he needed to apologize about last night—oh!" She crossed to where she'd laid her fleece jacket on the back of the sofa and pulled her cell phone from the pocket. "I played this for the police but not for you."

She punched a couple of buttons and a male voice

came out of the phone's tinny speaker. "Rachel, it's Davis again. Look, I'm sorry about last night, but he seemed to think you might be receptive. I've really missed you. I didn't like leaving you in that place. Please call me back so I can apologize."

"*He* thought you might be receptive," Seth repeated. That jibed with what Joe had told him, but who was the "he" Rogers had been talking about?

"I think maybe he tried to kiss me or something."

"And you didn't let him."

She shot Seth a look. "I broke up with Davis years ago. I still care about him, and I desperately hope you're wrong about how bad his condition was and that we find him alive and okay. But I'm not in love with him anymore."

"Is he in love with you?"

"I don't think he ever was," she said flatly. "I'm not sure Davis loves anyone quite as much as he loves himself." She pressed her fingers against her lips. "God, that sounds terrible, especially since he could be dead because he came here to see me."

"Remember how I told you I went to talk to Smoky Joe this morning, and that's how I knew to look for Davis?"

She nodded.

"Joe said the man you were with made a pass at you, and you rebuffed him. I figure that man must have been Davis Rogers."

"Why didn't you tell me before?"

"I thought it was something you'd prefer to remember on your own."

Her expression took on a slightly haughty air, reminding him that no matter how tempting he might find her, and how receptive she might be, there was a whole lifetime of differences between them, in experiences, in education, in culture and in outlook. "You had no right to make that decision for me."

"Won't happen again," he snapped back.

She closed her eyes. "I'm sorry. I shouldn't have barked at you."

His anger ebbed as quickly as it had risen. He had no right to get up on his high horse considering he was still keeping the secret about Adam Brand. "No harm done."

"I wonder what he meant—that 'he' seemed to think I might be receptive to Davis's advances," Rachel murmured thoughtfully. "Who's the 'he' Davis is talking about?"

"I was wondering that, too."

"I don't think Davis knows anyone here in Bitterwood besides me. I mean, he knew my dad, of course, but my father's dead. I guess he might have met Diane once—she and my dad married around the time Davis and I broke up—"

"What about your stepbrother?"

"Paul?" She frowned. "I don't think so. We've gotten fairly friendly over the past few months, dealing with the company and taking care of my father's last wishes, but—" She shook her head. "We were both adults when our parents met. We didn't form any kind of family bond, and I can't imagine him giving Davis advice about my love life."

Bailey didn't seem the matchmaker type, Seth conceded. Or the criminal type. He was an efficient, if perpetually distracted, office manager, helping George Davenport and his daughter keep the company going. But company scuttlebutt notwithstanding, Seth had never thought Paul seemed to want to run the company.

But someone did.

"How can we find out who's next in line for the CEO job if you can't step in?" he asked.

Rachel looked up at him. "The only thing I know for sure is that, until my father's will is executed and I'm declared in charge, the company is under the control of a trust. And even then, the trust managers can make a change within the first year if I were to die. In other words, I can't put the disposition of the CEO job in my own will until I've run the company for at least a year."

"What if you couldn't take the job from the outset?"

"I don't know. It hasn't been an issue, since I already agreed to take on the responsibility."

"Do you regret it?" he asked out of curiosity.

"Agreeing to run the company?" Her brow furrowed, and she gave the question the thought it deserved. "I don't regret keeping my father's company alive. I don't regret the time I spent with my dad learning the ropes, or the peace it gave him to know the company would be staying in the family."

"That's not entirely what I asked."

"I miss being a librarian," she admitted with a faint smile. "But I can volunteer on weekends. Or take time out to go read to the kids on story day."

"Is that enough?"

"It will be." Her voice was firm. "It has to be."

A shrill noise split the tense silence that fell briefly between them. They both reached for their cell phones.

It was Rachel's phone. "Hello?"

She listened for a moment, her expression so tight it made Seth's chest hurt. "Yes, I understand." Another brief pause and she added, "Yes. I can do that. Okay. Thank you."

She hung up the phone, her expression carefully still as she slowly lifted her gaze to meet Seth's. What her features lacked in expressiveness, her blue eyes made up for, blazing with pain and fear.

"What is it?" he asked carefully.

Her throat bobbed with a deep swallow. "That was Antoine Parsons. A motorist on the Great Smoky Mountains Parkway pulled over near Sevierville to take a picture of the mountains and spotted a man's body lying about twenty feet down an incline. The Sevier County police called the Bitterwood P.D. because of the APB they'd put out on Davis."

"Is it him?"

"He didn't have any identification on him, but he does have a few identifying marks. They want me to take a look at the body and see if it's him."

"No," he said flatly.

Her eyebrows lifted. "No?"

"They can't ask you to look at a body like that," he said firmly, remembering how the man in the bushes had looked. His recall of the event had been coming back to him slowly but surely, and what he remembered of the man's condition only strengthened his resolve. "The man I saw in the bushes was badly beaten. You might not even be able to recognize him—his face was a mess—"

"I don't think it's his face they want me to look at," she said quietly. "He has birthmarks and scars on his body that I'd be able to identify."

The sudden, entirely inappropriate flood of jealousy burning through his system only made him angrier—at himself, at the police for putting her in such a horrible position and, most of all, at the monster who was wreaking havoc all around her life for what seemed, to Seth, the most ridiculously petty reason he could think of—control of a moderately successful midsize trucking company.

How could the job of running Davenport Trucking be

worth five murders and the wholesale destruction of Rachel's life? It made no sense, but it was the only logical motive Seth had been able to come up with after weeks of pondering the question.

What was he missing?

"If you go, I'm going with you," he said firmly.

She sent him a look of gratitude. "I'd appreciate that."

He looked down at his borrowed clothes. "I'd better change."

"Right." She waved toward a door to the right. "There's a bedroom behind that door. You can have it tonight."

He took his overnight bag into the bedroom and closed the door behind him. As he dressed, he took a moment to call Adam Brand for an update.

The FBI agent sounded harried when he answered. "Not the greatest time, Seth—"

"A lot's happened." He outlined the events of the day as economically as he could. "I'm about to go with Rachel to take a look at the body."

"This is bad." Brand didn't sound surprised, Seth noticed.

"But not unexpected?"

There was a brief pause on Brand's end of the line. "Not entirely."

"You're not going to tell me what you know, are you?"

"Not yet. Just keep an eye on Ms. Davenport and let me know everything that happens. I promise I'll tell you what I know as soon as I have all my ducks in a row on my end."

"I'm going to tell her I'm working for the FBI."

"No."

"I'm not comfortable lying to her."

"Seth, one of the reasons you've been so valuable to us is the fact that you're a damned good liar. Don't pretend you're suddenly a paragon of virtue. Just do what you do well and don't try to do my part of the job."

"I'm not going to keep lying to her," Seth insisted firmly. "I don't need your permission. I'm just giving you a little warning."

"You could screw things up badly if you tell her."

*I could screw things up worse if I don't,* he thought. "I'll tell her she has to be discreet. She'll understand. She can be trusted."

"If it gets around that the FBI is looking into some little stalker case in Bitterwood, Tennessee, it could screw up a very big, ongoing investigation."

"An investigation into what?"

"I can't tell you that." Brand had the decency to sound as if he regretted keeping Seth in the dark, at least. But Seth was losing patience with the skullduggery.

"Good night, Adam." He used Brand's first name deliberately. Adam Brand wasn't his boss, even if he paid the bills, and Seth would be damned if he'd kowtow to the man.

He hung up and tucked his phone in his back pocket. Out in the front room, he found Rachel at the window, her forehead pressed against the windowpane. At the sound of his footsteps, she turned to look at him. She'd been crying, though her eyes were mostly dry now.

Forgetting his promise to keep his distance, he crossed to where she stood, wrapping her up in a fierce hug. She stood stiff for a second before she relaxed in his arms, her cheek against his collarbone. Her arms curled around his waist, pulling him closer.

"Tell me I can do this," she said.

He wanted to tell her she didn't have to. But he'd seen the desperation in her eyes, the fierce need to be in control.

To be all right.

He released a slow, deep breath. "You can do this."

She nodded, her expression firming into iron-hard determination. "Let's go." She let go of him and walked slowly to the door, leaving him to follow.

# Chapter Ten

She'd seen death twice in her life. First at the age of fifteen, when her mother's madness had led her to suicide. Some details were fuzzy in her memory but not all. Rachel still remembered the stark moment when she'd realized her mother had gone and wasn't coming back.

More recently, she'd watched her father die, a peaceful drift from slumber to utter stillness, protected from the cruelties of his life's end by the drugs his doctor had given him to make it easier to let go. They'd dulled his pain and given him a peace in death that his disease had denied him in life.

But until the moment the Sevier County morgue attendant pulled back the sheet on the battered body of Davis Rogers, she'd never seen death resulting from murder.

His face was battered almost beyond recognition, but the hourglass-shaped birthmark on his left biceps and the long white scar on his right knee filled in the blanks for her. It had been nearly seven years since she'd been in any kind of relationship with Davis, but he'd kept fit, the intervening years doing little to change the body she'd once known intimately.

Grief gouged a hole in her heart, and she turned away after nodding to the deputy sheriff who'd accompanied them into the morgue.

Seth stood just behind her, and it seemed as natural as breathing to walk into his arms when he reached out to her. He pulled her close for a moment before leading her out into the corridor, where the air seemed immediately lighter.

"I'm sorry," he murmured against her hair.

She wanted to cry, felt it burning its way into her chest, but she let it rise no further. She wasn't going to fall apart, especially not here in the midst of strangers like the deputy, who watched them both through narrowed eyes.

A few feet down the hallway, Antoine Parsons pushed away from the wall and crossed to where she, Seth and the deputy stood. "Is that the man you saw at Sequoyah House?" he asked Seth.

"Same clothes. Same condition." Seth moved his hand comfortingly up and down Rachel's back, but she felt tension gathering in him like a thunderstorm rising up a mountain. "I didn't think he had much of a chance of making it without help."

"We're still working on cause of death." The deputy, who'd introduced himself as John Mallory, seemed more interested in keeping his eye on Seth than meeting Antoine Parson's gaze. Seth himself seemed acutely aware of the deputy's scrutiny, though he tried not to show it.

He'd warned her, she thought. People looked at him differently because of who he was. What he'd been. And maybe if she'd never seen another side of him—the kind man, the brave protector—she'd be inclined to view him the same way.

She had viewed him with suspicion as recently as a few hours ago.

But that had been before he'd kissed her.

Was that all it took? Was that how easily she gave her trust?

She felt herself edging away from him, even as the thoughts roiled through her mind. He let go, let her move away, not looking at her as he did so. His gaze was fixed on John Mallory, his chin high and his mouth set with stubborn pride.

But even though he wasn't looking at her, she felt as if his defiant stance was meant for her as much as it was meant for the deputy. *This is who I am. This is what I deal with every day. If you can't handle it...*

"I'd like to request formal release of the body into the custody of the Bitterwood Police Department," Antoine said to Mallory. "Based on eyewitness testimony, we have reason to believe the assault leading to Davis Rogers's murder took place in the Bitterwood jurisdiction."

"Not so fast," Mallory said. "Until the C.O.D. is determined, the location of his death is still at issue."

"You really want this case?" Antoine argued. "You're about to have this man's family and their grief and questions crashing down on you. There's damned little evidence to go on, thanks to the rain and the removal of the body from the place where he was attacked. You're buying yourself a damned near unsolvable case, John."

"And you want it why, Antoine?"

"Because I think it may be connected to an open case in Bitterwood." Antoine flicked a quick look at Seth.

A slight twitch of Seth's eyes was his only response.

"I'll tell you what," Mallory said after a moment of consideration. "I'll talk to the sheriff, see if I can't get him to agree to a joint investigation, based on the testimony and pending the determination of the C.O.D. Then, if the cause of death suggests that the murder took place in the Bitterwood jurisdiction, we'll hand the whole thing over. Deal?"

Antoine didn't look happy, but he gave a nod. "I can live with that."

"Ms. Davenport gave us some information that should help us locate and inform Mr. Rogers's family of his death, so I'm going to go get the notifications started." Mallory shot Antoine a wry look. "Unless you'd like to handle that part of the investigation?"

Antoine smiled. "You found the body. You make the notifications."

Once Deputy Mallory was out of earshot, Antoine turned to Seth. "He really, really doesn't like you."

"I have that effect on a lot of people," Seth replied in a bone-dry tone. "I think in his case, it has more to do with Cleve Calhoun than with me. Cleve sucked Mallory's cousin into some land deal he's still holding a grudge about. Can't say I blame him. He lost a hell of a lot of money."

"If only he hadn't been so greedy, he could have avoided it?" Antoine asked. "Isn't that what you fellows say? Can't con an honest man?"

Seth slanted a look at Rachel, a hint of a smile curving his lips, though none of the amusement made it into his hard green eyes. "Something like that. I don't reckon that makes for much of an excuse, though."

"What happens now?" Rachel asked, finding the tense posturing between Seth and Antoine exhausting.

"Deputy Mallory will contact your friend's family. They'll make a formal identification for the record and, meanwhile, we'll get a warrant to search his room and his vehicle at Sequoyah House. I've already had it sealed off and posted a couple of officers at the bed-and-breakfast pending the warrant."

"Is there anything else we can do to help?"

Antoine looked at Seth. "If you could tell more about what you saw before you got hit on the head, we'd be better off. Maybe you saw the person who did it and you just don't remember."

Seth shook his head. "I doubt I'd be alive now if I'd seen who hit me." He glanced toward the door of the morgue. "Whoever did this doesn't seem interested in leaving witnesses behind."

"Witnesses to what?" Antoine asked.

Rachel wondered the same thing. What could Davis have seen that would warrant someone beating him to death? As far as she could tell, he'd come to town for her father's funeral. At most, he'd have been in Bitterwood for maybe a day before he was murdered.

The only thing he might have witnessed of any significance was what had happened to her at Smoky Joe's Saloon.

Which had to be the answer, Rachel realized.

"He was with me at Smoky Joe's Saloon last night," she said.

"I spoke to Joe Breslin earlier today," Seth explained as Antoine shot Rachel a curious look. "He told me he saw a man fitting Davis Rogers's description with Rachel last night at his bar. The man made a pass at Rachel, she rebuffed him and he left, according to Joe."

"Is that what his phone call was about?" Antoine asked. "The one you played for me?"

Seth looked at Rachel. "If he left before you did, what could he have possibly seen?"

"You think you were drugged." Antoine also looked at her. "Could Rogers have done it?"

She shook her head. "He wouldn't do that to me."

"It's been a few years since you were together," Seth

pointed out. "Maybe someone flashed a little cash at him—"

"He's a plaintiff's lawyer in Richmond and has done very well for himself. You saw where he was staying. Sequoyah House isn't cheap."

"Maybe he still holds a grudge about your breakup," Antoine suggested.

"He broke up with me," she answered bluntly. "I mean, it was mutual—we had both realized by then that we just wanted different things in life. But he was the one who finally made the move to end it. He's never tried to hurt me. You heard his message."

Her gut tightened as she realized the final call, the one she'd heard cut off with a thud, truly had been his last. At some point after that call had ended so abruptly, he'd been beaten to death.

Tears rose in her eyes, stinging hot. She blinked them back, but they kept coming, rolling down her cheeks in a sudden, unstoppable flood.

Seth's hands closed over her shoulders, warm and strong. It would be so easy to lean back against him, let herself melt in his solid heat.

But once she started depending on him, it might be difficult to stop. And he'd already made it clear that he wasn't in the market for any sort of entanglement.

"I'd like to borrow your phone again," Antoine said suddenly. "I'd like to record those last messages to you, if that's okay. Should have done it earlier. I could get a warrant, but this would be faster."

"Of course." She handed over her phone.

"I'll get it back to you as soon as I'm done. If you'd like to come to the station with me, I can record while you wait."

"Why don't we get something to eat?" Seth suggested.

"Ledbetter's Café is just around the corner." He looked up at Antoine. "Want us to bring you something?"

Antoine looked surprised by the offer. "Yeah. Sure. A pulled pork sandwich and some of Maisey's sweet potato fries." He pulled his wallet from the inside pocket of his jacket and handed Seth a ten, his eyes glinting with amusement. "You really are good at getting people to hand over their hard-earned money, aren't you, Hammond?"

Seth grinned back. "At least this time, you'll get a sandwich and fries out of it."

AFTER THE TRIP to the morgue, Rachel didn't have any appetite, but she let Seth cajole her into an omelet on toast. She managed to eat most of it, even though it seemed to stick in her throat. She sat back finally and watched Seth work his way through a plateful of barbecue ribs and Maisey Ledbetter's homemade slaw.

He ate with gusto, she noticed, like a man who appreciated a good, hot meal when one came his way. Even now, there was a hungry look about Seth Hammond that made her wonder how many times he'd been uncertain where his next meal would come from.

Seth ordered Antoine's barbecue plate as they got ready to leave, adding a slice of lemon meringue pie with a few dollars of his own money. At Rachel's questioning look, he shot her a sheepish grin. "I stole his pie at lunch one day in high school. He never knew who did it, but since I'm in the making-amends business these days—"

"Nice of you."

"Nice would have been if I hadn't nicked his pie in the first place."

Antoine raised an eyebrow at the unexpected slice of pie but thanked them and traded Rachel's cell phone for the food. He also had some information from the crime scene unit at Rachel's house. "They went over the place pretty thoroughly, but other than the piece of plastic and the shoe box you found, they couldn't find anything else of interest."

"What about the blood?"

"Not human. Animal of some kind, which wouldn't be hard to come by in a farming community like this."

She felt a rush of relief. "Thanks for checking."

"You're free to go back to your house, but if I were you, I'd change the locks as soon as you can. And put an alarm system in place."

"I'll definitely do that."

"I wish we had the manpower to send patrols by your house regularly, but we're already stretched pretty thin with a detective on leave and another recently retiring—"

"I understand," she said quickly, aware she was luckier than most people in her position. She could afford to hire protection if she needed it. Most people couldn't.

"I'm not going to ignore what's happening to you." Antoine's voice softened with concern. "I know this is the fifth murder connected to whatever's going on with you, and I won't avert my eyes and pretend it's not happening. I'm going to do my damnedest to figure out who's behind it."

"We've had some thoughts about that," Seth told him. He glanced at Rachel as if seeking permission to say anything further.

She gave a nod.

"The best I can tell, everything started about nine weeks ago, right?" Seth looked around the bull pen, his expression wary. "Is there someplace a little less open where we can discuss this?"

Antoine seemed surprised by the question, but he led

them down the hall to a small room equipped with a table, three chairs and a video camera mounted high in one corner. He showed them the button on the wall that controlled the camera. "It's off."

Seth looked at it closely, then took the lone chair on the far side of the table, leaving Rachel and Antoine to sit in the other two. "Sorry if I'm coming across paranoid, but I'm not sure who to trust these days."

Antoine shot him a wry look. "Tell me about it."

Rachel frowned. "What does that mean?"

"Are you suggesting there's someone on the police force involved with what's happening to Rachel?" Seth asked.

"I don't know. I don't have any particular reason to think so, but I have reservations about the way some things are done around here. I'm just saying I understand Hammond's caution."

"I'm wary of anyone with a badge," Seth said wryly. "Though a lot of that's my own damned fault."

"Too bad. We're having all kinds of trouble with fraud cases these days, the economy being what it is." Antoine sighed. "There are just too many ways to part good folks from their hard-earned money, and it wouldn't hurt to have an insider on our side."

"I'm wondering if money isn't the driving force behind what's going on at Davenport Trucking," Seth said.

Rachel looked at him, surprised. "We're pretty successful, I'll grant you, but I'm not sure we're five murders worth of successful."

"You'd be surprised how cheaply murder can be bought," Antoine muttered.

Seth twined his fingers on the table in front of him, the muscles and tendons flexing and unflexing, drawing

Rachel's gaze. A couple of hours ago, those hands had been on her. Touching her. Branding her.

She swallowed with difficulty.

"You said you think it started nine weeks ago?" Antoine nudged.

Rachel realized Seth's gaze was on her, green eyes blazing with awareness, as if he'd been reading her thoughts. She flushed.

"With the first murder. April Billings. Summer intern at Davenport Trucking. She'd just had her going-away party at the office the day she was killed. Remember?"

Rachel nodded, pain darting through her chest. "She was so excited to be going back to college. She had missed all her friends over the summer, and she had managed to get into a really popular class in her major that she was looking forward to attending." She blinked hard, fighting tears at the memory. "She made me want to go back to college all over again."

"You were close to her?" Antoine asked.

"Yeah. I guess she gravitated to me because I'm a librarian. I mean, I was. That was what she wanted to be, too. And she'd have been a good one." Rachel dashed away a tear that had slipped free of her control. "I really wanted that for her."

Seth's gaze softened. "She was a nice girl. She should've had that life she wanted."

"Who knew that you and April were friends?" Antoine asked Rachel.

"Anybody who worked there knew," Seth answered for her. "Rachel is big news around the company. Even the guys in the garage were speculating what it meant that Mr. Davenport had clearly brought her on to be his successor."

"You were?" Rachel hadn't realized.

"Well, sure. You'll be the boss. We aren't sure if you plan to keep running the place the way your daddy did or if you'll change things around." There were secrets in his green eyes but also amusement. Rachel realized there were things he could tell her—wanted to tell her—but not until they were alone.

That realization—that shock of intimacy—made her feel warm all over.

"Was anyone hostile to the idea?" Antoine asked.

Seth gave a quick shake of his head. "Worried, maybe. Jobs can be hard to come by these days. People feel lucky to be employed, and anything that threatens to change things—"

"But surely they knew the company was doing well, even with my father's illness," Rachel protested. "He worked hard to make everyone feel comfortable and secure with what was happening."

"It's easy to feel secure when you're not one paycheck away from ruin."

Even though she knew Seth didn't mean his words as a rebuke, they still stung a little. Because he was right. She'd never had to worry where her next meal would come from. Or whether or not she'd be able to make the next mortgage payment or pay the next utility bill.

"I still don't see how those worries constitute a motive for murder," she said more sharply than she'd intended.

"No," Seth agreed. "What's happening here is too personal."

"You mean this is all about hurting Ms. Davenport?" Antoine sounded skeptical, to Rachel's relief. Because the idea that someone hated her enough to kill people to torment her was utterly horrifying.

"Not that exactly," Seth said with a quick shake of his head. "But I do think that whoever's doing this knows enough about her life and her history to choose his actions to injure her in the worst possible way."

*He knows,* she realized, recognizing the hint of pity in Seth's eyes. *He knows about the missing year.*

*But how? How could he know?* Almost nobody outside of the clinic in North Carolina knew how she'd spent the year following her mother's death. Her father had told everyone that she'd gone to school abroad to get away from the aftermath of her mother's suicide, and nobody had questioned it because nobody but her father had seen the state she was in that night. He'd taken quick steps to protect her.

How could any of this be about what had happened fifteen years ago? How was that even possible?

"But what's the point?" Antoine asked. "What does hurting Ms. Davenport this way accomplish?"

"It could drive her out of the CEO position at Davenport Trucking," Seth suggested.

Rachel shook her head. "We don't pull in those kinds of profits. Sure, we do well. People get paid, and we make a comfortable profit. I'm not hurting for money. But no way are all these murders about taking over Davenport Trucking. There's no upside."

For the first time, Seth looked doubtful. "It's the only thing so far that's even close to answering all of the questions."

"Why not just kill me, then? Why torment me instead?"

"If you're killed now, what happens to the company?" Antoine asked. "Who gets your shares?"

"My mother's brother. Rafe. He owns about twenty percent of the company already because he put up seed money when the company started. But Uncle Rafe doesn't want to run the company. My father even offered the job to him before he brought me into the picture, and Uncle Rafe said no. He's a musician and a promoter."

"We need to find out what happens if you're still alive but unable to run the company," Seth said quietly. "It seems to be the point of trying to drive you crazy, and that appears to be what's going on here."

"I told you, I don't know. I've never asked that question." Maybe she should have, she realized, given her history.

"Who *would* know?" Antoine suddenly looked interested.

"My father's personal lawyer, of course. Maybe my stepmother, Diane—but she's out of town. It's possible he'd have told Garrett McKenzie—"

"Former mayor Garrett McKenzie?" Antoine whistled softly.

"Old family friend." She had never felt self-conscious about her family connections before, but both Antoine and Seth were making her feel like a pampered princess with their reactions.

Was that fair? Was she supposed to feel ashamed of having a father who had worked hard and provided well for his family?

"Anybody else?" Seth asked.

"The lawyer for sure. I'm not positive about Diane or anyone else." She risked another quick look at Seth, trying to read his expression. But he was suddenly closed off, impossible to read.

Just when she most needed to know what he was thinking.

# Chapter Eleven

The house was midnight quiet, even with all the lights blazing. Rachel had wanted to return to her father's house to spend the night rather than the cabin. There'd been a look of stubborn determination in her eyes when she'd told him her decision. They'd stopped to get their things at the cabin and arrived just as the grandfather clock in the den was chiming twelve.

Rachel watched him carry their bags inside with a look of apology in her weary eyes. "I know you think I'm crazy to come back here. But I won't be run out of my house. Not by the son of a bitch who's doing this."

He admired her determination, even if he'd prefer to stash her somewhere safer. "Understood."

"I must be taxing your patience."

"Oh, not for a few days yet."

The teasing reply earned him a tired smile. "You're a trouper."

"So are you."

Her response was another quick smile and a shake of her head as she dropped her car keys on the entry table and kicked off her shoes.

"You need sleep," he told her. "Go on up to bed. I'll lock up."

She caught his arm as he turned toward the door.

"How do you know about the time I spent in Westminster?"

He considered pretending he didn't know what she was talking about. But she deserved better than to be treated like a child. "Is that where you were? Is it a hospital?"

She took a small step back, her hand falling from his arm. "You don't know?"

*Great.* Now she thought he'd tricked her. "I didn't know the details. I just guessed the situation."

Her lips pressed into a thin line. "I can see why you were so good at what you used to do. You're really kind of spooky."

"I guessed about Westminster because it was the only thing that would explain the elaborate ruse in the attic."

Her brow lifted. "Restaging the moment of my big meltdown?"

"You were really shaken by what you saw. I could tell you were beginning to doubt yourself when we didn't find the evidence you expected right away."

She closed her eyes, as if she could blot out the memory of those moments. "I used to relive that night. Over and over again. Trying to stop it. Trying to reach her before she pulled the trigger. I went almost three months with no more than an hour or two of undisturbed sleep each night. I came really close to dying because of it. I couldn't eat. I lost a lot of weight. Couldn't think straight. All I could do was remember something I couldn't change, no matter how hard I tried."

He brushed his fingers against her face, unable to stop himself. She leaned into his touch, her face lifting even as she kept her eyes tightly shut. He brushed his lips against her furrowed brow. "I'm sorry."

She rested her head against his chest. "She wanted me to die with her."

His heart contracted. "She tried to kill you?"

She shook her head quickly. "Remember that window in the attic, the one by the trapdoor? When I got up to the attic, that window was open. The wind was blowing outside, whipping the curtains around. She told me she'd opened it for me. Because she knew how much I wanted to fly."

Seth closed his eyes, remembering Rachel's drug-induced words on the bridge. *She said I should fly.*

"I was fifteen going on thirty. I wanted to be grown, to be my own woman. When she was lucid, that idea seemed to terrify her. But when she was drowning in madness, she told me to fly."

He hugged her close. "I'm sorry."

"For a long time I couldn't remember much of it at all. I was terrified people were hiding things from me about her death, that I'd done something to hurt her."

"My God."

"Most of the memories came back on their own. And I knew what I didn't want to remember." She looked up at him with hard, shiny eyes. "There was a moment, right after she pulled the trigger and was lying there, bleeding all over that drop cloth, that the thought of flight seemed so sweet, so tempting. I remember, I walked past her body to the open window and stared down at the patio below. Those flagstones looked hard. Unforgiving. But it would be over in a flash, and then the pain would be gone."

He pressed his lips to her forehead again, swallowing the horror swirling in his chest at her words.

"I'm terrified of heights now. Just climbing the ladder into the attic scared the hell out of me. I think it comes from the memory of standing at that window, staring down at my own death."

He stroked her hair, hating her mother for doing such

a thing to her. "How many people know about West-minster?"

She looked up at him. "Almost nobody. My father came up with an elaborate story about my going to live with a great-aunt in England and going to school there. All my old friends didn't know what to say to a girl whose mother had killed herself, so it wasn't much trouble to discourage them from trying to reach me."

"I've never heard a word about it, and you know what a gossip mill this town can be."

"I've wondered whether my father was protecting him-self as much as he was protecting me. From the stigma of having a mentally ill daughter as well as a wife who committed suicide." She looked shamed by the admis-sion. "I shouldn't have said that. I know he was protect-ing me. And he didn't see me as mentally ill now or he wouldn't have left the business to me."

"And nobody else knew?"

"Well, my great-aunt in England knew, because she had to be the alibi. Uncle Rafe and Aunt Janeane—they live in Bryson City, near Winchester. My doctors and nurses at the clinic. My father, of course." She crossed her arms over her body, rubbing her arms as if she was cold.

Seth pulled off his denim jacket and wrapped it around her. "Better?"

The smoldering gaze she lifted to meet his almost made his knees buckle. "Thank you."

*Get your mind on the stalker. Think about the kind of payback you want against him.*

The ideas for revenge flooding his head helped cool his ardor, along with a slight step backward to take him out of the immediate impact of her delicate scent and sad-eyed vulnerability. "What about the trustees of your father's business? Would any of them know?"

"I don't think so. Well, maybe my stepmother. She's always treated me as if I'm a little fragile." Her brow creased again. "A lot of people do when they know my mother committed suicide."

"It's a trauma most people can't imagine."

"I hope they never have reason to know what it feels like." She shivered. "You don't suspect Diane, do you?"

Thanks to Mark Bramlett's final words, they knew the person who'd hired him to commit the first four murders had been a man. But Diane Davenport could have hired someone to do all the dirty work for her, he supposed. Even the solicitation. "How much would she stand to gain if you were removed as CEO?"

"As far as I know, nothing more than she'd gain if I remained CEO. That's something I need to ask my father's lawyer in the morning."

Seth wondered if he'd be able to turn off his mind tonight long enough to get some much-needed sleep. While logic told him it wasn't likely the intruder from earlier that day would repeat an invasion so soon after the police had scoured the place for evidence, instinct told him he needed to stay on full alert.

"Maybe I should sleep down here on the sofa," he suggested.

Her cheeks flushed pink as she smiled. "I'm way too tired to make any moves on you tonight. Your virtue is safe with me."

He smiled at her attempt to lighten the mood. "I appreciate that, but I was actually thinking about the best way to keep you safe."

Her smile faded. "From intruders?"

"I don't think it's likely anyone will try anything tonight, after all the police presence today, but my gut says better safe than sorry."

"You listen to your gut a lot?" The question was serious.

"I do."

She slowly walked toward him, closing the distance between them. He found himself unable to back away, frozen in place by the desire in her eyes. She laid her hand in the middle of his chest and let it slide slowly down to the flat of his stomach. "What does your gut tell you to do with me?"

He couldn't stop a dry laugh from spilling from his throat. "I don't think that's my gut talkin', sugar."

Her eyes widened slightly, then she laughed, the sound belly deep. It was a glorious sound, he thought. Rich and deep and utterly sane. If he'd harbored a doubt about her mental stability, that laugh crushed it to powder.

"I like you, Seth Hammond. I hope like hell you decide to stick around once this is all over." She rose to her tiptoes and pressed her mouth to his, the kiss light and undemanding.

It nearly unraveled him anyway. His whole body trembled as he watched her walk away, up the stairs and out of sight.

SETH DIDN'T LOOK as if he'd gotten much sleep when he greeted Rachel the next morning with a cup of hot coffee and a creditable omelet. "I think you should call the company lawyer as soon as his office opens. See if he can work us in this morning."

She took the omelet and cup of coffee to the small table in the kitchen nook, "Got our agenda all worked out for today, have you?"

"The sooner we figure this out, the better," he said firmly.

*The sooner you get to leave, you mean,* she thought

with a hint of morning-after bleakness. All her confidence of the night before had faded into doubts by the time she'd drifted to sleep. At least her subconscious had been certain of his ability to keep her safe. If she'd dreamed at all last night, she couldn't remember it and it hadn't disturbed her sleep.

She called the lawyer as soon as his office opened and he agreed to see her right away if she could get there before nine. His office was in Maryville, about twenty minutes away, but fortunately she'd showered and dressed before making the call, so they reached Maryville with time to spare.

"Am I going to be forced to fire you for ditching work?" she asked lightly as they passed the big Davenport Trucking sign on West Sperry Road.

"I took vacation days. Cleared it with your stepbrother before I went looking for Davis Rogers."

"Very conscientious."

"What about your stepbrother?" he asked with a sideways glance toward her. "If you were incapacitated, could he take over as the CEO?"

"I don't think he wants to be CEO. His passion is hospitality. He used to work at a big resort on the Mississippi Gulf Coast before things went bad down that way and a lot of people were laid off. I think he's still hoping to get back into that line of work someday. I think he's only stayed at Davenport Trucking this long because his mother married my father. I won't be surprised if he gives me his notice sooner rather than later."

"Okay." Seth fell silent until they reached Ed Blount's office in the Maryville downtown area. The lawyer's office was located in an old two-story white clapboard house converted to upstairs and downstairs offices. Blount's suite was on the lower floor, and he greeted

Rachel with an affectionate kiss on the cheek and a look of puzzlement.

"I didn't expect to see you this soon," Ed told her. "If you're here about the will reading—"

"It's not that," she said quickly. "I do have a question about my father's business, though."

"Okay." Ed spotted Seth, his sandy eyebrows lifting.

"Ed, this is Seth Hammond. Seth, Ed Blount."

Seth's face was a mask. "We've met."

From the look on the lawyer's face, it must not have been a pleasant acquaintance. "What is he doing here?"

"I can go," Seth said.

"No." She caught his wrist, holding him in place. She turned back to Ed. "Let's just stipulate that Seth was no doubt a complete ass in the past, and you have every right to distrust him for whatever it was he did to you—"

"It wasn't to him," Seth said. "It was his daughter."

She shot him a look. He met her gaze, unflinching for a moment. Then his eyes dropped, and he turned his head away.

"She thought you loved her," Ed growled.

"I know."

"That's it? You know?"

Seth's gaze lifted slowly. "I could tell you that I regret it, but you're not going to believe me, and it won't make her feel a damned bit better."

"What about her college money? Can you give that back to her?"

Rachel's heart sank painfully at the look of shame on Seth's face. But he didn't look away from Ed. "I tried."

Ed stared at him. "When?"

"About a year ago. She shoved it back to me and told me she didn't want my dirty money."

"Where is it now?"

"I gave it to the soup kitchen in Knoxville. I know Lauren used to volunteer there."

"That's where she met you," Ed snarled. "You played on her soft heart and convinced her you were just down on your luck and looking for someone to believe in you."

Seth's expression grew stony. His voice, when he spoke, was dry and uninflected. "I did."

"You broke her heart."

"I know."

"I'm sick of hearing that!" he bellowed, charging toward Seth.

"Ed." Rachel grabbed the lawyer's arm and put herself between him and Seth, struggling to keep a sudden tremor in her knees from spreading to the rest of her limbs. "You had to work me in and I don't want to run out of time because of this."

"I'll wait outside." Seth exited abruptly, closing the door behind him, leaving Rachel alone with Ed.

The lawyer glared with loathing at the closed door, his breathing coming in short, harsh grunts. "What the hell are you doing with that man?"

"It's a long story. And it's not relevant to what I'm here to find out."

Ed stared at her in consternation, visibly trying to collect himself. Finally, in a calmer tone of voice, he asked, "What are you here to find out?"

She nudged him toward his office door, shooting an apologetic smile toward the pretty red-haired receptionist who had watched the whole debacle with her mouth in an O of surprise. "I need to know what would happen to Davenport Trucking if I were no longer able to act as CEO."

WELL, THAT *had gone well.*

Seth sank onto the top porch step and stared across the tree-shaded street at the mostly full parking lot of a sprawling one-story medical clinic. Pediatrics, he realized as the cars came and went with their cargo of harried moms and coughing, sniffling children.

Maybe he should write Rachel a note, leave it on her windshield and walk back to Davenport Trucking. He could hang around until lunchtime and see if one of the guys in the fleet garage could drive him to the rental car place in Alcoa in exchange for lunch.

But before he talked himself to his feet, the door opened behind him and Rachel stepped out, stopping short as she spotted him on the porch step. "Oh. I was halfway expecting you to be gone."

He rose and turned to face her, his spine rigid with a combination of shame and stubborn pride. "I was halfway to talking myself into going."

"You warned me," she said quietly, nodding toward the car.

"I did." He fell into step with her as they walked to the Honda.

"Didn't you realize who we were going to see?"

"I didn't connect the names." He forced a grim smile. "Lots of Blounts in Blount County, Tennessee."

"Did you really try to pay her back?"

He slanted a look at her, trying not to be hurt by the question. "Yes."

"And when she refused, you gave the money to the soup kitchen?"

"Foundations of Hope. Downtown. Ask for Dave Pelletier."

She paused with her key halfway to the ignition. "You always sound as if you're telling the truth."

"And you can't trust that I am." It wasn't a question. He saw the doubt in her eyes.

"I want to."

"That's not enough. You have to be sure, and you can't afford to let time and experience prove my motives are sincere."

"I don't know who to trust at all." She looked so afraid, and he hated himself for adding to her distress.

"Sometimes you just have to trust your instincts," he said quietly. "What do your instincts tell you?"

She lifted her gaze to meet his. "That you want to keep me safe."

A strange sensation, part agony, part joy, burned a hole in the center of his chest. "You're crazy."

Even though tears shined in her eyes, she laughed. "That's not a nice thing to say to a woman with my mental health history."

He laughed, too, even though he felt like crying, as well. "I won't hurt you. Not if there's anything I can do to avoid it. And if you ever begin to doubt me, you say so and I'll be gone."

"Deal." She held out her hand.

He shook it, his fingers tingling where hers touched him. He resisted the powerful urge to pull her into his arms and let go, turning to buckle himself in. "What now? What did you learn?"

"A lot. But I'm not sure how it's going to help us."

# *Chapter Twelve*

"So the trustees choose the CEO?" Seth asked a few minutes later, after Rachel had summarized what Ed Blount had told her. "Is that the gist of it?"

Rachel nodded as she threaded her way through traffic on Lamar Alexander Parkway, heading toward the mountains. "There are parameters, of course. My father apparently left a list of approved candidates that the trustees have to choose from first. If none of those candidates is willing to take the job, the trustees are tasked with a circumscribed candidate search. My father apparently left detailed instructions."

"Blount wouldn't give you the details, though?"

"Not before the reading of the will next Tuesday…."

"But?" he prodded, apparently reading her hesitation.

"He mentioned that my uncle helped my father come up with the list. I think Uncle Rafe might be willing to tell me now if I ask him."

"So let's ask him."

She shot him a smile. "Where do you think we're heading?"

Her uncle lived across the state line in Bryson City, where he and his wife, Janeane, ran a music hall catering primarily to Smoky Mountains tourists. The drive from Maryville took over two hours, but Rachel couldn't complain much about the view as their route twisted through the Smokies, past bluffs cut into the earth and sweeping vistas of the mountains spreading north and east, their tips swallowed by lingering mists that even the sunny day had not completely dissipated.

They arrived at Song Valley Music Hall in time for lunch. The fall tourist season was just starting, which meant they didn't have their choice of tables when they walked into the dimly lit dining hall, but they didn't have to wait in line, either.

Uncle Rafe himself came out to greet them, menu in hand and a smile on his face. His eyes widened as he recognized her. "Rachel, my dolly! You should have called to let me know you were coming. I just gave away the last front-row table for the show!"

"That's okay—we'll enjoy it anyway." She gave her uncle a kiss and turned to Seth. He looked uncomfortable, which struck her as odd, considering his history as a con artist. Weren't con men chameleons? "Uncle Rafe, this is Seth Hammond, a friend of mine. Seth, this is my uncle Rafe Hunter."

Her uncle's blue eyes narrowed shrewdly. "Hammond."

Seth nodded. "Yes, sir."

"Any kin to Delbert Hammond?"

Seth's expression froze in place. "My father."

Uncle Rafe nodded slowly. "There's a resemblance."

Seth's mask slipped a bit, revealing dismay in his green eyes. "So I'm told."

Rafe cocked his head to one side. "You're the one got burned."

Rachel looked from her uncle to Seth. His left hand rose and settled against his right shoulder, kneading the skin through his shirt. "That's right. Long time ago."

"Heard you've been playing nursemaid to Cleve Calhoun for the last little while. That true?"

"Yes, sir." Seth's hand dropped away from his shoulder. "He's at a rehab place now, though. His son talked him into giving it a go."

"You couldn't get him to agree?"

"Don't reckon I tried, really. I've never had any luck talking Cleve into much of anything.

Uncle Rafe smiled a little at Seth's admission. "I'll buy that. You still in the life?"

"Uncle Rafe—"

"I am not," Seth answered.

"You sure?" Her uncle's gaze went from Seth's stony face to Rachel's.

"I've found there's no long-term job satisfaction in lying to people for a living."

Uncle Rafe's gaze swept back to meet Seth's. "I don't know, son. I'm a showman, and what is that but lying to people for a living? Putting on an act, sucking them into a narrative of my choosing?"

"The people at a show know what they're seeing isn't real," Seth answered slowly. "They're willing participants in their own deception."

Uncle Rafe's well-lined face creased with a smile. "Damn good answer, boy." He hooked his arm through Rachel's and led her to the second row of tables facing the large stage. "Gotta go start deceiving this room full of willing participants in their own deception," he said with a wink in Seth's direction. "You'll stick around after the show, of course?"

"Absolutely," Rachel agreed. "I need to ask you a few questions about the trucking company. Will you have time between lunch and dinner?"

"I'll make time, dolly girl." He gave her a quick kiss and headed for the back of the restaurant.

The food at her uncle's place was good, simple home cooking. Janeane ran the kitchen, while he booked the acts and kept the daily shows going, varying things up every few weeks to keep it fresh for returning customers, Rachel told Seth while they were waiting for their orders. "Probably sixty to seventy percent of their customers are tourists," she added. "But they get a lot of locals, too, who like to take in a show. He brings in a lot of young, upcoming bluegrass and country performers. He has a real talent for knowing who's going to be the next big thing."

"You're proud of him," Seth said with a smile.

"Yeah, I am."

His smile shifted slightly. "Nice to have someone to be proud of."

"You don't?"

"There's Dee. She's the real star of the family." Rachel could tell from the look in his eyes that he thought the world of his sister. "I knew when we were little she was going to be special. She never let anything that was going on around us faze her. She knew what she wanted, and she went after it. And she always did it the right way. No shortcuts. No stomping all over someone else to get ahead. I used to think my parents must have stolen her from some nice family, 'cause she wasn't a damned thing like the rest of us."

"Are you two close?"

The pain she occasionally glimpsed in his eyes was back. "No. My fault. I wore out my welcome with Delilah a long time ago."

"She helped you out with me."

He reached across the table, lightly tapping the back of her hand. "That was for you, sugar. Not for me."

"She doesn't believe you've changed?"

A mask of indifference came over his face. "Nobody does."

"I do," she said without thinking.

His gaze focused on hers, green eyes blazing. "You don't know me, Rachel. And most of what you've heard and seen should scare the hell out of you. Don't make up some fantasy about the misunderstood tough guy who just needs someone to care. I'm not misunderstood. People understand exactly who I was. I've earned their disgust."

"You're not pulling con jobs anymore—"

"So? I did. I did them willingly, with skill and determination."

"And then you stopped."

He shook his head. "Because I finally disgusted even myself! Do you understand what I did?"

She found herself floundering for an answer. "You lied to people and conned them out of money—"

"I hurt people," he said in a low, hard growl. "Not with a gun or a knife but with my lies. Do you know Lauren Blount, Rachel?"

She shook her head. "Not really."

"When I met her, she was nineteen. Pretty as a postcard and as sweet as Carolina honey. I convinced her I wanted a life with her, but because of my meth-dealing daddy and how he blew up my whole family, I couldn't catch a break. Showed her my burn scars, told her how I got them saving my mama from the burning house after my daddy nearly killed us all."

"Is that really what happened? That's what Uncle

Rafe was talking about earlier, right? About your getting burned."

He met her gaze. "So what if it was? That's what con men do, don't you get it? We take the truth and use it to sell our lies. I had burn scars from draggin' my mama out of that house 'cause she was too drunk to get out herself, and yeah, it makes a real pitiful story. Women see your scars, get all soft and gooey about how you're some hero, and they don't even see you're playing them like fiddles."

She looked away, feeling ill.

"I had Lauren eating out of my hand. I told her I had this idea for a business, see, and I needed some seed money, but no banks or businesspeople were going to take a chance on some old hillbilly like me. I made it sound like a sure thing. I made it sound like our future. And she ate it up. She saw the poor sad sack who just needed a good woman's love to make things okay for him, and she went for the bait in a heartbeat. Just like I knew she would."

"Then what did you do?"

"She gave me the money she'd saved up for her next two semesters of college. Cried a little as she did it, telling me that even if nobody else believed in me, she did."

Tears burned Rachel's eyes as she tried to picture herself in Lauren Blount's situation. Madly in love and wanting so much to help him out. Would she have given him the money?

She didn't think she liked the answer.

"I took the money and I left town. Left her a note telling her that she needs to be careful about who she trusts in the future." He smiled, but it was a horrible sight, full of anger and self-loathing. "She's taken that warning to heart. I don't think she trusts anyone anymore."

Silence fell between them. Finally, Rachel found the courage to speak. "Didn't she press charges against you?"

He shook his head. "She gave me the money willingly, and I was vague about what I planned to do with it. She would have had to try to prove her case in court, and she didn't want to face that kind of scrutiny." He grimace-smiled again. "Lucky me."

"My God."

His green eyes flashed at her again. "Now you're getting it."

She felt sick. "What made you quit the con game?"

"Cleve's stroke."

She narrowed her eyes. "Really."

"He was helpless for a long while. His own son didn't want to hear from him. He had no one in the world to take care of him but me. I realized I didn't want to give up even part of my life for the old bastard. What had he ever done for me but turn me into a criminal?"

"Why did you help him, then?"

"Because there was no one else. Someone had to."

"It could have been the state. Or he could have hired a caretaker. It didn't have to be you."

"It did." He looked down at the flatware bundle wrapped up in a slip of paper by his elbow. He pulled the flatware to him and began to play with the bundle, turning it slowly in a circle as if he needed time to organize his thoughts. After a minute, he pushed it aside and looked up at her. "It took a day or two, but I remembered that Cleve had taken me in when I had no one else. Everybody turned on my family, and especially me, because they all knew I was going to turn out like my daddy anyway. Why bother?"

"What about your mother? Couldn't she have helped you?"

"My mama is a drunk. Has been since I was a kid because it was the only way she could keep livin' with a man who beat her up for fun."

Rachel covered her mouth in dismay.

"Tawdry, ain't it?" He'd slipped easily back into the hard mountain twang of his raising. "That's the Hammonds of Smoky Ridge for you."

"What do you think would have happened if Cleve hadn't taken an interest in you?"

"I'd be in jail. Maybe even hooked on meth. Maybe dead."

"Cleve saved you from that."

"And introduced me to a life that seemed like a no-brainer at the time. I could lie with the best of them. I'd been lyin' all my life, coverin' up for what happened in that house." His lips curved slightly, but his gaze seemed focused somewhere far away. "It was so easy."

"Until it wasn't."

His gaze snapped back to hers. "You know what con men really do, Rachel? They kill your soul. You start out a normal person. Caring. Trusting. And then he strikes, and you're never the same. You trust no one. Nothing. You're afraid to be nice, because it makes you vulnerable. You're afraid to care because it makes you an easy mark. You meet a nice guy, a good guy, a guy who would treat you right, and you can't let yourself believe him because you know sweet words and a tender touch can hide a monster." He leaned toward her, his gaze so intense it made her stomach quiver. "That's what I did to Lauren Blount. It's what I did to God knows how many people along the way."

She didn't know what to say. She didn't even know what to feel.

"I did that." He sat back, looking away. "I don't know

how a man can forgive himself for that. I don't know how he lives with it. He can try to pay back the money, he can promise he'll never do anything like that again, but he can't change the fact that he had that kind of evil inside him and he let it have free rein. How do I live with that?"

She had no answer. The things he'd told her, the things he'd described, sickened her. Yet, the obvious guilt and remorse he felt touched her heart, as well. He'd been young and desperate, and while he was right—those facts weren't excuses for the things he'd done—they were, at least, mitigating factors.

At thirty, was Seth Hammond the same man he'd been at twenty? Obviously not. But was she crazy to take a chance on a man who'd lived the kind of life he had?

The food came, but she'd long since lost her appetite. Seth toyed with his food as well, eating little. He seemed determined not to look at her for the rest of the time, and it was a relief when the music started, giving them both somewhere to park their reluctant gazes for a while.

Uncle Rafe came back to their table after the music set was over and looked with dismay at their barely touched plates. "Didn't like the food?"

"My fault," Seth said quietly. "I brought up a stomach-turning topic just as the food arrived."

Uncle Rafe's eyes narrowed as he waved over a waitress and asked her to put the food in a couple of to-go boxes. "Take it with you. Maybe you'll be hungry later. Now. What was it that you needed to ask me about the trucking company?"

"This is going to sound like an odd question, but it's important. When Dad came to you to discuss his will, he asked you to help him make up a roster of preapproved candidates for the job of CEO if I were unable to fulfill my duties. I asked Ed Blount to give me the list, but he won't do it before the will reading next week. I need to see the list now."

"Goodness, girl, whatever for? You're the CEO, free and clear, so what does the list matter now?"

"Someone may be trying to change the situation," she said quietly.

Uncle Rafe leaned closer. "Change the situation how?"

Rachel glanced at Seth. He was looking at her, finally, his gaze intense. He gave a little nod, and she lifted her chin and met her uncle's troubled gaze. "I think someone's trying to drive me crazy."

# Chapter Thirteen

The Song Valley Music Hall's office was a small room in the back of the building, nestled between the large kitchen and the public restrooms. The decor was strictly old-fashioned country charm, but Seth was relieved to see that whatever his eccentricities, Rafe Hunter took his business seriously. A new computer with a flat screen monitor and an all-in-one printer/copier sat in one corner. Shiny steel file cabinets took up one wall, while a well-organized storage cubby occupied the other.

Rafe went straight to the computer and called up a document file. At a glance—all Seth got before Rafe sent the file to print and closed it up—there were six names on the list. "Do any of those people know Mr. Davenport was considering them as possible CEOs?" he asked.

"I believe George let them know. He wouldn't want to give the trustees a list of people unwilling to consider the job, after all."

The paper came out of the printer, and Rafe plucked it up and handed it to Rachel. "There's your list. I hope to God you're wrong about your suspicions, dolly. Maybe you should come stay here with Janeane and me for a while."

"It's not a bad idea." Seth tamped down the part of him that was begging her to tell her uncle no. It made sense for her to get out of Bitterwood for a while. She could let Seth look into that list of people while she stayed safely out of it.

Safely away from him, too.

"No," she said, and part of him nearly wilted with relief. "This is my life we're talking about. I'm tired of letting everyone else make decisions for me. I need to be part of ending this mess."

"Are you rethinking your decision to be the company CEO?" Rafe gave his niece a probing look.

"I don't know," she said finally. "I never thought I wanted to take over the company permanently, but I love the people there and I want the company to be a success. My dad believed I was the person who could do it, and the more time I've spent there over the past year, the more convinced I am that he's right. I can do this job. I can do it well and take care of our customers and our employees. And I really want to, at least for a while longer. I can always go back to being a librarian later."

Rafe cupped her cheek with one big hand. "Why don't you tell me what's been going on?"

As Rachel related the things that had happened around her for the past two months, Seth found himself watching Rafe carefully for his reaction. Could he have his own reasons for wanting control of the company? The music hall seemed to be successful, but appearances could be deceiving, as Seth well knew. Rafe could be neck-deep in debt. He might be a compulsive gambler or have a bad drug habit that sucked his profits dry.

It might have been too obvious to kill Rachel before her father's death, since Rafe would be the prime suspect. He was at the top of the list to get control of the company if she were dead. Which would also make him the prime suspect if her death was suspicious in any way.

But if she were unable to fulfill the requirements of the job due to mental health problems, Rafe would have a great deal of influence if he wanted it, and nobody would suspect he'd engineered the situation.

He'd helped create this list of people to take her place. Might he have taken an even greater role, as her closest living relative, if she were declared incompetent?

If he harbored such wicked thoughts, they certainly didn't show in his horrified expression as he listened to Rachel's story. "My God, you should have called your aunt Janeane and me for help."

"I wasn't sure what was going on," she admitted. "If Seth hadn't found me on that bridge, I don't even know if I'd be alive."

Rafe blanched, his hand shaking as he lifted it to her face again. "Who would do such a thing to you?"

"I don't know."

"We think it must have something to do with Davenport Trucking," Seth said. "That's why we need the list."

Rafe's gaze snapped up to meet his. "What is your part in all this?"

The easy answer, of course, was that FBI Special Agent in Charge Adam Brand had asked him to keep an eye on Rachel. But since he hadn't shared that information with her yet, he didn't think it was a good idea to spill the beans in front of her uncle.

"I work at Davenport Trucking," he answered. "The family's been good to me, and I know a little something about deception. I guess in some ways, I'm uniquely suited to unravel a plot against Rachel."

"Thank you kindly for your help, then. But I can take care of her now. Dolly, you need to pack up and come stay with Janeane and me."

"No." Rachel's response was quiet but firm. "I'm an adult, and I will take care of myself."

"Rachel—" Seth began.

She turned her cool blue gaze to him. "Yes?"

He didn't want to argue with her in front of her uncle, so he nodded toward the list. "Anything stand out?"

She took a look at the list, her brow furrowed. "Not really. Most of the people are Davenport Trucking employees—Stan Alvis, who's the chief financial officer, Drayton Lewis, our comptroller, your direct supervisor at the garage, Gary Adams—hmm." She frowned a little.

"What?" Seth asked.

"Paul is on this list." She looked up at her uncle. "If he was willing to be CEO, why didn't my dad give him the job outright?"

Rafe shrugged. "He wanted it to be you. In fact, I'm the one who suggested Paul. I figured Diane would be hurt if we didn't, and the boy has been a loyal employee for nearly a decade now."

Seth considered what he knew about Paul Bailey. The guy came across as a put-together, confident businessman, but even though he'd been with the company for years, he didn't haunt the doors of the place the way George Davenport had, or even some of the other people on the short list. Seth's own boss, Gary, worked long hours and was a stickler about getting the job done right. He was blue-collar and rednecked, but Gary was smart, too. What he lacked in formal education, he made up for with his inquisitive mind and strong work ethic.

If Seth were picking a new CEO, he'd definitely go for Gary Adams over Paul Bailey, despite the seeming disparity between the two men.

But he wasn't looking for a CEO.

He was looking for a killer. Which of the people on that list wanted the job badly enough to kill for it?

And why?

DELILAH HAMMOND HAD spent almost half her life away from Bitterwood and normally thought it a good thing. Her first eighteen years growing up on Smoky Ridge had been a long, exhausting exercise in avoidance. She'd dodged her father's blows and her mother's selfish neediness. She'd kept clear of Seth's self-destructive anger and the constant temptations of drugs, booze and sex, determined to get an education and get the hell out of the mountains with her future intact.

Good grades and hard work had earned her scholarships to college. More hard work had gotten her through the FBI Academy and onto a fast-paced domestic terrorism task force. Later, she'd left the bureau for the private sector and ended up where she was now, working for former marine Jesse Cooper and his family's security agency. She had a life. A purpose. Bitterwood, Tennessee, should have been in her rearview mirror, not her windshield.

But as she wound her way through the curves of Vesper Road toward Ivy Hawkins's house, closer and closer to the brushed-velvet peak of Smoky Ridge, she felt an odd, pulling sensation in the center of her chest.

*Home,* she thought, and bit her lip at the image. Just no getting away from it after all.

There was a black Jeep Wrangler parked in the driveway, she saw as she turned off Vesper Road. Ivy Hawkins was back.

As it turned out, so was Sutton Calhoun, Ivy's boyfriend and one of Delilah's oldest friends and a colleague at Cooper Security. He came out onto the porch before

Delilah had opened the driver's door of his truck, the expression on his tanned face fiercely grim.

Delilah's stomach cramped at the sight of him. Had something happened on his trip to northern Iraq? Nobody at Cooper Security had mentioned any trouble when she'd been there for the meeting last night.

"You're back," she greeted him, not bothering with a smile. He clearly wasn't in the mood.

Ivy Hawkins came out and stood beside him on the porch, her dark eyes blazing with anger. "Have you seen your brother lately?"

*Oh, no,* she thought. "Not since yesterday morning," she answered, climbing the steps slowly. "Why?"

Sutton gestured with his head for her to follow him inside the house. He led her into the study, where Ivy kept her computer. The laptop was open, and a photo of Rachel Davenport filled the screen.

Delilah walked closer, studying the photo with a frown. The photo had been taken at the funeral, she realized. Mourners were gathered around her, but she was definitely the focus of the image.

"Where did that come from?" She braced herself for the answer.

Sutton reached behind the laptop and pulled out a pair of sunglasses attached to a neck cord. It took a second look to realize the neck cord had a small connector jack built in. When Sutton picked up a small, rectangular plastic device and plugged in the cord, she realized what it really was.

"A spy camera." She looked up at Sutton. "Where'd you find this?"

"At my father's house." He put the unit down. "It was lying out in the open, next to the computer."

"And you think it's Seth's."

"Don't you?"

Delilah looked at the photo of Rachel Davenport still up on the computer screen. She'd caught Seth at the funeral and called him on being there, accusing him of trying to run some kind of con on Rachel.

He'd said he was there just to say goodbye to his employer. Clearly, he hadn't told her everything.

She closed her eyes. "How many photos?"

"About a hundred, spanning the past two weeks. He's been keeping an eye on Rachel Davenport primarily, although there were also some photos of the trucking company personnel. I don't know what your brother is up to, but it can't be good. He's put a hell of a lot of sweat and coin into following that woman around."

She forced herself to ask the obvious question, even though it made her sick to think about. "You think he's connected to the murders?"

The look of pity Sutton sent her way felt like a gut punch. "I honestly don't know."

"Where is Seth now?" Ivy asked. She was clipping her badge to the waistband of her jeans, Delilah realized.

"You're back on the job?" she asked. Ivy had been on administrative leave since Mark Bramlett's death.

"As of today," she said with a lopsided smile. "Never realized how much I'd want back on the job until I was forced off."

"What about you, Sutton? Still planning to give your notice and move back here to Hillbilly Heaven?"

Sutton put his hands on Ivy's shoulders. "Already gave my notice. The Iraq mission was my last one. I'm back in Bitterwood to stay."

Funny, Delilah thought, how a place so full of bad memories still had a way of getting under the skin. She'd never figured Sutton would come back to Bitterwood any more than she would. "Are you planning to arrest Seth?"

"Not sure we have what it takes to get a warrant," Ivy admitted. "But I'm definitely going to ask him a few questions."

"You should have stayed with your uncle and aunt."

The first words Seth had spoken in almost two hours came out so soft she almost didn't hear them. She turned down the radio and met his brooding gaze. "I'm not going to hide in Bryson City. If someone's screwing around with my life, I have a right to know about it."

"That doesn't mean you have to be in the crosshairs."

"If this is your way of backing out of the investigation, just say so."

"I'm not saying that," he said quickly.

She turned onto the narrow, winding road that led to her family home, her stomach tensing as she thought about what might await her at the end of the road. She hadn't yet called the locksmith to change the locks nor gotten an estimate from an alarm company. Maybe she'd been depending on Seth Hammond too much. She needed to be able to meet Seth on equal footing, not as a victim. That's not the way she wanted him to think of her. Not by a long shot.

"If you want out, I'll understand. I don't want you to see me as an obligation.

His unnerving silence stretched out long enough for them to reach the end of her driveway. As she turned down the drive, his next words nearly ran her off onto the lawn. "I'm working for an FBI agent."

She righted the car, put on the brakes and looked at him. "What?"

"I've done some informant jobs for an FBI agent my

sister once worked with. Mostly undercover kind of stuff, places I could easily go that the FBI couldn't. A few weeks ago, just after Mark Bramlett died, my FBI handler called me and asked me to keep an eye on you."

Rachel pulled up outside the garage doors and parked, turning to look at Seth. He gazed back at her, clear-eyed.

"Why?" she asked.

"He didn't say exactly."

"You didn't ask?"

"I asked. He didn't say. All he told me is that this one wasn't for the FBI. It was personal."

"Personal?" That answer made even less sense than the FBI being interested in her life. "What's his name?"

Seth looked reluctant, but he finally answered, "Adam Brand. He's a special agent in charge in the Washington D.C. field office."

"I've never heard of him."

"I don't think it's that kind of personal."

"There's more than one kind of personal?"

He gave a soft huff of laughter. "There's all kinds of personal, sugar. But what I mean is, I got the feeling he's talking about your situation being of interest to him for a personal reason."

"And you didn't press him on it?"

"We've always had a need-to-know kind of relationship," he explained with a half smile. "If I need to know, he'll tell me. If he doesn't tell me, I don't need to know."

"You're okay with that?"

"I'm not crazy about it," he admitted. "But I've helped the FBI stop some very bad people from doing terrible things." His grimace suggested some of those terrible things had come very close to happening to him. "Adam Brand is one of the good guys, and there aren't many of them willing to give me a break."

"So what did Agent Brand ask you do to, where I'm concerned?"

"Just keep an eye on you."

"Is that why you were on the spot to help me at Purgatory Bridge?"

He shook his head. "That was dumb luck. I was just heading to Smoky Joe's for a good time."

"And ended up plucking my sorry backside off a bridge." She gave him an apologetic look.

"I'm glad I was there." The warmth in his voice seemed to spread to her bone marrow.

"So am I."

Silence fell between them, sizzling with unspoken desires. He wanted her—it burned in his eyes, scorching her—but he made no move to take what he wanted. What they both wanted.

She made no move, either, tethered in place by caution. Desire was a chemical thing that didn't always take reality into consideration. Wanting him wasn't a good enough reason to throw caution to the wind.

Was it?

"We need to get inside and see if anyone's left you any new surprises." He dragged his gaze away and opened the passenger door.

She stifled a sigh. Even if she was willing to take a chance, clearly Seth had different ideas.

Maybe it was for the best.

A thorough room-by-room inspection of the house showed no sign of an intruder. Seth took a second look around while Rachel was making calls to the locksmith and the alarm company that handled the trucking company's security. He wandered back downstairs as she was jotting down the appointment time she'd set with the security company for the following day.

"Did Delilah say when she'd be back from Alabama?" he asked, dropping onto the sofa across from where she sat.

"No. Why?"

"I need to go see Cleve at the hospital in Knoxville. I promised him I'd stop in at least once a week, and I'm running out of week."

"I think maybe you're running, period."

His gaze whipped up to meet hers. "Meaning?"

"Ignoring this thing between us doesn't make it go away."

His brow furrowed. "Rachel, we agreed—"

"What scares you about it?" she asked.

"It scares me that you're not scared," he answered flatly. "You're a smart woman. You've got to know that I'm a risky bet."

"Every relationship is a risk."

"You've lost a lot already. You're vulnerable and lonely—"

"So, I'm emotionally incapable of knowing what I want? Is that what you're suggesting?"

He closed his eyes a moment, frustration lining his sharp features. When he opened his eyes, they blazed with helpless need. "You're a beautiful woman. You seem so cool and composed on the outside, but then you give me this glimpse of the passion you got roiling around inside you and I just want to bathe myself in it." Raw desire edged his voice. "I've got no right to want you so damned much, but I do. And if you don't stop me, I don't know if I can stop myself."

She felt the last fragile thread of caution snap, plunging her into the scary, exhilarating ether of pure, blind faith. She rose from the sofa and walked over to where he sat.

"I don't want to stop you." She touched his face, sliding her fingers along the edge of his jaw. "Don't stop."

He turned his face toward her touch, his eyes drifting closed. "Rachel—"

Bending, she pressed her mouth to his, thrilling as his lips parted beneath hers, his tongue brushing over her lower lip and slipping between her teeth to tangle with her own tongue. He tasted like sweet tea and sin.

He wrapped his arms around her waist, pulling her down to him until her legs straddled his. She settled over his lap, acutely aware of the hard ridge of his erection against her own sex. A guttural sound rose in her chest as she pressed her body more firmly against his, molding herself around the hard muscles and flat planes of his body.

His hands slid down her back and curved over her bottom, his fingers digging into the flesh there, pulling her even closer. His breath exploded from his throat when she rocked against him, building delicious friction between their bodies.

"What am I going to do with you?" he groaned against her throat, his lips tracing a fiery path along the tendons of her neck.

She whispered her answer in his ear and eased off his lap, pushing to her feet. She held out her hand, locking gazes with him.

She saw questions there, but also a fierce, blazing desire to give her what she'd asked for. Slowly, his hand rose and clasped hers, and he let her tug him to his feet.

Their bodies collided, tangled, then melded. He wrapped one arm around her waist, pulling her against him, while his free hand threaded through her hair to tug her head back. He claimed her mouth in a slow, hot kiss, no frantic clash of teeth and tongues but a thorough seduction, full of purpose and promise.

"You look so prim and proper on the outside," he whispered against her temple as he led her to the stairs. "But you've got a danger monkey inside you."

She laughed at the term. "Danger monkey?"

He didn't answer until they'd reached the door of her bedroom. He stopped there, turning to look at her. As always, the intensity of his gaze made her legs wobble a little, and she grabbed the front of his shirt to hold herself upright.

"Being with me is a risk, Rachel. People will look at you differently. They'll tell you you're crazy. Tell me you know that."

She could barely catch her breath, but she managed to find the words. "I know that. I don't care." Growing impatient, she tugged the hem of his T-shirt upward, baring the flat plane of his belly to her wandering hands. She splayed her fingers over his stomach and ran them upward, through the crisp dark hairs of his torso. They tangled in the light thatch on his chest, drawing a low groan from his throat.

Then her fingers ran across the rough flesh of his burn scar, and he froze.

Her gaze lifted to meet his. "Is that where you were burned?"

He nodded. "One of the places."

"Let me see."

He slid his shirt off, baring the scars on his chest and shoulder. She examined them first with her gaze, then with a featherlight touch of her fingers. "It must have hurt like hell."

"It did. They told me at the hospital that I was lucky.

Most of my burns were second degree, which would heal better. But one of the doctors said they also hurt worse."

"Your mother must have considered you her hero."

Her words seemed to wound him. "My mother stayed drunk for days after the fire. All she ever said to me was that I should have saved my father, too. I didn't have the heart to tell her there wasn't enough left of him after the explosion to save."

Rachel pressed her cheek against his scarred shoulder. "I'm sorry. That must have been so terrible for you."

He threaded his fingers through her hair and made her look at him. "Don't feel sorry for me. That's one thing I don't need from you."

Her pity melted in a scorching blaze of desire. "Okay. So what's one thing you *do* need from me?"

He dipped his head and kissed her again. She heard the rattle of the doorknob as he groped for it, felt the shift of their bodies as he backed into the bedroom, drawing her along with him.

The backs of her knees connected with the bed, and she tumbled backward onto the mattress, Seth's body falling with her. He settled into the cradle of her thighs, dragging his mouth away from hers.

"I've never wanted anything as much as I want you," he whispered.

A thrill of power coursed through her, making her heart pound and her head spin. She rolled him over until she was on top of him, her hands clasped with his, pinning him to the mattress. She lowered her head slowly, kissing her way from his clavicle to the sharp edge of his jaw. She stopped, finally, at the curve of his ear, nipping lightly at the lobe.

"Prove it," she answered.

With catlike grace, he flipped her onto her back again, feral desire blazing from his eyes.

Slowly, thoroughly, he did as she'd asked.

## Chapter Fourteen

"What did you want to be when you grew up?"

Rachel's sleepy voice pierced the hazy cloud of contentment on which Seth had been floating for the past few minutes. He roused himself enough to think about what she'd asked. "I think mostly I just wanted to grow up."

Her fingers walked lightly up his chest. "I guess there wasn't much room for dreams in that kind of life, huh?"

"I think the dreams were all unattainable on purpose," he answered after a moment of thought. "If you let yourself dream small, there was the possibility that it could come true. Which meant it hurt all the more when it didn't. But if you dreamed big, you knew from the start that it was impossible. So it couldn't really hurt you."

She was quiet for a long moment. "I used to want to be a writer."

"You did?" He supposed he could see it. She'd been a librarian, and her house was full of books. The temptation to create rather than simply consume was strong. He knew from his own experiences working as a mechanic the pleasure of being an active part of making something work. He'd always loved cars, even as a kid when having one of his own had seemed an impossibility. But he loved working on them even more, seeing what made them go, what could make them stop, how to make them work more efficiently.

"I did. But my father was always such a pragmatist. He liked to point out the odds against success in any endeavor. I don't think it occurred to me until much later on that he wasn't meaning to discourage me. He just wanted me to have the facts."

"And you let the facts deter you."

"I found an easier way to work with books."

"Easier isn't always better."

Rachel propped her head on her hand and looked down at him, her honey-brown hair falling in a curtain over his shoulder. "That's a very wise observation."

He laughed, shaking his head. "That's just bad experiences talking, sugar, not wisdom."

"Where you do think wisdom comes from?" She bent and kissed the scar on his chest, then touched it with her forefinger. "You checked the stove for a burner the other day."

He grimaced. "Fire and I don't mix well."

She slapped his chest lightly, making it sting in an oddly pleasurable way. "Like heights and me."

"You run from things that are bad for you." He gave her a pointed look. "Usually."

She rolled onto her back. "Stop it, Seth."

He turned onto his side to look at her, propping himself up on his elbow. She was only half-covered by the tangled sheets, her torso gloriously naked. In the golden late afternoon light slanting across the bed, she looked like a gilded goddess, all perfect curves and mysterious, shadowy clefts. She belonged in a better place than this, he thought. She deserved to be worshipped and adored by a worthy man.

What if he could never be that worthy, no matter how hard he tried?

"When I'm with you, I want to be perfect."

She met his gaze with smiling eyes. "Nobody's perfect."

"Wrong answer, gorgeous. You're supposed to say, 'But you are perfect, Seth. You're perfectly perfect. There's never been anyone more perfect in the history of the world.'"

She laughed. "Nobody sane would say that."

"Thanks a lot."

"I don't want perfect." She rose up on her elbow as well, facing him. "I want someone who makes the effort to do the right thing for the right reasons. When I look at you, when I watch you dealing with all the suspicion and temptations you have to deal with, that's what I see. I see a man who's made terrible mistakes that he still suffers for, but he tries. He tries so hard to be a better man."

Her words scared him. "What if I'm not that man?"

"You are," she insisted, pressing her hand flat on his chest. "You're just afraid to believe it."

He wanted to believe it. He had spent the first fifteen years of his life wishing away reality and he'd spent the last five years doing the same thing, though for different reasons.

Dreaming the impossible because it hurt less when it didn't come true.

But what if those dreams weren't really impossible? What if he could have a decent life, surrounded with good people who cared about him and wanted the best for him? Other people could live that life—what if he could, too? Was that really too impossible to believe?

A distant rapping sound filtered past his thoughts. After a few seconds of silence, the sound came again.

Rachel's head lifted toward the bedroom door. "Is that someone knocking on the door?"

The rapping downstairs had grown more insistent. With a low growl of impatience, Rachel swung her legs over the side of the bed and started gathering up her clothes, dressing as she went. Seth shrugged on his own clothes, joining her downstairs at the door.

"Wait." He put his arm in front of her as she started to open the door, holding her back. "Let me see who it is first."

He put one eye to the peephole and felt a ripple of surprise. Sutton Calhoun's face stared back at him through the fisheye lens.

"Who is it?" Rachel asked.

"An old friend." *Turned enemy,* he added silently. He unlocked the door and opened it.

The indistinct, distorted images that had flanked Sutton in the fisheye lens turned out to be Seth's sister, Delilah, and small, dark-eyed Detective Ivy Hawkins. Seth didn't know what he found more alarming, the grim looks on all three faces or the Bitterwood P.D. badge clipped to the front of Ivy's belt.

"Has something happened?" he asked.

"Seth Hammond, the Bitterwood Police Department would like to ask you some questions," Ivy said in a low, serious tone.

The sinking sensation in his chest intensified. "About what?"

Ivy's dark eyes flickered toward Rachel. "Your involvement in the harassment and stalking of Rachel Davenport."

"That's ridiculous," Rachel exclaimed, stepping forward. "Seth is not stalking me."

"We've found a disk of photos that would suggest otherwise," Sutton snapped, his gaze firmly fixed on Seth's face. Seth didn't miss the disgust, tinged with disappointment, in his old friend's eyes.

"You think I'm behind what's been happening to Rachel," he said.

"I saw the photos." Delilah sounded more hurt than angry. "I saw the sunglasses camera—that's expensive equipment. Where did you get the money?"

"Sunglasses camera?" For the first time, Rachel's voice held a hint of uncertainty.

"You were wearing them at the funeral," Delilah said, her gaze pleading with him to give her a reasonable excuse.

"He was snapping photos of you at your father's funeral," Sutton said.

Seth felt Rachel's gaze on him. He turned slowly to look at her.

Her blue eyes were dark with questions. "You were wearing sunglasses at the funeral. I remember that."

"I was," he agreed. "And they were camera glasses. Remember, I told you I was working for the FBI."

For a moment, some of the doubt cleared from Rachel's expression.

"Working for the FBI?" Delilah stared at him. "But how? You'd have had to pass background checks—" She stopped, shaking her head. "Seth, please—"

She wanted to believe him, he saw with some surprise. More than she doubted him. "Call Adam Brand," he said quietly. Urgently.

Delilah blanched at the mention of Brand's name, not for the first time. Seth had long suspected something bad had gone down between his sister and the FBI agent almost eight years earlier, when she was still working for the bureau.

Ivy pulled her phone from her pocket. "I'll call him."

As Delilah recited the D.C. office number from memory, Seth slanted a look at Rachel. She gazed back at him, trying to look supportive, but doubts circled in her blue eyes like crows in a winter sky.

"I'm not lying about this," he told her. But listening to his low, urgent tone, he could see why the doubt didn't immediately clear from her eyes. He sounded desperate and scared.

Because he was.

"He's not in his office," Ivy told them a moment later. "The person who answered said he'd taken a few days off and was out of pocket."

Seth frowned. Brand hadn't said anything to him about going on vacation. In fact, in all the time he'd been dealing with Brand, the man hadn't taken more than a day or two off at a time.

"He never goes on vacation," Delilah murmured, echoing his own thoughts.

"Why don't we go down to the station and sort through all of this?" Ivy suggested in a calm, commanding tone. Seth looked at her thoughtfully, remembering when she'd been a snot-nosed little brat who'd followed him and Sutton all over Smoky Ridge. She'd grown up, he realized, into a tough little bird.

He looked at Rachel again. Her eyes were on Delilah, her expression pensive. Seth followed her gaze and saw his sister staring at him with blazing hope rather than doubt.

She believed him, he realized with astonishment. "We'll keep calling," Delilah said quietly.

Sutton, however, was having none of it. "What's the point? You really think the FBI's going to hire a con man to keep tabs on a grieving heiress? That's like assigning an alligator to guard the pigpen."

Seth turned to look at Rachel. Her eyes had gone reflective. He couldn't tell what she was thinking, and that scared him to death. "Rachel—"

"Are you going to take him in?" She turned her cool gaze to Ivy.

Ivy nodded. "Yeah. I am."

Seth looked from Sutton's stony face to Ivy's. "You gonna cuff me?"

Ivy's left eyebrow peaked. "Is it going to be necessary?"

He was tempted to make it so. Go out in a blaze, since it's what everyone seemed to expect of him.

But he simply shook his head. "Let's get this over with."

He looked back as he walked out of the door, hoping to catch Rachel's eye and try one last time to make her see that he was telling the truth.

But she had turned away, her cell phone to her ear.

He trudged down the porch steps, feeling suddenly dead to the core.

RACHEL STOOD BENEATH the hot shower spray, her mind racing. She'd never been a woman of impulse, heedless of warning signs. Even as a child, she'd been a rule follower, thanks to her father, who'd always explained the reasons behind his strictures in ways she could understand.

Logic told her she should be down there at the police station right now, demanding that Seth explain his lies and machinations. But she just couldn't believe any of the allegations against him.

She knew all the reasons she should, of course. Though nobody had showed her any pictures, she didn't doubt they existed. Ivy Hawkins was a cop with no reason to lie. And even Seth's own sister had said she'd seen the photos.

But that didn't mean Seth had been doing something to hurt her. He'd told her he was working for the FBI, and she'd believed him. If he was following her on the orders of the mysterious Adam Brand, it made sense he might use covert surveillance equipment to do so.

She'd called the trucking company as soon as Ivy Hawkins had made it clear she was taking Seth in for questioning, wondering if there was any sort of fund available from the company to help employees with legal problems. But their lawyer had been doubtful. "What you're describing doesn't sound as if it's connected to the employee's work at the company," Alice Barton had told her. "He wouldn't qualify."

She'd known the legal fund idea was a long shot, but she had a feeling Seth might have been more open to accepting her help if it came from the company instead of her own resources. No matter. She was going to figure out a way to help him whether he liked it or not.

Out of the shower, she dressed quickly, letting her hair air dry as she pondered what to do next. She needed to see the photos, she realized. See the so-called evidence against Seth. There might be something in those photos that could clue her in to who was really trying to destroy her life.

Before Delilah had dropped her off at her car the day after the Purgatory Bridge incident, she'd given Rachel her business card with her cell phone number. Where had she put it?

She was digging through the drawers of her writing desk, looking for the card, when there was another insistent knock on the door. Distracted, she almost opened the door without looking through the peephole. She stopped at the last moment and took a peek.

It was her stepbrother, Paul.

Relaxing, she opened the door. "Oh. Hi."

He pushed past her into the house. He looked around, as if he expected to find someone else there with her. "Are you okay?"

"What's wrong?" she asked, closing the door behind them.

"I just got a call from Jim Hallifax at the locksmith's place down the street from the office. He said you were changing the locks here because you'd had an incident with an intruder."

She stared at him, confused. "Why on earth would Jim Hallifax call you about that?"

Paul stared back at her a moment, looking a little sheepish. "I, uh, mentioned in passing that you were taking your father's death badly and that I was worried about you being here all alone. I guess he thought I'd want to know that you'd had some trouble."

She shook her head. "He had no business telling you that."

"Are you angry that I know?"

She took a deep breath and let it out slowly. "No. But I'm fine. Really." At least, she had been while Seth was there. Now that she was alone, however, she felt vulnerable again.

"You shouldn't stay here alone. I could move in for a little while, at least until the locks are changed."

"I'm getting an alarm put in, too," she assured him. "Dad resisted it forever, but I just don't think it's safe to live here without some form of protection."

The phone rang, interrupting whatever Paul was going to say in response. For a second, Rachel thought it might be Seth, but she realized he'd have called her cell phone. She let it ring, not in the mood to talk to anyone else at the moment. The machine would pick up the message.

"Call from Brantley's Garage," the mechanized voice drifted in from the hallway where the phone was located. Rachel frowned, trying to remember why Brantley's Garage would be calling. As the message beep sounded, she remembered. Seth's car with the flat tires. They'd given Brantley her phone number in case he couldn't be reached by his cell.

She didn't reach the phone before the caller started leaving a message. "Mr. Hammond, this is Wally from Brantley's Garage. Your car is ready to pick up."

She grabbed the phone. "Wally, Mr. Hammond isn't here, but I'll be sure he gets the message. Thanks." Bracing herself, she hung up the phone and turned to look at her stepbrother.

He stared at her, his expression disbelieving. "Why would the garage call here to reach Seth Hammond?"

"Because he was staying here with me."

Paul stared at her as if she'd lost her mind. "Why?"

She sighed, realizing she was going to have to tell someone everything that had happened, sooner or later. There was no point in trying to hide from her choices any longer. She'd made them, and if they turned out to be mistakes, she'd have to live with them, because she had no intention of apologizing.

"It's a long story," she said. "And it started a couple of nights ago on Purgatory Bridge."

## Chapter Fifteen

"Are you charging me with something?" Seth blurted before Ivy Hawkins and Antoine Parsons asked the first question.

"Should we?" Ivy asked.

"Charge me or let me go," he said flatly.

"We can hold you for twenty-four hours without charging you for anything," Antoine said in a quiet tone. "I'd rather not do either, frankly. I'd like to believe you've gotten your act together, because I remember you as being an okay guy back in the day, before all that mess went down with your dad and you got sucked into Cleve Calhoun's world."

*So,* Seth thought, *Parsons gets to be the good cop.* He looked at Ivy, who was watching him with thoughtful eyes. "I've told you everything. Meanwhile, Rachel Davenport is home alone at a house that's been broken into at least once, after over a month of incidents targeting her and the people around her. Including five murders."

"Why did the FBI want you to keep an eye on Rachel Davenport?" Antoine asked.

"Adam Brand didn't say. All he told me was that it wasn't an official FBI inquiry."

"Was that unusual?"

"Never happened before," he admitted.

"And you didn't question the order?" Ivy interjected.

"Of course I did. But look—Adam Brand's an FBI agent, which means he's a secretive guy by default. He tells me only what he thinks I need to know in order to do the job he gives me. I didn't need to know why I was keeping an eye on Rachel."

"You weren't even curious?" Ivy sounded doubtful.

"Honestly? I didn't care. I was already keeping an eye on Rachel before he called." He gave her a pointed look. "But you already know that."

He saw Antoine slant a quick look at Ivy and realized the pretty little police detective apparently hadn't done much talking with her partner about Seth's part in bringing down serial killer Mark Bramlett. He supposed she might not have had time to tell him much before the police department put her on administrative leave.

"I certainly didn't know you were stalking her," Ivy denied.

"I'm not stalking her," he protested, though he supposed that an outside observer might think so. He'd been spending many of his off-work hours keeping an eye on Rachel Davenport and the people around her, ever since he'd started putting two and two together about the serial killer victims, all of whom had shared a connection with Rachel.

"You've been following her. Taking photos of her. Insinuating yourself in her life. Know what that sounds like to me?" she asked.

"Like a con man picking out a new mark," he answered.

She looked a little surprised to hear him say it out loud. "Then you see the issue I have with your story."

"And here's the issue I have with the way your department has handled this investigation," he snapped back.

"It took four murders before you'd so much as admit in public you were looking for a serial killer. And it took you longer still to tie all four people to Rachel Davenport."

"You knew earlier?" Antoine asked with a slight rise of one dark brow.

"Y'all never step foot into any of the beer joints around these parts, do you?" He shook his head. "You like to sit here in your nice, clean police station and pretend there's not any crime in these parts, not like there is in the big city, even though these hills are full of desperate, poor people. That's why someone can offer twenty grand to kill someone and you'll never hear a word of it, because you're too scared to get down in the dirt where the bad guys wallow."

Antoine looked surprised. But not Ivy. Because she was sleeping with Sutton Calhoun, of course. They were talking marriage and babies and the whole sappy lot, from what Seth had heard. Of course, Sutton had told her what Seth had told him about the twenty-grand hit he'd heard about.

"Sutton told me about that," Ivy said quietly. She gave Antoine an apologetic look. "I should have told you. I'm sorry. It was only hearsay, and Sutton didn't know who Seth had talked to."

"It would have helped with our investigation," he said. "You want to tell us who told you?"

"The guy's nowhere around these parts anymore. He got out of town not long after that happened. I don't even know his real name. Just the name he went by when we crossed paths now and then. Calls himself Luke, but he's fast to tell you it's short for Lucifer, because he's a fallen angel." Seth grimaced. "My theory, he's some poor preacher's black sheep son. His mama probably prays for him every night and cries about him every day."

"What did Luke tell you, exactly?" Antoine asked.

"That he had been offered a hit job."

"And you didn't think to mention this to us before now?"

"Luke didn't take the job, and if you snatched him up, he'd know I was the one who told. I might need information from him in the future."

Ivy's brow furrowed. "Information for what?"

"Anything. Everything." Seth leaned forward. "You don't know what it's like living outside proper society, do you? Sure, your mama's got a bit of a reputation for bringing home deadbeats, but people mostly understood that was just because she wanted someone to love her. They may not have approved, and I'm sure some of them thought she was stupid, but nobody ever thought she was a bad person."

Ivy gave a slight nod.

"Right now, I can't depend on society to see me as anything but trouble. And I'm not lookin' for sympathy when I say that—I know I brought on my own troubles. But it doesn't change my situation. There are times when I have to depend on people you wouldn't want to be seen with. Hell, I don't want to be seen with 'em, not anymore, because it makes it that much harder for me to try to fit in with good people." He shook his head. "But my opinion of what constitutes good people and bad people can be a little fluid."

He saw a hint of sympathy in Ivy's dark eyes. "Did you press Luke about who tried to hire him?"

"Not at the time. I hadn't connected it to the Davenports then. I was trying to keep my nose clean, stay out of messes, and I didn't want to know anything more." He felt a sharp pang of guilt. "If I'd pushed a little harder, maybe I could have stopped it. But I just wanted to stay clear of trouble."

"You should have told us," Antoine agreed. "Do you have any idea how to find this Luke person again?"

"I tried to find him a few weeks ago, but he wasn't anywhere around. I talked to some mutual acquaintances and they told me Luke had gone to Atlanta for a while to see if he could get any work down there."

"What kind of work did he do?"

Seth shot Antoine a pointed look.

"The kind of work you used to do?"

"Yeah, he runs cons when he can. If you can get your hands on Atlanta area mug shots from bunco arrests in the past three weeks, I could maybe pick him out of a lineup."

"We'll look into that," Ivy said. "Meanwhile, there's the issue of the photos you took of the funeral."

"I told you what that was about."

"And conveniently, your so-called contact at the FBI is out of pocket."

"Not very damned convenient for me," Seth disagreed. "And how many times do we have to go back over this same ground? You do realize you've left Rachel Davenport by herself, unprotected, in order to chase me around in circles for no good reason?"

Ivy and Antoine exchanged looks. As if they'd reached a silent agreement, Antoine got up and exited the interview room, leaving Ivy alone with Seth.

"Where's he going?"

"He'll get someone to check on Ms. Davenport."

"Look, Ivy—Detective." He couldn't help but make a little face as he corrected himself, a picture in his mind of Ivy Hawkins as a snub-nosed thirteen-year-old with shaggy hair, skinned knees and a crooked grin. It was hard to take her seriously as a police officer when he'd known her as a tagalong for so many years. "I know why you have to bring me in and ask me these questions. I'm trying to be patient and cooperative. I am. But you and Sutton painted a really bad picture of me for Rachel. I've been trying to help her, not hurt her. And it's got to be hard for her to trust anyone, especially someone like me—"

Ivy's eyes widened. "Oh my God. Are you involved with her?"

He sat back in consternation.

"Oh my God." Ivy sat back, too, staring across the table at him through widened eyes. "What exactly did we interrupt this afternoon?"

He made himself as opaque as he could and didn't answer.

"Oh my God."

"Will you please stop saying that?" he asked.

Ivy brought her hand up to her mouth, covering it as if it were the only way to keep from blurting out her shock again. The resulting image would have been comical if Seth hadn't been so worried.

A knock on the door drew Ivy out of her seat. A uniformed officer told her something, and she turned to Seth. "Stay here. I'll be right back."

"Is something up?"

"I'll be back in a minute." Ivy left the interview room, closing the door behind her.

Seth put his head in his hands, frustrated by the delay. Rachel probably thought the worst of him right now. And who could blame her? He'd kept things secret, as usual, not trusting her with the full measure of truth. He talked a good game about trying to earn her trust, but when it came right down to it, he hadn't trusted her enough to be completely honest.

And now, he had to pay for it. He just prayed Rachel didn't have to pay for it, as well. Because she'd already been alone in that house for too long, without anyone to protect her from whoever wanted to do her harm.

"You should have told me about all of this." Paul gave Rachel a stern look softened slightly by the sympathy in his brown eyes. "Why did you try to go through all of this alone?"

"I wasn't alone."

"And trusting a man like Seth Hammond is even crazier."

"He was very kind to me. He's taken some risks to help me out," she defended Seth, wondering why she was bothering. Paul would look at the evidence and assume the worst. Seth had tried to warn her that's how it would be. To anyone on the outside, all the evidence would seem to point to Seth's playing games with her. If she hadn't spent the past few days getting to know Seth intimately, she might concur.

Intellectually, she could see the warning signs, but she couldn't connect them to the Seth Hammond she knew. He had been nothing but kind to her, even when telling her a few hard truths. He'd been genuinely remorseful about the ways he'd hurt people in the past. He'd told her the truth when a lie would have served him better.

"Why would someone do all of this to you?" Paul asked her.

"I think it must have something to do with Davenport Trucking. Or, more specifically, my job there."

Paul's brow furrowed. "In what possible way?"

"Paul, what do you know about my father's will?"

He shrugged. "Only what scuttlebutt at the office says. Your father wanted you to be CEO when he died, and so you will be."

"Have you ever heard anyone speculating about what might happen if I weren't able to take the job?"

"Not that, exactly." Paul pressed his mouth into a thin line. "I guess people are wondering why you'd want the job. You always loved being a librarian. I think some people thought George was being unfair to ask you to take over his dream by leaving your own dream behind."

She'd felt the same way, at first. And felt a hell of a lot of guilt about it, considering her father's deteriorating condition. "I need them to realize I'm doing this job because I want to, not because I feel obligated to."

"Is that really how you feel?" Paul looked unconvinced.

"At least for the next few years."

"And then?"

"And then we'll see." She had a feeling she'd go back to the library sooner or later. But not before she was certain her father's legacy was in the best hands possible. She owed her father's memory that much.

He was silent for a long moment. "It would be easier on you if you stepped down."

"I'm not going to let someone scare me away from a job I've decided to do." She lifted her chin.

"You really think these murders are about you?"

"I know it sounds crazy."

"It sounds narcissistic," he said.

"It's neither. It's just what the evidence is pointing to. You think I want to believe people have been murdered to get to me? Believe me, I don't."

"But you've been listening to Seth Hammond. He's

not exactly the most reliable of tale-tellers. What if he's playing his own game with you?"

"I've thought about that." She'd thought about it a lot, especially over the past hour, testing her faith in him against the logic her father had taught her. "I just don't see what he gets out of it."

"Do you know how he used to make a living?"

"He was a con man."

"He was a particular kind of con man. He preyed on vulnerable women. Convinced them that he wanted them, that he loved them. That they should trust him. He bilked them, and then he was gone."

She didn't answer, knowing he wasn't telling her anything that Seth would deny.

"You're not falling for him, are you?"

"I know what he is," she answered. Her cell phone rang. She dug it from her pocket and saw an unfamiliar local number.

Was it Seth? He might be stuck at the police station, using his one phone call to get in touch with her. She punched the button and answered the call.

It wasn't Seth. It was a police officer. "Ms. Davenport, this is Jerry Polito with the Bitterwood Police Department. Detective Antoine Parsons asked me to check on you, see if you're okay there by yourself."

"I'm not by myself, Officer," she answered with a look at Paul. "My stepbrother is here."

"Good." The policeman sounded relieved. "Detective Parsons suggested you might want to have someone stay with you, given all that's been happening to you."

"Thank you." She hung up and turned to Paul. "The police. They were concerned about having left me here alone."

"You're not alone." Paul put his hand on her shoulder. "I'll stick around tonight, okay?"

He had stayed there plenty of times during his mother's marriage to her father, but she couldn't shake the feeling that she'd prefer to be alone than to have Paul stick around for the night. Maybe it was as simple as wanting to be free from scrutiny or unwelcome pity for a while.

And, if she was being honest with herself, she was hoping Seth would be released soon and come back to finish what they'd started that morning.

God, she needed to talk to him. She needed to hear his voice, to make sure he was okay.

"Why don't I make you some tea?" Paul suggested, nudging her toward the kitchen. "You still have some of that honey chamomile stuff you and my mom like so much?"

"I think so." She followed him into the warm room at the back of the house, trying not to remember the time she'd spent in there with Seth just that morning.

But the kitchen was no worse than the den, where she'd begun her earnest seduction of the most dangerous man she knew. Or the hallway, where they'd kissed up against the wall for a long, breathless moment before finding their way to the bedroom.

Even after her shower, she'd imagined she could still smell him on herself, a rich, musky male scent that made her toes curl and her heart pound. She wanted him there with her. Where he belonged. If he walked through the front door that very minute, she knew she'd tell Paul to go home and leave her alone with Seth. To hell with what Paul thought about it.

To hell with what anyone thought.

"PAUL BAILEY HAS a record," Ivy told Antoine. She spoke too quietly for Seth to hear her from his seat at the interview table, but he'd long ago learned how to read lips. Cleve had pounded into him the importance of equipping himself with all the tools necessary to do a thorough con job.

Being able to tell what people were discussing while out of earshot was just one of his skills. Another was reading body language. And Ivy Hawkins's body language screamed anxiety.

Antoine Parsons looked at the folder Ivy showed him, his brow furrowed. The anxiety seeped from her body into his, setting up a low, uneasy vibration in the room.

Seth couldn't stand the wait. "Why did you look at Paul Bailey's record?"

Both of the detectives turned to look at him as if they'd forgotten he was still in the room. "We've been looking at everyone at Davenport Trucking." Antoine sounded distracted. "The records from Mississippi just came through. He had some gambling problems when he was working casinos there. It's how he lost his job—skimming and setting up some cheats for money."

Seth sat back in his chair, surprised. He'd never thought of Paul Bailey as a possible suspect. The guy didn't seem interesting enough to earn suspicion.

"Even if he has a gambling problem, I'm not sure how taking control of Davenport Trucking could help him," Ivy answered. "I did some looking into the company back during the murder investigation. The CEO position's compensation package isn't all that large. Most of the profits are funneled back into the company. If Paul were to be made CEO, at most his pay would go up a hundred thousand."

"That's a lot of money," Antoine murmured.

"It can't just be about money," Seth said. "If he's the guy behind it, he was out there offering twenty grand for the hit. If he's so money-strapped, how can he pay twenty grand?"

Ivy and Antoine exchanged looks. "If it's not about money, what's it about?"

"I never said it wasn't about money. I said it's not *just* about money." Seth stood up from the interview table, bracing himself for one or both of the detectives to tell him to sit back down. But they didn't, so he continued, "I've been trying to figure out why anyone would target Rachel Davenport in the particular way they have, and it's got to be about Davenport Trucking, right? All the evidence points in that direction."

Ivy nodded slowly. "Agreed."

"Whoever targeted Rachel didn't kill her, because killing her creates a different set of events than just getting her out of contention for the job."

"What different set of events?" Antoine asked.

Seth outlined what he'd learned about the triggers that came into play depending on how the CEO job came to be vacated. "If she's dead, control of the company goes to her uncle Rafe, and he makes all the decisions without input from the trustees. But if she's merely incapacitated, the trustees make a decision based on recommendations already in place. There's a list of preapproved candidates for CEO. Paul Bailey, by the way, is one of those preapproved candidates."

"Does he know he's one of the candidates?"

"Probably. His mama is one of the trustees, and they seem to have a close relationship. Plus, from what Rachel's told me, Paul hasn't always been gung ho about working for the company, so I figure there must have been discussions between George Davenport and Paul for the old man to feel okay about including him on that list of candidates."

"But if the compensation's not that much better—" Antoine began.

"That's what's been bugging the hell out of me," Seth admitted. "But while I was waiting for y'all to get back in here, I started thinking about what the job would entail besides just money. It's long hours and a lot of stress, because you've got dozens of trucks at your command and you're responsible for where they go, what they haul, what fines have to be paid if you screw things up, what repairs and regular maintenance have to be done, and suddenly it hit me that I needed to stop thinking about it as a businessman and start considering how I might use it if I had criminal intentions."

Ivy shot him an amused look. "What a stretch for you."

He made a face at her. "If I was criminally inclined these days, there's a hell of a lot I could do with a fleet of trucks. I could move drugs back and forth. Illegal arms. Hell, I could traffic in people. Sex slaves, illegals, anything and everything. I could haul a dirty bomb from Central America to Washington, D.C., if I had my own fleet of trucks."

"I'm glad you don't," Antoine murmured.

"My point is, control of the trucks is control of a lot of potential income. If someone was inclined to use even a tenth of the fleet for illicit purposes—"

"They could make a fortune," Ivy finished for him.

There was a knock on the interview room door. Antoine grimaced at the interruption and went to answer the knock.

"If Paul Bailey still has a gambling problem, maybe he owes somebody very bad a lot of money," Ivy said grimly.

"It could be the mob, the Redneck Mafia, South American money launderers—"

"Could be anyone who wants to control a fleet of trucks for the small price of forgiving Paul Bailey's gambling debt," Ivy said. "Good God."

"And he's there with Rachel right now," Antoine said from the doorway, his expression dark. A uniformed policeman stood behind him.

Seth snapped his gaze up. "What?"

"Jerry just talked to her on the phone. Her stepbrother is there with her. She said he was going to stay there so she wouldn't be alone."

"Damn it!" Seth started toward the door, ready to bowl them both over if they tried to stop him.

Neither of them did.

# Chapter Sixteen

The chamomile tea was a little sweet for her taste, but Rachel wasn't going to complain. After the day she'd just survived, she wasn't about to be picky when someone gave her a little uncomplicated pampering.

Paul settled into the chair across from her at the kitchen table and sipped his own cup of tea. "I closed off that trapdoor to the attic while the tea was brewing."

"Yes, I know. I heard the hammering." She smiled.

"Speaking of the attic, I was actually planning to come here today before I talked to Jim Hallifax. Feel up to a little scavenger hunt?"

She raised her eyebrows over her cup of tea. "Scavenger hunt?"

"Mother called from Wilmington. She meant to take her wedding album with her to her sister's place but left it behind. I was planning to carry it with me when I visit her later this week, but I have no idea where she kept the album. She said she thought it might be in the attic?"

Rachel grimaced at the thought of going up there again. "I'm sure it's probably in an obvious place."

Paul gave her a teasing smile. "Oh, right, you're scared of high places, aren't you? Still haven't outgrown that?"

"It's not that, exactly." She stopped short of telling him what her phobia was really about. Funny, she thought, how she'd been able to share that deep, dark secret with Seth but balked at telling a man who was practically family. "And you're right. I should have outgrown it by now. Did Diane give you any idea where in the attic it might be?"

Paul smiled helplessly. "She said something about a box on the top of a bookshelf?"

*Oh great,* Rachel thought. *A high place within a high place.*

But this was a good test for her to prove, to herself if no one else, that she wasn't going to let her past define her any longer.

She put down her cup and pushed to her feet. "Fine. But you're coming with me to hold the stepladder."

"I KNEW YOU weren't involved with this." Delilah told Seth as they sped along the twists and turns of Copperhead Road, part of a three-vehicle rescue mission. Ivy's Jeep was in the lead, with Antoine right behind her. Delilah and Seth took up the rear, to his dismay, forced to go only as fast as the vehicles ahead of them.

"You knew?" He shot her a skeptical look.

"Okay, I wanted to believe." She looked apologetic. "I'm in this to help Rachel."

"I know. I'm sorry I didn't see it sooner."

"There was a lot you had to look past first." He tamped down a potent mixture of frustration and fear as he tried Rachel's cell phone again. It went directly to voice mail. "Why the hell isn't she answering?"

"Did you try the home phone?"

"Yeah. I get a busy signal."

Delilah didn't respond, but he could tell from the grim set of her jaw that she was worried.

"I think I love her," he said, even though he'd meant to say something entirely different.

Delilah's gaze flicked toward him. "What?"

"I think I love Rachel." He shook his head and corrected himself. "I know I love her."

"Oh my God."

"Why do people keep saying that? You think I'm not capable of loving someone?"

"I didn't say that. It's just—surprising."

He slammed his hand against the dashboard. "Can't we go faster?"

"These mountain roads are treacherous at normal speeds," Delilah said. "At high speeds, we could all end up dead, and how's that going to help Rachel?"

His heart felt as if it were going to pound right out of his chest. "I shouldn't have let y'all leave there without her. I should've protected her better. Damn it!"

"When did this happen? This thing with Rachel?"

He stared at her. "We're going to talk about my love life in the middle of all this?"

"You brought it up."

"I don't know," he growled. "I always thought she was pretty, of course. And I guess when I started suspecting the murders had something to do with Davenport Trucking, I started paying more attention to her."

"You suspected a connection all along?"

"After the second murder, when it was clear that both of the dead women had worked at Davenport, yeah. I did."

"This is so crazy. Her stepbrother."

"If he's in debt to the mob or someone connected like that, his life is on the line. He's already proved he's willing to kill to stay alive. He's not going to stop just because his stepsister is next on the list." He tried to keep his voice calm, but inside he was raging.

If, God forbid, they arrived too late—

"Oh, no," Delilah murmured.

He looked at her and found her gazing through the windshield ahead, her brow furrowed. He followed her gaze and saw what she had.

Smoke, rising in a black column over the treetops.

Something straight ahead was on fire.

And the only thing straight ahead was Rachel's house.

THE SLAMMING OF the attic door had caught Rachel by surprise. Already nervous, she'd jumped and whirled at the sound, ready to scold Paul for scaring the wits out of her.

But Paul wasn't there.

"Paul?" She'd been certain he was right behind her on the ladder. She'd felt his footfalls on the rungs below her, making her cling all the more tightly to the ladder as she climbed.

He hadn't answered, but she'd heard noise on the other side of the door. Reaching down to push the attic door open again, she'd discovered it wouldn't budge. "Paul, damn it! This isn't funny!"

More sounds of movement had come from below, but Paul hadn't answered.

Then she'd smelled it. The pungent odor of gasoline. "Paul?"

She'd heard a faint hiss, then a louder crackling noise on the other side of the door. The smell of smoke mixing with the fuel odor had spurred her into full-blown panic mode.

She'd grabbed the metal hasp of the attic door again to give it a tug and found it hot as blazes, making her snatch her hand back with a hiss of pain.

*Fire. The house is on fire.*

She wasn't sure how long she'd stood frozen in place

after that, trying to think. Long enough to realize there was more than just panic going on. Her brain seemed oddly sluggish, as if it took thoughts a longer time than usual to make it from idea to action.

Had she been drugged? Had he given her something in the chamomile tea? Something to slow her reaction time, to muddy her thinking so that she couldn't escape his trap?

She needed help. She needed—

She needed her phone. Digging in the pocket of her jeans, she'd expelled a soft sigh of sheer relief at finding it there. But when she tried to make a call, there was no signal.

*That's crazy*, she'd thought, trying to quell her rising fear long enough to think past the cottony confusion swirling in her brain. The house was one of the few places in Bitterwood where there was almost never any trouble getting a signal.

Unless, she realized, someone had a jammer.

Paul. Oh, no. It couldn't be.

*Okay, okay. Think.* She obviously couldn't get out the way she'd come in. Smoke already poured into the attic through the narrow seams in the door. Even if Paul hadn't wedged it shut behind her somehow, the fire would make getting out that way impossible.

But there was another trap door by the window.

She was halfway there before she remembered that Paul had already nailed it shut. Stumbling over the last few steps, she came to a stop against the window frame, sagging in despair.

He'd planned this, she realized. He'd come here today not to protect her but to kill her.

But why? Did he want to run Davenport Trucking so badly that he'd kill her for it? How did that make any sense? He'd never seen the job as anything more than a paycheck. He didn't even go to Christmas parties or participate in any of the interoffice morale projects.

But his interest had picked up in the past few months, hadn't it?

Why?

She felt certain the answer was somewhere just beyond the mists in her brain, so close she could almost feel it.

She banged her hand against the wall in frustration. "Paul!" she shouted, wondering if he could hear her over the rising din of crackling flames. "Paul, if you want the CEO job, I'll give it to you. Right now. In writing. Paul!"

Hell, he was probably nowhere near the house by now. The police knew he'd been there as recently as thirty minutes ago. He was probably already gone, off to set up an alibi for himself.

She turned and looked out the window, staring down the dizzying twenty-five-foot drop to the flagstone patio below.

Paul was gone, and she was trapped in her worst nightmare.

A DARK SEDAN swept past them on Copperhead Road, traveling in the opposite direction. So intent was Seth on the expanding column of smoking rising ahead of them that he almost ignored the passing motorist.

But a faint flicker of recognition sparked in his brain as the sedan reached them and passed. "That's Paul Bailey's car!"

Delilah's head twisted as the other vehicle passed. She shoved her cell phone at Seth. "Hit the *S* button. Sutton's on my speed dial."

Sutton answered on the first ring. "What?"

"The dark blue Toyota Camry that just passed us going south—that's Paul Bailey's car. Go after him."

A moment later, Ivy's Jeep pulled a sharp U-turn and headed off after the sedan. Antoine's department sedan braked and turned, as well. He slowed as they started to pass, and Delilah put on the brakes, rolling down the window at his gesture.

"I've called in Fire and Rescue, but they're across town. It may be up to y'all to get her out." He gunned the engine and swept off in pursuit of Ivy's Jeep and Bailey's Toyota.

Delilah pressed the accelerator to the floor, forcing Seth to grab the dashboard and hang on.

The house almost looked normal at first glance, but smoke was pouring from somewhere on the second floor, rising over the slanted eaves to coil like a slithering snake in the darkening sky. Seth jumped out of the truck before it stopped rolling, racing for the front door at a clip.

Delilah's footsteps pounded behind him on the flagstone walkway. "You don't have any protective gear!"

He ignored her, not letting himself think about what lay on the other side of the door. Tried not to smell the smoke or hear the crackle of the fire's hissing taunts. The heat was greater the closer he got, but he pretended he didn't feel it, because if he let himself feel it, if he let himself picture the licking flames and skin-searing heat, he wasn't sure he could do what he had to do.

"Rachel!" he shouted, taking the porch steps two at a time. He reached for the door handle.

"No!" Delilah's small, compact body slammed into him, knocking him to the floor of the porch. He struggled with her, but she was stronger than he remembered, pinning him against the rough plank floor. "Stop. There could be a back draft if you open the door right now! We have to do this right."

He stared at her, his heart hammering against his sternum, each thud laced with growing despair. "What if she's already dead?"

Delilah's gaze softened. "We'll find a way in. I promise."

She let him up, holding out her hand to help him to his feet. He gingerly put his hand on the doorknob and found it sizzling hot to the touch. Fear gripped him, a cold, tight fist squeezing his intestines until he felt light-headed. He could see the flicker of flames already climbing the curtains of the front windows and tried not to collapse into complete panic.

"Maybe the fire hasn't reached the back," Delilah said, her hand closing around his arm.

The back. Of course. If the fire hadn't gotten to the back of the house—

He forced his trembling legs into action, speeding back down the porch steps and around the corner of the house.

The back of the house showed no sign of fire yet. Even if the rest of the house was in flames, if Rachel was holed up somewhere the fire hadn't reached, he might be able to get her out through the trapdoors in the mudroom and closet.

But to do that, he had to go inside.

Where the fire was.

"Seth!" Delilah caught up with him and grabbed his arm, pointing up.

He followed her gaze and saw a pale face gazing down at him through the open attic window. Smoke slithered out around her, coiling her in its sinister grasp.

"Rachel," he breathed. She was alive.

"The trapdoor's nailed...shut..." She swayed forward,

grabbing the window frame in time to keep from toppling out. "I think...I'm drugged."

"We need a ladder," Delilah said urgently. "A tall one."

"Rachel, do you have a ladder? A long one?"

"No ladders!" She shook her head, sagging against the window frame. "No ladders. Please, no ladders." The last came out weakly, and she disappeared from the window.

"She's terrified of heights," he told Delilah. "But that may be the only way to get her. Go check the shed over there for a ladder."

"What are you going to do?" she asked, her dark eyes wide.

"I'm going to see if I can undo whatever Paul did to the trapdoors and get her out that way." It would still involve ladders, but shorter ones, not a rickety steel nightmare.

He could spare her that much, couldn't he? Even if it meant facing his own worst nightmare?

"You're really going into the fire?" Delilah stared at him as if she were seeing him for the first time.

"I have to," he answered, and put his hand on the back doorknob. It was only mildly warm to the touch. Taking care, he opened the door. Heat billowed out to greet him, but it didn't trigger any sort of combustion. He looked at his sister. "Go find a ladder, in case I fail."

She gave him a final, considering look before jogging off to the shed.

He entered the mudroom and tried the trapdoor, surprised but relieved to find it unlocked. He climbed into the second-floor bedroom closet, coughing as smoke seeped in under the bedroom door and burned his lungs.

It was a lot hotter in the closet, but he didn't let himself think about it. He turned on the closet light, which made the thick cloud of smoke in the small room all the more visible. Covering his mouth with his sleeve, he reached for the ladder to the attic trapdoor and stopped, gazing up in dismay. The door wasn't just nailed closed. It had been anchored in place with at least two dozen long nails. Even if he had a hammer—which he didn't—it would take long, precious minutes to pull out all those nails. And the police had confiscated his Swiss Army knife.

Painfully aware of the ticking clock, he reversed course and went back through the mudroom door. The heat here was stronger, pouring around him in slick, greasy waves. The odor of gasoline wafted toward him, and he realized there was an open container sitting right by the back door.

He set it outside quickly and looked toward the shed. The door was open and Delilah was inside, digging around. "I need a hammer!" he called to her. "Can you see a hammer?"

She emerged from the shed a moment later, carrying a large, old-looking claw-head hammer. He met her halfway to get it.

"The fire is spreading," he told her breathlessly as he took the hammer. "Even if I get up to her, we may not have any choice but to get down by ladder. The sooner the better. I'm not sure we can wait for the fire trucks to arrive. Have you found a ladder?"

"I spotted it in the back. I have to dig for it. You get into the attic. I'll get the ladder." She squeezed his arm, encouragement shining in her dark eyes. Warmth spread through his whole body like a booster shot of hope.

"See you on the other side of the window," he said.

He raced back into the burning house, dismayed to discover that in the few brief seconds he'd been outside, fire had licked closer to the mudroom. He could see flames dancing through the kitchen doorway, spreading inexorably closer. By the time he made it into the attic, the mudroom exit wasn't likely to be a viable escape route.

It was going to be the ladder or nothing.

The heat in the bedroom closet was oppressive, though the door had not yet become engulfed in flames. Still, eerie yellow light flickered through the narrow slit beneath the door, and smoke pouring through the crack limited visibility in the crowded space to inches.

He pulled down the trapdoor ladder as far as it would go with the door nailed shut and hauled himself up on the rungs, praying the wood was sturdy enough to hold his weight while he worked. So far, the electricity in the house was still on, giving him enough light to see the nails he had to remove.

"Rachel?" he called, wondering if she could hear him on the other side of the trapdoor. Was she even conscious anymore?

"Seth?" Her faint voice sounded remarkably close, as if she was just on the other side.

"I'm right here, sugar. I'm pulling out the nails. But you have to get off the door or you'll fall through, and I won't be able to catch you."

He heard scraping noises above him, then silence.

"Rachel, are you off the door now?"

When her voice came, it was faint. "You have to go. The fire…"

"You think I'm going to leave you up there alone?"

"It was Paul. Paul did this. I think he did everything."

"That's right, we know who it is now, so it's going to be okay. We'll get him, and then you'll be safe."

"You must hate me."

He smiled at the plaintive tone. "Never."

"I didn't listen to you."

"Yeah, you did," he said, his voice coming out in a soft

grunt as he struggled with a particularly difficult nail. "I told you I was trouble, and you listened. Smart girl."

"I didn't believe you—"

"I know. It's okay."

"No!" Her voice rose a little, her obvious fear tempered with frustration. "Listen to me. I didn't believe… you did it."

His fingers faltered on the hammer, nearly dropping it. "You didn't?"

"I know you. Who you are when you're not being a defensive jackass."

A helpless smile curved his lips. "You do, do you?"

She didn't answer.

His gut tightened, and he attacked the final nails with fierce determination, so focused that he didn't realize until the ladder dropped to open the trapdoor that the fire had finally breached the closet door, the crackling flames waiting for him as he dropped. Fire snapped at his pant legs and singed his shoes as he scrambled up the ladder and into the attic.

Rachel lay on her side a few feet away, her eyes closed and her breathing labored. Her face was sooty from the smoke rising through the rough slat flooring into the attic. He crouched beside her, his heart pounding.

Her pale eyes flickered open, and her soot-stained mouth curved into a weak smile. "I knew you were a hero."

He cradled her smudged face. "Yeah, well, we can debate that later. Right now, we're going to get you out of here. Okay?" He helped her to her feet and crossed to the open window, praying Delilah had come through.

She was standing below on the flagstone patio, locking the extension ladder into position. Struggling with the unwieldy contraption, she positioned it against the wall beneath the attic window. It didn't reach the windowsill, ending about five feet beneath.

*Damn it.* Seth gazed at the gap between himself and freedom.

"You'll have to climb down to it," Delilah called. "I've seen you monkey your way up a fir tree. You can do it!"

He could do it, but what about Rachel? She'd have to climb out of that window into nothing but her trust in his ability to keep her from falling.

Could she do that?

"Rachel?"

Her eyes fluttered up to meet his, her pupils dark and wide. "What?"

"I have to go out the window to the ladder."

She shook her head fiercely. "No ladder."

"We have to go out this way. The closet below is already on fire."

Her chin lifted. "Then you have to go without me."

"No," he said firmly. "We live together or we die together. Your choice. But I'm not going out there without you."

# Chapter Seventeen

"Please, Seth. I can't do it." Panic sizzled in Rachel's veins, driving out anything but fear, as black and deadly as the smoke filling the room at her back. "You go. Now."

His hands closed around her face, forcing her to look up at him. His face was soot-smudged and dripping sweat, but in his clear green eyes she saw a blaze of emotion that sucked the air right out of her aching lungs.

"I will not go without you." Each word rang with fierce resolve. His hands clutched her more tightly in place, as if he planned to drag her out the window with him, whatever the consequences.

"Okay." She peeled his hands from her face and gave him a little push toward the window. "Be careful!" she added with a rush of panic as he hauled himself onto the windowsill.

He disappeared over the side, only his fingers on the windowsill remaining in sight. After a harrowing moment, his face appeared over the sill again. "Okay, sugar. Your turn."

Terror gripped her gut, and she almost turned around and ran toward the trapdoor, preferring to take her chance with the fire. But his hand snaked over the side, grabbing her wrist as if he'd read the panic in her expression.

"You can do this. I braved the fire. You brave the heights."

*Fly, baby. You can fly.* Her mother's voice rang in her ears, a fierce, mean whisper of madness.

*No. I won't fly.*

*I'll climb down like a sane person.*

She closed her eyes a moment, mentally working her way through the next few seconds. She'd get settled on the windowsill, get her balance. Seth would be just below. He wouldn't let her fall.

He'd never let her fall.

She swung one trembling leg over the windowsill, clinging to the frame until she was straddling it, more or less balanced. But her imagination failed her. She couldn't visualize a way to get her other leg over the sill without plunging out the window.

"Take my hands, Rachel." Seth's voice gathered the scattered threads of her unraveling sense and tied them together. "Just take my hands and swing your leg over the edge."

She caught his hands. Fierce strength seemed to flow through his fingers into hers, and she swung her leg out of the window. She was hunched in an uncomfortable position, but she maintained her balance.

"This is the hardest point. Get this right, and we're home free." Seth released one of her hands and braced his against the wall. "I want you to slide off the ledge and onto my arm, turning around to face the wall as you do it. Okay?"

She stared at him. "That's your plan?"

He grinned up at her. "Take it or leave it."

She realized, in that scary, crazy moment, that she was helplessly in love with Seth Hammond. Faults and all. Any fire-phobic man who'd haul a drugged, acrophobic basket case out of a burning house was a man in a million. Whatever had driven him in his sin-laden past, he was a hell of a man in the present.

And if he thought he was going to talk her out of what she was feeling, then he had one hell of a surprise coming to him.

"Remember what we did this afternoon?" she asked, sliding her butt off the sill and into the curve of his arm.

His green eyes snapped up to meet hers. "Yes," he answered warily.

She slid the rest of the way into his grasp, anchoring her fingers on the ladder rungs. The hard heat of his body behind her felt like solid ground.

"As soon as I sober up, we're doing that again. Understood?"

She felt his body shake lightly behind her as laughter whispered in her ear. "Understood."

Step by careful step, they reached the safety of the patio together just as the fire trucks pulled into the driveway.

"THERE'S NOT MUCH to salvage, I'm afraid." Delilah kept her voice low as she crossed to where Seth sat next to Rachel's hospital bed. The E.R. doctor had insisted she stay overnight for observation, given how much smoke she'd inhaled. But he was optimistic that she'd be fine in a day or two.

"I know she'll hate losing the mementos of her family," he murmured, brushing his thumb against the back of her hand where it lay loosely in his palm. "But I don't think she'll miss that damned attic."

"You're right about that." Rachel's voice, thick with sleep, drew his attention back to the bed. Her eyes fluttered open. "So, we lived, huh?"

He squeezed her hands. "Yes, we did."

She rubbed her reddened eyes. "I feel like I swallowed a smokestack."

"You nearly did."

The door of the hospital room opened, and Rafe Hunter breezed into the room on the sheer force of his personality, his wife, Janeane, bringing up the rear. Rafe nudged Seth aside and grabbed his niece's hands. "Rachel, darling, are you all right?"

Rachel gave Seth a quick look over her uncle's shoulder.

"I'll be back in a little while," he promised her, backing out of the room to let her family have time with her. Delilah came with him, laying her hand on his arm as he started to slump against the wall.

"There's a waiting room down at the end of the hall," she said, hooking her arm through his. "Ivy and Sutton need to talk to you."

Seth didn't like the bleak tone of Delilah's voice. "What's going on?" he asked as she led him into the small waiting area at the end of the corridor.

Inside were a handful of hospital visitors scattered among the rows of chairs and benches. At the far end, near the big picture window looking out on the eastern side of Maryville, Sutton Calhoun and Ivy Hawkins had their heads together with a grim-looking Antoine Parsons.

All three turned when he and Delilah walked up. "What's happened?" Seth asked, his gut tight with dread.

"Paul Bailey is dead."

Seth stared at Antoine. "I thought you caught him and took him into custody."

"We did. We booked him, and he was waiting in his cell for his lawyer. The guard near his cell had to go referee a fight between a couple of drunks down the hall, and, when he got back, Bailey was dead."

"Murdered?"

"We're not sure." Antoine sounded apologetic. "We don't know if he ingested something or what. The coroner's got the body already and should have the autopsy done in a few days."

"He didn't do all of this by himself," Seth said firmly. "Someone was pulling his strings."

"That's what we think, too," Ivy assured him. "This case isn't over."

Seth ran his hand over his jaw, his palm rasping over the day's growth of beard. "Is Rachel still in danger?"

"Probably not," Sutton said gently. "Paul Bailey was clearly the link. If he was in charge of the company, then whoever had control of him had access to the trucks. Without him, there's no entry point. Whoever did this will just look for another fool to manipulate."

"So the man behind the curtain just gets away with five murders and weeks of tormenting Rachel?" Rage burned in Seth's gut, as hot and destructive as the fire that had licked at his heels in Rachel's house.

"He won't get away with it if we don't let him," Delilah said. "I've been thinking about what you told us. About Adam Brand."

There was an odd tone to his sister's voice that he hadn't heard before. A vulnerability that she'd never really shown, not even as a girl. He looked at her and saw anxiety shining in her dark eyes.

"What about him?" he asked.

"I've been trying to reach him, going around the obvious channels. I called some people we both knew back in the day. And that story about his being on vacation? It's bull. It's just the official story, at least for now."

"What's the real story?" Sutton asked curiously.

Delilah's expression went stony. "The real story is that he's gone AWOL. And the FBI is investigating him for espionage."

Seth shook his head firmly. "No way. Not Brand."

His sister's eyes blazed at him. "Something's really wrong, Seth. Because there's no way in hell Adam Brand would do anything to hurt this country. And now I'm wondering if what's going on with him has anything to do with his reason for having you follow Rachel."

"How?" Seth asked, not sure how to connect the two ideas together.

"I don't know," Delilah admitted. "I can't see an obvious connection." Her chin lifted. "But I'm going to find out."

She pulled out her cell phone and walked over to an empty spot on the other side of the room.

Sutton's gaze followed her movement briefly, then turned back to Seth. "I guess we owe you an apology."

Seth shook his head. "Not yet. Let me get a few more years of the straight and narrow under my belt and then maybe you'll owe me."

"You're really out of the life?" Ivy asked, more curious than disbelieving. "I hear it has a way of sucking you right back in."

"I don't want the guilt," he said simply. "It's not a life you can live if you have any sort of conscience, and apparently my daddy didn't blow mine up in that explosion after all."

Sutton looked at him through thoughtful eyes and gave a brief nod. "Good for you, Hammond. Prove everybody wrong."

"Speaking of daddies, you talked to yours recently?" Seth asked.

"I went by to see him once I was back in the country," Sutton answered. "He's getting back a lot more of his functions than I think he ever believed he would."

"I should have insisted he keep up with the therapy," Seth said with regret. "I'm sorry."

"He wasn't ready then. You couldn't have made him." Sutton shrugged. "You went above and beyond. I owe you."

"Not yet," Seth repeated with a faint smile.

He waited a few more minutes, giving Rachel time with her family, until he could stand it no longer. He left the waiting room and headed back down the hall to her room.

Her aunt and uncle had gone, but Rachel was still awake. "Where's the family?" he asked as she smiled sleepily at him.

"I asked them to call Diane," she told him, her smile fading. "To let her know what's going on with Paul."

She didn't know Paul was dead, he realized. He was tempted to keep that information from her until she felt better.

But that wasn't fair, was it? Keeping things from her would only convince her she couldn't trust him. He'd damned near been burned—literally—by his secrets. If he was serious about the straight and narrow, serious about becoming a man who could deserve a woman like Rachel Davenport, he had to start by telling the truth, even when it was unpleasant.

Even when it hurt.

He pulled up a chair by her bed and took her outstretched hand. "I just talked to Ivy and Antoine about Paul."

Her fingers tightened around his. "He's in really bad trouble, isn't he? That's why I wanted Uncle Rafe to talk to Diane. She's always liked him. He'll break it to her gently."

"I don't know how to say this but just say it. Paul is dead."

Her fingers went suddenly limp in his. "Dead? How?"

He told her what he knew. "It's possible he smuggled something into the jail. If we're right about someone pulling his strings, it may be that he found death preferable than whatever his puppet master had in store for him."

"He used to gamble in college—Diane used to bail him out all the time—but he went to rehab for it."

"Sometimes—a lot of the time—good intentions aren't enough. Sometimes, rehab doesn't stick."

Silence fell between them as they each considered the double meaning of his words. Rachel spoke first. "Someone made Paul do this. I don't think he'd have done anything this terrible if he wasn't under extreme pressure."

Seth wasn't as inclined to give Paul Bailey's motives the benefit of the doubt, but he couldn't argue with her logic. "The police are looking into Paul's background, trying to figure out who he owed. If we figure that out, we'll be able to protect you better."

"So you think I'm still in danger?" She sounded deflated.

"Not the way you were, no. We don't think so. Paul was the leverage to get a foothold in the trucking company. Without him, whoever was pulling his strings can't get control over the trucks, and we're pretty sure that's what he wanted."

"You don't have any idea why he wanted control of the trucks?"

"Obviously the idea is to use them to ship some sort of contraband. We just don't know what."

"Couldn't they buy their own trucks?"

"Probably not without greater scrutiny."

"So he might already be under investigation?"

Seth thought about Adam Brand. Had the FBI agent tugged the tail of the wrong tiger? "Probably. We just have to match the suspect to the crime."

"We do?" She quirked an eyebrow at him. "You've joined the Bitterwood P.D. now, hero?"

He smiled at the thought at first, but his smile quickly faded. It was a surprisingly tempting idea, he realized. And if he hadn't burned his reputation to the ground, maybe he'd have had a chance to try his hand at being one of the good guys. "No, but I'm interested in the outcome of the case."

Her lips curved again. "Because of me?"

Helpless to say no, he nodded. "Because of you."

Her smile widened briefly but quickly faded. Tears welled in her eyes, and she brushed them away with an angry swipe of her fingers. "Poor Diane. She's lost everyone."

"She didn't lose you. Right?"

Her fingers tightened around his. "Thanks to you."

He kissed her knuckles. "There were a few minutes there I thought I was going to have to stay in that attic with you until the fire got us."

"I wouldn't have let that happen," she said firmly.

He smiled at her confident tone. "Yeah, you say that now."

"I meant what I said up there."

Heat flushed through him as he remembered what she'd said, but he didn't want to assume they remembered the same thing. She'd been drugged, after all. "Which part?"

Her lopsided smirk reassured him that they *were* thinking of the same thing. "You know which part."

He shook his head. "What am I going to do with you?"

Her smirk grew into a full grin. "You need me to remind you?"

"I'm still a risky bet, Rachel. Not everyone's going to be able to see beyond my past. They're going to think you're crazy for wanting to be with me...."

She pushed herself upright in the bed, leaning toward him to place her hand on his cheek. "I'm a big girl. I can take it. What I can't take is life without you in it."

Gazing into her shining blue eyes, he realized she meant every word she was saying.

He closed his hand over hers where it lay on his cheek. "I'm going to do everything I can to make sure you never regret your decision. I promise."

She leaned closer, brushing her lips against his. "That's a good, solid start. Don't you think?"

He wrapped his arms around her, careful not to get tangled in her IV tube. "Yeah, it is," he growled in her ear, breathing in the smoky sweet smell of her, letting it fill him with hope. "It's a very good start."

\* \* \* \* \*

# *Join the Mills & Boon Book Club*

Subscribe to **Intrigue** today for
3, 6 or 12 months and you could
**save over £40!**

We'll also treat you to these fabulous extras:

- FREE L'Occitane gift set
  worth £10

- FREE home delivery

- Rewards scheme, exclusive
  offers…and much more!

*Subscribe now and save over £40*
www.millsandboon.co.uk/subscribeme

# The World of Mills & Boon®

There's a Mills & Boon® series that's perfect for you. We publish ten series and, with new titles every month, you never have to wait long for your favourite to come along.

---

**Blaze.**
*Scorching hot, sexy reads*
4 new stories every month

**By Request**
*Relive the romance with the best of the best*
9 new stories every month

**Cherish™**
*Romance to melt the heart every time*
12 new stories every month

**Desire™**
*Passionate and dramatic love stories*
8 new stories every month

# What will you treat yourself to next?

*Ignite your imagination,
step into the past...*
6 new stories every month

## INTRIGUE...

*Breathtaking romantic suspense*
Up to 8 new stories every month

*Captivating medical drama –
with heart*
6 new stories every month

## MODERN™

*International affairs,
seduction & passion guaranteed*
9 new stories every month

## n o c t u r n e™

*Deliciously wicked
paranormal romance*
Up to 4 new stories every month

## RIVA™

*Live life to the full –
give in to temptation*
3 new stories every month available
exclusively via our Book Club